Fiery Deeps

Fiery Deeps

TEN STORIES OF UNDERGROUND CAVERNS, FANTASTIC
TECHNOLOGY, AND FEMININE POWER

Edited by J.S. Fields & Heather Tracy

CONTENTS

Introduction

We're back again...for the very last time!

Fiery Deeps completes this (completely unplanned) sapphic elemental series. I can't tell you how much I've been looking forward to this one and the inevitable destruction. You'll find numerous other authors also realized fire was an easy excuse to rid characters of their clothes (myself included). Not everyone gets naked, but we do once again have sapphic protagonists in a host of unique situations, including pirate ships, fabric stores, burning buildings (hello firefighters!), smithies (hello black-smiths!!), underground tunnels, and Charon's boat. The anthology also involves just about every kind of witch imagina-ble, and magic of all sorts.

Through absolutely no planning of our own, the nine stories in this anthology are remarkably cohesive in their chaos. We've got a great line up of authors including several debuts, and of course my old writing group is still present and accounted for. As always, stories cut a wide swath of the sapphic experience and include aro/ace protagonists, nonbinary lesbians, and bi and pan women. There's a little offering for everyone, but don't expect to come away unscathed. There's a lot more heat in this anthology than the past installments—a fitting end to the World's Apart anthology series.

If you've made it through the previous three, welcome back! If this is your first introduction to the anthology series...come on in and have a seat. Just don't expect to leave with your clothes on.

—J. S. Fields, August 2024

Distant Gardens
Farther Reefs
Lofty Mountains
Fiery Deeps

When Worlds Apart
Become aligned
Then lovers' limbs
Are now entwined

William C. Tracy
August 2024

A NOTE ON THE STORIES CONTAINED HEREIN:

Each tale is marked on the title page with what sapphic representation is involved, as well as any content warnings. There is also a "Heat Level" if you wish to read or not read particular sexual content. The scale is as follows:

Low/None: There may be talk of sex, holding hands, or possibly kissing.

Medium: Mention of body parts, touching, and make-out sessions, but all scenes are "fade to black."

Hot!: Has at least one full sex scene, start to finish. You have been warned (or encouraged...).

The Fire Swamp is for Lovers

Rosiee Thor

Sapphic Representation: Lesbian, Bi
Heat Level: Hot!
Content Warnings: Fowl puns, Indigestion

True love was a sham and it smelled of farts. The swamp was hardly Rhoda's idea of a romantic destination, which was probably why Gracelyn had elected not to come. Rhoda was reluctant to go anywhere without her lady, but all it had taken was a sweet smile and a hair toss to send Rhoda spelunking through humid caves and ankle-deep bog water that reeked to high heaven.

"Eugh," Rhoda groaned as a geyser released a putrid jet of steam.

"Whoever smelt it dealt it!"

Rhoda halted, causing her companion to topple into her. He had at least five inches on her and biceps about which his someday-biographers would wax poetic, but no combination of broad shoulders and shiny, blond tresses could knock Rhoda down (he probably skipped leg day). Blayze Bristlebug—or whatever he called himself—was no match for Rhoda. Not in war, not in peace, and certainly not in matters of love.

And love was why they were in such a wretched place, after all.

The quest: seek a single phoenix feather from the Fire Swamp.

The prize: Lady Gracelyn's hand in marriage.

Rhoda would not allow herself to be bested. Not by the greatest swordsmen in the land. And certainly not by Blayze.

"It was the swamp," Rhoda said without humor. It was a marvel how such an enormous head could house so few thoughts. She didn't know if Blayze even had the capacity to understand the scientific phenomena around them—from the complex pressure system beneath their feet to the unique mineral makeup of the water trickling on either side of the barely beaten path they followed.

She opted for simplicity. "It's the sulfur that causes the smell."

"Whoever denied it supplied it!"

Rhoda got out her knife.

All the rumors she'd heard of the fire swamp spoke of its volatile nature in vague platitudes, the dangers within naught but a treacherous silhouette of some boogeyman or another. When she was a child, her father told her stories of a witch who dwelled within. Her anger and hatred were so pungent that even the swamp did not want her. The cyclical flames of a phoenix purged the land of her wretchedness over and over as they fought for dominance.

Now that Rhoda was a few miles in, however, the swamp didn't seem so bad. Yes, there were the troublesome geysers and pesky mosquitos, not to mention the stench, but so far, the place had only halfway lived up to its name, with plenty of swamp but a distinct lack of fire. Something was off.

"Be quiet," she growled, eyes narrowing as the trail sloped down. She cut the edge of her tunic and tied the excess cloth around her nose and mouth.

"Quiet, quiet, yes right, I can do that," Blayze said. "The epitome of stealth, that's me!"

Rhoda was surprised his vocabulary was large enough to include the word *epitome.*

What Gracelyn saw in this oaf, Rhoda would never understand. He didn't have two brain cells to rub together, though she supposed Gracelyn's uses for him might be more recreational than academic. As Rhoda paused to cut away a curtain of vines blocking their path, she glanced back at the man in question. Perhaps it was the cherubic dimples in his cheeks or his impressive abdominal muscles perpetually on display. Oh, how Rhoda longed to introduce him to the concept of shirts.

Rhoda did not engage in such gaudy displays. She showed her strength in the way she chopped wood for her lady's fire, or the way she slew game for her lady's dinner, or the way she held her lady's thighs as she fucked her. The corners of Rhoda's lips twitched as the details of their last entanglement washed over her. Nobility on the whole were a rotten lot, but the taste of Lady Gracelyn was still fresh on her tongue, her moans and whimpers like birdsong. No, Rhoda was not so insecure as to be threatened by Blayze Bumblewort.

Only, Lady Gracelyn of Daggerhold couldn't marry them both. That much was clear.

Rhoda would have been content to share her. She would have remained her lady's steadfast lover, no matter how many others she took, but she couldn't stand by and let someone else make her their bride, not when the honor could be hers. And someone like Blayze... Rhoda did not think she could bear it if she lost to such a clown.

Rhoda really should have left Blayze behind at the first sign of trouble. She should have gutted him like the pig he was.

Beside her, Blayze sawed away at the thick vines with his cutlass, a pinched expression wrinkling his face. Rhoda sighed and turned the blade in his hands so the sharp end faced the vines. A look of delight danced in his eyes as the vines came free.

Rhoda issued a silent apology to pigs everywhere. They did not deserve to be lumped in with such company.

"Why don't we play a game?" Blayze asked after no more than a few minutes of silence.

"I don't like games."

"Sure, you do!" Blayze clapped her on the shoulder.

She shrugged him off.

"The archery contest, the foxhunt, the joust..."

"Those hardly count."

"Why not?"

"I don't think a duel and I Spy are on the same level."

Blayze only shrugged. "They are both games. Admit it: you like to play!"

"I like to *compete*."

"But you agreed to Lady Gracelyn's challenge—what is this if not a game?" Blayze gestured to their dreary surroundings.

Rhoda wrinkled her nose, and not just at the stench. If she was honest with herself, the whole ordeal irked her. She proved herself to Gracelyn every day, and no marriage contract would stop her. Love was not something that could be tested by a quest or measured through comparison. It was either enough or it wasn't, and Rhoda knew how earnestly, how passionately, how selflessly she would love Lady Gracelyn if she let her.

Rhoda didn't want to play a stupid game. She didn't want to be stuck in the fire swamp with Blayze Bolsterburg for company. Rhoda's organs seemed to grind together in protest, but she gritted her teeth and soldiered on. For her lady, there was nothing she wouldn't do.

"Fine, I'll go again," said Blayze. "I spy with my little eye something beginning with M."

"Is it me *murdering* you?"

"Mushrooms!" Blayze exclaimed with the air of someone seeing a mushroom for the first time.

He pointed to a patch of fungus on a nearby stump: long, thick stems were concealed behind a yellowish web topped with conical blush-red caps. The bark of the old oak was blackened and charred from recent fire, but the fungus was all the more vibrant for it. Blayze's eyes actually *twinkled* as he stared, the infatuation in his gaze far more compelling than any look Rhoda had seen him give Lady Gracelyn.

Rhoda, who spoke often with grocers and foragers, had never seen anything like it. Well, she'd never seen a *mushroom* like it. Unfortunately, its shape and coloring reminded her all too sickeningly of a certain appendage she did not possess herself. Besides which, her father had taught her not to eat anything unfamiliar that was more vivid than her own coloring.

Not Blayze, though. He charged ahead, cutlass in hand like a chef's knife.

Before Rhoda could call him back, flames erupted—from the earth, from the trees, from the sky.

She squinted, but she couldn't see for the haze of heat before her. Smoke choked her lungs and stung her eyes. The world upended itself as her brain was starved of oxygen. She hit the hard trunk of a nearby tree with her shoulder and the ground seared her palms when she caught herself.

Scrambling away from the blistering heat, she pressed the cloth over her nose and mouth and regained her footing. The sound of crackling fire chased her from the beaten path, away from Blayze, or whatever remained of him. A fissure of guilt threatened to slice through to her, but Rhoda pushed the feeling away. She had to focus on saving her own skin. Blayze was beyond her help now.

Despite herself, Rhoda turned back toward the flames, orange and hungry as they erupted from the ground, consuming leaves and sticks and every molecule of oxygen around. Her stomach sank as she watched a silhouette sweep through the heart of the inferno unscathed.

It was a bird, feathers shimmering a brilliant gold through the haze. Its wings fanned the flames, spanning the length of a horse. Perhaps her eyes were playing tricks on her, too watery and aching from the smoke to be trusted. Rhoda watched with held breath as it landed in the center of the firestorm, the light around it flickering like the blue center of a candle. For a moment, everything stilled as it turned to look directly at Rhoda. Its face was alight with the power of the sun, but its eyes were the color of midnight, a void in the blazing heat.

They were the last things she saw before breath fled her body and she fell to the ground, unconscious.

* * *

Rhoda woke to the smell of lavender. Memories trickled across the surface of her mind like syrup: lazy mornings wrapped in satin sheets, lounging in the spill of sunlight from the window, her lips ghosting the silken skin of

Gracelyn's throat. She sank into the warmth, breathing in the scent of her lover.

Only Lady Gracelyn did not smell also of honey and turmeric and...was that garlic?

A sharp pain stung her scalp.

Rhoda's eyes opened on a scene altogether too strange for comprehension. She blinked, and blinked again, trying to bring her circumstances into clearer focus.

She lay on a bed of dried grass and moss on the forest floor, a crochet blanket covering the lower half of her body. Nearby, a fire crackled beneath a soup pot the size of Rhoda's dinner table. As for the pain, the source of it became clear almost immediately as the shrill crow of a rooster sounded alarmingly close to her ear.

Rhoda shot up, scrambling away from the bird. Her hands came away covered in detritus, dirt and twigs adhering to her skin. A salve, sticky and sweet-smelling, coated her palms. It was all too much.

"Hah!" she half-laughed-half-cried as she made eye-contact with the chicken.

For an absurd moment, Rhoda thought perhaps this was the fabled witch of the fire swamp. The blanket, the cauldron, the dried herbs hanging from a laundry line above her... Yes, it all made sense. The witch was in her bird form, now. A common chicken, meant to lull her into a false sense of security.

"Nugget!" came a gruff voice. "You leave our guest alone, you hear?"

The chicken was not deterred, advancing on Rhoda with its speckled head bobbing eagerly. Either "Nugget" did not understand human language, or he had some avian form of oppositional defiant disorder.

Rhoda growled, low and menacing. Or at least, she tried to be as menacing as one could be whilst facing off with a chicken. The absurdity of it all washed over her like a cool plunge. Perhaps this was all some hallucination. The last thing she remembered was the feeling of lightheadedness, the rising heat, the chalky texture of her tongue...

It came back to her in fragments, pieces of memory like shattered glass. Blayze and the mushroom, Blayze and the fire, Blayze and the *phoenix*.

Anger boiled in Rhoda's stomach, perhaps misplaced against all birdkind. She grasped for something—anything—to use as a weapon, her own sword nowhere to be found. Her fingers closed around the handle of *something*, and she levied it at her foe.

A spatula. Still, it would have to do.

"Stay back, foul beast!"

"Now, now, there's no need for pun-based humor," came the voice again, this time from behind her.

Rhoda whirled around, losing her footing in the process. Steady hands caught her by the elbow and waist.

"Careful. You're still weak."

The last time Rhoda had been called weak she'd been in her adolescence, bruised and bloodied, knees in the dirt with a blade levied at her chin. At least then, she'd fought. Now, she found herself woozy, her vision cloudy, her breath labored at even the merest hint of exertion. If not for the arms around her, she would have surely fallen.

Weak was exactly what she was.

She let herself be guided toward the bubbling cauldron in the center of the clearing and onto a tree stump to sit. Rough hands tried to pry the spatula from her fingers, but Rhoda clung tight. It was all she had to defend herself.

"Why don't you put the spatula down and I'll give you something more suitable?"

Was it a threat? This would be a prime opportunity to gut her and be done with it all.

But she was not offered a sword—by either the dull or pointy end—but instead a simple wooden spoon, followed by a steaming bowl of some sort of soup. Rhoda didn't dare to eat in case of poison, despite the painful clench of her stomach, so instead she looked up, blinking the stranger into focus.

This was a witch, if ever Rhoda had seen one. She was all soft curves—her cheeks, her shoulders, her hips. A round face carried the sly smirk of youth and the wise creases of age in equal measure, dark freckles spilling across her rosy-brown skin like stars. What was visible of her arms was speckled likewise, her hands and forearms covered by leather armlets. She wore a green apron embroidered with vines over a brown skirt, hitched up and tucked into her belt to reveal wide leg trousers beneath. Branches and feathers were tangled in a halo of burnished gold curls, and on top, rested a wide brimmed hat covered in small yellow flowers.

A witch, indeed.

"Salt?" she asked, passing Rhoda a small ceramic dish. "I don't often have guests, so I never know how much will be to others' liking."

"I'm not a guest," Rhoda said through gritted teeth. "And I won't be eating anything you give me."

The witch set her seasonings aside with a heavy sigh. "Suit yourself, but you'll recover your strength much quicker if you eat."

She eyed the substance in her bowl carefully: a brilliant orange broth with small chunks of onion and pepper, garnished with fresh green herbs. It smelled sweet and spicy at the same time. It made her mouth water.

"I know better than to eat food I haven't cooked myself," Rhoda said with an unconvincing waver to her voice.

The witch's eyes crinkled, dark forest green irises sparkling with hidden depth as she reached to take the bowl.

Rhoda let out an involuntary whimper, but the witch only tipped it against her lips and drank before returning it to Rhoda.

"See? Not dead." The witch pointed to herself. "It's safe to eat, I promise."

"Not sure what good a promise is from a witch," Rhoda grumbled, but she spooned some of the broth into her mouth. It tasted better than it smelled. She had to hold back what was sure to be an unseemly sound as the flavor hit her tongue: ginger and garlic, turmeric and honey, with a light flavor of coriander running through it all. It was nothing to the lavish feasts Lady Gracelyn hosted—wild pheasant, herbed potatoes, roasted carrots, and whipped raspberry pudding—but Rhoda's palate practically sang as she took a second spoonful and a third.

"A witch, eh?" Humor curled at the edges of the witch's lips. "Is that what they're calling me?"

"Is that not what you are?" Rhoda was too weary to feel the fear that normally accompanied such accusations. If the witch had wanted to kill her, she would have already.

But the witch didn't look offended, merely cocked her head and said, "I am Agatha."

"Agatha." Rhoda tried the name on her tongue, syllables tangling with the savory flavor of the broth.

"And you?"

"Rhoda."

"Like Rhododendron?" The witch—Agatha—brightened, her eyes practically sparkling with delight at the connection. "They are the first flowers to grow back after a forest fire." She plucked lovingly at the long flat leaves of a bush with budding purple flowers behind her. "Resilient things. No wonder you've recovered so quickly. A testament to your namesake, perhaps."

Rhoda had never been compared to a flower before. She did not have the gentle grace or smooth complexion to garner such compliments. No one remarked on rosy cheeks or full lips or twilit eyes when they looked at her. Instead, they praised her skill with a sword, her diligent spirit, her resourceful manner. She didn't let it bother her. She was proud of those traits, after all. What did it matter that she had a square face and a crooked mouth? That she had broad shoulders unsuited for delicate gowns and jagged hair she'd cut herself? She was not so pretty as her lady, but Gracelyn did not seem to mind. So why did Agatha's comparison make her face flush uncomfortably?

"How long was I down?" The question came small and bitter. Better to focus on the practical. Rhoda didn't like to admit defeat, but it was clear to her now that if not for Agatha's hospitality, she might have found herself in different circumstances...or maybe she wouldn't have found herself at all.

"Today marks the second you've been in my care," said Agatha.

"Two days?!" Rhoda shot to her feet, spilling the rest of her soup on her boots. She hadn't planned to be gone from Lady Gracelyn's side for more than a week. With the journey back to Daggerhold from the swamp, she was left little time in which to find the phoenix. "I need to—"

"Are you in a hurry?" Agatha's voice remained airy and unbothered.

"I must be going, but I thank you for the hospitality." The word felt insufficient for what Agatha had done for her, and she knew the moment it left her lips that no verbal gratitude could counterbalance the debt she owed. "Just as soon as I repay you. What service might I render that you would deem equivalent for saving my life?"

"Nonsense," Agatha scoffed. "You are in no state to travel on your own."

"I will have to try."

"What is so urgent?"

"I am on a quest. I seek a single phoenix feather, and..." Rhoda swallowed with difficulty. Her throat was still sore from smoke inhalation. "I hope to find my companion, or discover what's become of him."

"Well, perhaps I can help!"

"I have leaned on your kindness enough, I should think."

Agatha frowned, wrinkles overtaking her visage, rivulets and eddies that spoke of years Agatha could not have lived at her apparent age. Then, it all melted away into an expression of sheer, youthful delight.

"I know what I shall require of you!" she exclaimed.

Rhoda straightened, her knight's training instilling rigid posture into her shoulders as she awaited orders.

"My supply of firewood is running low. Restock my stores, and your debt will be repaid."

Rhoda blinked. It was too simple, too pedestrian. "Is that all?"

Agatha smiled and pointed just beyond the hearth toward an axe leaning against a small house of splintering red maple.

Rhoda looked from the witch to the axe and back again. Easy enough. Getting to her feet, she crossed the clearing, stepping over Nugget the chicken on her way. She grasped the axe's smooth ash handle—though it pained her tender palms—and hoisted it up onto her shoulder. Or rather, she tried to. Instead of the usual ease with which she was accustomed to wielding an axe, her arms felt leaden with the weight. Even the short jaunt from the fire to the house had sent her heart racing, her lungs wheezing to catch up. She tried again and managed to lift the axe a few feet off the ground, but the wooden handle scraped uncomfortably against her the raw skin of her palms, and she careened into the wall.

"I suppose you'll just have let me nurse you back to health until you're well enough to complete the task," Agatha said, chipper as could be.

Rhoda heaved a sigh and slid down the side of the house until she was sitting on a patch of moss. "You did this on purpose."

"Whatever do you mean?"

Closing her eyes, Rhoda leaned her head back with a clunk. So, she was stuck here, at the mercy of her failing body. And a witch was promising to help her recover.

Rhoda couldn't remember the last time someone had offered her help. She was always the one helping others. She lived to serve—the honor of her family, the whims of the realm, the passions of Lady Gracelyn. Rest was not for people like her. Pain bloomed in her chest that had nothing to do with physical exertion.

"Thank you," she murmured, her eyes fluttering open.

Agatha stood, crossing the clearing to offer her a hand up. Her palms were calloused, her grip firm. Rhoda was slow to detangle herself. Perhaps it was just the exhaustion, but something about Agatha's sturdy presence made her feel just a little stronger—or like she didn't have to be.

"I'm sorry I called you a witch, Agatha."

"Don't be." Agatha loosened her grip, but didn't let go. Her sorrel green eyes danced with the light of the high noon sun filtering through the trees. "Witches have names, too, you know."

* * *

Witches had much more than names, Rhoda discovered the following day. They also had prisoners.

"Blayze?" Rhoda nearly leapt from her boots. "Is that you?"

He didn't respond, but she didn't need him to. It was undeniably him, not a single swoopy hair on his head was so much as singed. He looked entirely unbothered, eyes closed in slumber. He lay on a cushy mattress surrounded by pillows, a large quilt draped over his lower half. If not for the gentle rise and fall of his chest, she might have thought him a corpse.

Agatha had sent her inside to fetch something—a ladle? a larger soup pot? a basket of herbs? Blayze's sudden appearance had shocked the memory from her. She stood over him, watching in silence, unsure what she should do. She wasn't strong enough to run away on her own yet, let alone lugging Blayze's limp body with her. Perhaps she could pretend she hadn't seen him and bide her time until she had recovered enough to free them both.

"Be careful not to wake him yet."

Rhoda jumped as Agatha slipped in through the door behind her, but she didn't look angry.

"Huh?" Rhoda said, unimpressively.

"The antidote is still working its way through his system. It's best to let him sleep through the worst of it."

"Antidote?"

"Your friend ingested a highly toxic mushroom."

"The smelly one?" Rhoda's nostrils flared at the memory of the stench.

"Indeed. Untreated, consuming a raw *Phallus flammeus* can cause irreversible damage to the liver and colon."

"*Phallus flammeus...*" Rhoda echoed, recalling the bright hue and elongated shape of the fungus in question. "Is that because it's shaped like a—"

"Mycologists have such a gift for comedy!"

The witch's face split into a grin.

Rhoda stared at her, mouth agape.

Blayze loudly suckled his thumb.

"It will be days before he wakes, I expect. He won't be much of a conversationalist till then."

"Your expectations of his verbal discourse may be too high."

Agatha chuckled and took Rhoda by the elbow. "Come, let's leave him to his rest." She guided her back toward the door, plucking a coil of twine from a shelf on her way out.

Maybe Agatha was going to strangle her with it. Rhoda wrinkled her nose at the thought. The witch had been nothing but kind to her since she'd woken the day prior. She'd even saved Blayze's life. It wouldn't hurt to be a little kinder, even if only internally.

* * *

They passed the time companionably enough, tying herbs in bundles and adding the occasional spice to the soup. Rhoda came to know Agatha's daily routine—the early hour at which she rose, the gentle tones she used when feeding her chickens, and the quiet hum of pleasure when she tasted a good broth. Twice a day, Rhoda helped Agatha administer Blayze's medicine. She hoped he woke soon, if only because he was beginning to smell, and *she* certainly wasn't going to wash him. Rhoda's own strength returned to her muscles before her lungs, but she still managed to chop enough firewood for Agatha's hearth each day. No matter how many logs she stacked by the house, however, they were gone by morning.

"It's the perfect amount!" Agatha would declare whenever Rhoda expressed frustration that she could not keep up with the witch's demand. "You are doing splendidly. Now, here, try a honey-roasted beet."

She was never alone, a phenomenon Rhoda had left behind in childhood, and yet she did not find the witch's presence grating. She was used to ample time spent in solitude—Lady Gracelyn did not have time to while away the hours with her (she had a stronghold to run) and Rhoda's siblings labored most of the day (they had families to feed). In fact, she'd spent more time with Blayze Blubberbutt in recent history than with anyone else. Even before their ill-fated quest, he'd always seemed to be wherever she was needed. Most often, her leisure time was spent in silent contemplation as she groomed her horse or sharpened her sword or polished her armor. Agatha's quiet companionship was a welcome balm to a wound she'd not truly realized was open.

Around mid-afternoon, as the sun bent lower in the sky, the light filtering into the clearing through jagged tree branches, exhaustion softened Rhoda. Agatha insisted she sleep for a while, but Rhoda caught sight of the witch stealing away into the trees through her eyelashes and returning just before dusk. It was the only time of any consequence they were apart.

After one such excursion, Agatha prodded Rhoda to consciousness, a plate outstretched before her bearing two fried eggs with crispy edges and crushed herbs and chili flakes sprinkled on top.

"Eat," Agatha insisted, pushing the eggs toward her. "You need protein to regain your strength."

Rhoda moved to the stump close to the fire to eat her meal. "Isn't Nugget a rooster?" she asked through a mouthful of egg.

"He is."

"Roosters don't lay eggs, I thought."

"They don't." Agatha pointed into the bushes.

Rhoda narrowed her eyes, gaze catching on the movement of two golden feathered hens weaving between the roots of a nearby tree and pecking at the ground with laser focus.

"Gorgonzola and Gladiator keep me well fed."

Rhoda nearly choked on the second egg, but thought better of questioning Agatha's naming conventions. Instead, she asked, "Why keep the rooster, then?"

"Nugget?" Agatha's gaze snapped to her, sharp as an arrow. "Now, why would you ask something like that?"

"I just thought since he doesn't lay eggs, he's not actually useful, right?"

"Does he need to be?"

The question was asked without edge, but Rhoda still felt herself harden. "We all need a purpose. It's what gives our lives meaning."

Agatha's tongue clicked against her teeth. "Who on earth told you that?"

"Who told me?" Rhoda's eyebrows shot up. "No one needed to *tell* me. Isn't that a universal truth?"

"How universal can it be if I don't believe it?"

"Maybe things are different for you, but where I come from, I perform a service for the stronghold, and in exchange receive protection and a wage. The greater the service, the higher I am held in esteem. If I was not useful, there would be no point in keeping me around."

Agatha's lips twitched into a frown. "I'm sorry. That's terrible."

"Terrible? That I receive rewards for my good work?"

"Terrible that you have been made to feel as though you are only as worthy as your deeds."

"That's just how society works."

"Oh, Rhoda." Agatha shook her head in the manner of a disappointed teacher. She sank to her knees in the dirt, hands finding Rhoda's legs as she spoke in an earnest tone. "Society is not a fixed thing. Society is what we make it."

Rhoda didn't know what to say to that, so she looked down, worrying a mossy stone with her fingernail. It was the color of Agatha's eyes—green and gray with speckles of gold. Agatha's thumb seemed to trace the same pattern in the fabric over Rhoda's knee.

She liked the rules of society—they told her where she belonged, what she deserved. How else was she meant to measure her accomplishments? It felt good, she'd always told herself, to earn her keep, to earn her trophies, to earn her lady's time. What was worth having that was not honestly won?

"A single phoenix feather," Rhoda whispered.

"What's that, now?"

"The cost of my lady's hand in marriage."

"They're making you *buy* her?" Agatha's expression soured.

"No, no. It's what she wants from us—me and Blayze. Whoever brings her the feather will win her eternal love."

"And what of yours?"

"My what?"

"Your eternal love?"

"It is hers—I give it freely."

Agatha looked at her expectantly, as though there was more to be said, another step to be taken.

"Oh." Rhoda's gaze faltered as her logic crumbled before her like crispy dried oregano.

Rhoda had been bold in her affections, and Lady Gracelyn had accepted her eager acts of service. She'd accepted them, but never returned them. Rhoda would have gladly spent the rest of her life pleasing her lady, but would it ever be reciprocated? There was the ugly truth of it. She could love Lady Gracelyn with every muscle in her body, with every ounce of her spirit, but the best she could hope for was that Lady Gracelyn would let her. She could not hope to be loved in return.

"I'm sorry," Agatha said, finally, a whispered lament.

"You have nothing to apologize for." Rhoda averted her gaze. She did not think she could look into Agatha's verdant eyes without crying. "You only led me to the truth."

Rhoda's knee went cold with the absence of Agatha's hand, and she keened. She'd not realized how much the other woman's touch was grounding her until she lost it. But then, Agatha's thumb found her chin and tilted Rhoda's face until they were eye to eye.

"I'm not apologizing," she said. "I'm *sorry*. There is a difference."

"There is?" Rhoda barely managed, breathless at the intensity in Agatha's gaze.

"I'm sorry you have not been loved the way you deserve."

"Deserve? I don't know that I deserve—"

Agatha pressed her thumb against Rhoda's lips, quieting her. "You deserve," she said firmly. "You deserve to be loved freely. You deserve to be loved with the same vigor with which you love. You deserve to be loved in a way that makes you feel worthy of it. Every day."

Rhoda's lips parted on a sharp inhale as Agatha rose up and leaned forward, coming to rest between Rhoda's thighs. They were mere inches apart, and Rhoda was acutely aware of all the places they touched, of the bead of sweat dampening the golden curls framing Agatha's face, of the flush of freckled skin just below Agatha's collar bones.

Around Gracelyn, Rhoda's mouth felt dry, and her skin felt clammy. The woman made her nervous beyond belief, the fear that her lady might toss her aside at any time, a deep ache in her bones. But she was not thinking of Gracelyn now. The careful angles of noble cheekbones, the dark sweep of shiny hair, the smooth unweathered skin that had seen no labor...it had once been her only focus. But now, she preferred this bright, sunny spot of reality.

Exhaling, Rhoda's tongue touched the tip of Agatha's thumb, eliciting a smile from the witch. Agatha dragged her thumb over Rhoda's bottom lip, a playful tug, a gentle tease. Rhoda's heart seemed to stutter in her chest, and the realization crashed over her that she had never really *been* kissed—not like this. She'd always been the one to do the kissing. So, even though she wanted it, even though she felt herself lean into Agatha's touch like a compass to north, she waited for Agatha to cross the remaining distance until their breath tangled and finally, *finally*...

"My tummy hurts!" came the unmistakable whine of Blayze Blunderbuss. He stood on the threshold of Agatha's little hut with the imprint of a pillow pressed firmly onto one side of his face and look of consternation in his eyes. He held up a soiled bit of cloth and said, "Can one of you come smell this and tell me if it's normal?"

* * *

Now that Blayze was decidedly alive, Rhoda had never wished him deader. Before he woke, there had been a gentleness to the witch's glade—the patches of sunlight, the pockets of silence, the camaraderie she'd built with Agatha that felt so easy and so right. After, it was as if a tempest had ripped through it all, casting everything into disarray.

Now, there were three of them.

And it was time to leave.

Rhoda knew it, even if Blayze did not. He seemed content to make his mark on the place. He sprawled across the clearing like an enormous cat luxuriating in a sun spot. His things were scattered everywhere, and he was simply too loud. He walked loudly, he chewed loudly, and he even *thought* loudly—speaking his every notion as if they were a sharing-circle and he had eternal possession of the sharing stick.

Rhoda could think of a place she'd like to shove that stick. Instead, she channeled her energy into chopping wood. She was no longer so physically tired that she could not complete the task the witch had set her. It was time to stop dallying. She needed to replenish the witch's wood pile and return to hunting the phoenix, wherever it might be.

What came after that...she could not bring herself to think about in detail. Gracelyn's face was naught but a blur in her mind's eye, a prize she was too afraid to think about lest it spoil.

"That's enough," came Agatha's mild tone as Rhoda swung the axe above her head for the umpteenth time.

"Not hardly," Rhoda replied with a grunt before letting the axe fall and splitting the log in two. "I estimate I have halfway to go still."

Agatha's hand found Rhoda's bare shoulder, quieting her—body and spirit. Rhoda's grip on the axe slackened as the tension in her jaw bled away. Agatha didn't speak for a moment, letting her searching gaze sweep over Rhoda. The little desperate part of Rhoda's brain, all needy and indulgent, came to life under Agatha's soft touch. She wondered briefly what the witch saw as she studied her form. Was Rhoda the capable soldier, all glistening sweat over rippling muscles? Or was she the invalid, still too weak to meet the witch's needs?

Despite herself, Rhoda flexed just a little.

"I was just about to go for an egg hunt, if you care to join me. Gorgonzola's a creature of habit, but I think Gladiator may have found a new laying spot and I intend to sniff it out," Agatha said, gaze darting toward the shadow of the trees.

Blayze belched loudly, the sound carrying all the way around the back of Agatha's house.

Rhoda threw down the axe. "Yes, alright. A break sounds nice."

It felt good to stretch her legs. She was unaccustomed to sore muscles from inactivity. It was altogether a different kind of pain. She vastly preferred the sort that spoke of a job well done, an enemy well fought, or a lover well pleased. But trudging through the ankle-deep shrubbery of the forest floor felt like learning to walk all over again, her muscles stiff and her joints unyielding.

"Letting your chickens roam free seems an awful risk to take in a place like this," Rhoda said once they were out of view of the camp. "Aren't you worried they'll run off?"

Agatha's expression pinched. "Why would they? This is home."

"Sure, but aren't there other risks?"

"Like what?"

"Like...poisonous mushrooms?"

"They know better than we do which plants are toxic and which are safe to eat."

"Okay, what about dangerous animals?"

Agatha scoffed. "They can take care of themselves, believe me."

Rhoda tried to imagine a chicken facing off against a cougar or a bear and grimaced. She wasn't entirely familiar with the fauna of the fire swamp, but surely the place had grizzly wildlife to offer, like...

"What about the phoenix?"

Agatha fixed Rhoda with a penetrating stare, searching, seeking...

"Is that what you fear most in these woods?"

Rhoda shrugged. "I do not think I am so weak of spirit..."

"Naming your fear is not a thing that makes you weak, Rhoda." Agatha took a step toward her, then another. "It is the unspoken fears that hold power over us. They devour you from the inside, in solitude. When you speak the fear aloud, then you do not have to fight it alone."

"I'm not afraid of the phoenix," Rhoda said firmly. "I am not afraid of beasts—physical manifestations of power I can fight with my blade." She'd fought worse than phoenixes, of course: wyverns and chimeras and harpies. All of them had left her with scars, but she'd come away victorious in the end. No, she did not fear the fight.

Agatha took yet another step toward her, forcing Rhoda to cede the space until her back hit the trunk of a tree.

"Then what is it that you fear?"

Rhoda made a face. "Had I known a walk in the woods with you would include such an interrogation, I might have stayed with Blayze and his unfortunate gaseous emissions."

"I'm sorry." Agatha rocked back on her heels. "I did not mean to make you feel cornered." The intensity waned from her eyes and her gaze slid from Rhoda's face.

Rhoda started forward, Agatha's surrender feeling less like victory and more like loss. She reached for the witch's arm, determined to see this—whatever it was—through to the end. But before she could catch Agatha, she slipped through Rhoda's fingers and lunged toward the ground.

"Aha! Found you!"

In a tangle of roots protruding from the ground lay a golden ball of feathers that could only be Gladiator, the chicken, who let out an indignant cluck. Agatha lifted her carefully with both hands, murmuring gentle nonsense.

For a moment, Rhoda imagined how it might feel to be so small, to be lifted from her feet—Agatha's left hand splayed across her chest, the right pinned against her shoulder blades.

Before she could dispel herself of the notion, Rhoda stepped close to Agatha so when the other woman stood, they were nearly touching. "I am not afraid of a phoenix," she said again. "I know what the future holds if I complete my quest, but I'm not sure I want that future anymore. But without it...I am afraid I will no longer be myself." Rhoda's eyes grew heavy as her confession broke from her chest. "I am afraid of letting go and discovering there is no one waiting to catch me."

Agatha dropped the chicken. With one hand, she pulled Rhoda to her by the forearm, her other hand fisting itself in Rhoda's tunic. Heat bloomed between them, as Agatha's whispered answer was swallowed by their kiss:

"I'll catch you."

Kissing Agatha was like watching a sunrise. Her lips were rays of light—gold and coral and lilac—washing over Rhoda to melt the exhaustion from her limbs and heart. She gripped Agatha's waist, barely daring to touch the sliver of exposed skin between layers of cloth. Agatha's body molded to hers like a heavy syrup, gentle and slow. It felt rapturous: to hold the witch in her arms, to be held in return.

Agatha pulled away, a mortifying whine escaping Rhoda, but Agatha did not let her suffer for long, trailing kisses down her throat and across her collar, hot and blistering. It was nothing to the heat that pooled low in Rhoda's belly, along her thighs, at her very center. Her eyes fluttered closed as she tipped her head back.

She never closed her eyes with Gracelyn.

The thought hit her like a ton of bricks. She didn't want to think of Gracelyn now. She didn't want to compare them.

"I'm sorry." Agatha stepped back, hands splayed in a gesture of surrender. "That was too much?"

Rhoda blinked, taking in the sight of the witch. Her hat was askew, lips swollen, virescent gaze thick like honey mead. Rhoda knew desire when she saw it. Gracelyn, for all that she did not love Rhoda in return, had certainly *wanted* her. She summoned Rhoda to her chambers often enough, commanded Rhoda to take her with fingers, with fist, with tongue. Rhoda had seen eyes drunk with pleasure and passion. She had never seen them drunk with hunger—for *her*.

Rhoda stumbled over roots to take Agatha's hand in her own. "Not too much," she said, breathless. "Not enough."

A smile unfurled on Agatha's lips as she pushed up onto her toes to meet Rhoda in a kiss. They stumbled together back toward the solid support of the tree, a languid dance of limbs and clothes as they shed their layers. Rhoda's tunic, Agatha's apron, their shoes and socks became a tapestry of discarded barriers.

Rhoda's hands were greedy in their touch as she trailed her fingers across freckled skin, connecting the constellations on the apex of Agatha's shoulders, the rounded crests of her hips, the hollow between her breasts. Agatha mirrored her exploration, touch catching on the ridges of muscle on Rhoda's back and the crease of her thigh.

It had never been like this before—two navigators in uncharted territory. Rhoda had never thought overlong about her body, about whether it would be pleasing to others. It hadn't been *for* others in such a very long time.

"Can I…" she whispered as her hand came to rest just below Agatha's breast.

Agatha nodded, reaching for Rhoda's hand and moving it up…up…up…

Brushing her thumb over a wine-dark nipple, taut with desire, Rhoda bent her head to take the other in her mouth. Agatha tasted of salt and sage and the fresh dew after a cold night. Her fingers tangled in Rhoda's hair, pulling gently at the nape as a moan echoed between them. A pang of need swept through her, and Rhoda's legs trembled slightly as she lowered herself to her knees. She'd never been one for religion, nor had she cared for the ways of heathens, but here in the grove of the fire swamp, she was prepared to worship the body of a witch.

"Wait," Agatha said, pulling Rhoda back to her feet. "Wait."

"What's wrong?" Rhoda's tongue felt heavy. Her heart thundered against her ribs, her core suddenly cold at the rejection. If she could not be good at this, then what was she? "You don't want—"

"Oh, I want." Agatha smirked as she traced a line down Rhoda's chest, coming to rest just above the thicket of curls at her center. "But I want *you* first."

Agatha pulled Rhoda's hips forward and spun them so Rhoda's back was once more against the tree. She laced their fingers together before pressing in for another kiss, slow and deep. Rhoda's breath caught and her eyelids shuttered as Agatha ran her nails lightly up her stomach. A shiver coursed through Rhoda, and she reached for Agatha instinctually.

Agatha tutted. "Can't have you getting distracted," she purred before pinning Rhoda's hands above her head. "I want you focused."

"But I—"

Agatha silenced her with a kiss, teasing her bottom lip with her teeth as she drew away. "But what?"

Rhoda's words felt stupid and thick on her tongue as she put voice to the tightness in her chest. "I'm better at the other part. I'm good, I promise. If you'll just let me—"

"If you don't want this, just say the word." Agatha loosened her grip on Rhoda's hands, but didn't let go. "But if your only objection is that you might not be good at receiving pleasure, let me prove you wrong."

Rhoda only knew how to love in acts of service. She didn't know how to receive them, herself. It was where she was comfortable, practiced. But maybe it was time to try something new.

"Prove me wrong," she said, wishing her words sounded more like a challenge than a plea.

"With pleasure."

It was Agatha's words as much as her touch that made Rhoda's stomach swoop, her need building with every passing second.

"You're pretty when you let go," Agatha said before running her tongue over the sensitive peak of Rhoda's breast. "So pretty."

Rhoda arched, following the retreat of Agatha's mouth, but the witch whispered the words again, her breath a cool balm against Rhoda's skin. She lowered herself between Rhoda's legs, one hand braced against her hip, their gazes locked. The rhythm of Rhoda's heart felt uneven and unpredictable, a nervous tremor. Still, though she'd known Agatha only a matter of days, she knew Agatha would take care of her. She was the first person who'd ever wanted to, and that felt like a small miracle.

Rhoda watched, rapt as Agatha sank lower at an agonizing pace. She burned kisses into the hollow of Rhoda's hip like a brand. Her fingers danced lower, coming to rest at the base of Rhoda's spine.

Rhoda couldn't help herself. She parted her legs, an invitation.

"Eager, are we?" Agatha gave her a sly smile before turning her attention to the tender flesh of Rhoda's inner thigh.

Rhoda tipped her head back further as Agatha inched her way toward her center, brushing her knuckles against Rhoda's curls. A whimper escaped her at the merest contact, and she opened her legs wider.

"I don't know," Agatha said as she licked up Rhoda's thigh. "I rather like it over here."

Rhoda failed to hold back a whine.

"No?" Agatha asked, a teasing quality to her voice. "Tell me, where should I touch you?"

Rhoda couldn't put it to words. She was used to Gracelyn making demands in the bedroom, but it felt somehow wrong or embarrassing to verbalize her own desires. Instead, she reached for Agatha's hand and drew it down. Agatha's gaze caught hers, heat building where Agatha cupped her. For a moment, they stayed just like that, with Rhoda standing against the tree and Agatha on her knees. It felt reverent, it felt revelatory.

Then, Agatha touched her, running a finger along her entrance and up her slit. "Amazing," Agatha whispered. "You're amazing." She circled her clit once, twice.

All Rhoda had done was stand there, her folds a slick providence of desire. But as Agatha murmured affirmations against the skin of her belly, her fingers stoking her into a ball of nerves and tension, Rhoda found herself believing. She did not have to be anyone or do anything to deserve this. When Agatha touched her, Rhoda wasn't a knight or a peasant or even a damn good lumberjack. She was just herself.

"Can I taste you?"

It took Rhoda a moment to realize Agatha had asked her a question amid the medley of pretty words and gentle ministrations. Agatha's fingers carved a labyrinthine path around her clit that made Rhoda's limbs quiver. She felt weak, but somehow not broken.

"Yes," Rhoda replied, barely a whisper. This was how it felt to surrender without losing.

Agatha bent her head and lifted Rhoda's leg over her shoulder. Then, Agatha's mouth was on her, warm breath like embers. Her tongue dragged pleasure from the depths of Rhoda's body. She licked and sucked in patterns Rhoda couldn't fathom, a maddening rhythm. When she dipped a finger into Rhoda's opening, it was almost too much.

"So good," Agatha said against her clit, the words rumbling through Rhoda's entire body. "Perfect."

Rhoda fisted her fingers in Agatha's hair as she came, arching against the rough bark of the tree. Her vision went white as her body clenched around Agatha's fingers. It felt like falling, like flying, like a gods-damned metamorphosis.

Agatha was true to her word; she caught her, lowering them both toward the forest floor. She nuzzled Rhoda's neck, pressing a soft kiss to her throat, her temple, then her lips.

"See?" she said through a grin, removing her fingers from Rhoda's folds and licking them clean. "I told you you'd be good at this."

There was a hazy sort of indulgence to the moments after, with Agatha's body curled around her, the witch tracing invisible lines along her breast bone. Rhoda was used to the perfunctory scuttle to resume her work after such entanglements—with Lady Gracelyn or by herself. There wasn't time in the strict schedule of Daggerhold for relaxation. Maybe that was how Gracelyn preferred it— without time for reciprocity.

"Give me a second and I can—"

Agatha pressed a finger to her lips. "There's no reason to rush."

Rhoda pushed herself up on her elbows. "But you—"

Without ceremony, Agatha threw her leg over Rhoda's hips, straddling her and pinning her to the ground. "But I am content." She stroked Rhoda's hair, smoothing it and tucking the short strands behind her ear. "I like looking at you."

Truth be told, Rhoda liked looking at Agatha, too. It didn't hurt that the witch was utterly celestial above her, brown skin bathed in the afternoon glow. She reached for Agatha, unable to stand another second without kissing her beautiful mouth. As she hitched her hips to bring the witch closer, their lips mere inches apart, there came a loud squawk and a flurry of feathers. Gladiator scurried up Agatha's back to perch directly in her hair, beady eyes gazing through the trees.

Laughter bubbled up from Rhoda's throat, bright and unrestrained. "I'm sorry," she said, wiping tears from the corners of her eyes. "I just didn't except to be cock blocked quite so literally."

Smile lines creased Agatha's face, bracketing her mouth in perfect symmetry. Rhoda couldn't help but kiss her. She sat up as best she could with Agatha planted above her, but before their lips touched, the chicken squawked again, a shrill and urgent tone. Agatha shoved Rhoda away, hand covering her entire face as Agatha pushed her against the forest floor.

Just in time, too. A jet of hot orange flame erupted from the chicken's beak, scorching the foliage above Rhoda's head.

"What the—"

"We've got visitors." Agatha got to her feet.

Rhoda followed suit, casting her gaze about the clearing. She didn't see anyone, but she heard the sound of heavy footfalls crunching the underbrush nearby. If Blayze had followed them all the way out here to ruin yet another intimate moment, she really was going to have to resort to unsavory methods of disposal.

It wasn't Blayze.

The silver glint of armor shone through the trees as two knights of the realm advanced. They wore full plate armor embossed with the crest of Daggerhold and carried spears.

"Halt!" one of them shouted.

"Drop your weapon!" called the other.

Rhoda reached for her hip where she normally carried her sword, but she'd left it back at Agatha's camp. Besides which, she and Agatha were both entirely naked.

Agatha, however, arched a brow and indicated the chicken still nested atop her hair. "You mean this old bird?"

While the knights bent their helmeted heads to confer, Agatha mirrored them.

"This can't be good," she whispered.

Rhoda was inclined to agree. Though she stood perfectly still, her mind was a flurry of activity. What were guards doing here? Who had sent them? Back at Daggerhold, the sight of fully armored knights would hardly have phased her, but here in the swamp, they were more of a surprise than fire-breathing chickens.

Agatha brushed Rhoda's arm with her own, grounding her to the moment. "I want you to do me a favor," she said. "Don't ask any questions, just do one thing for me."

Rhoda didn't even have to think about it. "Anything."

"On my signal, run."

Cowardice had been bled and beaten from Rhoda's spirit long ago. Her instinct was to stand and fight, always, against all odds. But Agatha was no warrior, and Rhoda wouldn't force her into conflict she didn't welcome. Besides which, Rhoda wasn't confident they could do much unarmed and undressed against two knights. Not even with a fire-breathing chicken on their side.

"You're to come with us," said one of the knights. "Our orders are to retrieve any transients by whatever means necessary."

"Well, then I suppose we have but one choice." Agatha's lips quirked slightly. "Run!"

Following orders was what Rhoda did best, so she turned tail and sprinted for the cover of the trees. It wasn't until she felt the heat at her back and heard a scream that she realized Agatha wasn't with her. She turned, eyes widening at the sight.

Fire filled the air with Agatha at its very center. She swayed, hips and shoulders moving in a hypnotic pattern as she gathered flames around her like a cloak. Flesh turned to feathers before Rhoda's very eyes, taking a form she'd seen before.

Agatha *was* the phoenix.

"Don't—don't come any closer." One of the knights had fallen and was scooting away from the towering bird. The other was pinned against the trunk of a tree.

The phoenix stepped toward the knights, graceful and commanding in its intention: *flee or burn.*

Rhoda didn't wait to find out the knights' fate. She sped through the trees, branches scraping her arms and legs as she went. It wasn't until she broke through a thicket of brambles and found herself on a narrow but distinct path that she realized she was lost. Without the witch by her side, she had no idea what direction her camp lay. She looked up and down the path for a sign of familiarity.

Instead, she found a feather.

Red and orange plumage fell from the sky like ash, bright against the green canopy above her. Rhoda stood with reverent stillness as one of the feathers drifted down toward her, landing in her open palm. It was still warm to touch.

"Rhoda?"

Her name was a melody, spoken curiously with the same sweetness that filled the air. Rhoda closed her eyes, barely willing to believe it would not be some deception of the swamp. But when she turned to look, it was she.

Lady Gracelyn.

Dressed in a gown of white silk, Gracelyn looked like a dainty pearl. The fabric shimmered as she moved, giving it an almost liquid quality. Dark hair fell in perfect waves down her back, adorned with teardrop diamonds hanging from a silver circlet. She was the embodiment of a snowflake in a world of fire.

"Why haven't you any clothes?" she asked with just a hint of humor.

Rhoda looked down at her naked body and thought of her tunic discarded in the wake of her and Agatha's passions. It was probably burnt to a crisp now.

"Never mind. We'll find you something suitable on the way back." Gracelyn beckoned her forward, indicating her palanquin bracketed by four servants. She picked up her skirts and led the way.

Rhoda stayed rooted to the spot.

"What are you doing here?" she asked, voice crackling.

Gracelyn whipped around, though her hair stayed perfectly still. "I should've thought that was obvious. I came to fetch you, of course." Her gaze, a brilliant blue, sliced into Rhoda like blades. "You were gone so long, I feared the witch had got you." Incredulous laughter scraped at her like shrapnel. "But of course that was a ridiculous notion."

Rhoda still didn't follow, looking from the feather in her palm to the derisive smile on Lady Gracelyn's perfect full lips.

"Come, now." Gracelyn reached for her hand. "You have completed your quest and may return to Daggerhold in triumph to collect your prize." She said it with a sultry air, a private insinuation just for her. "You've earned it."

It was all Rhoda had ever wanted.

It was no longer enough.

"What about Blayze?" Rhoda heard herself ask. It wasn't the question she wanted answered, but she didn't know how to put voice to all the thoughts swirling in her mind.

"Who?" Gracelyn furrowed her brow.

"Blayze. You know, Blayze... Bl...ayze." Rhoda fished around her memory for his surname and came up empty. "You know, the other contender. Do you not wish to bring him back as well?"

Gracelyn shook her head. "I know not of whom you speak."

Well, that was inconceivable. Blayze was her rival, her opponent, her enemy. Wasn't he? She thought back to all their time together, but without the shroud of competition, she found the memories softer, rosier. He was a companion, a peer, maybe someday even a friend.

"Hark, foes!" A form rushed from the trees, a streak of rippled muscle and...feathers. Blayze stood between them, shirtless and cradling a chicken in each of his palms. "Cower before my fire power. Oh hey, that rhymed! A poet, and I wasn't even aware!"

Gorgonzola clucked, letting out a spark, while Nugget simply pecked at Blayze's fingers.

A thousand questions rose in her mind—like how did he know she was there, and how did he know the chickens could breathe fire, and what was his real last name—but the one she gave breath to was, "Do you even want to marry Lady Gracelyn?"

"Of course not!" Blayze lowered the chicken slightly.

"Then why on earth did you come on this quest?"

"Couldn't let you go alone, could I?" He chuckled as though it was the most obvious thing in the world. "You're my best friend, after all."

Rhoda's cheeks heated with shame at all the horrible things she'd thought about him. Though she'd never voiced a one, her animosity for him had been unfair and entirely avoidable. Blayze Buddybum, a friend.

Gracelyn looked at the entire tableau with thinly veiled disgust. "Well, this certainly has been...it has *been*."

Blayze's eyes almost skipped over Gracelyn, as though she were a quotidian decoration like a landscape painting or a potted plant. Instead, his gaze fell on the feather cupped in Rhoda's hand. "You've done it!" he gasped, dropping Gorgonzola, who promptly scurried back into the underbrush. Nugget looked on with longing—or as much longing as a chicken could muster. "You found the phoenix!"

"Or the phoenix found me," Rhoda muttered.

"My Gods! It wasn't Gladiator, was it? She was obviously the ring leader."

Ignoring Blayze, Rhoda opened Gracelyn's palm and placed the feather there, stark against ivory skin. It was what she'd set out to do, and like any good knight, Rhoda did not leave her quests undone.

"There," she said, folding Gracelyn's fingers over the feather and letting her thumb run over soft unburdened skin. "You have what you came for."

Gracelyn smiled, a perfunctory gesture. "Time to depart." She turned toward the palanquin, her servants standing to attention, but Rhoda held her in place, hand braced on Gracelyn's arm.

"I won't be going with you." Rhoda thought she would feel some shadow of fear when she said it aloud, but no regret haunted her words. "This is goodbye."

Gracelyn fixed her with a perplexed expression. "I don't understand. You found the phoenix feather. You've completed the quest. Now we may leave together..." She blinked several times in rapid succession. "To be married, Rhoda."

"Is that what you want?" Rhoda asked.

"Why must you ask such insipid questions? The quest is complete, the criteria fulfilled. As per the stipulations of our agreement, we must now be wed."

The laugh tore from Rhoda's chest, a painful bark. "So romantic of you."

She had imagined returning to the Daggerhold on horseback (though she'd taken no horse to the swamp), dressed in a fine doublet embroidered with golden thread (though she owned no such garment). She would ascend the steps to her lady's grand hall and kneel before her on the marble floor to offer a phoenix feather for her love. It would have been a proposal for the ages. Someone (not her) would write poems about it.

No one would write about this.

"I used to think love was something to achieve, like a medal or a trophy," Rhoda began. "I thought if I was good enough, then love would be mine. But love isn't about being good or accomplished or revered. Love is something you give, it's something you receive. It's not something you take."

"You think me greedy?" Gracelyn stared at her, no malice in her gaze.

It was an honest question, so Rhoda answered with the truth.

"I think your needs are different from mine. You need someone whose pleasure lies solely in being your pillar. You need someone steadfast, someone brilliant, someone who needs to make you happy."

"And that isn't you?"

"I thought it could be, but...I need someone who wants to make me happy, too."

Gracelyn swallowed, her throat working as she surveyed Rhoda. "I thought you were happy with me."

"Someone will be—I know that. Someone who wants to make you their world, someone who does not want the things I want..."

"What do you want?" Gracelyn asked in a small voice.

"I want to be held by someone who wants to hold me. I want to wake up to the smell of breakfast already cooking. I want to braid lavender and watch it dry while talking about everything and nothing. I want to live my life *with* someone instead of for them, and—"

"And you have found that someone?"

Rhoda's chest constricted. Had she? Agatha had not said whether her affections were for the moment or forever. Rhoda hoped it was the latter, but it had no bearing on her decision now.

"I know it's not you."

Gracelyn nodded slowly. "I see." She set her shoulders and held the phoenix feather to her chest. "Then I suppose I came here for nothing."

If it wasn't for the single tear that raced down Gracelyn's cheek, Rhoda would have thought it was true. She fought the urge to reach out and wipe it away. It wasn't her job anymore.

She stood in silence, watching as Gracelyn's servants carried her away on the palanquin until the lady she'd loved was only a speck in the distance.

"You know I'm not romantically or sexually inclined, right?" asked Blayze.

Rhoda jumped. She'd quite forgotten he was there. "What?"

"I'm afraid your love for me is doomed to be unrequited."

Rhoda stalked back into the forest without a word.

* * *

Rhoda found Agatha curled in the roots of a tree, her arms and legs pulled tight around her body. The only signs of fire were the scorch marks on the trees and burned underbrush around her, but no flames remained. Her eyes were closed, but her chest rose and fell in shallow breaths.

"Agatha?"

She didn't stir.

Rhoda's heart rocketed into her throat as she knelt beside her. She was cold to the touch, as if all her flames had stolen her heat. That was how phoenixes worked, she supposed, but that didn't stop the jolt of panic through her body. Gathering Agatha in her arms, Rhoda held her close. She could share her warmth if nothing else.

When at last they reached the camp, Rhoda bent to set Agatha down in the makeshift bed where Rhoda herself had slept.

"Too cold," Agatha whispered into Rhoda's shoulder, snuggling closer.

"I know, I know." Rhoda laid her down in the bed and pulled the crochet blanket up over Agatha's body. It was her turn to take care of the witch. "I'll only be a moment."

She made quick work of it, moving about the camp like it was her own. She had a fire going in no time, sending a warm glow over the entire camp. In the soup pot, she did her best imitation of Agatha's broth, adding herbs as she stirred and tasting it until it was passable enough to serve.

"Eat this." Rhoda held out a spoonful of broth for Agatha, waiting for the witch to drink every last drop before she climbed onto the mossy bed beside her, wrapping arms around her body and pulling her close. She smelled like charcoal and earth.

"You're here," Agatha murmured against Rhoda's chest.

"Is that all right? I wouldn't want to exceed my welcome..."

Agatha gripped Rhoda tighter, as though afraid she would fly away—never mind Agatha was the one with wings. "She came for you, didn't she?"

"She did." Rhoda had only wanted to end things between her and the lady. Now, she was ready to start anew. "I sent her back alone."

"You did?" Agatha tilted her head back to look at Rhoda, gaze quivering.

"I hope that was all right—" Rhoda stopped herself short. She'd spent a lifetime letting someone else's desires dictate her life. No more. "What I mean to say is that there is no other place I'd rather be—not now. Maybe not for a long while."

Agatha blinked at her, patient as ever.

"You have changed my world," Rhoda continued. "I thought I understood what it was to live, but before I met you, I was only surviving, only worthy if I provided service to others." A smile flitted unbidden to her lips. "Here I feel...beyond value."

"That is because you are," Agatha murmured. "You are enough, exactly as you are."

Rhoda felt the truth surround her like a twin crochet blanket, warm and worn and made with love. "Do you suppose that means I can stop chopping your firewood?"

Agatha cackled, a bright and brilliant sound like fire snapping. "I'm a witch, Rhoda. I don't need wood to make a fire."

"So...can I stay?" Rhoda asked.

"Yes! Yes!" As she repeated the affirmative, Agatha planted kisses on Rhoda's forehead, her cheeks, her nose, her jaw until she fell back into her arms. "I hoped you would, only...I wasn't sure you'd want to."

"Why wouldn't I?" Rhoda lowered her head, hovering her lips just above the witch's. "This is home."

"Home sweet home!" Came Blayze's cheerful voice from just behind them.

Rhoda deflated. Though her affection for the man had grown significantly that day, she wearied of his interruptions. A conversation about boundaries was certainly in order, perhaps best saved for a time when they were all adequately clothed.

"Let's go inside," Agatha suggested, eyes dancing with mischief. "I believe we have some unfinished business, and we are still naked, after all."

"Excellent notion." Rhoda pulled the witch to her feet and hurried toward the hut. She was barely inside before Agatha had her pinned to the door, lips on hers. Whatever exhaustion she'd suffered on account of her transformation seemed to melt away with every touch. If her display of fire had been a death, then perhaps this was the rebirth.

Rhoda met Agatha's voracity with her own. Their tangle in the woods had been only the prelude, and Rhoda could not wait to discover what other pleasure there was to be had at the hands of the witch—hands that were currently exploring her most eagerly, fingers already drawing shivers from Rhoda's body as they worked against her.

Two could play at that game. Rhoda nudged her leg between Agatha's, letting the witch ride her thigh until they were both panting, barely holding each other up as the world went hazy and Rhoda felt so wound she might never fully unravel.

"Guys? Can I come in?" Blayze asked through the door. "Gorgonzola and Gladiator won't stop staring at me. I think they're plotting something."

Rhoda groaned. "Please tell me your door locks."

There was an audible click, and Rhoda let herself succumb to bliss.

"The Fire Swamp is for Lovers" is a stand-alone short story by Rosiee Thor, whose short fiction can be found in anthologies such as *Lofty Mountains, The House Where Death Lives,* and *Being Ace.* In longer form, Rosiee is the author of young adult novels *Tarnished are the Stars* and *Fire Becomes Her,* the picture book *The Meaning of Pride,* and official tie-in novels for franchises like *Life is Strange* and *Firefly.* You can find Rosiee online at www.rosieethor.com or on social media @rosieethor.

The Flamesmith

William C. Tracy

Sapphic Representation: Lesbian
Heat Level: Medium
Content Warnings: Violence, Discussion of death and abuse, Plague

I put down my pack and stretch my back, staring at the dark entrance to the cave of the flamesmith. Even from here, I can see lights dancing in the darkness, as if fire itself jumps from one place to another. I have traveled long weeks all the way from the other side of the island, from the ashes of my village. All my hopes and dreams are pinned on the answer the flamesmith will give me.

She must grant my desire.

My pack has only a few stale rinds of bread, a quarter of a skin of water, and a few other necessary items. I have no coins to pay for the flamesmith's services, but I don't let that stop me. This is the only goal left in my life now, a journey, a pilgrimage for one thing only.

To feel again.

The cave entrance is a welcome respite from the hot midday sun, and I pause to let my eyes adjust to the dimness. But there are lights in here, placed around the cave. It is bigger than I first assumed and is even hotter than outside. The ground must slope gently down here, the entrance opening to an underground amphitheater. As I slowly pan across the dark walls, I see evidence of the cave's expansion from its natural state, to make places for treasures beyond my imagination. Each gently glows red, or orange, or yellow on its pedestal. A rose here. Several bronze staves. A helm of flames. A cup filled with orange light. At the back of the room is a hearth dug into the wall, flames leaping from a blaze that makes the chamber stifling.

But in the center of the room is my target. The object of my weeks of travel across swampy lands infested with crocodiles and hippos, of biting insects the size of my thumb.

The flamesmith is a behemoth of a woman, head and shoulders taller than me, her skin blending in with the earthen shadows. Her back is turned to me and her arms bulge with muscle as she wrestles with an object out of my sight. Her mighty legs are thick and strong, thighs glistening with sweat as she stands astride a small workbench, backside clenched. Flashes of red and orange sneak around her figure, as I rustle my sandals on the dirt to announce my presence.

The flamesmith turns to me, even more impressive from the front than the rear. Her black hair is braided close to her head, in rows and swirled in a pattern that must be circular from above. Sweat drips down a prominent hooked nose, black eyes staring a challenge at me.

"What's your request?" she asks. Her hands work at a flame nestled between them, channeling the powers of the gods, fingers obviously straining even in the dim light to keep it from escaping her. "Quickly, before I lose this."

I want to plan my request, but the words I have labored over pop out before I can reign them in. "I need to connect with others again."

"If you lost that ability, I can't get it back for you. Something can't be made from nothing." The flamesmith's answer is short and she turns away, as if the flame in her hands is pulling her.

But the step turns into a hop, the woman coming down hard into a squat, clutching the flame in front of her. Then she's back up, jumping. She twirls in midair, graceful for such a large person, and comes down in a squat facing the other direction. The hearth illuminates half her face, lips pulled back in a grimace. She sways one way, then the other, cradling the flame like a small child, and I am reminded of my daughter, now taken from me.

She continues leaping, swaying, a rhythm behind her moves, though unheard. She ignores me completely, locked in a battle with the flame. It's hotter now, the color slightly brighter red. She finishes with a flourish, arms straight up, the flame above her head, but it's no longer a flame. It's a bright red bowl, flickering flames trapped within its walls. She brings it down in front of her, chest lifting and falling like bellows.

"You're still here." She stares straight at me, flat and unconcerned. Little wonder. She could turn any person I knew, including my late disgrace of a husband, into a twisted stick with those muscles.

"I want to connect with others again," I repeat. "I need to feel once more." I have traveled weeks to say that. I will not simply go away.

The flamesmith doesn't answer, instead displaying the bowl with flames encased in its sides. "You know what this does?"

I shake my head.

"A woman came to me yesterday because she wanted a bowl to hold three times as much as what she usually carries from the local well, and for it to be small and weigh little." She hefts the bowl easily. "It'll never be heavier than this, and it'll hold easily three times as much as a bucket." She points to a wooden slat bucket off to the side. "I do this day in and day out. Most of my commissions are such idiocy. Why not ask for a bowl that never empties? Why not ten times as much instead of three? She traded me precious items she'll never be able to afford again, all to save two trips to the well." She places the bowl down carefully, looking as if she wants to throw it. Her eyes travel to mine and I nearly step back at the intent behind them. "I'd die happy if I could make items every day that truly take my talent. Instead, I make baubles for imbeciles. So believe me when I say I would love to give you the ability to truly know others once more, but it is impossible. It is beyond my ability."

"But you are the greatest flamesmith on the island!" I cannot help myself. "All others pointed me to you."

The woman gives a sharp nod. "They're correct. No one is more competent than Rehema the Flamesmith."

I cross my arms. "If you are the greatest, then you can fulfill my desire, just as you fulfill those...lesser desires." Her disgust for the nearby villagers is palpable.

"And what payment do you have for such a request?" She eyes my ragged clothes and small bag.

I swallow and lift my head. "Ask anything you wish. I will get it for you, though it takes me the rest of my life."

"Then you come to me, asking for the impossible, with no incentive for me to exert myself, and empty promises." Her eyes are narrow, face pinched in distaste.

If I keep raising my chin, I will be staring at the ceiling of the cave soon. But I literally have nothing else. Despite her scorn and harsh words, I wonder if there is a light of interest in her eyes. She is still speaking with me, and has not bodily throw me out, which she could easily do.

"Are you the greatest or not?" I challenge. "I will go to no other."

Rehema laughs now, and the sound is rich, and deep, and warm. If I could feel anything, I might have been drawn in. But I can't. It is why I am here. To me, it is just a laugh.

"Look upon my creations and tell me what you think!" She spreads her hands wide, and I realize I have forgotten about the other wondrous items strewn about the cave.

"I've a better connection to the gods of our island than anyone else. These are only the unclaimed items, or ones where the requester asked for an item beyond their ability to pay for." She gives me a long look, before stalking to the edge of the cave, unnaturally graceful for her muscles and size.

On the left is a collection of spears, staves, bowls, and other common objects. They are all dull red or bronze, some reaching toward a brighter glow.

"These're the dullards." Rehema points back to the bowl she's just made, left near the hearth. "They require little imagination, little effort, and fulfill common needs. More of a thing, a sharper point, a stronger material. They're objects barely worth my time, when the person asking could have achieved the same result with some effort."

She turns away from them quickly. These are the most populous items, and I am shocked even these simple items people could not pay for. How much does the flamesmith charge?

But she is on to the next section, filled with warm, bright orange objects. These are more fanciful. A reaching hand, a single flower, a globe with swirling orange motes within it, the helm of flames.

"These're the desires people had to reach for. They couldn't have achieved the results on their own without much time or effort, perhaps even more than in one life." She cups the rose. "The ability to poison a person's thoughts toward another." The reaching hand. "The touch of slow and lingering misfortune." The globe. "The ability to heal from all but the direst injury." The helm. "To be ever untouched in battle."

I have taken a step forward before I realize it. These are true treasures, lying forgotten in the flamesmith's cave. Even one of them could change the circumstances of my life.

She hears the scuffle of my feet and glances toward me with sly grin. "Could I interest you in one? The original claimants are all dead or horribly poor now. I'm certain I could find a suitable price for any one of them. It may only take you the next twenty or thirty years to collect."

I swallow and shake my head. Rehema has already confirmed my request is greater than this. "I will not budge. I repeat my original commission."

"No need. I heard you the first time." She turns away again, but not before I see what looks like satisfaction. Why? But she seems to enjoy showing off her collection.

Next are two bright yellow objects, so bright most of the light in the room comes from them, though there are many more of the others. One is a miniature tree cycling through the seasons in seconds, dropping miniscule leaves even as new ones grow from its branches. The other is a coiled snake, which I nearly dismiss until I see its tongue flick out lazily. It turns its head just slightly to stare at me, unblinking, and my eyes instantly water from the brightness.

Rehema moves her hand over the tree, a scant finger's width from its tiny branches. "A means to guarantee a kingdom's rule in perpetuity. Have you heard of the empire of Kempt?"

"I know of most kingdoms on this island. That is not one of them."

"It no longer exists, nor does any memory of it. Half the court pooled their wealth for me to craft this item. The other half..." She moved her hand to the snake, running a single strong finger down the back of its head. It rears slightly into her touch. "They required me to make a device which would select the favored few, the ones who *should* rule the entire island."

She turned back to me. "Simply the *completion* of these items, each of which took a year, affected Kempt. No one ever came to retrieve them, and only I now remember their kingdom."

"And you think my request is greater than *this*?"

Instead of answering, she holds up a finger and returns to the pedestal next to the hearth, carelessly swiping the bowl she recently finished to the ground. It does not break.

She sets her great legs, thighs straining as she twists. I jump as the top of the pedestal opens with a sharp *crack*, and I shield my eyes. The light fills the room like noonday sun.

"Come, come," she beckons, and for the first time I step farther into the cave, walking with hesitant steps to the source of the light.

Next to Rehema, I see the object is a bright white crown, bejeweled and delicate, a color of flame I have never seen, pressed into physical form.

"What is it?" This close, I can smell Rehema's scent, like rosemary mixed with roses, covered over by the warm, burning scent of fire.

"A wish to become a god," Rehema whispers. Even she is in awe of her creation. "I made it for my mistress, when she told me her deepest desire. She wished to ascend, as in the stories of old. Her skill was greater than mine, though her strength was lacking. I trained for twenty years with her, from a young girl to a woman. She was the greatest person I've ever known."

"What...what happened to her?" I breathe.

"She died. Instantly, when she touched the crown." Rehema's voice was rough. "She didn't have the strength to ascend. I have wondered since if I'd"—her hand strays forward, then back—"but I dare not test myself."

I understand why she locks this prize away in darkness, away from anyone's touch. As if with a physical effort, she tears her gaze away from the crown and to me. "You see what I am capable of. Have I satisfied your curiosity?"

I cannot understand why what I ask for is so precious. "I simply wish to connect with others. To be part of something again. When my daughter died, I felt all hope and love die too. I want it back."

Rehema's face is lit from underneath by the spectral crown, and she places the top of the stone pedestal back, wrenching it closed again with a rasp of stone on stone. I blink, squinting to see, though I thought the two yellow flame creations were bright before.

It is dark enough I do not see Rehema's hand until it is close to my face. I almost step back, but hold firm. As my eyes clear I stare into her strong face, her hooked nose, her closely braided hair, and her dark eyes. She is perhaps not pretty, but she is powerful, and so obviously self-assured her presence is like a lure. We are of an age, I think. Old enough to have had a family and lived through loss, though I do not know if Rehema has done the first. I can see the second in her eyes.

"What's your name?" Her hand is close to my cheek, hot like fire, and she passes it down my face, shoulder, and arm, never touching, almost scorching, as if she searches for something.

As if the words are pulled from me, I say, "I am Bennu. Of nowhere and nothing. After the plague that decimated our village, the first to leave was my pitiful excuse for a husband, slinking off to join our enemies, opening the village gates for them to enter in the middle of the night. Spears and clubs were our lullabies that night as I saw everyone I had ever known struck down. My mother's head was bashed to pulp before my eyes as she fought warriors twice her size with a cooking spoon. I felt my regard for others wither then. My husband's head was carried on a stick by the attackers—suitable payment for his betrayal. I fended off warriors twice my size all night to keep myself and my little girl safe. Then she died the day after, her sickness resurfacing from the stress—the one I had carried within me, fed of myself, and taught to be what I could not—and that was when all else died within me. I feel nothing. I wander the world without connection, unable to settle, unable to form new bonds. I even feel nothing from the great goddess Sekh, nor any of the lesser gods. They ignore my pleas. My only drive is to get that back because I *remember* what I once felt, even if I cannot any longer."

I stop for a breath, amazed how the story has flowed from me. I have never told that to anyone else, not that I had many chances, wandering alone these past weeks. But even to the few lonely merchants to which I traded my last coins for food, I never had a reason to tell my past.

Rehema lowers her hand, her face grave. "Yes, I think your request is greater than any of these other treasures. For each of these I've created, there was a spark to work with. Some pride, or lust, or ambition. You have none of these. No connection to anyone. You are completely alone."

Her eyes bore into me. I should be stung by the words, but they are the simple truth.

"And you say it is impossible to fix this?" I ask.

For just a moment, I see a light of challenge in her eyes, but then it disappears.

"Yes. It is impossible. I can create war from argument, heal a limb from a partial one, cause plague from a fever, and generate a new thought from an idea. I cannot make something from nothing. It is best you leave." She turns away, picking up the bowl that carries three buckets of water.

I offer one last challenge. "And you will be satisfied with lost kingdoms and simple requests? Will the greatest flamesmith not attempt the impossible?"

She only waves a hand over her muscled shoulder.

Truly I have nothing. I exit the cave and in the slanted light of afternoon, I look for a place to make camp nearby. I will not leave.

* * *

I watch the other woman—Bennu—make her way from my cave. She's pretty, in a petite way. But then everyone is petite to me. She's also a fool.

I know she's a fool because she quests after the impossible. I can feel the lack of connection to the gods in her body. She's cut herself off completely and the gods are fickle. To reforge that connection would take more effort than the rest of my creations together.

I also know she's a fool because I am one too. I take jobs from anyone, for ill or good, because I must have more. Red, orange, and yellow—these are the colors of the flame, and every true flamesmith can use them. I'm the only one to create a white flame, worthy of the gods, though my mistress was not.

Yet there's more. My mistress whispered it once, when she thought I couldn't hear. The greatest of the flames.

Blue flame.

To channel that much of the gods' power would be my masterpiece. It was the only reason I invited the fool woman in, showed her the white flame crown. To see if there was a chance her request could drive me to even greater creation.

But no. Once I realized she's completely cut off, from others, from the land, the gods, I knew it was impossible. She's a dead woman, a ghost still walking.

There's nothing I can do for her, and I force her from my mind. I have plenty of commissions from people across the island, one of which is due tomorrow morning.

I return to the hearth, my forge, watching the flames jump and dive there. This flame has been burning since my mistress's mistress was a girl, and I'll not let it die in my lifetime, though I have never found an apprentice worth my teaching. After I am gone, this flame will gutter out, and my treasures will be fair game to anyone who can take them. It will plunge this island into chaos. Fortunately, I will no longer care.

I stare into the fire. There's a man who's paying well to curse his enemies in another village of his kingdom, much like some other flamesmith must have allowed Bennu's village to be cursed, though I didn't tell her that.

I pick a strong orange flame, ripe with anger. It resists my pull and my muscles strain to wrest it from the fire. Sweat breaks out across my brow, but not because of the heat. I'm very familiar with that. I feel the pull of Sekh at the core of the planet, where all the gods and goddesses live. I must make the connection to her.

It is time to dance.

My hips begin to sway side to side. One foot steps forward, then back. The other follows it. I twirl and the flame separates from the blaze. I wrestle it into a spin, letting the steps of the dance build my connection to Sekh.

At first, I cradle the flame in my arms, as if it's a babe, then hold it out as it grows scorching, even to my skin. Each twirl, each swing and sway, makes the aura about me brighter. The rings of colors surround me, first rust red, then another of bright red. I stretch the flame in front of me, beginning the process to confine the transient fire to a solid shape. It's graduated from a babe in arms to an object with a purpose. Vibrant orange joins the other rings around me, then diamond yellow.

I am in the throes of the dance now, and I jump, because that is what is needed next. I come down in a low squat, presenting the object above my head. Even I do not know what its final shape will be.

Finally, pure white joins the other colors around me, the extent of my power. But not the last color. Ever-elusive, the final blue of the hottest fire. Someday I will reach it. It is the pinnacle of my craft. But not today. I dance, and Sekh blesses me with magic. The wrath to smite one's enemies is poured into the elongated flame I wrestle into submission, like a dance partner refusing to follow. My size and muscle are merely a byproduct of my training in this magic, for my will is what burns hottest, devising the next step in my dance to conquer this flame.

With my full power gathered, the flame slowly takes the form of a solid red trident, and my steps slow to a gentle sway, cradling my new creation. Finally, I stop, and Sekh's aura fades away.

I place the trident on the pedestal which hides the crown, waiting for it to cool and solidify into its shape. The man will be back the next day to pick it up and curse his rivals. Unbidden, Bennu's face comes into my mind, with her tale of plague and betrayal. It must have been a flamesmith who was behind the plague. Otherwise, a flamesmith would have healed it. It meant there was some original agent who caused her daughter's death. But no. There was no reason to tell her. She was gone and said plainly she felt nothing. Neither did I.

* * *

The next day, I am at the entrance to Rehema's cave's when she arrives from a humble shack nearby. It is smaller even than the one-room home I shared with my husband and daughter. Rehema blocks my way, hands on her hips, standing in front of the entrance.

"You're back. Why?"

She's as direct as always. There has to be a way to convince this rock of a woman. I will pay anything I can earn, find, or steal.

"I told you I wasn't giving up. What can I give you? Money? Favors? Blood? Time? What do you want?"

"Several of those you will certainly pay if I were to make your desire manifest, but I've told you it's impossible." She spreads her hands, taking in the cave. "I want for nothing. I have so many demands I can barely keep up."

"Yet you still live here alone."

That finally seems to hit a chord and Rehema pauses. Her face closes for just a moment, then she is back with another glower for me.

"You should try other flamesmiths. Maybe they can help."

"You have already showed me you are the best, and I will accept no less. If you cannot help me, how can anyone else?"

Rehema lifts her proud head to argue, but then her eyes focus behind me, and I turn to confront the heavy footsteps approaching.

An old man comes over the rise of the hill. No, not old. I see he is old before his time, wrinkled and crumpled with hate. His feet are like spikes into the ground, his fingers like claws.

"Do you have it?" he spits at Rehema.

The flamesmith stares down at the crumpled man from her impressive height.

"I have your wrath, if you have my payment."

The old man—no, the *cruel* man—seems to crinkle even further inward, like dry wood crumbling. I can tell he does not want to part with his payment, but he wants his "wrath"—whatever that is—even more.

He unhooks a pack from his bag, changing his silhouette. It is nearly as dark as his skin, and that had added to my assumption of his age. He is deathly thin but was not actually humpbacked.

"Three bags of my best grain. You should know this is a significant part of my harvest. I had to sell part of my farm to buy the higher-quality seed. I can barely afford—"

"But you *can* afford it," Rehema says, snatching the bags from his hands. I have the distinct feeling this man is wealthy far beyond what I will ever see. Any part of his wealth leaving his grasp causes him as much pain as I felt when the plague came and took people I had known since I was a child. Back when I could feel.

Rehema peers into each bag, swirling the contents with a massive finger. "At least there are no weevils this time."

"My commission?" The man stares with open greed at Rehema's massive chest, which is right at his eye level. Rehema seems not to notice.

"There is one more requirement." She disappears into her cave and comes back with a trident of living orange flame which seems to wriggle in her hands, as if trying to get free of its form. She presents it on flat palms.

"Quickly now, before it is in the air too long. For a spell this potent, you must claim it fast."

The cruel man grimaces, but takes a knife from his belt and pierces his finger with a wince, squeezing the tip between the neighboring finger and thumb. A single drop of bright red blood beads, and drops with a hiss onto the surface of the trident. But rather than calm it, the weapon goes wild, bucking in Rehema's hands and she thrusts it at him.

The man grabs it greedily, and as soon as he does, the trident goes still, cooling in his hands. I take a step back before I realize it, away from the cold coiling rage emanating from it now. It is like a serpent, hidden in the grass, and I'm thankful when the man capers off with his prize.

I turn back to Rehema. "I see your power. You made this weapon after I left yesterday. Why is that scourge so easy for you, when you refuse me my request?" I do not know what the cruel man will do with his trident, and I do not care.

She steps closer to me, head and shoulders above me. The heat from her body is like the midday sun, burning away the morning fog. She reaches one hand up to cup my chin, and I let her turn my face side to side, peering at me as if I am a prize chicken to sell.

"You've abandoned every part of yourself but this shell." Her voice is low and husky. "I can't connect what is not there. That man was filled with wrath. Merely his presence in the nearby village was enough to fuel my dance. You have nothing. No money, no valuables, not even your cares." She pulls away and my head sags without her support, as if she tugs away a crutch I've been leaning on.

What *do* I have? Why have I even come here?

I only knew I must come here, to restore the emptiness inside.

I stare back at Rehema for a full minute, and she lets me, considering the same way she did the day before. She still has not forced me away, but simply said my request was impossible. It is as if she waits for something more.

But what can I offer? I have nothing.

Then the words bubble up within me. "You say I must have a spark, but that is exactly what I am requesting. You are the greatest flamesmith on the island. Can you not fill me with your fire?"

"And burn you to a crisp?" Rehema opens her great hand in front of my face. That one hand could reach around my skull. "I've had an entire lifetime to hone my craft and learn to resist the flame."

"Then it is possible." I grab for the chance. "Can your flame itself act as the connection I need? A way to make me feel again?" A strange desire sweeps through me. "Could I...be your apprentice? Learn from you?"

Now it is Rehema's turn to consider me. Her eyes rake me in, like flames over dead leaves, and I wonder if my skin will begin to burn.

Finally, she cocks one hip, hand on the other. It is a strange pose.

"Bennu, have you ever tried to dance?"

* * *

Bennu's dead eyes have a small light in them for the first time since she arrived yesterday. She straightens just slightly at my words.

"Dance? Like the flamesmiths do? Like you do?"

This scrap of a woman has planted the idea in me. Well, if she won't go away, then she may as well be useful. I doubt she'll ever amount to anything, wounded as she is, but as I told her, I have too many requests. A helper—an apprentice—will take the burden off me. I must confess, at least to myself, that her request interests me. Can something be made from nothing? If she were near me, I could continue to study her condition. Perhaps learn if anything else can be done for her. I'm interested in her story—the first time in a long time.

I nod, keeping my thoughts from my face. "To dance as a flamesmith. If you won't leave, then at least you can help."

She throws back her shoulders, chest proud. "I am a strong worker. I told you I will do whatever you require. I can learn to dance."

"Then come with me." I have only simple commissions for the next few days—ignorant requests like the water bowl. Bennu won't be too much of a burden.

I turn back to my cave, listening to her follow behind me, but turn back at the trudging, slipping steps.

"That's how you walk?"

Bennu looks confused. "What does that matter?"

"If you are going to learn the flame, you must move like the flame. Graceful. Sinuous." I walk back toward her, letting my hips take my weight, rolling my shoulders. It won't get me anywhere fast, but it captures the eyes, the attention. It can make a connection with the goddess Sekh.

Her eyes follow my hips too, the most intent I've seen her. I stop a breath away from her, looking down at her as she stares at my waist.

"Like this. Follow me." I step back, then turn, arms coming up, then spreading out. This far from the hearth, the aura doesn't come immediately, but it vibrates deep in my core.

Bennu surprises me by stepping around me, taking my hand in hers, raising it to turn underneath. It's clumsy and rigid, but she's trying.

"I said I will do anything. I am a fast learner." She lets my hand go and twirls in front of me, self-aware and awkward.

This woman is a mystery. Lacking any emotion or connection, yet so eager to be filled. A mystery I can solve.

"It's a start," I say, and take her hand, swaying as I dance my steps back to the cave. She's stiff, but follows my lead.

Inside the welcome heat of the cave, I show her my treasures in more detail, and tell her how the dance draws the essence of the flame into the body, starting the connection with Sekh.

I show her again how I dance, making my next commission, a means to balance scales quicker when selling rice. It's a simple thing, and the flame takes form as a dull red block, its weight unnaturally heavy in my hand.

"There's only one more ingredient needed to fix the flame in its final form," I tell her.

"Blood, yes?" Bennu eyes the weight.

"Technically any part of the requestor's body will work. Hair, spit, flesh. People like blood as a symbol. It makes the object worth more to them if they have to bleed for it."

We fall to talking the rest of the day. Bennu attempts to dance, but she trips halfway through and falls against the hearth. I'm by her side before I know it. The hearth is blazing hot for those who are not used to it, and I support her as she moves away, cradling her forearm, now red and blistered. But she doesn't cry out, nor make a fuss as we walk to the nearby river to wash and bandage her arm. She is well and truly broken inside, disconnected from the world.

I feel the challenge growing within me. It should be impossible, but as Bennu keeps saying, am I not the greatest flamesmith on the island? What would it take to make her feel once more? Perhaps I don't need to craft something from nothing, but to temper an old, broken thing into a new one—burn her up and mold her again. It will be a long, hard, and painful process. But then, there is always a price.

* * *

My first week under Rehema's apprenticeship is torture. The burn on my arm is still healing, and I would stay clear of the hearth save that is what everything Rehema does revolves around. Sometimes one a day, sometimes two, she makes simple creations for unimaginative people. The only redeeming part of them is that I get to watch her dance.

Rehema is the most powerful woman I have ever met, a monolith of muscle, skin, and sweat. Yet when she moves, it is like a river flowing, taking the quickest path from here to there, interpreting the flame differently each time for that particular item. And when she dances, I feel as if she brings the hearth to my middle, burning me from the inside out. Why do I stay with this pain? I could simply leave, and continue my meaningless life on the island.

But there is more here. I do not know how, but I know it. I attempt a dance, but I am still clumsy. Rehema says I need to feel the flame to learn the steps, but that is entirely the problem. It, and Rehema, are both strangers to me, though I sleep in her hut, warming myself next to the fire of her body. We do not touch, but the proximity is enough to stave off any chill as the year wanders into autumn.

* * *

Two weeks with Bennu shadowing my footsteps, and my aura comes quicker each time I dance. I don't know why. Is it because someone watches me? Have I been striving for an audience all my life? I don't think myself vain, but perhaps that is it. I haven't danced this freely since I was a child under my mistress's tutelage, while she told me how and where to curb my exuberance and focus it into controlling the flame.

Was she...wrong? My mistress had incredible skill, but she never even crafted a white flame. Am I binding myself unnecessarily?

So, I let myself free on these simple, ignorant requests. I jump, and grind, and gesticulate as I dance, sometimes letting strange words fall from my lips.

I secretly delight in the few times our hands touch as we sleep together. Until Bennu wakes up screaming, that is. She says the nightmares are getting better, but it's hard to tell. When she's fully awake, she says nothing of them.

Still, a hammer which always hits the nail glows with inner orange light, rather than dull red, as the woman who requested it applies a drop of her blood.

The nearly lightless hoe I create, which will never dull, burns with cherry red light.

The bowl that will never spill or tip glimmers with hidden heat as the man takes it from me, blood on his fingertips.

Bennu watches my dance each time, her eyes following my arms, my hips, my feet. It's as if she pours more flame into my work, without even knowing it.

* * *

I gasp as a dull red glimmer surrounds my hands, but I do not stop my simple dance, back and forth along a grid. It is a training exercise. I have been with Rehema a month now, and neither of us has even mentioned my request again. I watch her create, day after day, and try to follow along.

Only this last day have I felt the heat from the hearth enter me. There is a connection deep beneath me, into the center of the earth, like a string of blazing energy.

"An aura, mechanically created, but there." Rehema looks smug, as if she knew I would do this eventually. I was not so certain.

"What do I do with it?" The heat makes sweat run down my back, but I keep my feet moving.

"Anything you want. Make something for yourself this time."

I focus my thought on what I want. Firstly, a way to keep this heat from affecting me so much. I reach for the fire in the hearth, amazed as my fingers wrap around a small flame and grasp it! It barely burns my fingers and I know soon that will not matter at all. The larger burn on my arm is nearly healed, though the shiny scar will be with me always.

I wrest the flame away, much smaller than what Rehema crafts with, and cradle it in my arms. It touches my burn and I hiss at the pain. That debt is paid then. Rather than blood, I've already given it a bit of my flesh. My feet go through the rhythms I've practiced every day as my arms draw the flame into a protective skin. It flattens into a thin sheet, which I wrap around myself like a shawl. I sigh as the heat of the hearth becomes bearable for the first time.

Rehema approaches. "This is good work, especially for a beginner." Her hand engulfs my shoulder and for once, it is not like I have gotten too close to a fire.

It feels...comfortable.

* * *

Bennu has been with me two months, and I'm starting to really question if her request is impossible. The quality of my craft is improving, especially since I can give the easiest jobs to Bennu. I'm barely capable of making dull red objects any longer. Even with no effort, I produce a cherry-red flame.

As she shows me the crude goblet she's made to keep water from spilling, I take her forearm in mine—the one that was burned. It's healed, but the skin is shiny and tight there. My hand reaches from her wrist to elbow. She's so brittle she would snap like a twig with any force.

She looks a question down at my hand, then back up to me.

"You still feel nothing? You're doing good work here."

But her eyes hold barely a spark of triumph in her creation. "I know the goddess must have blessed me to be here. The movements create the object from the flame. That is all there is."

On a whim, I lean close to her. She smells as much of the hearth as I do now, but underneath is her own scent, that of sweet fennel and clover. We've seen each other's bodies many times, living in my small close hut, but though I have caught her eyes tracing my thighs, hips, breasts, and arms, she never acts. Maybe that is for me to do, since she lacks that impulse.

My nose touches hers, then our lips meet. She doesn't resist, but neither leans in. It has been long since I tasted another woman, though, and I pull back, licking my lips.

"You feel nothing from that, then?"

"I will not deny the sensation is pleasant," Bennu tells me. "But no. There is nothing."

"I will simply have to research this more, then," I tease her. The side of her mouth lifts, but it is hesitant. I've never heard Bennu laugh. "Would you like me to continue? To continue to search for the spark?"

Am I imagining a flicker of the dullest ember in Bennu's eyes? One struggling to survive a mighty wind?

"Yes," she says, and puts her lips again to mine.

* * *

I have trained with Rehema for a year now. I barely remember what it was to travel by myself across the island. We have a rhythm between us. A dance, as it were.

The nightmares still come, but Rehema soothes them away for me when I wake, kneading my sore muscles from working at the hearth, kissing my worries away, and probing deep within my being with her strong fingers until I scream with urgency rather than fear. I try to return the favor as best I can. The pleasure is a release, but it is still not like the memories I have from before. I know there is a void within me that warmth, pleasure, companionship, or work cannot fill.

The dance comes easier, and I have abandoned the training lines Rehema drew for me, venturing out into my own creations. She teases me that I am still rigid and inflexible in my movements, but I am getting better. Less withheld.

At the same time, I see how much Rehema has grown in skill while I have been with her. We discuss it at length, how her movement fills the hearth now, embracing the flames, and my attention, to herself with a wild abandon I could never hope to replicate. Admirers come from afar simply to request a commission and watch her dance its creation. I watch them, wishing I could be the one to see Rehema move for the first time again.

I feel like sheets of ice are melting around me, though I do not know what lies under them. Is there anything of me, or only unfeeling walls? Will I simply dissolve once there are none left?

* * *

The years are kind to Bennu and I, and with the money from the many projects we craft, I hire builders to craft a better house for the two of us, with a proper bed instead of a mat on the floor. We eat well, and Bennu displays a surprisingly good head for business and for sewing. We receive rich silk fabric as part of the payment for my next yellow flame project—an open hand, which gives fortune to everyone in that kingdom. Bennu makes it into a stunning wrap, which shows off her hips, finally starting to fill in after a life of starvation. The kingdom, or at least its rulers, willingly pays the rest of the price. They suffer through five years of blight and drought, but those that survive become wealthy beyond measure, armed with the glowing yellow hand.

Bennu is more lithe and graceful than ever before, and we've even collaborated on several commissions, lending our flames to each other as we create. Yet there is always a veil between her and me. She still doesn't feel, just as I've never yet achieved the blue flame. She is my greatest project, tempering loss to plenty, molding what was broken into what is whole.

My research over the years makes me think the two are related. To solve one is to solve the other.

* * *

I have everything I ever wanted. A house, good food and clothes, and a partner who adores me. I know this is true. Yet still I am the wretched refugee inside. I cannot feel the trauma that shaped me, but it lingers in my bones.

Rehema and I dance together, forging flames into wishes, but I can tell I hold her back, even as her strength grows. If I could return the affection she has for me, her strength would double. Triple.

I pour my frustration into my work until I make my first orange flame. Rehema finds me, drenched with sweat, spinning around the forge, blessed by the goddess Sekh.

"What will you make?" Her voice is quiet, but cuts through the underground cavern. I realize I have poured everything into my dance, with no output. I know enough to understand it will burn me up if I let it, protections or no. I hold a swirling flame in my hands as I dance, and it is frustration incarnate. My thoughts go back to that hunched man, his wrath bending him into a parody of age.

I keep my gaze locked on Rehema, because if I do not, the raging currents will take me away from her. I spit into the flame I hold, and it sizzles as my frustration becomes solid—a crouched jackal, hair raised and teeth bared. It wriggles in my grasp, and I hastily set it on one of the pedestals in the cave. It will bring only misery to anyone who touches it.

My strength fails as I do this, and Rehema catches me before I fall senseless. I nestle into her arms, my skin itching and raw.

Another veil lifted between me and her. Hesitantly, I touch her cheek with my hand. I realize I have never initiated contact between us like this. Always it is Rehema leading, supporting.

"How much will it take to make the impossible possible?" We have not spoken of my original request in years, but always it sits between us.

"More than this," she answers.

* * *

Many years later, as I watch Bennu dance near the hearth, the old scar on her forearm catching the light, it suddenly comes to me. I have lately been focused on the impossible once more, as both our skills have grown. A small collection of poisonous creations litters my hearth. The snarling jackal, a screaming buzzard, a charging hippo. None of these can ever be sold to another without dire consequences. Few come to us nowadays. Our prices are too steep, our creations too fine. Bennu is trying so hard, but it is not enough. I'm not enough.

And I have it. The price of an impossibility. I know what the payment for a blue flame must be: a lifetime.

The realization sparks a fire in my belly, as if Bennu has put her skillful fingers to work on me. I take the first step, arm coming up in front of me. Bennu is instantly aware, as always, and her steps change as I sway in time to a rhythm only the two of us can hear. She knows as well as I do that it's time.

Her dance becomes a mirror of mine, though less complex. Feet stomp, then my head rocks forward and back, in time with the beat playing in the back of my mind.

Bennu's arm jerks up, as if pulled toward me, and the hearth flares with light.

The goddess Sekh fills me in an instant.

I twirl around the podium that hides the white crown and the old seal cracks as I dance around it, leaking light.

My fingers reach out to play against hers as we move in tandem around the room. We do not need to communicate, save by our feet and our eyes, both locked in the mirror of each other.

She hefts an old dull red spear that has been here as long as she has and hefts it toward the ceiling. It dissolves into a shower of light, feeding both our auras.

We spin past each other, and I grab several more staves and tridents. As my fingers touch them, they blossom into sprays of light. The hearth shimmers into orange light.

Bennu grabs the rose as I gather up the globe of orange light. Together, we eat through my old treasures, fueling this thing growing between us. Destroying my past as we create the future. My mind reels at what it must be, but I push the thought away. There is only the dance, and Bennu.

She is the one to offer up the animal instincts once within her, and the jackal, buzzard and hippo become manifest, dancing with us, complicating our duo. I grit my teeth, trying to hold everything together.

Finally, the three animals burn themselves out, and Bennu's face loses a tightness that has been there since she first came here. It makes her even more beautiful.

She takes the brilliant yellow snake and wraps it around her shoulders as I lift the miniature tree above my head. The snake shimmers into diamonds down Bennu's front, marking her dress with stars. The tree's leaves become tiny comets around my head as the trunk disintegrates in a flash of light.

The hearth blazes with white light, and I know what must be next.

We move around the pedestal, now on one side, now on the other. Stamping, jumping, flailing as if Sekh moves us like puppets. We dance with no regard for anything. The aura grows around us: red, orange, yellow, and then white. There is nothing left of my treasures except the one I keep hidden from all.

With trembling hands, even as I keep my feet crossing and moving, I lift the top off the pedestal and toss it aside.

Bennu's eyes are wide—the most emotion I've ever seen from her in the years we're shared together. As she dances, she shakes her head, though she must know we've come too far. There is no turning back now.

I nod, finally certain. Both of my hands reach out, grasping the white-hot crown, and it is like a sunrise in my bones.

I scream and throw my head back as light erupts from my eyes and mouth.

I screw my eyes closed and grit my teeth. I am not dead, and that means I am worthy. Finally.

I lift the crown on my head and reach for Bennu's hands, bedecked with treasures of flame. We rotate around each other, now out in the middle of the floor. The hearth threatens to spill over into the room in a liquid blaze. We have, both of us, given everything.

I feel the blue coming before it is visible, a wave of heat like molten rock under the ground, spilling up through my body to make me burst into flame like a torch.

But I don't, because Bennu is there, with me, taking the burden when I can't. The blue is too much for one person.

But maybe it isn't for two.

I know how able a flamesmith she has become, though she restricts herself to simpler projects. The blue light reveals all.

We spin closer together, our hands locked, then our hips, then our lips. My white crown reflects the diamonds on her dress, even our clothes submitting to apotheosis.

Around us, the aura glows blue and a single thread grows above our heads. I cannot see it, as my eyes are closed, but I can feel it. It joins us in more ways than I can count, forged over the years. A connection, something forged from nothing. It is tiny, and unremarkable, but also the most powerful thing I have—we have—ever crafted.

"Rehema," Bennu breathes as our kiss ends, and my name has never sounded so sweet.

"My love," I whisper back.

"My...love," she repeats. "I *love* you, flamesmith."

And then Bennu laughs. In all our years, she never has. Is it like sapphires falling on glass. It is the crackling of flame.

We separate, but the blue flame remains above us, stretching as far apart as we are from each other. We end our dance with a spin around the cave, testing the limits. There are none.

We are one.

"The Flamesmith" is a short story by William C. Tracy, based in the same world as his upcoming progression fantasy series. Want to read more of his works?

Join his mailing list at **www.spacewizardsciencefantasy.com** and get a free story at the same time!

If you want to read along with his new stories, check out William's Patreon at **www.patreon.com/wctracy.**

Rank and File

N. Romaine White

Sapphic Representation: Lesbian, Ace
Heat Level: Low
Content Warnings: Coarse Language, Violence, Abuse

The war for the mortal kingdoms began hundreds of leagues below the oldest and lowest mountains, in caverns first carved by dwarves, massive serpents, and lovers of dark places. In Lord Helnor's mines—where lava flowed, and ogres fed furnaces and forged with molten metal, and hoblins ran underfoot carrying wares and weapons and messages for their betters—Abscess was thinking of skulls. And glory. But mostly skulls.

The skulls would signify glory of course, if she were allowed to keep any. She was only a foot soldier, after all. She and her kin were Petramori, and the mortal kingdoms had never seen their like before, creatures bred in darkness with smoke and acid in their lungs. They reeked of brimstone, their heads many-horned, their hands many-clawed, and their hides many-scaled. They were made only for war and knew nothing else, only that the skulls of the enemy, be they human or elf or dwarf, made fine decoration.

"What's that face, Abscess? You look like you're thinkin' too hard."

Captain Pokeweed cuffed Abscess on the shoulder before she could turn around. She was grinning. A jagged scar crossed her face, leaving a hole where the right eye once was and splitting her top lip so that a hint of her soot-stained teeth was always showing. Of all the captains, Captain Pokeweed had the best battle scars.

"Counting salamanders, waiting for you," said Abscess. "Are we going topside or what?"

"Always ready to go topside." Captain Pokeweed walked past, and Abscess followed. "Should I just leave ya up there this time?"

"Maybe you should! Give me time to find the Mountain Witch. I'll drag her back to Lord Helnor myself."

Captain Pokeweed laughed and Abscess's guts bobbed merrily. She lived for the thrill of battle, but the thrill of making her captain laugh was nearly as satisfying.

"All right you sulfur breathers, enough tongue-wagging," Captain Pokeweed shouted to the rest of the company. Under the high arches of the Serpent's Entrails, where tunnels crossed to form a cavernous atrium, a hundred Petramori clamored to attention. They lined up in rows of twenty. Abscess joined them, gripping a scarred double axe in front of her.

"Let's move out, fiends!" called the captain.

Abscess and the Petramori met the call with a roar and chant as they filed into the tunnels that led upward. "Hut! Hut! Hut!"

The tunnel wound up and up, the way lit intermittently by flickering torches. Abscess knew when they neared the surface by the change in the incline and in the air. She inhaled the mist that clung to the Harrowed Forest, droplets of clean water collecting like dew on her nose hairs, tasting the smell of sun-drenched leaves, lilac and mint, and rich, dark earth on the back of her tongue.

She sputtered. Gross.

Abscess hated going topside. Everything was cold and wet and squishy. The air in the mines could be humid, but in a bracing, cleansing sort of way. It was a heat that burned away all the sharp dust and mold that got between your scales. On the surface, it was a cloying sort of humidity, like a merquid hugging you. As soon as she met her first humans, though, all the unpleasant quirks of topside made sense. Humans, too, were cold and wet and squishy. They lacked horns, scales, and quills. Their outsides should have been their insides for all the protection they offered. Such simpering beasts could not survive in the mines. The Cloud Dwellers saw fit to make a cage for them as plush and delicate as they were, for whatever reason.

They raided, and it was *okay*. It was much like Abscess's very first outing, only six months after she was hatched. She was scrawnier and slimier then. And that raid had been bigger—six hundred hoblins, one hundred and fifty

Petramori, and twelve two-headed vultria, each bearing one rider and diving upon the walled city from above.

She watched Pokeweed with wonder that first time as she piled head upon head in the town square and selected her ten favorites to take back to the mines. She could have had the hoblins do the work for her, but no, Pokeweed boiled and cured the skulls her very self. It was then that Abscess learned the potential of skulls and vowed to begin a collection of her own. One day, when she'd made a reputation for herself.

In the early dawn light, the houses of scant human villages stood among the trees like ghosts. They herded villagers into a circle, guarded by a handful of Petramori while the rest emptied the houses of their belongings. Captain Pokeweed would look through it all for anything valuable, then the company would have its turn, and the rest they'd light on fire and be on their way.

"Come on Brimbreath, hurry it up," said Abscess. Brimbreath was in an unshapely corner of a one-room hut puttering with a little box.

"Look, Abs," he said, staring at the box with wonder. "There's a funny little bird inside."

Brimbreath opened the box, and it began to sing. It was a strange sound, like shards of obsidian slipping through fingers and falling to the ground, and yet there was an order to it.

"Shut that horrible noise," Tarpith snapped from a corner. Brimbreath closed the box gently.

"What a piece of junk," Abscess laughed.

Brimbreath held the box close, as if afraid Abscess might get spittle on it. "Iounno. I think it's interesting. Do you think Captain would let me keep it?"

"Not like she's gonna notice, anyway," said Abscess, as Brimbreath followed her out of the house and into the square. Captain Pokeweed had gone off again, and Abscess didn't bother asking where. It was becoming a regular thing whenever they went topside. Eventually the captain would be back and say she'd gone to check the perimeter, or was investigating a report from the scouts, or was emptying her glands, and that would be the end of it.

Abscess simply shook her head and glanced over at Brimbreath, who was fawning over the box like the head of a freshly forged flail. "Just keep your mouth shut. Only you would want such a strange little..."

The rest of whatever Abscess said was lost in a roaring gust of wind that took Abscess off her feet.

Dust whipped through the air. Abscess shielded her eyes reflexively, even as she wanted to stay focused on her comrades. Bodies and branches scattered through the trees. She forced her eyelids open.

A white dragon, glimmering blue and pearl in the pre-dawn light, shuddered with the force of its landing. The trees around Abscess collapsed. Something gurgled and quivered under the beast's back foot, which it lifted. Abscess saw what was left of Brimbreath, not quite dead, but no longer anything that could be considered alive.

Before Abscess and her comrades, the dragon reduced. The wings withdrew and shriveled, like a butterfly's metamorphosis in reverse. The limbs shortened, but the scales remained and became plates of armor, shining like porcelain.

What stood before them could have been a human knight, except her white hair spilling from her helmet retained the spiny quality of the dragon's crown of feathers, and her eyes blazed like sunlight. There was no mistaking her for anything but one of the immortal children of the clouds, sworn allies of the Mountain Witch.

More of her kin landed and recoiled into their humanoid forms, but Abscess was only aware of the knight before her. She saw her in a haze of fury and wonder. This sensation felt very much like the first time Abscess emerged from the mines and saw the sun breaking over the black trees of the Harrowed Forest. What the human lands offered was a different kind of light from the red fire that bore Abscess, a light that caused her to tremble with loathing and awe, then turn away from its piercing brightness.

Abscess raised her axe and bore down on the dragon with a roar. Her swing was met with a long sword, the metal shining like a mirror.

They struck, blocked, and danced. A battle unfolded around them, footsteps and cries and beating wings filling the air, but Abscess only had eyes for her dragon. She was an excellent fighter, better than any Abscess had ever met on the battlefield, better than any she'd ever sparred against among the horde. Under the fury, Abscess felt her heart hammering. She was... excited.

"My name is Abscess," she said to the dragon knight. "And I'm going to kill you!"

The knight said nothing, which was uncommonly rude, even by Petramori standards. She did not so much as acknowledge that Abscess spoke at all. Abscess struck harder, though every blow was parried masterfully.

"Too out of breath to speak?!" she shouted over the ringing of their blades.

The dragon smiled. "No. I am only in awe of the many openings you leave in your form."

"What openings—"

That was the last thing Abscess remembered of their battle.

When Abscess awoke, she was deep in the mines surrounded by the rhythms of broiling steam and pounding metal, her whole body was sore, and she was miserable with nightmare after nightmare where she battled some dazzling white specter while Brimbreath's rotting corpse jeered at her from the corner of her vision.

Saline and Felsic told her everything she missed when she was coherent enough to listen. Three, then four, then six dragons had landed, and human and elf knights poured into the clearing from the trees, and suddenly their company was overrun and fighting for their lives. Captain

Pokeweed emerged from wherever she had gone, called a retreat, and directed the Petramori to grab what spoils they could while the hoblins and vultrion covered their backs. They lost the vultrion, and its rider, too, and most of the hoblins, though Saline and Felsic did not say how many. No one cared much about hoblins.

Aside from Brimbreath, they lost three other Petramori. Abscess gritted her teeth. The priests could hatch more, of course, but the Petramori were important to the cause. Hoblins couldn't go toe-to-toe with the elves and dwarves, let alone the dragons, like Petramori could.

"We saved this for you," said Saline quietly. She reached down beside her leg and came up with Brimbreath's singing box. It was missing a nail in one of the hinges that held the top on. It no longer closed all the way. It was scuffed and grimy in places, but the lacquer and all the rest were more or less intact. It fared much better than Brimbreath had, Abscess thought, and that made her guts do a strange, hurty flip.

"Heard the captain talking you up yesterday," Felsic said, the corner of their mouth lifted in a grin. "Takin' on a dragon all on your own, and livin' too? That's big, Abs. That's what captains are made of."

Abscess's guts were flipping again, and this time it was not so hurty.

"Did she come by while I was out?" said Abscess.

Felsic and Saline looked at one another. "Captain's in the dungeons," said Saline.

Abscess was silent for a moment. "On what grounds?"

"Treason," said Felsic miserably.

Abscess was on bed rest for three days after that. She stashed Brimbreath's box under her cot, and now and then she took it out. She imagined it was the dragon knight's pretty skull, and that made her cling to the box a little protectively.

When the healers finally let her go, Abscess went straight to the dungeons. She was turned away by the hoblins, then the guards when she pushed past the hoblins, and then bodily carried out and threatened with dismemberment and worse.

And so, Abscess steeled herself and went to see Commander Render.

Abscess had never spoken to the commander herself. That was something only captains did. But Commander Render surprised Abscess by allowing her into her private bath, fed by a boiling underground spring, and surprised her again by knowing her name.

"You fought the dragon," said Commander Render, her black scales glistening under the steam.

One of Commander Render's personal pages escorted Abscess past the dungeon guards and to Captain Pokeweed's cell. The captain sat on the ground, legs crossed, her body almost lost in shadow. But Abscess could see the chains tethering her to the wall. It seemed a little excessive, what with the cell's bars, and beyond those the guards, and beyond them the entire horde. Captain Pokeweed would never leave the mines again. For a quiet moment, Abscess did not know what to say.

The captain lifted her head, green eyes catching the light from the torches.

"Hey, Captain. Heard you were tellin' stories about me."

Abscess tried to smile. She defaulted, as always, to trying to make Captain Pokeweed laugh.

The captain answered with a rough, hollow chuckle. "Whatever you heard, it's all true," she said.

Abscess frowned. "And what about the stories I'm hearing about you?"

"Aw, kid," said Captain Pokeweed.

They fell to silence. When the captain did not answer, Abscess said, "Why did you do it?"

Abscess had badgered Felsic until they told her everything. Commander Render and Lord Helnor himself accused Captain Pokeweed of spying for the Mountain Witch. She used raids to rendezvous with humans and elves or leave messages. Her treason was giving the enemy an advantage and continuing the war.

"Because," said Captain Pokeweed quietly. "Because it was right."

Abscess slammed her claws against the bars. "It was right to betray the commander? Your company?"

Me? said Abscess's guts, flipping, twisting unpleasantly.

Captain Pokeweed's eyes narrowed to slits, but they held no anger. Something else, though, something that made Abscess feel miserable.

"Yeah. And I know you don't get it now, but one day you might."

Abscess's hands fell away from the bars. "What's that supposed to mean?"

In the shadows, Abscess could see a flash of Captain Pokeweed's teeth as she grinned. "You always think too hard, Abscess. Don't stop now."

Pokeweed's execution was performed in the Bowl with all the personnel that was present in the mines at the time. That was two thirds of the horde: fifty-six infantry battalions, sixteen thousand cavalry, eight thousand vultriers, and all of the captains and generals. The miners, the forgers, and the foremen were also there, and the cook staff, the custodial staff, and Commander Render, and Lord Helnor, and his priests, and the priests' supplicants. The Bowl was nearly full, and in the crush of bodies, all was still as the executioner's axe fell upon Pokeweed's neck.

Abscess did not cry. For one thing, that's not what a Petramori's tear ducts were for. If what Abscess was feeling could be called sadness, the synapses that would carry the information from her brain to other parts of her body did not travel to the eyes. A Petramori's circuitry simply wasn't built that way.

For the other thing, if Abscess were to cry in this moment, then presumably it would be an outward expression of loss and grief. That would imply some deep interpersonal attachment that Petramori were not engineered to feel. They were not humans, after all. They had a social order. They had an instinctual desire to be with other Petramori. They were not related in the way that humans and other top worlders may observe. They did not understand relations. They barely understood friendship. To expect one to grieve a comrade was like expecting two chickens to celebrate a wedding anniversary.

What Abscess did feel, without a doubt, was anger and disappointment, though not just toward Pokeweed. In fact, the majority of this suffocating feeling was directed at herself.

I should have known sooner, Abscess thought to herself over and over again. *Pokeweed is a topside name.*

The last thing she felt was a smoldering rage, and this she reserved entirely for the white dragon knight. Surely, all the Mountain Witch's force deserved it, but Abscess was not unrealistic. It would take her a very long time to smite the Mountain Witch's entire army, and she wanted to make them to hurt *now*.

Pokeweed would tell her to focus. If the task is too big to chew, break it into bite-size pieces. Abscess did not have to fight the entire army. She only had to fight one soldier, a high-ranking, beloved knight. Claiming the dragon's head and serving it to the Mountain Witch on a platter would surely make them hurt. It was the dragon that took Brimbreath, and in a way it was also the dragon that took Pokeweed, so it was only logical for the dragon to feel the full force of Abscess's...everything.

The day after the execution, Abscess was made captain of her company. She was summoned to Commander Render's tunnels. The Commander was there, and Lord Helnor.

"Commander Render told me how you fought one of the Adversary's top generals single-handed," said Lord Helnor in a low, gentle voice that made the flesh under Abscess's scales tingle.

She was silent. She knew she should say something, but her tongue wouldn't work properly. At last, she managed a strangled grunt.

Lord Helnor graciously continued. "She is called Luriel Pearlwing. It is a moniker fitting for those sinister, deceptive creatures. Your bravery and loyalty are admirable. It's soldiers like you that set the right example for the rest."

"We look forward to how you will exemplify yourself next," said Commander Render with a pleased grin.

Abscess did not risk another attempt at speech and simply bowed stiffly.

Abscess's company was in an uproar when they got the news and followed her around, calling, "Ho, captain here! It's Captain Abscess! Make way for our captain!"

"All right, shut it," Abscess snapped.

"Shut it, for the captain," they whispered. "Make way, make way!"

Abscess wished she could feel their jubilation. She had dreamed for years of this moment, but it was tainted by thoughts of Captain Pokeweed. Of Brimbreath. Of Luriel Pearlwing.

"Luriel Pearlwing," Abscess whispered, tasting the name on her tongue.

And so, Abscess had a nemesis.

The dragon was in Abscess's mind day and night, in sleep and in waking. It felt as if every nerve and tendon in her body was pulling her topside. She'd never felt this way before. She had never craved revenge, never hated so purely. Never had she been so consumed by anything, not even dreams of promotion. All her new title meant was the opportunity to meet Luriel Pearlwing again, so that she could part the knight's head from her shining shoulders.

They marched. They raided. They clobbered. They marched. They hacked. They slashed. Abscess missed no opportunity to volunteer her company for topside action. They lost a Petramori now and then. They were replaced and her company's numbers remained strong. That was life for the Petramori, of course. They were bred and hatched to be Lord Helnor's ultimate soldiers in a dark and ceaseless war. War and death were all that existed for the Petramori, and Abscess had resolved long ago that if that was the case, then she would be the very best soldier she could be. She would make this bloody, infernal life exemplary.

At last, Abscess got her wish. Commander Render organized an extended campaign into the Midlands of the continent. It was a major operation, and they would be away from the mines for several months. Their first move was to seize the valley the humans called Herrydown. The Mountain Witch could not ignore such a brazen invasion of her territory.

Commander Render called them to march in the dead of night deep into the valley. As dawn broke, they met the enemy's forces, horde against horde. First came volleys of arrows, then dragons clashed with vultria, and then foot soldiers were slamming together, blade against blade. Abscess hacked and slashed her way through any enemy that came into her path, heedless of whether they fell or not.

Then she saw her, the knight with white hair and iridescent armor. Luriel Pearlwing shone in the dawn light like an avenging star, striking down hoblin and Petramori alike.

Abscess beat her way through the throng, rending the Mountain Witch's soldiers with her axe, pushing her own comrades out of the way.

"Luriel Pearlwing!" Abscess roared. She'd practiced for this moment.

The dragon turned and looked her way, gaze lofty and cool. It was to be expected of a Cloud Dweller. Perhaps she did not even remember their fight. Abscess let that thought fill her with rage.

Then the dragon said, "Abscess."

Abscess smiled. She swung her axe at Luriel's neck.

Luriel deftly twisted out of the way and lifted her sword.

"You remember me," said Abscess as they circled one another. To her own ears, she sounded a little too pleased.

"Of course. How could I forget such an unfortunate name?"

"It's because my breath smelled like pus when I was hatched!"

Their blades cut through the air and rang together. Soldiers instinctively cleared a circle around them, repelled by the ferocity of their battle.

Fighting Luriel required all of her strength and wits to match Luriel's fluid movements, but Abscess had prepared for this. She would not be knocked unconscious this time.

She promised herself this, because Luriel fought with impressive fury. She was fast and unrelenting. She did not seem bored, and Abscess was secretly pleased with that. She had not realized that it was something she even cared about, but they were nemeses. Abscess would be her perfect match.

Abscess swung her axe and Luriel reeled out of the way, but Abscess saw the thread of silver blood fly. She had cut Luriel right below the left eye. Luriel came in low and took Abscess's feet out from under her. Suddenly Abscess was on the ground, looking up as Luriel loomed over her and raised her sword.

Then Cutworm and Felsic were between them.

"No—" Abscess shouted. She did not want help.

With an effortless swing, Luriel cut Cutworm's head from his shoulders. Felsic leapt forward.

"Felsic, *no!*" Abscess scrambled to her feet, but then more bodies rushed in, pushing her back. She tried to break through, but in the crush of bodies, she could not find Luriel's white glow.

The Mountain Witch's forces retreated. Lord Helnor claimed the valley. The horde celebrated that night and into the next, and Abscess made a good show of celebrating with them. It did not feel so much like a victory to her. She lost Cutworm and twelve members of her company in the battle. More than that, she had lost Luriel Pearlwing and had no clue of the knight's fate. Surely she hadn't died, for the horde had claimed three of the Mountain Witch's generals and now paraded their bodies around the bonfires, and none were dragons.

So perhaps Luriel had survived, and Abscess would get another chance. She did not relish the idea of having to try again. She wanted her battle with Luriel to be decisive. Revenge didn't seem quite so satisfying if you had to make multiple attempts.

And yet, her guts twisted when she thought of meeting Luriel again, the sensation somehow both hurty and pleasing.

Luriel fought with passion, as if she, too, wanted something, though Abscess could not imagine what. They fought as if nothing in the world existed but the other. The two of them were bound, now. Luriel Pearlwing was pure light, burning bright like a fireball, from her golden eyes to the tip of her mirror sword. Abscess wanted to experience that heat again, warming her to the marrow. She wanted to know what it was like to burn.

Despite the victory, the war's pace did not slow down. Abscess applied herself even more to excursions into the human lands. They marched. They slashed. They hacked.

Then Tarpith transferred to another company. He'd at least had the decency to yell at Abscess, first.

"What are ya at, ya hob-brained slavedriver?"

Abscess was stunned. Tarpith had always had a short fuse, but he usually spent it on the hoblins or the meeker Petramori. Not ever her.

"Since when are you afraid of a little hard work?" she replied.

"Aye, it's all hard work around here, but you've had us topside day after day for months! You want us right in the thick of things and we go with ya. We win a battle and it's hardly a pat on the back before ya got us toiling again. Are ya tryin' to kill us, like ya killed Brimbreath and Cutworm?"

The words hit Abscess like a punch to the gut. Then she growled, "Clearly not hard enough."

Tarpith didn't like that. "I ain't marchin' with a power-drunk maniac. Go die on yer own! Leave me out of it!"

The next she saw Tarpith was at the mess, deep in bitterbeer and laughter with Captain Marrow's company as if he'd always been there. If Tarpith saw her looking, he gave no indication.

This made Abscess more determined. She wasn't sure why. She had nothing to prove to Tarpith, but thoughts of him made her annoyed, and she took that annoyance and bent it to pining for her quarry.

Abscess marched into that topside world again and again, each time breathing deep the cursed heavy air, nostrils flaring. It smelled of cloying fog and decay and promise. She savored it.

"All right, you fiends! Let's move out!" she called as she always did. As Captain Pokeweed once did.

"Hut! Hut! Hut!"

Each foray was long and monotonous, and Abscess took Tarpith's words to heart, after all. She did what she could to spare her company. She studied the maps for shortcuts. She lingered at rest areas. She let the company hunt and fish for a little extra protein. She even avoided fights if they could help it, and if it was clear there was nothing to gain.

The war escalated, and so did the activities of the horde. Villages and towns burned. The hoblins cut down the Harrowed Forest and carried its lumber down to the mines. When Abscess saw it next, the lush forest was an empty expanse dotted with wide, black stumps. Here and there a sapling stood defiantly, as if trying to start the forest anew, but the leaves and stems were coated in ash and Abscess could not tell at a glance whether it still lived.

Their next march would take them through the Sandmarshes and to the southern isles. It was a month's journey under normal conditions. Commander Render expected them back in half the time. It was a killer pace that made even Abscess balk.

"Wouldn't it be safer if we went around the Sandmarshes?" she found herself asking.

"Safer, but not relevant," said Commander Render with surprising patience. "I need intel from the Sandmarshes."

"Are we looking for anything in particular?"

"You are looking for the *enemy*, and any news worth reporting."

"And...anything else? Specifically?"

"Are you dissatisfied with my instructions, Captain?"

They stared at one another for a long moment, but by now, Abscess was in too deep to backtrack.

"I am just wondering...why...we are doing this. Is all."

Commander Render leaned forward. "You are doing this because I am the commander, and I command it."

Abscess chose her party carefully. She needed fresh bodies. Her companions for the previous patrol were all excused, to their immense relief. She, herself, would be stretched to her limit, but she was a captain, and saying no was not an option.

The ground was gentle and the way easygoing for the first few days, and that helped. Her good cheer lasted well into the fifth day, when they entered the Sandmarshes—an expansive desert with tricky patches where water emerged from underground channels and created deep, sticky bogs of cloying mud nearly indistinguishable from solid ground. They ran. At this pace, so long as nothing waylaid them, it would take two days and two nights to cross the Sandmarshes, but Abscess found herself flagging after only the first day. She was too tired to truly panic about it, which was a blessing.

On the second day, Leechmeat fell into a patch of cactus. She laughed it off, then after a few hours began limping, and a few hours later stumbled to the ground. She would need to be carried, but they did not have the time for it. They ran on, with Leechmeat lying in the sand, calling for them to wait.

That was their only loss before they made it out of the Sandmarshes and to the coast, where the clean ocean breeze was a cool, blessed relief.

Abscess and her party had run day and night with no food and no water for seven days, and now they turned and looked once more into the expanse of the Sandmarshes. That's when the real losses began. First Sixhorn misstepped and fell to a bog pit, then Thorntoe when they tried to get him out. It nearly took Saline too, who had also attempted the rescue, but Abscess managed to pull her back.

Then they stopped to rest for an hour, and Grop did not rise when the group did. She simply lay against a rock, mouth agape, staring into the sky and seeing nothing.

They made it out of the Sandmarshes somehow, and still Putri collapsed mid-run. He had lost a great deal of weight. They all had. Abscess felt like little more than a shadow, propelled along only by instinct.

At last, she had it. Abscess called a halt for rest. The Petramori lay on the ground as if corpses. There were seven left of their initial twelve.

"Saline," she called before Saline had a chance to sit down. Abscess could not be sure that she would rise again if she did.

The two of them walked until they heard the telltale sound of running water. They followed the sound to a wide stream, the water bubbling over rocks and fallen branches. Without waiting for invitation, Saline fell to her knees and plunged her entire face into the water.

Abscess copied her. She drank deeply. Then she came up and wretched onto the ground. She rolled over, head swimming, breathing hard, and stared up at the canopy. Then she rolled over and drank again, slower this time.

Her head came up again, and before her, on the other side of the stream, stood two deer. A big one and a little one. They drank, then the big one looked up and met Abscess's eyes.

They stared at one another. Abscess could not bring herself to move. She had no strength to move, anyway. The deer twitched an ear, then seemed satisfied there was no danger and went back to drinking.

Abscess continued to watch the deer drink. The forest was quiet, save for the stream and bird calls overhead. Sunlight filtered green through the leaves. It was cool and peaceful. It reminded her of how the Harrowed Forest used to be. That thought tugged at something inside of her and made her feel a moment's sadness, though she could not understand why. Something like...loss, or regret, even though she'd never cared anything for topside forests before.

The deer looked up sharply, ears turning this way and that, then they dashed quietly through the trees. Abscess tensed. They weren't leaving that quickly for nothing.

At first, she could not believe her eyes. She thought she must have been delirious from the march, or from drinking too fast. She blinked and shook her head, but the image of Luriel Pearlwing before her would not dissipate.

The dragon had shed her armor, which should have been Abscess's first clue that this was not an illusion, for she had never seen Luriel without her scales. She was in a state of undress, trousers rolled up to the knee, shirt draped over an arm, and feet bare. And she looked tired. Surely Abscess could not be imagining that, either. The whole picture made the dragon seem vulnerable, nothing more than a farm girl in desperate need of a bath, save for the long white hair around her shoulders that glowed in the dim light of the forest's understory.

Luriel seemed just as surprised to see Abscess and Saline sprawled on the other bank as they were to see her. After several seconds of staring, Abscess realized that Luriel was unarmed, and she could have the advantage if she got her ass up already.

"Lurrr..." she growled. Further syllables seemed beyond her. No matter. She needed action, not words. She splashed into the stream, raised her axe and took a mighty swing...and missed.

And no wonder. She was a good five feet away from Luriel. How had she misjudged so completely? Luriel was staring at her wide-eyed, equally stunned by the mistake.

Abscess gritted her teeth and closed the distance, and at last Luriel was forced to move. Abscess swung with all her strength. Luriel twisted this way and that, evading every strike.

"Fight me!" Abscess yelled, swinging again, while Luriel calmly stepped out of the way and said nothing.

"Can't fight me without your army behind you?" Abscess goaded, lunging, and too late could feel that her feet weren't in position to catch her weight.

Luriel, at that moment, pushed forward and hit Abscess squarely in the chest with her shoulder. Abscess lost her balance completely and landed in the stream.

"This is no fight," said Luriel calmly, looking down at Abscess. Her legs glistened with some of the droplets Abscess had splashed on her, but other than that she looked completely unfussed.

Abscess stared up at the dragon and could, for the first time, feel the leagues of difference between them. Luriel Pearlwing was a Cloud Dweller, born to rule the mortal lands from the heavens. Abscess wasn't even a topsider. She was a creature of the underworld, conceived so far beneath the dragon knight's gaze that she should never have garnered notice.

That thought infuriated Abscess. She was panting, but it did not clear her head. Her heart felt big in her chest like it might burst at any moment.

"Why are you just standing there, then?" she asked. "Go on, stomp on me. Isn't that all we are to you? Just creatures to trample?"

Luriel raised her brows and continued to stare at Abscess with her infuriatingly level expression.

"You are creatures of unchecked, senseless destruction," she said gently, "but I get no joy from killing the vulnerable."

"You lie!" Abscess felt no stronger, but she gathered herself to stand anyway. "Killing is all dragons know!"

"With all due respect, I am not the one with the axe."

"Don't mock me!"

"I'm not. I am only curious why you—"

"Rarr!" Abscess, with all of her strength, swung her axe at Luriel's neck and pictured the blade parting the flesh in a shower of silver blood. She imagined the dragon's head rolling into the stream, the feathery hair floating on the water. She imagined presenting the head to Commander Render, and how she would then skin and boil the skull herself, like Captain Pokeweed. Then she would place the skull of Luriel Pearlwing over her cot, right next to Brimbreath's box.

Instead, Abscess fell face first in the stream, she and her axe sending up a wave of water. When Saline shook her awake, Luriel was gone.

The party arrived in the mines two days late, haggard and thin, but alive. Commander Render dressed Abscess down thoroughly over the delay. Abscess took it quietly. The Commander went in about the elite status of the Petramori, how she expected flawlessness, how their strength and endurance were a tribute to Lord Helnor and they owed their undying loyalty to the horde. Abscess had heard it before. This speech always lit a fire in her before battles, but this time the words scraped over her scales unpleasantly.

Finally, Commander Render dismissed her, and Abscess went back to her cot. She lay there a while, listening to the sounds of fire, steam, metal ringing, hoblins and Petramori shouting through drills. She missed the furnace of the mines, the blistering, boiling heat and how it soothed her skin, and yet she found herself thinking of the southern coast's cool, salty breeze, and the forest's shade by the stream. She thought of the deer, then she thought of Luriel Pearlwing, but she was too bone tired to summon the rage that thoughts of Luriel normally ignited. She only felt the frustration of unanswered longing.

She pulled out Brimbreath's little singing box. The music was hidden enough in the noise of the mines that no one looked in to see what she was doing, so she set the box on her chest, lay back, and closed her eyes. She thought of sunlight glowing through leaves, of water rolling over rocks, of the call of birds, and sunlight on Luriel Pearlwing's armor long after the music stopped.

Within a week, they were on the march again.

"All right, you fiends! Let's move out!" she called as she always did. As Pokeweed once did.

"Hut! Hut! Hut!"

Abscess took her company topside. She breathed deeply and smelled the usual wetness and decay as she always did, but she lingered at it longer than usual.

Tarpith returned to the company one thundery night. Captain Marrow's company had been taken out completely, ambushed by dwarves. Tarpith was the only survivor. He was thin now, even by his standards, his hide streaked with soot and scars Abscess did not remember. He rejoined their marches without a word, and Abscess said nothing of their ugly parting.

So, Abscess found herself leading her company topside once more through mortal hills and mortal fields. It was all blurring together. She marched, hacked, slashed, raided, marched, slashed.

She wandered away from her company to relieve herself in the shadow of a knoll, the only privacy to be had in one, lonely meadow. When she stood, she found herself shielding her eyes against a light so bright she took it for the sun. Then she blinked.

Luriel Pearlwing stared down at her from the very top of the knoll.

They regarded one another. Luriel was armored neck to foot, fully covered now. Only her head was bare, her helmet under one arm and her long hair rippling in a light breeze. Abscess could not imagine how she had not noticed her there before, except that Abscess was too tired to notice much of anything.

It even took her a moment to remember what she should do at this moment. But as she pulled the axe from her back, Luriel held up a hand.

"If it's all the same to you," said the dragon, "I would rather not fight right now."

Abscess blinked. She surely did not hear her right. After waiting for Luriel to clarify and getting nothing, she said, "Wuh?"

Luriel, unfathomably, sat down and then, unfathomablier still, gestured for Abscess to do the same.

A smarter, quicker Petramori might have seized this moment of vulnerability and lashed out at Luriel with their axe. Or maybe that was a thing only a dumber, more impulsive Petramori would do, for surely a dragon was never truly vulnerable.

In any case, Abscess found herself climbing the knoll on hands and knees. Near the top, she rolled onto her rear. She did not want to admit to herself that she had not been ready for a fight. No self-respecting Petramori would ever admit such a thing.

So, they sat. Abscess wiggled her hind around. The ground was mossy and damp, but not unpleasantly so. She stretched out her legs. She laid her axe across them, then thought better of it and laid the axe down beside her. Luriel was quite still, staring up at the sky and the white clouds drifting lazily above. Abscess followed her gaze, letting it trail to the trees on the gentle slopes around them, their leaves fluttering in the breeze that wound through the valley.

Abscess ached everywhere; old wounds and weariness that had nearly always been there, she thought, but she had never let herself feel them, really. They were only signs of life, and thus fortuitous, but now she felt them keenly and before she knew it, she was heaving a great sigh from her nostrils.

Beside her, Luriel did not stir, did not so much as look at her.

Underneath the aching, Abscess was wound tight. It was trouble to sit in such a prone state so close to the enemy, and even greater trouble if one of her comrades saw her. What would she say should Saline or Felsic appear? What would she do if Commander Render found out?

But she still did not move. There was something about this clearing that reminded her of that brief moment by the stream, when Abscess looked up and saw the deer and its hatchling drinking. Mouths to the water, just like she and Saline. She had felt a strange flop in her guts in that moment. A pull. She felt a kinship, somehow.

At last, Luriel spoke.

"I was hatched in a clearing much like this one," she said frankly.

Abscess stared at her, wondering why she would say such a thing. Wondering what this had to do with anything at all, and why Luriel expected Abscess to care. What a strange, pointless, self-involved observation.

But Abscess found herself answering, "Here? On human lands?" She snorted. "I would have thought you were born in the sky like the rest of your kin."

"I was raised among humans," said Luriel. "And elves. They are kin to me as much as the Cloud Dwellers."

"So you are the Mountain Witch's creature through and through," said Abscess with understanding.

Luriel looked at Abscess from the corner of her eye. Abscess could feel the dragon's dagger-shaped pupil on her. "Is that how you style Queen Islinder?"

"It is how I style a usurper and a slavedriver," said Abscess matter-of-factly.

Luriel's eyes widened minutely, regarding Abscess and not immediately responding.

"What?" said Abscess, when she finally got tired of waiting.

"Nothing." Luriel shrugged. "You only catch me by surprise. I always assumed you and your kind were aware of the evil you do in Lord Helnor's name, but now I—"

"The evil *we* do?" said Abscess, sputtering. "We do no evil! We're proud warriors! We're the only thing standing against the tyranny of the Mountain Witch!"

Luriel blinked slowly. "You burn forests, fields, and villages indiscriminately. You murder children as easily as you murder soldiers. You leave a path of destruction everywhere you go."

Abscess was ready to rebut, but for a brief moment, her tongue stuck in her mouth. The image of the Harrowed Forest, flattened and gray, passed through her mind. She recovered and said, "Humans are parasites. We cull their numbers so as not to be overrun by them."

"You call yourselves fiends. You call your army a horde."

Abscess threw up her hands. "It's tongue-in-cheek! All we do every day is march and maim and kill and die! We've gotta do something to lighten the mood! If someone has a broken leg, we keep marching! They either keep up, or they don't, and if they don't..."

She faltered here, too. The patrols were fresh wounds, still aching. She pushed on before unpleasant memories could make themselves felt. "We don't do anything until we're told. If Commander Render doesn't tell us to eat, we don't eat. If she doesn't tell us to drink, we don't drink. If she doesn't tell us to stop, we don't stop. I've walked all day and night without noticing the sky change. I was too busy watching my soldiers' feet to be sure they didn't stumble."

It all spilled out before she knew what she was saying.

Luriel watched her with bright golden eyes, and said, "Ah. Perhaps Queen Islinder is not the only 'slavedriver,' then?"

"I'm no slave!" Abscess replied, and something strained in her voice. Even she heard what a silly declaration it was, she who had never done anything but what she was told.

Luriel did not speak.

"I am a soldier," Abscess said, as if only to herself. "A captain. I worked so hard to be here. To meet *you* again."

Abscess looked at Luriel fiercely. The dragon met her gaze, and there was warmth there. Not a burning heat, but something reassuring. It made Abscess feel...weak.

She looked across the hills, glowing under the setting sun, and sighed. "I've traveled miles and miles over this wretched swamp, and all I've seen is battlefield after battlefield. Is that all there is? Is that all there is in the world?"

Luriel turned to look out at the valley with her. "Our previous conversation was cut short," she said.

Abscess could feel the unspoken *because you fainted in a stream*. Her face burned, and Luriel continued, "I did not ask the thing that was on my mind, then. Why are you here?"

Abscess stared at her. "Uh. 'Cause you invited me."

"I mean, why do you serve Lord Helnor?" said Luriel, with the infinite patience of ageless Cloud Dwellers. "This isn't your war. You don't have to fight."

"Do you have any idea how hard it's been for me? To be worthy! To be valuable!" Abscess growled. She did not know why she bothered saying it, only that she could not help herself.

She could not help but want to be understood. By a dragon. How strange.

Luriel pressed on. "Valuable? Are you only a precious stone, like the ones you mine? Or are you a weapon, just a piece of property to be wielded, and not the wielder herself?"

"Shut up!"

"It is not your war! If you do not wish to fight, then simply walk away."

"You first. You walk away, if it's so easy!"

"I do not fight because it is commanded of me. I do it because it is right."

The words rang inside of Abscess, taking her back to the mines and their dark, steaming dungeons, and eyes glowing green in the dark.

Because. Because it was right.

"And you?" Luriel continued. "Why do you fight?"

"Because I—"

Nothing came out. Rebuttal after rebuttal bounced off her skull. She could not imagine any would stand up to Luriel's scrutiny. *Because I have to. Because it's what my kin do. Because it's what I was told to do. Because it's what I was made to do.* These answers would only prove Luriel right.

Her silence, though, was even worse. Luriel took it for what it was—confirmation that Abscess had no good reason to fight for the horde. She did not look satisfied, though.

Abscess made a deep, coughing sound—a laugh—and said, "What would I do if not this?"

Luriel seemed ready for this. "Dream. Go where you may, do as you may, without sword or shield to weigh your steps. Heed the call of no lords or commanders save your very own heart."

Abscess gaped at Luriel and these ridiculous words. She shook her head. Luriel did not understand, after all.

Then she asked, "If I throw down my sword...would you take me with you?"

Luriel blinked, then turned her gaze to the sky. Abscess, of course, did not expect a serious answer. She wondered why she had asked such a question, only that she should get to be as ridiculous as Luriel. They were still nemeses, after all, and this single afternoon was a fluke. They would leave this place and do battle once more, and eventually one would kill the other, or perhaps they would die together. Abscess did not hate the notion.

Then Luriel stood to make her parting. Abscess watched as she checked her sword, checked her belt, and stretched, half-waiting for a surprise attack, half-wondering if she had the energy to defend herself if it came.

Then Luriel looked down and extended her gloveless hand.

Abscess stared at the pale calloused flesh of Luriel's palm, vulnerable and inviting. When Abscess looked at Luriel's face, she found something unexpectedly familiar in her eyes. She thought of the glade and the deer once more, and felt kinship.

Leaves rustled a few hundred feet away. Abscess whipped her head toward the sound. When she looked back, Luriel was gone, wings beating a hot wind down on where Abscess sat, her great, iridescent mass disappearing against the clouds. Her company climbed the knoll, shouting, "Dragon!" but Luriel was well out of range.

In the days following their meeting, the sharp pang of loss cut through Abscess's numbness. She felt like she was missing something but could not remember what. She played the singing box to try and remember. She played it dangerously frequently, but could not convince herself that there was any reason to be cautious.

When Saline died, it was truly the beginning of the end. Abscess's company had run into a band of hunting elves. This should have been quick work, since the Petramori had the numbers, and yet the elves were wily and shrewd opponents that hid in the trees and used arrows. Saline took one in the eye. It was quick and nearly bloodless.

For days, Abscess could not make sense of it. Saline had been a hatch mate, one of the first creatures Abscess ever knew. She was quiet and perhaps not lively company, but she had always been with Abscess, stoic and steadfast like a shadow. Abscess felt her absence keenly and did not know what to do. It...hurt. She felt sadness, and disappointment, and rage. Astonishingly, she felt betrayed. She knew this was unfair. Saline had done nothing wrong but die, and yet Abscess could not banish the thought.

There was no discussing it with anyone, either. Petramori did not brood. They did not bond over anything but lewd jokes and trophies from raids. And anyway, there was no one left to tell. When Abscess looked out over her company, she saw unfamiliar faces. Brimbreath, Cutworm, Leechmeat, Sixhorn, and Saline were all dead. Felsic lost an arm in a recent raid and was still on a sick bed waiting for it to regrow. Half of who remained were soldiers she had never known terribly well, and the other half were new hatches and she had not bothered to learn their names. The only familiar face was Tarpith. She was pondering the merits of confiding in him when a hoblin appeared with a summons from Commander Render.

Abscess followed the creature to the commander's tent, erected against a rock wall. The Commander stood behind the war table with Lord Helnor. A few of Lord Helnor's priests skulked in the corners. Abscess felt haggard and worn, but held herself tall.

"Captain Abscess," said Commander Render. "Report. How has your company fared on your recent patrols?"

Abscess made her usual observations, if a bit stilted. It struck her as strange that Lord Helnor and his priests would be present for a mere status report.

There was a brief silence that came when Abscess was done. Commander did not write anything down. She did not study the map laid out before her, like she often did. She just stared at Abscess with blazing red eyes.

"Is that all?" she said.

"That is all," Abscess replied.

Lord Helnor spoke then in his deep, quiet voice. "We've heard that you had another encounter with the knight Luriel Pearlwing. Is there a reason you did not mention it?"

Abscess blinked. "I encounter many knights topside, Your...um...Excellency. I did not think it important to clarify."

"Really?" he said, tilting his head. "You did battle against one of the Mountain Witch's greatest warriors. Surely that is an accomplishment worth noting. Even I expect my captains to brag about their conquests."

"Oh," said Abscess dumbly. "Well, um. We...battled, but she got away, so I didn't think..."

"Tarpith tells me he saw you and Pearlwing talking together," said Commander Render. "What did you talk about?"

Abscess heard buzzing between her ears. She could not summon a single thought other than a variety of curses for Tarpith, who she had never liked, not since the day he hatched.

"Perhaps you also consider your conversation with Pearlwing too unimportant to clarify?" said Lord Helnor sweetly, but Abscess sensed the danger.

Lord Helnor extended a hand to his priests. One stepped forward and removed a wooden box from their robes and placed it in Lord Helnor's hand. It was Brimbreath's singing box. They had gone through Abscess's things. The buzzing between her ears intensified.

"A lovely trinket," said Lord Helnor. "Seized on the battlefield, I am sure. But has a Petramori who has pleasant chats with the enemy earned such a trophy?"

He balanced the box between his fingers, caressing the scratched wood.

"What else do you keep from me?" said Lord Helnor.

Reflexively, Abscess replied, "Nothing."

"What have I done to earn your scorn, Abscess?" he said.

"Nothing, Your Excellency."

"Have I not provided you with your heart's desires? I gave you life. I have given you food, shelter, intelligence, and strength. I have elevated you, the Petramori, above the hoblins and even the vultria. You are a superior race. You are the culmination of my efforts against the tyranny of the Mountain Witch. And when this war is finally over, it is you who will inherit the earth."

Abscess had heard these words countless times, all her life, and yet now a small voice deep within her said, *But it's not your war.*

She would never have dared let such a thought enter her mind before, but now it was there and as she tried to shake it, a fiery anger bloomed inside of her.

"I did earn it," she said quietly.

Lord Helnor and Commander Render stared at Abscess. She could even feel the priests staring. "What?" said Lord Helnor.

"Brimbreath found the box in a raid. He gave it to me before he was killed by Luriel Pearlwing. I fought Luriel Pearlwing in Brimbreath's name and risked my life to avenge him. I have earned that box."

She had always been loyal. She had given her entire life, her entire existence to a lie, the lie that if she did so, that she would be rewarded. That the horde would answer her loyalty in kind. She would be loved, and protected, and honored.

Instead, whatever she gave, they took, and demanded more. And when she gave over everything she had, and there was nothing else, they would move onto the next Petramori without so much as a glance back. Just the same as Pokeweed, and Brimbreath, and Leechmeat, and Felsic, and Saline, and all the rest. Every moment of everyday Abscess was tired, aching, hungry, thirsty, angry, and scared, and it meant nothing, and it would never end, and it would keep on meaning nothing.

Abscess was having a thought, at last. She was thinking that maybe it wasn't Luriel Pearlwing that took Brimbreath and Pokeweed and all her friends from her. Maybe it was Commander Render, and Lord Helnor, and the priests, and the horde.

Abscess sensed danger, but the thought was in her head now, and she could not make it go away.

A silence emerged in the wake of Abscess's words. Commander Render's eyes were round like red-hot coals. Abscess did not think she'd ever seen the commander look so surprised.

Then Lord Helnor hurled the singing box into the rock wall that loomed at the back of the tent. A beautiful, sad note burst through the splintering wood, then the whole thing fell to the ground.

"You have earned *nothing!*" Lord Helnor screamed. He breathed heavily, wheezing as if the sudden outburst cost him, but it was the most emotion Abscess had ever seen their lord express.

Abscess did not quite remember all the things that Lord Helnor and Commander Render said to her after that. It did not matter, anyway, since they were not satisfied with her replies. Perhaps there was nothing she could have said to save herself.

So, she found herself in the Bowl, though this was a very different viewpoint than last time. From the stage at the very center of the amphitheater, arms bound and knees bent, Abscess looked up at thousands and thousands of faces rising in a circle around her. This must have been what Captain Pokeweed saw. She wondered briefly if her captain looked for her the way she now looked for any face that she might know, even Tarpith's traitorous jowls, but the faces were all too distant and numerous for her to focus on.

Somewhere behind her, Commander Render yelled out Abscess's many treasonous crimes. Another captain turned Mountain Witch's creature, betraying the sanctity of the horde. Abscess wanted to answer her, to say that she was not the one who had been disloyal. She wanted to warn the other Petramori, even the hoblins. All that awaited them was pain, sorrow, and a thankless, loveless death. She could not summon the words, however.

Instead, she hummed quietly. She did not remember all the melody of the singing box, but she hummed the parts she knew.

Behind her, Commander Render's voice faltered. Lord Helnor took over, speaking so loudly that Abscess almost lost the thread of the melody, but she pushed on. She closed her eyes and thought of the Harrowed Forest as it once was. She thought of deer drinking from clear running water. She thought of the smell of rain and soil and the sun and the clouds and all the things topside that she loathed and loved. Somewhere above her, the executioner lifted their axe. The buzzing between her ears returned and soon she could not hear her humming.

The buzzing grew cacophonous. Abscess realized it was not coming from between her ears at all. She opened her eyes. Soldiers in armor and leather poured into the Bowl, swinging swords, axes, and poles. Hoblins were running. Petramori were fighting. Growls and screams mingled with the clang of metal. It was mayhem.

The axe fell to the ground, along with the executioner's hands still gripping the handle. Abscess moved one knee in order to twist and look behind her. Lord Helnor stood there, arms out, stunned at the sword buried deep into his chest.

Abscess knew that long blade and its mirror surface, now covered in Lord Helnor's blood. He bled red, just like any human.

Luriel Pearlwing twisted the sword away and left Lord Helnor's body to fall. She stood over Abscess, her iridescent armor blazing in the hellish glow of the mines.

Then, Luriel held out her hand.

Abscess moved a hand to steady herself, only then realizing that she could move her arms. She did not know when her bonds had been cut.

The dragon knight dazzled like the sun, and Abscess was sure she was the most beautiful thing she had ever seen.

"Luriel Pearlwing," said Abscess.

Luriel grinned. "Abscess."

Abscess reached for the executioner's axe, and with a strong jerk, sent the severed limbs flying. With the opposite hand, she took Luriel's, and the dragon's flesh was as soft and radiant as Abscess had imagined.

They turned toward the battle and Abscess smiled.

"Rank and File" is a stand-alone short by N. Romaine White. You can find more of Romaine's work, social media links, and news about what she's up to at nromainewhite.com.

The Emerald Queen

Robin C.M. Duncan

Sapphic Representation: Lesbian
Heat Level: Medium
Content Warnings: Coarse Language, Violence, Abuse, Torture

1

My people, the enemy seeks to destroy us, we who have ruled these islands for generations. They think by stealing our magic, they have left us powerless, but our great navy still fights! We still win victories. We will take back the islands we have lost. We will reclaim the magic that is our birthright. We will capture the traitors among us, as we captured the treacherous Vermillion, and we will forge new magic. Lineca never will be defeated!

- Address by Apanato, Princex of the Hundred Isles

I'm here for an execution. Hopefully not my own. They'll have to catch me first.

I never could have imagined being a fugitive in my own city, my way of life under threat, the pain of losing my love—Mehdina who now hunts me for the Princex—the royal greed for the paradigms finally driving us apart. But I still have my magic, the artefact that belonged to my mother, now mine, and for that I am hunted.

This noon I stood disguised among the crowd in Cardoon Square, listened to the Princex—may they rot forever in a private hell—spout falsehoods and fakery while the nation slides into ruin. Lineca of the Hundred Isles is *losing*. Islands are captured weekly, but most heinous of the Princex's lies? There is no enemy: Linecans fight themselves, kill each other for nothing but the Princex's vainglory, the greed and stubbornness of our monarch. Yet Mehdina can't see it as Vermillion did, and now I do. As each island falls to the rebels, its people are freed, and join the uprising. The Princex is doomed, their reign crumbling. Without the wonderous paradigms and the abilities those artifacts conferred, the Princex's eyrs are reduced to common sailors. The once-indomitable Linecan navy relies on the skill and wit of its captains, increasingly outmatched by rebel cunning and numbers. The tide has turned with the bravery of one woman,

Mehdina's lover before me, scourge of the high seas, firebrand pirate, fearless buccaneer. But tomorrow Vermillion dies. And that's where I come in.

2

AH: *In summary, your lordship: one, the Institutes continue assiduously to research how to enter the Melavorna volcano where four of the five paradigms are lost, in order to reclaim them; two, our philosophers, alchemists and engineers strive Sun span and Moon turn to discover a technique to harvest the power residue from the stone of Cardoon's paradigm vault, or the rock of Melavorna Isle, assuming the same leaching effect occurs there; three—*

LLS: *Academician Hankani, you also are charged to discover how to make new paradigms.*

AH: *Has Astrid Opanimo been found, your lordship? Her paradigm recovered?*

LLS: *No. And it is not her paradigm. Magical artefacts belong to the Princex—may the shield of their wisdom protect us. Measures are in hand. We will acquire the Winged Paradigm soon. When we do, you'll have few turns to complete your task.*

AH: *You know where Astrid is?*

LLS: *We know where her family lives.*

*- Record of Principal Academician Hankani's audience
with Lord Lamyn Sakaria, Chair of the Royal Council*

Tomorrow morn, I'll visit my family, from whom I'm too long absented. I've sought knowledge of the paradigms far and wide to best determine how to reclaim them, but only Mother can explain how mine came first into her hands. How will my welcome be, when I'm hunted everywhere, as my love Mehdina and I hunted Vermillion, before I understood her mission to free Lineca? Will Mehdina ever come to see Vermillion was right about the silencing of dissent, the quiet removal of righteous resistance, or will we always be enemies now, her cleaving to her orders that I be hog tied, dragged to the Institute to be sliced open in search of what makes me fly, milked, or my paradigm melted down in search of their lost power? I fear not.

I do struggle to reconcile Vermillion's trip to the gallows. As a terror of the seas, she sent many good and honest sailors to their death. I should despise her. As the woman who loved Captain Mehdina Taradel before I did, who lost her before I did, who had Mehdina longer, I should envy her. As the thief who stole the Princex's paradigms, and who tried to steal mine to dispose of with the others into a blasted volcano...should I admire her courage, her selflessness? Because I know now Vermillion was right. I discovered the hard way, from abandoning closeted ignorance in the dusty Institute of Antiquities to follow my dream (and hopeless, then unrequited love); to finding freedom on the ocean; to flying when the power of my mother's charm was revealed; but most dearly in lying with the captain of the Scarlet Sword, floating on her sheets, drowning in her pillows, gasping through our kisses, cresting the wave of her hips.

On this incredible journey I've found new currents. Finally, I must acknowledge I believe in Vermillion's cause. Even when every loyal soldier and sailor—Mehdina too—would drag me to face examination. Even then, I've come to Cardoon to free Vermillion. We must retrieve the paradigms before the Institute reclaims them. But I can't do it alone, and she stole them once before. I need her.

The city's evening-dark streets are redolent of my fear. It stinks higher than streetlamps, cooking oil, dog piss and sea salt. Even the pressgangs don't work at night. The populace is past the point of cowering. They will fight anyone to keep their loved ones. (Did I fight hard enough to keep Mehdina?) And when the Princex and his cronies lose the power of fear, as they have lost the paradigms, who knows what happens next?

I've come abroad to meet a friend. A risk with such tension in the thick, hot air, and with so many refugees around, but I need help. If I'm accosted by miscreants or the guard, using my power of flight could bring a quick death, even under cover of dim-lit night, but I have other strengths now. The timid mouse is gone. A year at sea hardened me. Three months of running wore me sharp. Will Corina recognise me shaven headed, just a dirty stubble left of my raven locks?

Two City Guard clump up the steep street I descend, boots scuffing dusty cobbles, half-armour clanking, breath puffing. Cruel memory plays another scene, me running down this way to the harbour when I first met Mehdina. How can she hunt me now when we shared a bed, shared our bodies for so long? I push the thought away. Vigilance!

"Ho, boy! What ship?" calls one, hand on hilt. The other lowers his spear, ready, jumpy from turning away undesirables who cannot pay their way through Cardoon's gates. Before I can answer, the same clanking sounds behind me.

I stifle a flinch, manage to call, "No ship, lads," dropping my pitch, my cabin boy shape aiding the lie. "A sailmaker's life for me, span and turn for glory o' the Princex—may they last forever," rotting in a dungeon. I swallow a knot and start forward. The boots behind follow, unconvinced. The guards ahead block my last twenty paces to The Brewer's Droop. The taller, fatter, older one draws his stubby sword. The short, jumpy youngster hefts his spear.

My heart hammers my ribs. Is this my end, already? Do something, Astrid. Change the script.

"I'd buy a round, lads, but—" I stop, hands on hips, twist to size up the reinforcements: Two handy-looking sods. One's leer speaks of happy times strip-searching cadets, which he clearly thinks I am. Confidence, Astrid. We're all Linecans together. "I'm meeting a lady."

"No, yer not," sneers the nasty one, hands his pike to his comrade, closes on me, arms wide to stop me bolting.

I could fly, manage two strides downhill, leap into the night before they can grab me, but my game would be up. I could knife Nasty Lad when he grapples me, and he will—lustful eyes glinting even in this poor light. If I'm taken, they'll work me over, discover who I am. I'll be hauled away. They'll go to work on me, because the Princex must have their power back. Would Mehdina stand by and see me experimented upon? Nasty Lad's big hand grabs my shoulder. My chance to fly is gone. He hauls me around.

"Stand down, you wasters!"

Nasty ignores the new command, jerks my hood back, and grins.

"I said stand down, you waste of balls! A dick's a privilege can be taken away."

My past shipmate, Corina, strides from the tavern door, helm in hand, past the first two guards, ten feet tall in command though she's an inch below me. Nasty's grip slackens, seeing Corina's pips. Her swing's a wide arc, helm clattering his shoulder. Nasty yelps, whimpers. Corina whips out a knife.

"Who'll drop his breeches first? I aim to confiscate a prick for this insubordination." They gawp at her then snap to attention, all but Nasty, still bent, clutching his shoulder. "Oh, just fuck off then, if you can't take a joke."

The guardsmen hurry to obey as Corina throws an arm around my shoulders, pulls me in, all joviality, hissing through her thin-lipped smile. "How long were you at sea, idiot? Did you forget cities have corners?"

3

Vermillion now she languishes, upon Princex's pleasure,
her crimes will be her epitaph, no briny grave for she.
And as she lies in prison deep, she thinks upon her lover,
The brave Mehdina Taradel, who fights to save us all.

Mehdina seeks the rebel eyr, the traitor Opanimo,
As-trid who has abandoned us, denying us her power.
But when she's caught, the Institutes will wrest her secrets from her,
New paradigms then will be forged, to fight the rebel horde.

> *Scrub the decks.*
> > *Away with yea.*
> *Pull the lines.*
> > *Away with yea.*
> *Ship the oars.*
> > *Away with yea.*
> *Vermillion is her name, oh.*

(Low, ponderous.)
Vermillion goes to face her death, the noose, the rack, the halberd,
she will die, her body torn, at noon upon the day.
So will end Vermillion's tale, her song come to an end then;
Victory to the Princex, may they reign a thousand years.

(Chorus twice.)

- The Ballad of Vermillion (new verses) – Anonymous

Applause and catcalls cut through smoky air. The bard salutes, rattles a mostly empty flagon. Coins sail towards him. Corina flips him a miller. The brass coin hits the man's shoulder as he stoops to harvest earnings from the floor. She is such a handy blade. I must have her aid in this.

"Why the hells come here?" she mutters into her cider. "I should have you chained. Mehdina's torn twenty dosshouses apart, ransacked holds and warehouses, sailed the Home Isles twice to unearth you."

"To feed me to the Institutes," I growl. "Cut me open to see my workings."

"If you hadn't run—"

"They'd have filleted me by now," I say lightly, smiling because sour faces and bitter words in a happy crowd draw glances. And because Corie's been a firm friend since the Princex ordered my capture, and Dina rejected me. My

Mehdina, no longer. I miss lying together in swathes of clifftop flowers, naked chases through salty surf, sharing spicey crabsticks from One-arm's barrow on Dock Street. I miss her like laughter.

I touch my cheek. "Is Hankani close to retrieving the paradigms?"

Corina shrugs. "Learning to walk into a volcano takes time, apparently."

"Corie, you're naval liaison because you were on Melavorna when those geegaws went over the edge into brimstone and smoke. That weasel Sakaria trusts you. You'll be among the first to know." I glance at my untouched shot of runa. It can never taste as it did when I sucked it greedily from Mehdina's mouth, or lapped it from her stomach, my tingling tongue trailing down her belly to her lips, setting her writhing.

I lift the shot, tap it twice on the table, slug it down. I crank my arm to throw the glass at the fireplace then stop, put it down, and wave for the bottle.

"You can't go home," says Corina. "Mehdina put spies on your family. If you would throw yourself at her feet that's the way."

Corina's short, sweet-looking, but the fight and fury she carries scares me. That fire drew me to her friendship, and I need it now. "Help me free Vermillion, Corie," I murmur. "She was right, and I need her help. You don't love the Princex. The people will win. Don't be on the wrong side."

"I'm an officer," she replies. "Rebels burn villages. I protect the rule of law."

"Laws that chain us to the plough, the oars, the adze, hauling our own gravestones around till we're too broken to question." She scowls, but I fancy her grey eyes hold doubt. "Imagine freedom from greed, serving only the will of the people. Help me," I plead. "This is our only chance."

She drains her glass. Her grey gaze gives me hope.

"Convince Mehdina," she says. "I'll follow her."

"Might as well say convince the Princex." I scowl.

"Exactly."

* * *

Nearby The Brewer's stands Cardoon's tallest inn. I demand the attic room. The porter scowls. "The drudges sleep there 'tween shifts. It won't do." He slides the ground floor key forward again.

I put three silver sergeants on the counter. "It'll do for me."

His eyes narrow. "Twice that; I could fill it with refugees." I drop three more coins. He nods.

In near-darkness, I lie awake under creaking wood, gusting wind rattling the tiles, boards groaning. I'll never sleep. I think to calm myself, but my fingers are poor substitute for Dina's passion, her urgency, never knowing where she'll kiss next. Delicious, intoxicating, unpredictable. I had her, I had everything, but I think I knew it couldn't last. Vermillion hung over us: Mehdina's guilt, my jealousy, a wedge between us, and the Princex drove it home. But why did Mehdina side with them?

Thoughts of her—even conflicting ones—bring me to the edge of sleep, where urges, hopes, fears and all else besides topple into the abyss.

A creak, not in the roof. On the stairs.

4

You said watch for a girl, shifty, angry eyes. She's got my attic room, or I've not run inns forty year. Bring swords.

- Message to Mehdina Taradel, PFP, Cardoon Garrison

I twitch upright. Moonlight streams through the window, pearlescence painting the floor.

The creak again.

Hell's teeth. I'm done for, but I won't surrender. Never. Not even to Dina.

I leap up, still dressed because I'm not an idiot. Halfway to the window, the door bursts in, molten lamplight floods the room.

"Astrid, hold!"

I glance at that familiar, grating voice. Uniforms spill past burly, bearded Brogine—once Mehdina's eyrhearer, Scarlet Sword's first mate, a former friend.

"Hold."

I don't stop, push the unlatched skylight wide, climb onto the roof.

"Hear me out!" Brogine tries to command but knows from our voyages he may as well piss to windward. "Dina said come back, patch it up. She's no royal lacky. She'll mind the Institutes don' hurt ye."

"The Princex's day is gone," I shout back. "Dina can't see it. While your blade's all *I* see, Brogine." I turn and leap into soft night air.

Amber lamps, shining cobbles, moonlit roofs tip and flow, sweeping beneath me. I curve into the darkling sky and a net falls on me. I scream, arms twisting and snagging, legs buckling, trapped fast, falling. Foolhardy, impulsive, imprudent I was, but not stupid. My power resists the net's drag, slows my dash to the cobbles. I wrestle out my knife, slashing manically.

Still dropping, still cutting. An arrow skitters off tile, then another: a roof—

I slam into slates, hot pain lancing my hip, numbing my side. I roll down the pitch—less steep than some—net twisting around me, get an arm free, reach, sprawl best I can, slowing, shrug my shoulders free, slower. Stop.

I gasp, searching for breath. Another shaft clicks the slates, and another, another.

"Belay that shooting!"

Distance muffles Brogine's shout. My pained stupor clears enough to see I put a street and a roof between us.

They're firing blind. I still have a chance, and now I have a choice. Surrender, let Mehdina deliver me to the Institutes to harvest what power they can from me, or fight on. Easy choice. Life at sea made me stubborn, as stubborn and resolute as her. So, damn her, Brogine too, and Corina if she won't help, maybe even betrayed me.

I roll over sideways, push up to hands and knees on the rough slates. Tired and sore, I kick my legs free just as the black shape of a head and shoulders appears below me at the roof's edge.

Without thinking, I heft the net up over my head—balance shifting dangerously—fling the heavy trap down, staggering as I do. A man shouts in surprise and fear. I don't linger to see his fate, but rush—pumping and puffing—up the roof, reach the peak and jump, flying away through the smoky night.

5

She got away. Killed Tomwal. If yer right, ye'll have 'er soon. Always telled ye she was a wrong 'un.

- Message by runner, Eyrhearer Brogine to Mehdina Taradel, PFP

Wind chills the sweat on my skin as I climb. New pains appear, but streaming air supports my aching limbs. I push higher still as I learned from Loqa, the Melavornan girl, winged like all her people. Clouds wet my face, clearing my head. It seems I'm awaited at home, and there's no aid from Corina. Must I abandon asking Mother about my charm's origin? Is my plan to snatch Vermillion from her own neck-stretching death?

Soaked, exhausted, hope ebbing, in straits now, hunted, plotted against, yet desperate to fight for Lineca, *not* the Princex—may they see their end coming—I must do what

Vermillion would. I must fly in the face of all expectation, even Mehdina's.

I bank away from my course home, sweep my arms down, plunge back towards the city. Vermillion never gave up hope, even when Mehdina and I caught her, and the dozen times when we *thought* we had her, she fooled us with the unexpected. I will do the same. I'll visit my old mentor, now charged to reap my power. Because Hankani will know what's happening, and she will tell me.

6

Months passed in fruitless effort. After smelting hinges, locks and ironwork of the paradigm vault, casting new paradigms produced some effect (Notebook D7), but it quickly waned. Burning the vault doors, using the ash; frustratingly ineffective. Powdering the vault's very stone; not the slightest positive outcome.

Still, my staff and I strive light span and dark turn. I hoped Acady Yilzma's investigations of the eyrs themselves would bring advances. The once-powerful arrived (or were brought) to the Institute of Physiognomy; they lined the street outside. Yilzma questioned every one, at length. I heard Sakaria drove him relentlessly. Some subjects required the infirmary.

I fear (though less than I might if this were not set down in my own obscure cypher) what tortures Sakaria will mete out next, on Astrid if they catch her; Lineca's last eyr. Wayward, rebellious maybe, nowadays, but she was my charge. Still, I'd surrender her to spare the suffering of others.

- Principal Academician Hankani, journal extract

One great boon of my power is that I rarely tire in flight. Now, I circle the Institute till the guards reach their limits, tucking in my too-long-unwashed clothes against the possibility of noisy flapping.

I descend slowly into warmer air, touch the tiles of the Institute of Antiquities with tipped toes, a skipping step along the roof's peak, as I slow to a stop. I drop to my stomach, slide downwards, glancing back, feet fishing for a skylight.

I have no magic for this. I assault the slopping window's latch with a slender blade then slip inside, dropping softly into a dry and dusty space, cramped with clutter, the Institute's abandoned finds, boxed and forgotten. An eyrseer or eyrtaster might have navigated this place without light, but power gone, they'd be left like me, groping between crates and dust-sheeted jumble, feeling gingerly to find the protruding ladder then the square hole.

Memories press in as I pad through the Institute's quiet, lamplit corridors. I know the way, and how to avoid the few guards committed to the interior. Hankani's office is unguarded, as expected. The acady is a harmless scientist. But this one now is under the direction of the Princex's hubris, their exploitation, their greed, and I am a target.

I knock on the oak door. As heavy silence settles again, I hear the pad of slippered feet beyond.

The door swings open.

"Astrid!"

My former mentor steps back, maybe shaken enough to drop her candle, set her nightdress ablaze. I stride into the room, catch her forearm, take the candleholder. Acady Hankani pulls away from me.

"The guards—"

"Still out there, but would you give me up to torture and vivisection?" I can't help my spiteful inflection.

She's still pulling away. I release her, and she turns, grey hair swinging at her shoulders, sits on the bed's edge, grips the lap of her nightdress to still her nobbled hands. "You're dirty and bruised. I'd scarcely believe you could get any thinner. What are you doing, running from your duty? Why come here? You'll not have my aid."

I touch the five-turn-old, almost forgotten bruise on my cheek. I look a sight: little sleep; fleeing and hiding; begging, borrowing, stowing away to get back here. I think I knew this fair, insightful, trustworthy woman would not help me. How could I expect sympathy or succour? Hankani's life is lived at the mercy of the Princex—damn their eyes. How can she not see her duty is a curse? Unless she can.

"I hoped your time teaching me meant something, that the values you instilled remain in you, Acady. Some of our talks..." I lower my voice. "I thought I heard resistance in you."

"Astrid!" she hisses, stands, no longer shaking, closes on me, grips my shoulders. Wiry strength is fuelled by the concern behind bright eyes. Her elegant face wears badges of age won from love's laughter and scholarly work. Close enough for our noses to touch, she can breathe the words. "Now is not the time."

Hope! "When then? What better time to save a country from tyranny? Thousands dead, thousands displaced, gathering hungry and rootless in alleyways. Our production feeding the Princex's machine that harvests the world like their personal farm, plantation, mine."

Hankani's grasp eases enough for pain to register. "Astrid, you are one woman, barely past girlhood."

"I'm here for help. Vermillion."

A look of horror paints her face red and dark, blood searing her cheeks, candlelight shadowing her eyes. "Madness! How?"

I reach to my grimy neck and grip my mother's winged charm. "My paradigm."

"They'll shoot you down, Astrid." She clasps my arms again, tenderly this time.

"Before you experiment on me?" The acady bows her head, gaining years with each breath. "I hoped that in your heart, or at least in your head, you hated the Princex too."

Her mouth's a thin line, gaze intent. Weighing up her life as I have done mine? How she will spend the remainder?

Hesitantly at first, Hankani speaks. "The Institutes of Alchemy and Geology have worked closely in recent weeks, and feverishly, messengers scurrying like ants. Deliveries flow into their buildings as if the ants are nesting in the corner of Institute Square where Alchemy and Geology sit. A scaffold went up last week, sawing and hammering into the night. They've hoarded off the square's corner. Access is controlled."

"You must know what's happening. You chair the Institutes this year." My stomach clenches, mouth drying, thoughts drag up unwilling images of Vermillion hanging, and me dropping next, skin flayed in the search for paradigm power.

"Three turns past the clanking began, the hollow ring of metal tubes and plates. Sakaria sequesters the details, but they are building a machine, clearly, have been for spans. Not a war engine, I think. At night, their endless braising throws shadows on the buildings. The machine is large, a massive, threaded cone at its end. A digging machine, a tunneller. The only commands now are retrieve the paradigms, make new ones. They plan to breach the caldera of the Melavorna volcano."

"And the Princex will go on," I say, hearing my own hollowness.

"You can't stop them, even with a hundred times your resources."

I close my eyes, nodding repeatedly. "Can't stop them, Acady, but I can beat them. A metal engine is heavy and slow. A fast ship can reach Melavorna days ahead."

"But you can't enter the volcano."

An ache pierces my chest. Hankani has not called the guards. Maybe she's afraid to oppose the Princex, but she's thinking now how I might succeed.

"Ever since I left the isle, as you taught me, I've read all I can of Melavorna. Sources are few and almost never name the isle. Vermillion hid there for years. I'm guessing, Acady. Help me search Antiquities' library, please."

Indecision hunts across her features for an answer. Finally, her lips narrow, and she raises her head, once again my stern tutor. "I cannot. I will be accused." I close my eyes, sigh, fatigue settling on me. "But I will not stop you looking."

My second sigh is pure relief. Unthinkably, I grasp her in a bony hug. She pushes me away, not roughly and only after two breaths, reaches to her nightstand, and pushes a crumpled, lumpy paper into my hand. "Boiled sweets," she humphs. "You'll need something to keep awake."

Evading the guards, I spend the dark span between today and tomorrow among the bookcases ranked in the Institute's dry and dusty cellar. The work is hard, but Hankani trained me for it. Slowly, surely, knowledge flows.

7

You asked me to report urgently any news of Astrid Opanimo. Be advised she was here, in Antiquities' corridors, this evening. She interrogated me on your lordship's strategy. I told her nothing not already evident to any person in the street.

- Message from Principal Academician Hankani, to Lord Lamyn Sakaria

Today, Vermillion dies.

That's the nub, prime reason Dina and I fell apart. Long spans at sea my obsession grew. Waking in Mehdina's protecting arms I understood Vermillion a little more, and Lineca less and less. How could the Princex permit their cronies to scour the land for profit? How can they let the lords take and take, then wring their hands and say there's nothing to give when folk lose their farms and their boats to debt? How can they countenance the destruction of even one acre for the sake only of power?

I groan and ache, early morn's chill soaks into me, only my own arms clutching stiff, weary shoulders. I sit up from the angle of roof and chimney where I slept, stretch my limbs, my neck. Lilac and peach at the skyline promise more heat. Vermillion will have a glow when they stretch her neck at noon.

Loosened, but still hungry, I crouch to the edge of the Institute's roof. The street below looks dim and cold, untouched by the sun. I push off, take flight, the half-light affording some protection. I wheel upwards, catching glimpses over the hoardings in the square, get a peek at their precious machine. A bulbous hulk, leaden grey like storm clouds, sporting a swept back chimney, bands of riveted bracing around its hull. A small-wheeled but massive iron cylinder longer than any carriage. Big enough to carry a platoon of idiots into a volcano and cook them through as it does. Fools.

I carry my own heat away across Cardoon Bay, anger coursing through me. I must beat them to Melavorna, and I must have Vermillion to stand a chance, since I've lost my love, Mehdina. I would see her once more before I leave, though it's a sore risk, but I can't quiz my mother without running it, without springing the trap Corina confirmed. So, I fly east, high above the water as the swelling dawn warms my cheeks, towards the distant headland. Maybe Mehdina waits, but I know my parents' land like drawing breath. I refuse to be caught.

* * *

The verdant headland where Vuntino sits hugs Cardoon Bay like a mother holds her child. The sun is up, burning off the chill.

I land on the grass strip between vegetable plot and raised beds, tall corn and cane-fixed beans hiding me from the house. Mehdina's soldiers saw me land, of course. I emerge from the alley of green leaves to meet two guards at the cottage door. Two more approach from the orchard behind me, pushing me forward through the herb garden. I let my fingers trail in bright marigold, past vibrant dahlias, brush rosemary to smell its tang. Mother steps from the open doorway, chin up, defiant, joy and worry warring in her gaze.

"Astrid—"

"Astrid," says Mehdina, moving respectfully but forcefully past Mother to block the porch steps, arms akimbo, boots apart, challenging me in so many ways.

"I haven't come for you," I snap. A lie—my skin yearns for her. "Let me see my family then leave."

Mehdina's features twitch with ire and frustration. "To do what? Destroy my country? Hide away somewhere, save yourself? You'll go to the Institutes, be useful."

Goddess, I wish she would make use of me again. I miss her. "I'll fly from here and you'll never see me again. Or would you cut me down? Not much use then."

My mother flinches, scowls, ready to do someone injury, including me for being rude to guests, even unwanted ones. "Enough," she commands. "You'll sit in the parlour, you two, drink tea, and talk civilly under my roof." The guards start to move me forward, but Mother's glare pins them, finger accusing. "You dirty boots can stay in the garden. Your tea will be brought out."

The parlour's cool, shaded from the brightening sun. Dina and I sit at table, chairs creaking comfortably. Father, brothers, sister out in the field, or sailing to the lobster pots. Kettle on the range, steaming teapot appears with magical speed. No cakes: punishment.

Mehdina sighs heavily. "Astrid—"

"Vermillion dies at noon." I glance at Mother as she sits. "She was your lover. Is hanging to be my fate?"

"She betrayed Princex, Lineca, and me; you're well on your way to doing the same."

"I can't speak about you, but she stole the paradigms *for* Lineca, cast them into the volcano for *her* people, to save them from the eyes-damned Princex!"

"Astrid Opanimo!" Mother bristles. "If you'd curse the Princex in my parlour, use a civil tone, if you please. And Mehdina Taradel"—Mother's mouth pinches—"please state your intent towards my eldest."

Dina's eyebrows rise, and my heart swells to see the briefest smirk touch those lips. "She must be examined at the Institute. She may hold the key to making more paradigms to replace those lost."

"Will she be harmed?" Mother's gaze holds steel.

"Not while I'm there," says Mehdina, her clear eyes holding mine. "As I told her more times than I can count."

"It's not about me." I look away. "And you would not always be there. I'm done kowtowing. The paradigms must be destroyed, the Princex's well-mannered tyranny with them."

"Even your own paradigm?" asks Dina, not unkindly. "Is that what you want?"

I do not answer. I want her. Anger flares in me that no camomile, mint, and blackberry leaves will quench. "It doesn't belong to them. I don't owe them anything, but they owe all of us. The Princex must stop excavating the world, felling it, smelting it, drilling it, burning it. I want the sky and the sea and the land. I want to soar over it and dive into it, and I want to love you, Mehdina, but your duty won't allow it!"

"What should I do then?" Dina's words are terse.

It's easy to push my yearning for her into earnest words. "Act out of love. Give duty to family and friends before you give it to rulers and ministers."

"Oh, Astrid." Is she thawing, will hardness melt into a smile? "You're so naïve."

I gape. Has love left her entirely? She looks sad, and I feel sadness too, that she can't find it in her heart to put love before duty. I suppose that only works if love exists. I want to cry, but swallow the lump in my throat. She's decided it for me. Time to go.

I look at my mother and she smiles slightly, blinks in place of a nod; she understands. I surge up from the table, spinning my chair at Mehdina, who stumbles over it. I launch myself across the parlour at the corner ladder to the attic room, fly through the hatch, push the ladder down behind me, smirking at Dina's loud and colourful curse.

I fly across the dim, stuffy bedroom to the window, push it open and jump out, shoot up and away from my home. When shouts go up, I'm already beyond the range of whipping bowstrings, and the hot, blue air has dried my tears.

8

Opanimo is at large, preparing to disrupt your plans, lordship. I've no notion what she'll do but it'll be madcap risky. Guard what you hold most important.

- Message from Mehdina Taradel PFP to Lord Lamyn Sakaria

She cannot harm the Caldera Engine, only spoil its sheen by her blood staining the metal. Let her try to disrupt the execution, we are ready.

- Response from Lord Lamyn Sakaria to Mehdina Taradel PFP

I pierce the clouds, rain on my face, pain in my heart. How could I think she'd change her mind? For love of silly little Astrid Opanimo, bookish, unworldly, sleeves dusty again from Antiquities' shelves like the day we met?

So it is then, all I have left to risk is my neck. What can I do alone? I lifted Vermillion before, saved her in the caldera so she could die today. But volcanic air was soup thick, supporting, and I barely shifted us before help came. What now?

It's time. I lower my head, drop my arms, and plunge. Cardoon swells from a map to a street plan to a slate and cobble landscape. I target the centre, no misdirection, feint or finesse. I have one chance.

Cardoon Square expands in my view so fast that fear grips me. I bank away to make my approach down Victory Boulevard, the route they'll bring Vermillion in, paraded so she can see how loathed she is by those she would save. Raucous yelling reaches me, thousands thronging the street for a glimpse. I flatten my flight, drop below the roofline to shoot along the street. The air whips gasps and shouts away. I see the open wagon ahead. Vermillion strands proud, bound to a T-shaped iron frame. Beyond the dark-walled canyon of grand buildings, in the bright square, lies her fate and mine.

Arrows fly from rooftop archers. I'd drop lower, but I don't trust they'd stop shooting to spare the crowd beneath their misses. I push harder. Speed should fox their aim. The wagon enters grandiose Cardoon Square. Jeers echo between the buildings. A few more breaths and I'll be there.

A cloud of smoke drifts across the square, thickening.

I burst from the blocky cleft into a haze. Grey smoke masks the crowd, but I hear their shouting, bellowing. Dim shapes pass buckets in a ragged, half-seen line towards a fire in the corner of the square. Corina? Dare I hope?

Then I'm in it.

I knock one guard from the wagon as I land, two hands in her back, swing my leg hard to hobble the other guard with a groin kick, push him off.

"Astrid," Vermillion grins. "You Goddess-damned idiot." Her hands are chained behind her around the iron post, the T-bar stopping an enterprising prisoner climbing to freedom. She rattles the chains. "Not going anywhere, sorry."

Guards run in through drifting, stinking smoke. The driver grabs for me. I knock his grasping hand away, knee him in the face, spin back to Vermillion and step in close. I hug her to me. She raises an eyebrow. I strain to lift us both from the wagon, heave her up to the top of the post. She twists over the bar, dragging her manacled hands to the post's top, dropping her weight onto the crosspiece's junction. I drop my weight on the bar's cantilevered end. The weld breaks and Vermillion falls to the wagon bed.

Soldiers arrive, but only three diverted from the confusion of the blaze. Still enough to stop us dead. Then Corina stalks from the smoke, Brogine, Marin and Jantino, and three of Vermillion's crew behind. They subdue the soldiers as I scrabble for the reins.

"What the hells, Gine?"

He grins. "I 'ate Princey twice times Vermin here, an' tenfold more than you. Corie told me it's time to clean house. I believe 'er."

"Well, get aboard if you're coming," I yell, pausing two breaths before laying leather on the horses. They fight the reins, clattering the cobbles in a tight arc. Smoke, heat, flames. Combatants swearing and cursing, steel clashing as our group fights a melee with arriving soldiers. Horses bellowing, they drag us around. The poor, frightened beasts whiney and bolt from the fire and fighting. Not all of our folk get onto the wagon. The pursuing soldiers drop away behind. Smoke hides the diminishing gallows. We speed for the docks, toward freedom.

A line of City Guard dashes out ahead to block the boulevard, but they may as well scatter petals before us. The horses are not for stopping, and the guardsmen scatter from flashing hooves. Brogine (it can only be him) hoots back at them, then everyone flinches and ducks as arrows rattle in.

"I reckon I'm for rebellion!" hollers Gine.

"Get used to pain," Vermillion barks, but she's grinning like a lunatic, red hair streaming in the carriage's wake, the very spirit of resistance.

9

All Under Control

Vermillion is at large again, but she is hunted. Mehdina Taradel caught her before and will again. Vermillion and the rebel Astrid Opanimo will be put to death on sight.

The Princex—eternal is their reign—has blessed the great Caldera Engine. It sailed this day to reclaim the paradigms. All will be well. The Princex will prevail. We will prevail. Lineca's greatness is assured.

Lord Lamyn Sakaria

- Billposter about the High City

I don't know how we escaped. The chaos surely helped. Corina's wagon fire caught on the Institute of Justice. Flames climbed to the roof and hundreds fought till dusk to subdue the conflagration. So we heard from a passing gutter rat. Corina saved us, and I remember the impassive look on her face, standing amongst the madness as the horses turned, watching us flee as she remained.

Six of us made the docks, left the carriage in a lane, arrived in ones and twos drawing fewer eyes. Vermillion— I still wonder that she and I crouched in a dank, fish-smelling alley making hurried plans, others clustering round, Brogine watching the street. We stole a fast brig, slipped the harbour, and ran for open sea.

Three spans past, that brave, foolhardy escape. The first span was all fuss and bother, learning *Wavewitch*'s temperament, but Vermillion cowed her soon enough, whipping our crew of six into quick industry. Brogine knew her, of course, from the time Vermillion loved Mehdina. The others fell into line, used to running after orders on one ship or another. So, the *Wavewitch* ran for Melavorna, towards the paradigms and the volcano, with Mehdina and the Caldera Engine pressing us all the way.

"How do you keep going?" I ask Vermillion, who has *Wavewitch*'s helm as the sun sets. She laughs, tosses her head back, red hair aflame like the sky. She *is* bewitching.

"I possess the oldest magic there is, Astrid: desire. I never stop, I give everything. People admire that, desire my company, lust after what I have." She grins, ties off the wheel and stalks me where I stand at the rail.

"And what do you desire?"

She stops before me, salt wind tossing her tresses like flickering flames. Her arm circles my waist, pulls me against her. My first thought is how long I wanted to kill her. But she's right, I need her now. She's joined my fight, or I've joined hers. Her all too human magic brings heat to my face in the chill sea breeze. I've missed Mehdina so long now, and maybe I'm done fighting that battle, for one turn anyway.

I grasp the back of Vermillion's neck. She pulls against my grip, but she's not fighting, she's playing, smiling. I use both hands, pull her mouth onto mine, taste her hesitantly, as if her kiss might kill me dead on the spot. She breaks the kiss and I gasp, "I fucking hate you."

And she growls, "Show me how much."

10

I lie washed up in some other captain's sheets, twisted in linen, Vermillion's fingers trailing through the sweat on my back, lit by soft morning light.

"Little Astrid Opanimo is a tiger," she smirks huskily, hair tumbling. "The mother cats of Melavorna better mind their kittens."

Have I betrayed Mehdina when *she* abandoned *me* first? Dina's love was wild and free; but Vermillion tipped me like a hurricane tosses a clipper on thunderous swells, took me to disaster's brink, left me crest-hung, dropped me into dark, damp ecstasy.

A bang on the cabin door rattles me upright, hauling the sheet to my chest. Brogine pushes in. "Bah, stinks o' twat in here," he announces. "Island ho. Landfall afore sunset."

He scowls at me, but how would he understand my need to feel I hurt Mehdina back? Awkwardness stifles the cabin's air. It's the latitude, humidity of a lush, green isle, but I know I'm sweating my tryst with Vermillion. Even dressing, back to her, she reads me like a book opening before her. "Mehdina wouldn't blame you. She's supped from this cup, knows it's hard to resist."

I turn on her to vent fear and frustration, but she's smirking like those tigers do. "You're perfect for Dina, Astrid, but for now you must fight the Princex for her. That was our problem too, her blind duty came first." She laughs, crosses the floor naked, starts pulling on clothes from the locker.

After a dip in the sea, I stand with Vermillion and Brogine on the poop deck as I approach Melavorna again. So many greens swathe the mountain's skirts, grey rock scaling the peak to the truncated top where smoke issues. I've no words. Here we fought and almost died, Dina and me against Vermillion, and we captured her, but only once she threw the paradigms into that hot, poisonous place. And if I *can* find the lost four, can I destroy them? And my own?

* * *

The Melavornans, so long hidden from the world, fly out to greet us, a gaggle of youngsters, all soft-feathered flapping, a handful land on deck. Loqa is with them, hisses at Vermillion who kept her captive once from under tousled dark hair, a startling contrast to her light-feathered body.

"Why is she here?" Loqa snaps.

"Because I need her," I say. "We want the same things."

"You want the box." Loqa's brow furrows.

"Yon box'll be smashed to shards," growls Brogine.

I aim to calm the waters. "Your folk can spot it for us, if you will."

Our welcome on the beach is no warmer. Not only did Vermillion bring violence to this peaceful, once-hidden isle, but Lord Lamyn Sakaria arrived in her wake, and royal surveyors followed him. They have already clear cut an area beside the beach and built a jetty. It cuts into the crystal water like a scar from above the tide line.

There's no time for niceties, we're six strangers with a mission that could save Lineca and this place, too. We forge inland from our stolen ship, our reception committee flying above us as we battle through dripping, biting jungle to the village.

The elders greet us, but hesitance clouds eyes once clear in welcome. The women—who are taller and hold sway in this no longer hidden society—keep a wary silence, surveying our exchange with the male elders.

"Only woe came with you last time. What do you give now?" asks the least well preserved of our hosts.

"And now more sail on the sky!" says a youngster, arriving from the bay.

"Say fast and say true," demands the elder.

Vermillion's eyes bore into mine, thrumming to hear my next madcap scheme. Last night, I sensed glorious abandon in her, like she felt dead already, on borrowed time. Maybe now she sees some way to live.

"Since last I was here, I've searched Lineca's libraries, burgled scholars' homes, questioned explorers. Many turns wasted, but finally I found a text in Tenholm Monastery pointing the way. A tapestry in Roonland's Temple of Qinziui'i confirmed it. Yeluren fisherfolk sing of a woman entering Melavorna's green-limned sea caves, returning a decade later. She spoke of a city *beneath* Melavorna." Vermillion shakes her head. "Unbelievable, but I've heard enough, seen enough to believe it. There's a way inside the volcano. Is it true?"

The elders share questioning looks in the heavy shade of this neat and tidy building that feels part of the jungle. A woman moves forward, not the oldest or the tallest; the one with the widest wings, I think.

"It is true. You can go, but you will not come back soon."

Her eyes are hard. This leader—from her bearing, her belief—fights for her people as hard as Vermillion and I do ours, even those blind to their servitude, the harm their ethos does to all. And now Melavorna is threatened by yet another Linecan incursion, and there will be another after that, and another, and another as the flood gates open and natural life here is swept away.

Marin, breathless, bursts into the building, leaves and vine strands in their hair from tree climbing. "More sails! Two, three squadrons behind the flagship."

"They will be here by dark," says the chief elder. I wager she's weighing our fate; hard, grey eyes empty. I want to speak, stress their fate is twined with ours, that we can save all by ending the Princex's reign, putting our ruler's power beyond reach forever.

Vermillion touches my arm. Strangely gentle for this woman forever burning with emotion. "She knows, Astrid." And I can't help remembering last night, then I think of Mehdina and the Princex's machine, closing on us.

"We will show you." The elder's words are flat. "Let Her pick your fate."

11

*Start engine soonest. Make inland all haste. Begin
tunnel first suitable site. Assume Vermillion will succeed.
No time left.*

*- Signal, Lord Sakaria, institute cutter Future's Edge to
Captain Taradel PFP, Scarlet Sword*

The island folk and I fly to the cave mouth. The rest can only walk. Vermillion left the village cutting through jungle like she hated it, defying vine, stem and branch to stand before her blade. It's clear why Dina loved her; passion raw and pure shines from her.

The elder's name is Qara. We fliers arrive first, dropping through warm, coastal wind into verdant heat that cloys the lungs like syrup. It must be worse for Vermillion and crew. Qara, Loqa, two nameless males and I land in a clearing they must maintain, or the jungle would quickly reclaim it. This place's purpose is obvious enough; a dark tunnel of impressive bore gapes at me across bare earth. Vines and ferns festoon its edge, mosses and lichens coat walls and floor wetted by steady dripping from the roof. The cave is dark, ready to swallow any sign of us.

My feet begin to tremble, as if a low, steady peel of laughter issued from the cave.

"Does the mountain scorn me?" I ask Loqa.

Qara grunts. "When Melavorna cries, all hear."

The vibration continues beneath audibility. Then the walkers arrive in a flurry of slashing undergrowth, and in remarkable time, too.

"We have to go," Vermillion snaps, striding to the middle of the clearing.

"A torch?" I ask Qara but Loqa brings a cloth-wrapped brand from the cave. Brogine produces an ocular, focusses the sun, and the brand smokes into pitch-stinking life. He takes the torch, walks into the cave, Vermillion following, then Loqa (despite hating Vermillion). Qara sends the males away, then follows me into the mountain.

Fifty yards into the dark the sun may as well never have shone a day. The vibration's a shudder now, dragging my mind to even darker places. We walk a good time, following Brogine's torch. The tunnel starts sloping down. The heat increases, all water gone. Dryness scratches my throat. The rumble still permeating the rock nags like a husband. I hate it.

"The machine," says Vermillion as we're skirting a rockfall. "The Princex's Goddess-cursed engine. Pray it's not the death of us all."

The tunnel steepens further, to the point I fear treachery from the gravel underfoot. A new heart-deep thrum impinges on the Princex's engine, that paces us somewhere within the mountain. Every face is sheened with sweat. It pours off me. I can barely swallow. The air stinks of brimstone now, and a glow stains the walls. Our path flattens, expands, presents us with a view of hell.

Breathing is hard. The thunderous spit and bubble of flowing lava swamps all signs of the engine. This cavern's vast, two hundred yards around, domed ceiling, channels of earthly fury paying tribute to one great river of molten rock bisecting the hellish plain.

Qara points through the shimmering air, and I see the bridge.

"Our part is done," the elder Melavornan announces. "That is the way."

"To where?" I yell.

"To your fate," she says. "One of you. Loqa came to see. She has seen."

Qara turns to go. I can't reach her, but I grab Loqa's arm, careful not to disturb the white feathers of her wing. "Wait! Tell us more. How do you know the paradigms are here? They could have fallen anywhere. Did you see them fall here? How?"

Qara's face is a mask of distrust, and I see, maybe even feel, some of the loathing she has for Linecans. "Past the span, the hole in the cave wall."

I squint, blinking gritty eyes. "I see it." A dark opening exists. "But how do you know?" I insist.

"Even gods come home."

12

Beyond the river,
across the bridge,
the dark hole.

- Recorded by Lord Sakaria, found scratched in rock,
Melavorna Volcano

I think I left the clue for Mehdina because I still harbour hope for her, cannot believe she can cleave to wrongheaded loyalty after what she must have seen these past many turns. Good, honest people fighting for freedom, defending bold and fair ideals from a ruler's greed; not lust for more power or gold or glory, but greed for more of everything. If I could just talk to Dina again...

Vermillion grabs my arm, pulls me on. "Stay with us, damn you. Almost there."

She grimaces like a demon, flame reflected in her eyes. I nod, move forward. I don't know how we cross the floor of this furnace. My steps change. We must be on the bridge. My head swims. Brogine's leading, coaxing me on, grinning like a maniac, pulling me, my small hand in his rough, scarred one. Then we're at the hole in the wall, and by some miracle, cool air greets us.

I stagger forward like a dying woman in a desert, fearless of this mystery, seeing only salvation. This tunnel too drops down, dark and smooth. Vermillion's beside me, Marin close behind. Brogine's torch is redundant in the gentle glow permeating this tunnel. None speaks, only breathing, grunts of relief. Up ahead, the tunnel ends in light.

We emerge—

Standing on the shore of a lake, a vast dark mirror stretches away from our rock landing. Twice the size of the last chamber, roof twice as high. Crystalline veins thread the rock arching overhead, out across the still surface, and from those veins soft pearlescent light falls on the water. All is still.

"A boat." The chamber flattens Gine's growl, swallows it up such that I doubt he even spoke, but Vermillion advances, boards, takes up the oars, the boat rocking gently.

"Time, Astrid," she says, not harshly. "We have none. And while this stinks of no plan at all, it's where we are."

I step down into the boat, sit facing Vermillion, resist the urge to trail my fingers through the mirror of the lake.

The boat is big enough for four, but Brogine—suspicion in his eyes says, "We'll guard the landing." Marin turns to watch back up the tunnel.

Wordlessly, Vermillion rows us away from the landing. Oars dip the surface, dim reflection of the rock ceiling barely shifting, like rowing through mercury, perhaps. Out on the lake, a structure protrudes from the water, perhaps two or three feet tall, a low, stonework construction. Vermillion's making for it, saw it from shore likely, with her sea captain's eyes.

I turn to glance back and the sight makes me gasp. Where our wake should be, two edges of a curtain peel back. The reflection of the ceiling slowly disappears from an apex at the boat's stern in a wide fan of deep, clear darkness. And that darkness continues to broaden, the fan-shaped window on the lake becoming wider and wider, the edges rotating ahead of us, forming a vast midnight lily pad.

"Vermillion..."

"I see it. Never seen stranger, but keep your head, Astrid. Remember the task."

"But how did— Oh. Qara said the paradigms came home. Oh!"

I gasp as the crystal light from above penetrates the lake's gloomy depth, touches roofs, dusts cupolas, illuminates domes beneath the surface, walls revealed, silvered by the light, tinted algal green. I stare disbelieving, stomach hollow, heart pounding. There are cobbled streets, sunken markets, inundated squares, and now I see the structure ahead is a tower, its top the only part of the sunken city above the water's surface. And—

A figure waits for us there.

She wears a simple dress in the same shade of green slime, but does not glisten with dampness. She watches us approach, her jewels shining like the ceiling's crystal luminescence, a circlet of green stones glinting, a cluster necklace around her neck.

Vermillion works the oars, slowing us, turning us. When we bump the tower's stonework, the sound making everything suddenly real. The lady does not assist, just watches calmly as Vermillion jumps the tower's crenelated wall and ties up the boat. I climb up after. Vermillion clasps my arm, hauls me over the stone battlement.

"You are two," says the tall, elegant figure, her jewels and circlet glimmering. "Unexpected, still, I welcome you to Melavorna, the lost city found again."

I can't contain the buzzing questions. "Qara said the paradigms came home. What does that mean? Do you have them? How did—?"

And then I see. The chains decorating her neck. Plural, several, multiple: not a complex necklace, but two fistfuls of charms on chains of silver, gold, brass, copper; a cluster of sigils hanging in her plunging neckline. There hangs the cruciform paradigm of the Eyrtasters, the diamond of the Eyrhearers, the star is there and the pyramid. I'm open-mouthed. She has them, the paradigms are here before me.

We're so close to success, but... There are other charms round this woman's neck: a silver crescent, a copper flash, a square—black as if tarnished, a crook, an arrow, a circle, others hidden in the pile.

"What are these?" I whisper, wide-eyed. I'm so sure I know the answer that it makes my stomach churn. Vermillion looks ready to vomit.

The woman looks at us in turn, long, dark hair braided at her back, skin paler than a Melavornan's or a Linecan's. She's not a young woman.

"Pardon, lady, but can I ask where you're from?"

She smiles slightly, sadly. "I came from Yelur to find my sister. I searched three years before finding her here and, when I learned what had to be done, I took her place as the Emerald Queen. One of you must do the same for me."

"What do you mean 'must'?" says Vermillion, squaring up to her—this queen. "How will you make us? We've come to destroy these, Astrid's too." My stomach flips. I knew that was coming.

"The truth is horror enough to convince any decent person," says the queen of...what? The castle? The drowned city? Melavorna itself? "These trinkets you call paradigms, of which there are nineteen, with yours"—bile rises in my throat—"were crafted by Melavornans a thousand years ago, before they had wings. None knows how to destroy them. I took my turn to try and failed. One of you may do the same, at your leisure. But now"—she glances at my chest, and I can't help clutching my winged charm—"there is no time. Those cutting through the mountain are close. Their leader will not rest at reclaiming what Lineca lost."

"What—" I can't breathe or swallow. "What do the others do?"

"Powers to haunt your nightmares," she says. "Things your fears cannot conceive."

"Astrid Opanimo! Vermillion Desandi!"

Our names echo across distance and dead water. "Surrender to the forces of the Princex! Your ship and comrades are captive. Your escape is cut off. You're trapped! Surrender or die."

13

Figures move on the distant rock landing, a boat splashes into the water, oars clatter rowlocks, reverberating through the vast chamber.

"Astrid!" Mehdina calls, voice small, for now. "Don't be a fool! Do as Sakaria says. Please!"

"No," growls Vermillion. "You promised an end to this."

The sounds of rowing swell. I snatch a glance. A longboat, six or eight aboard, Mehdina in the prow, sword drawn.

"What are these new things?" I gesture at the charms. "What influence do they give?"

"Like yours they influence the elements," says the Queen, placid despite the forces descending.

"Astrid, they can't have this arsenal," spits Vermillion. "You're the magic one, do something. Now." She turns, red hair flying, knife drawn, to face the threat, but even the legendary Vermillion cannot hold for long. Little good can I do with flight, but if I had the elemental power of the volcano.

"Can you give me fire and earth?" I demand of the Emerald Queen.

She takes from her neck first the arrow pendant, then the black square. I take one in each fist, spin, dart to the parapet, step up, and jump into the air. There's no time to experiment. I circle high, think of the lava spitting and flowing, remember sails burning, stab down with my left fist and bark "Fire." Nothing. I yell "Fire!" Cool darkness pervades all. Then I remember the prayer I last spoke in

Antiquities hundreds of turns before, its last line, and know I don't even need to speak it.

Heart of the fire, I welcome thee.

A great gout of flame rages from my fist towards the longboat.

"Mehdina, I love you, get out!"

The last thing I see before fire fills my vision is Captain Mehdina Taradel diving for the water. Flame bathes the craft. People scream, jumping overboard.

I fly to the landing, spray fire at waiting soldiers, send them jumping and running. I fly into the tunnel, burst into the volcanic chamber, too full of purpose to think until later that I felt no heat at all. How can these wonders be made by humankind?

The Princex's engine has ruptured the tunnel wall just beyond the lava chamber. It lies like a monstrous beetle, great drilling cone grinding slowly, ready to chew through the mountain's heart once more carrying Sakaria away to gift the Princex terrible new ways to break the world. I fly to the wall, strike it with my black square-wrapping fist. *Soul of the land, I feel thee.* Rock tumbles down. I dart back, gravel hits me, I barely escape the crushing downfall. The engine's panels burst, rivets popping, thick metal skin twisting, bulging and bending as the mountain destroys it, burying the engine's carcass.

There is more to be done, and I have the power and the will to do it.

Within the volcano, this power is dreamlike, but bursting into the light it feels so real and vast. I sweep into the sky, wheeling around the island, and fly at the ships in the bay. I pour fire over Sakaria's flotilla, slalom through the tall sails, setting every ship ablaze, rushing air drying my tears as they form.

When all the ships are burning, I stop, look west towards Cardoon.

With this power, I could level the palace, cast the Institutes down, dethrone the Princex and burn all their greed with them.

I could change the world. No one could stop me.

And Vermillion would hate me as she does the Princex. Lineca would fear me, my family haunted by what I did. And I never could win Mehdina back.

So, I soar out of the bay, circle high above Melavorna's smoking summit, then swoop down into the clearing. I fly into the tunnels making light when I need it, find my way back through dark and fire to the lake. The sailors have righted the longboat, ferried the wounded back to the landing. I pass some trudging from the cavern, heads hung in defeat, wounds wrapped with ripped clothing.

I fly across still surface to the sunken tower, the inundated city glimmering below the water's surface. I land among Mehdina and Vermillion, Sakaria and the Emerald Queen. Finally, I unclench my fists and let these dreadful new paradigms dangle, swinging on their chains.

"Lord Sakaria," I say. "Your squadron is burning. You are defeated. Go from here and pack up your house. Soon you'll be gone from Cardoon, and from Lineca."

I'm surprised to see him not angry, but thoughtful.

Mehdina stands rigid, blade gripped tightly but pointing down at the stone. She's looking at me, and—Goddess preserve us—she's unsure.

"What did you do, Astrid?"

I destroyed twenty boats, may have killed many sailors, destroyed the Princex's engine. I'm sorry, Dina. I love you. Come back to me. Save me from this awful power. I need you. "I did what I thought right."

Mehdina hangs her head. The moment of truth. When she looks up it's at Vermillion, lips tight, eyes narrowed. "So, you were always right?"

"What do they give us that we need, Dina?" Vermillion asks. "And what do they take that we would do better to keep?"

"This discourse is done," says the Emerald Queen, not haughty, but with a chilling finality. "These charms must be hidden again from the likes of the Princex, and him"—she nods at Sakaria—"whose eyes reflect these chains like a mirror shows a flaw."

"How can we hide them now?" I ask.

Sakaria confirms my assessment. "The Princex will build another engine, this power will be theirs. Give me the paradigms now, ease the retribution coming to you all."

The queen considers Sakaria as she would a misguided child. "One boon of the artefacts is that they will hide themselves. Earth and fire, Astrid Opanimo."

I regard the charms still dangling from my hands, and I know what to do.

"But you cannot leave until someone takes my place. I have served Melavorna with resolution for ten years, but my will is tired. I will find my sister, who served before me."

"This at least is easy to determine," says Mehdina heavily. "If I've been wrong all this time, done the Princex's will to the harm of my people, then I have a debt to repay. Duty is something I do well."

"No, Dina!" My yelp is like a child's. Typical; Mehdina does the noble, selfless thing and I snap like a brat. I hate it, but how can I let her go again? "I need you now more than ever, Mehdina, and I think you need me."

"I do," says she, foremost privateer, my heart's thief. "But duty calls the loudest—"

"Oh, Goddess spare us another round of your sanctimonious bullshit, Dina! You deserve to be happy."

Vermillion steps into Mehdina, spins, grabs Dina's wrist then twists away with her sword in hand. Vermillion's motion continues, blade singing at neck height, and she decapitates Lord Lamyn Sakaria, chair of the Royal Council. His body tumbles to the stone, head bouncing twice before resting against the wall.

"He knew too much," says Vermillion. "I'll not spend a ten-year here awaiting my door being smashed in every time some lickspittle builds an engine."

"Vermillion—" Mehdina and I say together. She cuts us off, slicing the air with her empty hand. "I won't go back to the gallows, which surely awaits me regardless of who rules Lineca. Me and Queeny here have work to do, and so do you, Astrid." She tucks the sword in her belt, her hands firmly frame my face, and she kisses me deep and long. When she breaks away, she says, "Give them earth and fire, darlin'."

* * *

As I fly up from the jungle, square and arrow charms gripped in my fists again, Mehdina is spreading the warning. I sweep around and up the volcano's side, soaring high above then diving down at the caldera. Smoke streams past my face, my breath held until the crater floor resolves. I bring my fists together, locking thumbs against the force pulling them apart.

The common prayer takes on new meaning, and I add a third stanza of my own.

Soul of the land, I feel thee. Joy of the air, I embrace thee. Heart of the fire, I welcome thee. Body of stone, I command thee.

Fire pours from my hands down the volcano's throat. I feel I will shake apart and explode with the force, or blackout and fall into the expanding rent in the mountain. Bright fire spews forth, as if the mountain hurls death at me. Lava is vomited upwards as I drop yet further. *Pull up, pull up!* I banish my daze and turn, back straining, aching, upwards out of hell and into the sky.

When I'm high enough I pause, open one fist then the other, watch chains and charms tumble from my hands, quickly disappearing into that fire to find their way home.

14

Melavorna's eruption followed old, familiar flows. The village remained safe, as if they have always known the mountain's ways. The Melavornans aided the sailors' departure, the Linecans dismantling their own jetty for wood to repair ships enough to carry them away. Our stolen brig remained intact, and Brogine drummed up a full crew.

Now we sail for open water, course set for Cardoon. Events we, Vermillion most of all, have set in train must be seen through to the end. We expect a fight, but Mehdina and I are together. That's all the strength I need to face what comes. I still have my charm though. Mehdina made me keep it, a tactical advantage.

As dusk light spills gently through smoke-marked glass, I move slowly up Mehdina's skin, dropping kisses as I go. She has just been satisfied, and it's my turn to achieve an eruption of my own. Her skin is the map to a city of pleasure, one I've lingered in before. When I find my way north of her neck, she cups my chin and kisses me. "That's two stacks you've blown today, Astrid. You'll get a reputation."

I bring my hips to hers and cannot contain a whimper. "If you consort with rebels, love, expect rough seas and rowdy action."

"The Emerald Queen" is the last of three tales featuring Astrid Opanimo and Mehdina Taradel. The story of these intrepid and swashbuckling buccaneers began in Space Wizard's *Farther Reefs* anthology (2022) with "The Vermillion Lady", continuing with "The Cerulean Princess" in the *Lofty Mountains* anthology (2023). Is this the end for Astrid and Mehdina? Perhaps that depends on whether you believe in happy ever after...

Aubade

Maya Gittelman

Sapphic Representation: Lesbian
Heat Level: Low
Content Warnings: Coarse Language, Violence

On the seven hundred seventy-seventh year of the seventh age, the disparate peoples of the land will unite under The Wielder to surge forth across the seas and claim the Forgotten Realms as their own, Armed with The Axe to Cleave The World, the hero will lead the peoples to valiant triumph, leaving behind the shame of their common lives to dwell in glory and fortune for generations henceforth.

Astraea

"Eyes forward, Wielder."

Astraea straightened her spine and rolled her eyes before turning them, appropriately, *forward*.

"I saw that," said Felric Ceranduil. The elf pulled his unicorn ahead, looking daggers at Stray. "We are half a day's ride from the Master Forger's domain. It wouldn't do for the One Who Cleaves the World to tumble from her mount and split her head open on the very journey for which she was born."

"But it's *hot*."

Fell stiffened, and Straea stifled a grin. Even Mr. Holier-than-Thou couldn't argue with *that*. He'd spent the last decade in the more austere sect of the elfin forests as Astraea had, raised in commitment to Keeping the Prophecy. He may have been the cangue about her neck, but he was bound by it too. The latest annoying thing about being the prophesied Chosen One who brings about the dawning of a new age of prosperity by means of decimating existing society is, no one teaches you just how *hot* the midday sun is as it glances off the mountain lakes.

Astraea was no stranger to riding, but none of her afternoon sojourns or training jousts had prepared her for the utter physicality of this heat, enrobing the whole world, it seemed, in its humid power. She'd read the air was thinner by the mountains than in the elves' forest dwellings where Astraea had spent most of her life;

certainly more than the muggy coasts where she was born. Before her parents allowed the elves to carry her to her prophesied future and consequently, the end of the world. Still, no secondhand scientific language between the pages of a cold book could have conveyed the sweat, the press of it. Astraea thought of how she'd write about this heat when she finally put quill to notebook, but her mind, so often overflowing with words about the world she was never allowed to live in, felt sluggish in the heat.

It wasn't entirely unpleasant. She didn't want to think about what they were riding to.

As far as Chosen Ones go, Astraea was more curious about the world than usual, or so her devout Elf Mentors told her. Most Chosen Ones, according to Stray's Prophesied Keepers, did as they're told and focused on lessons like Wielding and Slaying and Purging the Earth of Unrighteousness. They *understood* the transience of this world, as laid out by the Great Oracles of the Past, understood their role as one of service, delivering this realm unto its next necessary stage. Only one as troublesome as Astraea skipped training and broke into the archives to read about the world she was destined to destroy.

So, no one had ever taught her how vast and varied the world was.

She supposed it made sense, given that she was born and raised to end it. Still, she *had* considered herself an expert on the universe, being the prophesied center of it. She'd read far more than required; indeed, sneaking into the forbidden areas of the court archives had been one of her only pleasures in the large estate of her early childhood, a favorite pastime prior to her deliverance to the elves.

Confined to the Keepers' coldly exquisite residences, Astraea had been welcome to read as much as she could about the world she wasn't allowed to experience. The stories were different in the elven voice, in pace and perspective.

She'd read widely, without focus, more concerned with the possibilities between the pages than in categorizing those stories into anything resembling strategy. Everything, even history and biology books, she read as fantasy. None of it really mattered to her, none of it ever would. She was too well-monitored and unpracticed at sneaking to get *away* with much, but given her very specific role, no one really cared if she went reading, as long as it didn't pull focus from her single-minded training.

Her other siblings gained power for the family in the ways theirs had done for generations. Through politics, textiles, livestock, basic potions. But since Astraea had the dubious privilege of being born under the proper conditions to fulfill the Prophecy, her parents— uninterested in children as a whole, careless as to the fate of a bookish seventh daughter—had no qualms about promising her to the elves at her birth, delivering her to her Chosen Keeper to raise like a lamb to slaughter.

Except Astraea was to be the knife.

The unicorn felt like a furnace between her thighs. Astraea had never really considered the merits of her nut-brown skin, but she was grateful for it now, watching the back of the pale elf's neck turn an inelegant, sweaty pink. She kept her grin to herself, pleased at witnessing one of the rare glimpses of Felric's physicality. His preternatural elfin self-importance couldn't protect him from the midday sun.

"I thought the cosmic hellsfire wasn't supposed to come until *after* I Wielded the axe," Astraea muttered.

"It's *cosmotic* hellsfire," Felric Ceranduil hissed (irreverence for Prophesied Titles would never not be the easiest way to get beneath his pearly skin), "and mortal penance—"

"—means immortal reward, I know. You *know* I know." Stray rolled her eyes. Let the mounts go on a bit before she piped back up. "...it's hot as a dragon's asshole out here though, Fell. I don't think the prophets are going to judge you for admitting it."

"Hush your impudent mouth," Felric said, sweating irritably. "We'll be there soon."

There was probably a spell that could provide some comfort, but Felric's preparations for this voyage began and ended with The Prophecy. When it came to the sect that desperately wanted to fulfill The Prophecy, all their power and planning was about the world to come after.

This one didn't matter.

It had been written in the stars, and you can't rewrite that.

What Astraea *could* write, at their next brief rest stop, was a good bit of nasty venting about Fell's sunburn. Her notebook was her most treasured possession, the only part of her that was truly private, truly *hers*, not promised to the universe. The fraught and narrow path of her life would have been unsurvivable if not for the soft magic of sharing her heart with the page.

Felric had told her, before they set out, not to pay the world much mind. *Eyes forward, Wielder. Keep your focus. Find the Master Forger. Get her to Forge your Axe.* Don't think about the destruction she was to bring to everything she could cast her gaze upon. Their descendants would thank her—worship her—when she brought about the next age of prosperity.

It had seemed to make sense in theory. Astraea had always been on the outside of the rest of the world. She yearned for it on some level, grieving an imagined version of herself who could choose her own path—but this was all she knew. She'd looked to this journey with something like relief before setting out: at last, the next phase could begin. She itched for this bit to be done, so long had its prospect haunted her, and had been steadfastly avoiding thinking about what came *after* the Wielding.

Yet confronted with the world around her at last, it was so *hard* not to take it in! Vast crops lush with strange plump vegetation, sprawling villages woven into the land rather than cut through, forests thrumming with magic Stray didn't have the language to know.

And she never would. So it wouldn't do to look.

Eyes forward, Wielder.

There was no alternative.

She filled her journal with the cruelest words she had for Felric's sunburn. *I hope it peels, you wretched creature. I hope it itches terribly and leaves a scar.* It wouldn't, his elf-flesh would heal before the night came. Bastard. She wished, not for the first time, that she had crueler words for him.

Then he refilled her waterskin, shoved it at her gruffly, and clambered back on his mount with less finesse than usual, wincing at the heat.

Astraea scratched the words from the page. She didn't regret writing her irritation down, but she didn't need to carry it with her. She had just needed to vent to her book and found she could no longer bring herself to make poetry about the world she was destined to end.

By the time they drew close to the dwarven mountains, she had a sunburn prickling herself.

"Send word to the Master Forger," Fell told the messenger goblins at the threshold of the dwarven domain. "The Wielder has come for her Axe."

Saga

Saga cast her gaze about her forge. Her apprentices merrily churning away. This month's deliveries right on schedule: farm sickles, fishing anchors, baby cradles. None of it would matter with the Prophecy set in motion.

She'd always known the Wielder might be coming, but that dread had been a distant, abstract sort of thing, easily avoided among the day-to-day mechanics of her life.

She felt sick.

"No."

"Well, yes," Glinrod said anxiously. "The archivists verified her identity, and her retinue assures us the One Who Harvests is ready to fulfill her duties."

"*No.*"

Saga held the unicorn shoe to the anvil. Raised her hammer high, her soft face unguarded. Glinrod flinched—but when Saga brought it down, the blow was careful, quiet, though her knuckles were white on the handle. She breathed hard, savoring the familiar thick scent of her forge.

Everyone knew about The Prophecy. It had the capitals and everything, little dwarflings memorized it along with the common alphabets and intro to smithing, before they'd even chosen a specialty at tenth-grown.

Whether you believed in it was determined—like many other things—roughly by where you grew up. Thing with prophecies is it doesn't *matter* if you believe or not, unless you're the one it actually affects. Well, theoretically it would affect every living being, but no one could *do* anything about it aside from those mentioned. Which left the bulk of its serious-taking to its more fanatic elfin acolytes, the specific human born at the right time for said elves to hone into a weapon—and, annoyingly for Saga, the Master Forger who was to make the Wielder's mighty axe, to fell the tree and start the war.

Yes, this was meant to happen every so often, once every star cycle or something. Saga didn't subscribe to any of it. She knew it was *possible* such a Hero might show up during her tenure as Master Forger, but had clung to a naïve hope the potential Wielder had befallen an untimely death, or that perhaps the elves had forgotten.

But the end of the world found her, just as scheduled.

"As I have always said," Saga said, reining herself into the cage of her patience, "I will not suffer bloodthirsty childishness simply because of a *prophecy*."

An unfamiliar sound rang out through the clouds of smoke. It was almost a laugh, but uglier.

"Lessons on childishness from one who bangs hot sticks about all day, is it?"

The words cut across Saga's beloved steam like a pick of ice. Two tall unfamiliar figures were making their way through the fires to Saga's Forge.

Glinrod shifted nervously. Saga sighed and shook her head.

"You can wait in the cauldron cupboard," she muttered. She handed the little goblin leftovers from her afternoon meal. "It's alright. Set the closing signal fires for me before you go, yeah?"

Glinrod nodded gratefully, scampering away. Saga watched the flare of signals, the other blacksmiths dutifully making themselves scarce after flashing a glance to ensure their leader's safety.

The two figures drew closer as the forge-fires dimmed. They never *stopped*—it was always dragon's-breath-hot in the forge, it had to be and Saga liked it besides—but it did cool a bit with the lack of active flamework. Saga's frown deepened as the chill set in with the intruders.

"Is such privacy truly required for such an *un*-secret ask?" said that same sinewy voice. Up close, Saga could register the accent. Her heart sank, the last hopes that this was some terrible prank fading away. Rarely did anyone ranked from those settlements venture this far, preferring to send messengers into the sunless caverns.

"Yes," Saga said simply. She settled into her Master's seat, the stone carved to her comfort, the height of the dais allowing her to look down on her intruders. She folded her arms, the weight of her everyday side-axe comfortable at her thigh, cloaked beneath her smithing garb. "The

Wielder, I presume?" Saga didn't put all her vitriol for the title in her voice, but she didn't hold back much.

"You flatter me." The words felt glacial. Slippery, enormous, eerily plain in their danger.

At last, the two figures drew into view. An elf, and a human.

While a good amount of elves had taken to weaving their lives quite comfortably alongside the more mortal inhabitants of the realm, there were a few sects, Saga knew, who still hewed closely to the days of Chaos, before the Fallow Period. The elf who stepped into Saga's space carried himself with the self-important gravitas of one who kept to tradition. Who believed himself an inheritor of a long-suffering victimhood: the powerlessness that comes from existing on this earth without proving oneself by literally dominating another. A generation that believes peace is weakness, and a lack of choice instead of the strongest, the only.

"I am Felric Ceranduil. Seventh Son of the Long Night's Forest, Starborn Elf. I have inherited the mantle of Keeper of the Sacred Prophecy, Guardian to The Wielder, the One Who Harvests, and it is my birth-given duty by the weavers of the universe to ensure that when the conditions are right as they are this stone season, the Axe be forged so my charge may fulfill—"

"Your charge is here to bring about the end of days and they can't speak for themself?"

The elf's oil-black eyes went wide, then narrow. He opened his mouth, but the second figure put a hand on his cloaked arm.

"His *charge* thought it fair to allow her Guardian the chore of introductions, Master Forger."

Saga raised a brow, eyeing the human. "Is that right?"

"Indeed it is," said the Chosen One, Ender of All Things. "And we extend our humblest apologies at disturbing your workday, it's just that our diviners have assured us the three-day window has begun, and as prophesied, we will need the Master Forger to craft me the Axe so I may fulfill our everlasting duties." She sniffed in the settling smoke, rubbing her knuckle across her nose. "I'm Astraea, by the way."

"Princess Astraea, the ninth of her name, destined to be the Chosen One, the Wielder of the Great Axe to Cleave the World, the Bringer About of—"

"She gets it, Fell," Astraea hissed. Felric Ceranduil went quiet, looking put out.

She was short for a human. Soft, as they go. Skin a warmer brown than either Saga's or the elf's, hair darker than Saga's own but smooth where the forger's curled and frizzed, and she was beardless. She wasn't slim, but there wasn't much muscle beneath her curves. Her clothes were simple, clearly worn from their ride here, but subtly expensive.

She was built for heroics: that is, for show. Saga knew the Prophecy better than she wished she did, haunted by the bloodshed that was her inheritance as much as, and intrinsically tied to, the forge she loved so much. The life she loved, the dwarf she was. The Prophecy called for a noble descendent, because of course it did—and indeed, the Chosen One likely hadn't lifted a hammer in her life, nor so much as a finger for anything that wasn't tourney training or embroidery. Nothing wrong with either, but it only calls into sharp relief how insane the very concept of this prophecy was, how removed from the realities of the world and what those who live it actually need.

If Saga *had* any interest in forging The Great Axe to Cleave the World, she doubted the prophesied Wielder could so much as pick it up, much less fell the Great Tree that was meant to bring forth a new age.

A thing she would've told the girl, had the oily elf not been hovering over her.

"The answer's still no."

Ceranduil's fingers twitched again; this time Saga knew she didn't imagine the silver light flashing between the folds of his sleeves. She didn't put her hand on her axe-handle, but noted their positioning, nonetheless.

"Master Forger, you know the Prophecy," said the elf. The injected patience in his voice was more unnerving than a yell. "The prophesied alignment is days away, and unlikely to reoccur within this lifetime."

"*Our* lifetimes, at least," Saga pointed out, gesturing at herself and the human. "*You* are more than welcome to wait it out for a future Master to make your weapons and end the world."

The guests were suffering in the close heat of the forge. A Master Forger beholden to pomp or tradition would've long since offered to continue this conversation elsewhere; literally anywhere else in the mountain was cooler than the Master's Forge.

Saga's pity didn't come so easily. Her respect was a hard-won thing, which is why it mattered.

"My *immortality,*" gritted the elf, "only redoubles my commitment to maintaining the proper order! To keeping the Prophecy, and ensuring the realm reaches its destined potential, else the prior bloodshed was for nought!" Ooh, a touchy point. Saga noted his passion, looking closer at Felric Ceranduil—it's hard to tell elf ages, but he could be old enough to have fought in The Last War. To have lost people, like Saga had.

He also could be not far from the age of the Wielder, who, up close, wasn't quite as young as her bearing suggested.

...he was still talking. It came across naïve, but Saga was well aware anxious yapping could affect all ages. He sure yapped enough to rival Great Uncle Marricet the Bowmaker, who routinely forced Saga and her cousins to draw straws for who had to bear the brunt of his company at solstice brunches.

"Rest assured, Master Forger," said the Chosen One. "My Keeper's fervor is merely a reflection of his commitment to the realm." She stepped forward. She was decidedly ordinary looking. The epitome of how most mountain dwarves would envision *girl with wealth from the human villages who happened to be born at the right time to pick up The Prophecy.* Capitals and all. "I apologize if his brusque nature has swayed you from the importance of our task."

"There is no *our*," Saga said, gentle but firm.

Felric Ceranduil laughed. It was a harsh sound from such a coldly elegant figure.

"Would that that were so," he said, bitterly. "Would that we could proceed without your *skills*, Master, but by some twist only the oracles knew, we cannot fulfill *our* duties until you have enacted yours."

"And why do you think that might have been?" Saga pushed herself to standing, stepping close and shrinking the distance between her and the intruders. Ceranduil flinched, sparks flaring at his fingers, but Astraea didn't move. She was frowning at Saga. "Why do you think they saw fit to refuse you dominion without convincing a smith their labor ought be turned to destruction?"

"We don't question divine rule," said the Chosen One. "It's not our place. The duty is an honor—our birthright."

Saga pitied this Astraea. It wasn't her fault, really, that she'd been sold this narrative. Saga had a choice in what to become, it so happened smithing aligned with her lot in life, aside from this damned Prophecy inheritance. She couldn't imagine being raised for such a violent task, a voiceless path.

"I don't keep promises to dead oracles," Saga said. "I keep the ones I choose to make. And when I stepped into the role of Master Forger, I promised myself and my people to use the power of the forge to grow and build alone. Never to harm."

"You would fail the entire realm for the sake of your own cowardice," hissed the elf. "Content with squalor and smallness, you would doom the rest of the world to an eternity of it rather than step into your destiny!"

Saga tilted her head.

"You speak like one who fought in the Last War."

The elf paled. A bead of sweat trickled down his marble-smooth cheek. "I did not have that honor. I was too young."

Raised by those who subscribed to its propaganda, then. Saga gentled her tone. "I know of the great losses the elves faced to bring about this peace. My parents and other elders have made it known, the great losses across species to earn the respite we have the privilege of living within. They made it clear too," Saga added, "how different grief hits when one is deathless, and one's only options after war are to leave home or live in the aftermath and build something from the wreckage. That is why we welcome all in the Mirkulag Mountains, though few of the elves choose our caverns."

Ceranduil was sweating openly now, his ire redoubling as his pretty face went ruddy. He muttered something that sounded like *coward*.

"I know peace makes you restless." Saga peered at him. He *was* young, for an elf. There was something almost adolescent in his hot-headedness, his self-righteousness. "But our rebuilding efforts since that war *are* the triumph. Conquering others won't fill your heart—it'll only drain you further. Peace is the best vengeance. Indeed, it's the only one worth pursuing."

The elf was losing his composure, muttering about *sacred duty* and so on. Astraea seemed unhappy as well, frustration etched in her brow.

"I honor your perspectives," she said, and Saga didn't hold back an incredulous laugh. "I'm afraid we do not have the time to convince you."

"Then succumb to the truth faster!" Saga too was losing her patience.

"You are mad," said the elf.

"Maybe you don't understand," tried Astraea, and at that Saga drew herself to full stature, looking down from her dais.

"Oh, I understand, Princess. I cannot control whether my answer sates, but know this: I will not create an axe unless I believe the cutting of the tree is the best choice for the people in its wake." Saga was breathing hard. Felric opened his mouth, but she continued before he could speak. "I'm going to have to ask you to leave."

"You'll come around," Felric said. "You will."

"You'll die waiting," Saga snapped, and sank back into her seat with her head in her hands. When she looked up again, Astraea had dragged him off.

Presently, Glinrod emerged from the cauldron cupboard.

Saga sighed, rubbing her forehead. She looked at her day's projects glumly. What good were fenceposts and unicorn horseshoes when everything was going to burn anyway?

"Hold my messages, Glinrod," she said, yanking off her forge-gear. "I need a drink."

Astraea

"Well, that could have gone better," Astraea said.

Astraea's Keeper was furious, practically steaming at his pointy, sunburnt ears.

"She'll come around. She has to. Let us get out of this godsforsaken place," Fell huffed.

Astraea followed obediently, but found herself dragging her heels.

She didn't want to leave. Stray thought the journey *here* was mind-altering, but she'd never seen anything like the forge. There was so much more to the realm than she knew! No wonder the elves never let her live in the world. One could argue—and indeed, argue their prophesied

Forger did—that by a great many measures, there was prosperity already.

Then there was Saga herself. Stray never really thought about what the Master Forger might be like, but nothing could have prepared her for *that*.

Astraea felt inundated with the world, exhausted by her lifelong burden of remaking it. Perhaps it was *because* her adolescence had been so terribly busy that she'd never realized her life was quite so narrow.

Funny. Pursuing the Prophecy, the thing that had narrowed it, somehow became the one thing that finally broadened her experience.

Felric was still muttering to himself, but at the threshold he spoke to Stray.

"You know what this means."

Astraea did. She always did. She knew like she knew every element of her birthright. *The Axe is your destiny. At all costs.*

"Yes, Keeper. I do."

Astraea cast one last look into the Master's Forge, the heartsfires of the realm. She thought she might have seen something gleaming in the depths. It must have been the embers of something big, dying away.

Saga

"Same again?" asked the bar dwarf.

Saga wanted to switch to whiskey. Badly.

"Yes please," she grunted. The barkeep jerked a nod, and the next round showed up alongside a bowl of fresh cherrynuts and a warm scone. Saga smiled her thanks, gut churning with guilt.

The Gorgon's Gully was the oldest, most beloved alehouse in the mountains. Like most such establishments, it bore the history of its inhabitants in its making. Paintings and engravings adorned the walls, rife with reference and legacy.

And there, behind bottles of the bar, was a great mural of dwarven triumph in the Last Battle, a prior Master Forger bedecked in intricate, powerful armor, thrusting their axe into the bloodred sky.

Such art was as familiar as stamps, at least in the older structures of the realm.

"I suppose," Saga said glumly, "it *is* destiny."

She stared at the painted Master Forger, there behind the wine bottles.

This is what dwarves were built for, they'd been taught.

"But we've *tried* it before, this whole Cleave the World thing." She frowned into her cup. "The apocalypse didn't make the world start over—it just hurt a lot of people."

"You can say that again, Forgemaster," agreed the bar dwarf, helping herself to the nuts. "That was the whole point of naming it The *Last* War! When did people forget!"

Saga shook her head. "What a hopeful name. A prayer for peace, really."

There weren't many who still held to the old traditions, who believed the Prophecy was inevitable—but those who did held fast.

"Take it from a barkeep," said the barkeep, "peace is the hard thing to maintain. It's easy to fall into fighting. It feels predetermined." She stretched, flinging her dishrag over her shoulder. "Turns into a sunk-cost thing once you've started, for some people, and that's the thing I wish more understood—it's alright to get riled. But it's never too late to stop."

Saga nodded, frowning. The scone was good, it was helping.

The thing with this prophecy is that there's no "*or else.*" *Saga* was the "*or else*"—well, Astraea and Saga together. They were the devil's advocate, the curse and the scourge. Astraea, or at least Felric Ceranduil, didn't see a choice.

"And alright," says the barkeep, "say dwarves *were* built for war. Say wombs were built for babies. Say sparrows were built as food for eagles and harpies. Doesn't mean I need to put babies in myself, any more than it means the sparrow should crack through her egg and offer her soft self up to the talons. Don't throw yourself down a path of pain because you believe it's inevitable. If it's coming, it's coming. But you might as well find out what else is out there first."

"Thank you," Saga said, and the barkeep grinned before turning to her other guests. Saga blushed—there was a number on the napkin she left behind.

The guilt in Saga's gut twisted, shifting into something closer to certainty. She drowned the lingering doubt in drink.

As a rule, Saga didn't like disappointing people. She liked a routine, a rhythm, getting the job done. She had no interest in making enemies out of this foolhardy princess or the pretty fanatic of her Keeper—but she wouldn't do as they asked.

Peace is hard, but worth it. Good work that helps people build good lives. Fresh scones, and the promise of future flirting with someone kind and clever.

No theoretical, bloodstained "victory" could be worth risking that.

So engrossed was Saga in her thoughts, she hardly heard the murmur go through the pub. The mountains see all sorts, but news of the prophesied Wielder had certainly invited attention and unease.

"Another of whatever she's having, and I'll have the same, please." Astraea placed her money on the table. The barkeeper looked at Saga.

"It's alright," Saga told her, and then turned to tell the pub the same. "The princess is only here to indulge in the great hospitality the Gorgon's Gully has to offer. No prophecy talk."

The conversational hum of the alehouse picked up again, though Saga still felt worried glances on them. She tucked away the barkeep's napkin, her resolve stiffening.

The Wielder was older than she looked. She perched awkwardly on the barstool. It wasn't her height—like most public seating, the Gully's stools were crafted with a variety of species in mind and enchanted to shift to whatever height allows their inhabitant to use the thing they're seated at. Saga made such seats herself, touched up the charmwork and footrests in this very bar, in fact, though they hardly required repairs, crafted by her ancestor's apprentices.

No, Astraea simply *was* awkward, clearly desperate to take in every sight of the bar but aware of the violence of her presence, trying not to attract attention. She was sweating in her expensive travel cloak, obviously ill-suited to the warm closeness of the mountains. The cider made her dark eyes wide, confronted with new taste and its strange, sour pleasure.

Figures, Saga thought, *when you're raised and bred for a single purpose, one which decidedly does not include much socialization.*

"Who told you where to find me?" Saga said.

"No one, I just asked where to get the best drink in town." Astraea grinned, sipping the cider appreciatively. "*Mm!* Lucky me you've got good taste. Glorious, thanks a thousand," she said in earnest, delivering the barkeeper a hefty tip. "The look on your face when Fell harangued you for absconding from your duties—" she shook her head. "Let's just say it's a familiar one. Sends me to my cups too."

Curious. From what Saga had seen, the Wielder had betrayed little lack of allegiance to her Guardian. But Astraea's voice was different, now he wasn't around. Not as taut.

"Let me get your next round," Astraea said, watching Saga drain her cup. "Something stronger, perhaps—as delicious as this cider is, I know my presence in your life merits a real drinking occasion."

Saga snorted as Astraea squinted at the carved menu above the bar.

"If you think my allegiance to your death cult of a prophecy can be bought with one of Mikaisma's ales, you'd—"

"Two Ferrier's Flights, please," Astraea said, grinning at the barkeeper. "You were saying?"

Saga rubbed the back of her neck.

"—better keep trying," she finished. Astraea beamed at her, and Saga rolled her eyes.

"This won't endear you to me, you know," Saga told her, after downing a third of her flight.

"I didn't come here to convince you. Fell will," Astraea said calmly, starting on her second glass. "He's already booked us a room at the inn from now 'til the Prophecy date, and I know he's not letting us leave without that axe. *Gods* this is good."

They drank in quiet.

Saga had tried very hard not to picture what a Wielder might look like if she had the bad luck of encountering one, but she wouldn't have pictured *this*—curious and mild at the same time, ravenous but respectful. She was a threat, certainly, but almost a silly one. She seemed so sure Saga would cave. It might be easy enough, after all, to persuade her to see reason.

The Wielder wasn't much taller than Saga herself. Saga didn't count herself an expert on the varieties of human by a long shot, but up close she could hazard a good guess Astraea came from a village on the coast. Thick dark hair that moved like a curtain, rather than the cloud-like frizz of Saga's dwarven curls when they weren't braided out of her way.

"You're really going to make me ask?"

"What?"

"If not to convince me," Saga said, "why are you here?"

Astraea's eyes widened, a delicate lower lip flicking between her teeth. She took a deep breath at her cup, then turned to Saga.

"I," she started. "I wanted to know what you were making. Before we interrupted you."

Saga blinked. Whatever she could've expected, this was the last on the list.

"Hmm," she said.

"I didn't realize how different dwarven smithing was from that of my kind, or even other surface-dwellers—foolish of me, I know, to have assumed the renown of your skill was anything comparable to human practices." She sipped from her flight, tightening at the taste of the whiskey. "But this forge is unlike anything I knew possible! The size, the *spells*, the way your apprentices move, I—! I'd observed farmers and blacksmiths and other professions on the ride over, and indeed, even the inland smithing isn't far from what we have on the coasts. It's nothing like this."

"'On the ride over,'" Saga said slowly. "Do you often make a habit of watching other people do their jobs? Or is it only when you're hellsbent on rending the very land they sow, and so on, Wielder?"

Astraea, to her credit, flinched.

"Well, it's not like *my* job requires much expertise. I never had the chance to actually hone a skill aside from being *The Wielder*. I was raised to destroy, not create. The way my keepers see it, this realm is destined to enter a new age once I Cleave the World, so why bother creating anything of virtue in it before it? Why learn how to function in a society I've only been destined to destroy?"

Saga stared at her.

"Come to me tomorrow."

Astraea coughed on her drink. "What?"

"Early morning, before Ceranduil wraps you in his agenda. Come to the forge, I'll show you what I was making."

Astraea was already shaking her head.

"He'd catch me," she said. Something dark crossed her eyes, and something in Saga tightened unpleasantly.

"Guess we'd better go now, then," she said. "Coming?"

The Wielder's chest heaved. Her eyes were very bright, and Saga had a nagging suspicion it wasn't only from the whiskey.

"Yes, please," Astraea said, and followed the path Saga carved through the bar.

Astraea

Saga looked so *right* in her forge. All stout, scruffy muscle, entirely at home in this heart of the mountain where everything was made, even the end of the world.

She was talking about smithing basics, and Astraea did her best to genuinely focus, because she was curious, but then the smith hoisted the hammer above her head, and with the fall of it to her anvil, Astraea's whole world changed.

She'd never seen expertise like this before. Oh, it was fucking *music* in its own dimension—her entire body looked like a poem—no, no, because how could words capture her power? It made the entire written world pale in comparison to the fact of her. Stray ached, almost violently, at the thought of being so at home in your predetermined lot. Though of course, Saga suited every role of Master Forger except the most important one of their generation: the one Astraea needed her for.

Focus! *Eyes forward, Wielder.* She did her best to take in what Saga showed her, but she was so distracted watching her work.

Saga was a song like this. Filled the caverns with the music of her making. Wielded her tools and instruments like they're part of her, as she freed her vision from the iron. She moved quick and sure. She was radiant.

"You want to give it a try?" Saga asked.

Yes. Yes. Astraea wanted. She wanted to learn. She wanted to write about it. She wanted to watch the smith forever. She wanted to *be* her, sure and stubborn and nearly free. She wanted, she wanted, she wanted.

"Alright," she said.

* * *

"I think I've had enough."

"You're doing fine, honestly—"

"*Don't* humor me, Forge Master," Astraea hissed through gritted teeth. She brought the hammer down to the anvil, the force of it shoving a yell from her gut. Sweat flowed like streams from her brow—even though she'd shed her outer clothes and Saga had provided an apprentice's cooling smock, the sheer heat of the forge seeped into her blood. "I don't think even the most desperate would pay for this quality." She looked at the little mangled shape forlornly. "It's like a children's illustration of what a unicorn shoe might look like."

The Forge Master chuckled. Her energy had eased, as Astraea had hoped, since returning to the place of her authority without Fell.

"You're not bad for a beginner," Saga said softly. "You hold the tools like weapons, but you move like it's choreography. It suits you."

Blood raced in Astraea's ears.

"Fuck off, I'm shit at this."

"You're not! Here, we can try something less intricate, give you a larger practice point."

"No!" How was Astraea meant to muster the legendary strength to Wield the Axe if she couldn't even forge a godsforsaken unicorn shoe? No, the skill sets didn't necessarily overlap, but she *had* been trained at a variety of weapons. None of her training required this level of finesse or precision, though. She did *not* like to be confronted with her own inadequacies. This was embarrassing. She steadied her stance. "I can do this."

Saga gave her a curious look.

"Alright then," she said. "Follow me. Breathe with the hammer, yeah? Breathe."

It became surprisingly easy to let Saga's instructions wash over her. No strategy, no prophecy—just mimicking the masterful movements of the dwarf's sturdy body, the enormous physical effort filling up all the usually frantic space in Astraea's mind.

Soon her limbs felt like molten honey. Astraea'd been built into the Wielder, the One Who Harvests. She had arms that knew a sparring sword like some would know a loom, a body that wouldn't tire after three days' ride—or at least, one that could wield that sword mechanically through exhaustion.

This was something else entirely.

It wasn't about muscle, but the rhythm. Never had Astraea experienced *awe* like she did now, looking over the forge.

Astrea had thought she knew heat.

Like most things, though, fire still had a way of surprising her.

She'd never known heat like this in her own body.

The way her muscles went molten under the rhythmic shocks of the hammer against steel. Sweat sloughing like soup, 'til she bit a hem from her cloak in frustration and bound it about her brow in a cheap but effective imitation of the Master Forger's.

It was more than that, though, as much as she fought to deny it—

The way Saga looked at her was heat, in its purest, simplest form, and it lit Astraea up from within.

If Astraea didn't know better, she might have thought it a spell, what the smith sparked in her with naught but a look. The tilt of her brow, the turn of her sentences. The warm, almost wet timbre of her voice. Astraea felt drawn to her by this heat, bound by it. The forge is an extension of the forger, and Astraea found herself pulled to its magnetism like hammer to stone.

Presently she slumped against the hammer, content to watch as Saga fixed her mess and set to the next project.

It was creation, Astraea realized, watching Saga shape metal like music. Like the gods with clay and life, or a child on the shore with a sandcastle.

Astraea had been trained before, but it was always about tuning her body for its singular task. It was different, observing Saga's sheer expertise and trying to imitate her. As her muscles strained, sweat sloughed from her brow, odd heat roiled in her very gut.

She recognized, with a sort of distant horror, that it was probably *desire.*

She had never felt this before. Or perhaps she'd always felt it, too broadly and vaguely to name.

Now it was focused, sharpened. Astraea's entire body felt like a flame, here in the hot cling the forge made of the caverns.

The Forge Master kept her hair braided tight, her beard shorn to a close contour—so she didn't have to worry about it catching fire again, she explained to Astraea. Saga liked to get close to her work—and alas, dwarven hair didn't have the same resistance to flame as dwarven skin does.

"So many stories of battlefield heroics, and not a single ode to the blacksmith. Yet it's the battle of steel and flame that enables every battle," Astraea mused. "The beginning of all things."

The effort and skill of it all. It took as much, if not more, than what she'd been taught. And she'd been taught to lead a war.

Saga snorted like she'd said something obvious. Astraea went hot because of course she had—of course Saga knows.

"Look at who wrote the stories you grew up with," the forger said. "Who has the time and resources to write one's own tale, what they choose as important to document? The victors write the history books, and they justify every atrocity when they do. No one wants to waste pages on the tool-maker—they write of the terrible power of the weapon. Perhaps because if one imagines a life behind the creation of the weapon, they'd see how fucked it is that we create things solely to harm each other."

Of course Stray knew all of this, had recognized the difference in the writings she found in her human home versus the elven archives—but she'd never extended the line of thought quite this far.

Not to herself and her own fate, certainly. That had seemed as set in stone as the very foundations of the earth.

"If anyone *had* written any odes to forgers or welders or farmers," Astraea said, "they'd never get to me anyway. I only had access to the books I could sneak from my family, or the elves, and they never had anything that challenged the divine rights of the Prophecy." She frowned, flushed face going even redder. "Which means maybe those stories *do* exist. They're just not the ones I was taught to value."

Saga grinned crookedly at her.

"It's alright, Wielder." The dwarf wasn't sweating like Astraea, but she was glistening with a thin layer of perspiration, her muscles thick and flushed with effort. "Just glad you can see it now."

Saga

It was...odd. Astraea proved predictably unsuited to the actual tasks of smithing, but she came alive with the hammer in her hand as much as any of Saga's apprentices, even with an absolute dearth of magic or dwarven talent in her blood.

Usually, the only sounds of the forge were mine-songs to keep the rhythm and pass the time, but Astraea chose to fill the quiet between her efforts with story.

Strangely, Saga found she didn't much mind.

Astraea told her about the coast, where she was from. The fresh air there sounded as lovely and thick as in Saga's mines. The jungles too. Saga had never been that interested in the rest of the world, but the way Astraea told it, the woman became a lens through which Saga could see beauty and possibility she hadn't before—feelings so simple and pure in their loveliness Saga, at some point, thought she must have outgrown them.

Watching this stranger who could—who *should* be the end of everything—take up Saga's life's work and breathe fresh energy into it—eager and irritated and messy in her motions, sweaty and ashen and *beaming* at Saga...

Astraea looked like a beginning.

Like a phoenix, anew.

"In my homeland," said the princess, when she paused to catch her breath, "we think of the forge as a dreary place. Industrial. Pottery and fence-bolts."

Saga arched a brow.

"When you measure the success of the realm by the freedom and joy of the many rather than the conquests of the few," she said, "something like shame for forging fence-bolts comes across, well..."

"Pathetic," Astraea said in earnest. Saga snorted and gave a pleased nod. "We *were*. I understand now," she said, casting her bright, tired gaze over Saga's forge. "I think I do, at least. This is your blood. Your sweat, your veins, your spit. It's a rhythm, the work you do. It's genesis, it's the very foundations of our world!"

Saga would find this wide-eyed naïveté far more tiring if she wasn't coming to truly feel for the girl—clearly, Astraea hadn't chosen this life. It wasn't her fault her Keeper had to be such a stickler. She'd been chosen by the oracles just as Saga had, and maybe if Saga could just show her what she herself knew, it would convince her too to let the world keep turning, Prophecy be damned.

"The forge has a life of its own," Saga murmured. "Not like ours, but less unalike than we give it credit for."

"Yes," agreed Astraea. "It has a heartbeat—no, it *is* a heartbeat."

Saga grinned. She could still feel the whiskey and cider in her system, churning alongside the familiar bodily ache and pleasure of working her forge.

"You're not a soldier, you're a poet," she said. Astraea lit up, then flinched, casting her gaze back at her hands. Clearly Saga cleaved too close to the truth of things.

"Thank you," she said. Her voice was different again, rough and quiet. "Bard, perhaps, in another life—one in which I was given the choice to choose my own fate. In this one, I was made to understand such tendencies would cause the death of everyone I've ever loved."

"That explains a lot," Saga said, and Astraea gave a half-bitter laugh. Saga shook her head. "You really want to Fell the Tree? To bring about the end of all things, to fight endless hordes of monsters until the earth is soaked in blood and the—"

"No one knows *exactly* what will happen—"

"But we do! We do know!" Saga's breathing had gone hard. "It's a commitment to war above all else, the undefined goalposts of its end ever shifting!"

"It could be a metaphor," Astraea offered. Was that Felric's influence, or was she more naïve than Saga had thought? "The Prophecy is intended to bring about progress, eventually—revolution is a *good* thing—"

"Revolution yes, when a system is corrupt, but what we have built is working!" Saga stared at her. "Unquestioned subservience to a higher power is only harmless until you've got a weapon in your hand."

Astraea opened her mouth, then closed it, frowning deeper than ever.

"I was made to believe the sacrifices of the Prophecy were ultimately in the best interest of the realm."

"You and every soldier who's ever chosen a superior's orders over the fact of the life in front of them!" Saga spoke clearly, but not loudly. "You are not asking me for defense, or prosperity. You are asking me for the end of the world."

The look on Astraea's face told Saga she'd never considered it quite like that.

"See you tomorrow, Princess," she said, and left the Wielder alone in her forge.

Astraea

Astraea also knew *helplessness,* or she thought she did. She'd never known anything but a choiceless path and had never met anyone in her life who might be able to relate. The closest possibility was Fell, the Chosen Watcher of the Chosen One, and he was the one person in the universe who'd most eagerly condemn her to it.

She's never known helplessness like this.

Never had her path felt so constrictive before this dwarven forger came looming into it—but no, she was always there. Saga was the Master Forger of Astraea's time. Their paths were inextricable—in so many ways the same—yet Saga didn't see it so. Or if she did, she'd chosen a different destination, one more unknowable than the end of the world.

For the first time in her life, what Fell wanted from Astraea was exactly what she wanted to do. She knew she wasn't thinking clearly. She knew she was being cruel, and selfish. She didn't care. She'd never known wanting like this.

Saga had just made it to the entrance of her dwelling when Astraea, panting, caught up with her. She shoved

Saga bodily against her door. Her tired muscles hardly had power in them. Saga liked the way the princess moved her.

"How could you leave me with *that?*" Astraea said, almost angrily. She was in Saga's face, all sweat and heaving and hot sweetness. "Break everything I've ever known, right when I was *finally* going to do the one thing I was made for?"

Saga grinned at her, buoyant.

"You've got far more to look forward to than the end of the world, Astraea." She was so close. She was so warm. "And if only you tell that Guardian of yours to shove it, I might show you what I mean."

"Please," growled the princess. Saga smirked before she kissed her, and then all that beautiful heat was sparkling and melting at once. Saga dragged her inside and barred the door.

Glinrod

It was nearly daybreak when Glinrod startled awake, peeling their face from a honeypot. After the rest of their route, they'd scampered back inside the cauldron cupboard to finish the snacks they'd abandoned and must've fallen asleep—not an uncommon occurrence.

What *was* uncommon was that the forge wasn't empty, though the morning fires weren't lit—meaning Saga hadn't arrived yet. Glinrod was about to tell off the intruder before they recognized the hushed, slimy voice of the Keeper. They froze, trying not to make a sound.

"—as expected," the Keeper was saying. "You're sure she didn't hear you sneak out this morning?"

"She didn't," came the Wielder's miserable voice. Glinrod clapped all three hands over their mouth. The Keeper gave that horrible laugh.

"Tired her out, did you?"

"It wasn't like that," Astraea started, but then her words cut off with a sharp breath. Glinrod trembled. Whatever power this Felric Ceranduil had over Astraea, it was dangerous.

"Keep telling yourself that," Felric said coldly. "Here, take it. One dose in her breakfast will do it."

"You're sure it's safe?"

"She'll wake up in three days," Felric said dismissively. "I swore I wouldn't hurt her unless I had to, didn't I? We just need her incapacitated so we can force her apprentices to forge the axe, and unconscious long enough to use her palm print to bless the metal and activate the Prophecy. I've researched this, Astraea. I expected this. I'm prepared."

"She won't be safe in three days," Astraea said. "None of us will be. She's going to wake to the end of the world."

Felric laughed.

"Yes, Princess," he said. *"Finally.* Now get back to your little lover before she wakes up."

But Glinrod saw the oily elf consider Astrea's back, then slip out a side door.

Astraea

Astraea's mind *wanted* to race, but it had gone numb. Everything was numb and too much all at once. Her legs felt leaden as she trod the same path as last night, only this was Fell's path, not hers, as last night had been. She felt outside herself like she never had been before: possibilities spiraling out before her of a life unlimited by predestiny. A life of creation, of nurturing things, of finding music where she'd once thought there was only soot. What else of the world might fill her with joy and hope like this—like her own calling never did?

Astraea could never truly renege on Fell, there was too much at stake, and he too powerful. She made up her mind, though, to tell Saga the truth—then at least the two of them could figure out what to do together. Saga would understand, she saw Fell for who he was.

More than that, she saw Astraea. And that's what had done it, really.

But when she arrived at Saga's dwelling, the Master Forger wasn't alone.

Saga

"Fell, what are you *doing!*" Astraea shrieked. Saga hardly heard her over the clash of steel on sparks. The elf was a blastedly skilled enchanter, his magic a worrying match for Saga's smallsword, the closest thing to a weapon she kept on hand.

"What I could clearly see you would not," Felric hissed over his shoulder at her.

Thankfully, while Saga might not like to fight, she could.

"For a famous pacifist you fight terribly well," panted the elf, hair falling across his eyes.

"You may have been too young for the wars, elf," Saga said, parrying, "but just because I don't like to fight doesn't mean I can't when I have to."

Felric snarled, lurching forward.

"You swore you wouldn't hurt her!" cried Astraea.

Saga's chest went cold.

Felric grinned meanly.

No.

No.

"There's no tool that cannot be used as a weapon, Master Forger," crowed Felric. "You were right when you said if the Prophecy circumstances were to occur when you were Master Forger, we'd lose the chance for centuries, if not forever. Everyone knows you didn't want to fulfill the Prophecy. Some have made their own peace with that, but some of us have faith in the gods and prophets! Some of us know what it is to pursue purpose!"

He punctuated the words with flashing sparks. Saga's steel held, but only just.

"You know nothing of purpose," Saga said, her eyes growing hot.

"Saga the Steady," the Keeper said mockingly. "Only has one weakness..."

Saga could not remember ever feeling this sick.

The elf smirked. "...*pretty girls.*"

Astraea

How do you build a life you expected to die from?

What is your purpose when it's not the end of all things?

How different the impact of the smallest moments—a butterfly, a simple meal—when they're not in service of fueling your body for the singular purpose it's been shaped for. Astraea felt sick with freedom.

It would be easier to do as Fell said.

It would be easier to do what she'd been told, to follow the path of the Prophecy, as she had done her whole life.

"Haven't I taken care of you?" he'd asked, and the worst of it was that he thought he had.

Astraea might throw up. It had only ever been theoretical—she could see that now. Saga was right, sh*e had* been childish, all of this was. Her path had felt so simple when she thought there was no alternative. The Master Forger was only ever supposed to be a tool, just as much as the axe. Anything could be justified when it was to uphold the will of the Prophecy.

But now she knew the taste of Saga's skin, and she would never be able to undo what it did to her.

"You betrayed me," Saga said.

"No!" cried Astraea, foolish and instinctive. She'd never known Fell was such a skilled fighter. He wasn't supposed to be here. What other secrets had he been keeping?

"There is no valor in peace," spat Felric.

"And there it is," Saga shouted, her muscles gleaming in the torchlight. Saga swung her sword, Fell dodging just in time. "You would sacrifice the world for a chance to prove you're better than it! That's not just sick, it's *pathetic*."

"There's no triumph in cowardice!"

"Your words aren't your own, Guardian! You let dead oracles puppet your pretty form as if they've got their ghostly hands shoved up your—ah!"

Felric laughed. Blood splattered the stone. It wasn't a deep cut, but it spanned nearly Saga's forearm, knocking her weapon away, and Astraea's gut boiled.

Somewhere outside the mountain, day was breaking. Here in the throes of the forge, there was only close, cloying heat. The only light came from fire. Astraea's own breathing filled her ears. The sweat on her skin was not only hers. That arm that was bleeding, that arm *Fell cut,* that very arm had been wrapped around Astraea hours ago. Strong and steady and, perhaps, everything.

Felric Ceranduil raised his hands. Astraea could recognize a hex brewing between them. He drew back—

And his magic clanged against Saga's sword, in Astraea's hands.

"*Fuck,* that's heavy," Astraea said, sagging from the blow.

If Saga's expression at her betrayal hadn't already broken Astraea's heart, Fell's face would have. Before it settled into the stone of cruel determination, there was a flicker of hurt so deep *he* had to have a heart to feel it. Astraea was probably the only person alive in this realm who could recognize it for what it was, and that had to count for something.

"I should have known," Felric growled. He lashed out again, more anger than finesse.

"You were sold a promise, when you were small," Astraea said. Sweat and tears dripped down her face. "And then you taught it to me. But this is already a triumph! There is nothing here to save."

Felric's face twisted terribly. Out of the corner of her eye, Astraea saw Saga moving, slowly, toward her tools.

"I wish I could've done this myself," Felric growled.

"But you can't! There is no halcyon paradise to kill for. We can't go back to before the Last War, we can only choose to prevent the next one!" Astraea swung Saga's sword with the surety the dwarf gave her, and the strength the elf once had. She had never been in a proper fight before, but she breathed as Saga taught her. And she had nothing left to lose. "Saga's right," she said. "It's not peace that makes you weak. It's the inability to sit with yourself in the quiet."

Fell snarled and opened his mouth to recite. "*Since the dawn of time the world gets made and destroyed and remade by the one who Wields the Axe; only through this battle can the realm achieve true prosperity—*"

"What if the prophets got it wrong?" Astraea cried. "What if there is another way to remake the world, without ending it! What if we don't have to keep the cycle of violence going? What if the prophets wrote out of a dying land, desperate to believe the hell of their lifetimes was *worth* something, *for* something? What if they couldn't have dreamt of a peace like this?"

It had seemed for so long that she and Saga were made for each other, for better or for worse. The Forger and the Wielder. But perhaps Fell was part of that too, her assigned Keeper. You couldn't break free unless you wanted to. And she wasn't sure she could convince him to want to.

But she'd never known an alternative until Saga showed it to her. Maybe she could show him.

So focused he was on Astraea, Fell didn't notice Saga coming at him with Astraea's ill-formed horseshoe 'til it was too late. The iron clanged against his skull, knocking him into Saga's sturdy grip.

"No!" Felric squirmed fitfully, dazed but not mortally wounded.

"We don't have to pick up arms for a war we inherited," Saga said. "When we've only known calms followed by tempests, sometimes that sense of quiet feels like a looming horror we have to get ahead of before it catches up." She held him firm, and Astraea could see the charmed chain in her hands that must be countering Fell's magic. "Let go of the idea you have to prove your valor, Sir Keeper. A life in pursuit of peace is enough."

"Discord will come—"

"How? There are no land disputes. When everyone has enough, they don't need to be at each other's throats."

"Discord is as certain as death."

"Alright, but we don't need to self-fulfill that prophecy. The prophets didn't actually give us an *or else.*"

"The *or else* is ignominy and the shame of a never-satisfied life!"

"Don't be ashamed of being insatiable, O Keeper," Saga winked, and Fell *blushed*. Astraea could've fallen down from surprise. "What if we don't have to destroy everything? What if we grow through the hard parts instead? What if we do the work of peace, instead of succumbing to chaos and death?"

Fell muttered something, slack in Saga's arms.

"What's that?" Astraea asked.

Felric Ceranduil swore colorfully. "I don't know who I am outside of this!" he said, sounding furious at himself.

"I do," Astraea said, flashing a look at Saga. Saga nodded. "Or at least, I know enough of it that I think there's something in there worth saving." Astraea stepped close, and Saga handed her the unicorn horseshoe. "Peace will be hard. But don't worry, dear Keeper. We'll find something for you to do." She raised the horseshoe and knocked him out cold.

"Got grunt work galore, that's for sure," Saga said, frowning at Fell. "You're sure enough we should keep him alive for it?"

"As sure as you were with me," Astraea said.

Saga cocked a brow.

"You're telling me that was a *good* example of trust?" She set about binding his wrists though.

"I won't kill him," said the once-Wielder. "I won't kill anyone. Ever."

Saga looked at her, and Astraea knew she understood.

A fresh poem began in Stray's heart, the one she'd been fighting not to write since the moment she laid eyes on the forger. An ode to the dawn of her, breaking free from the shackles of prophecy into a terrifying, glorious realm of possibility.

O firesmith, cycle breaker, refuser to the call! You were born to end the world but remade mine instead...

Saga

"I'm so sorry," Astraea said, again.

Saga was finalizing a set of precautionary cuffs that would stall out Fell's more violent spells until she could trust him—at least until the circumstances of the Prophecy passed. She made Astraea wait until she'd finished them and secured them around his delicate wrists before she relented.

"I believe you," she said, and the hope in Astraea's eyes made her feel fucking aglow. Time went blurry, a bit, when Saga allowed herself to be enveloped in Astraea's embrace.

"I can't believe he beat me here," Astraea said, her breath pleasantly warm on Saga's face. Her voice had lost all façade, all squeak and sweetness. "Thank the gods you were awake!"

"Thank the gods Glinrod knew a shortcut to my house," Saga said. "If it weren't for them, he might've drugged me in my sleep somehow and we'd never have had a chance."

Astraea's eyes went wide.

"I'm going to give them a *huge* hug when I see them next," she said. "A lifetime guarantee of pastries."

"You'll regret that promise," Saga laughed. She stretched, shaking her head.

"So."

Astraea looked at her.

"You didn't forge the weapon, Princess. You didn't fulfill the Prophecy." Saga brushed Astraea's sweaty hair from her eyes. "What now?"

The smile that spread across Astraea's face, then—oh, Sigurn the Steady, ninth of her name, Solaris of the Inner Sanctums and inheritor of the role of Master Forger to the realm had never, *ever* felt heat like that before.

"For the first time in my life, I don't know," Astraea said. "For the first time in my life, I cannot wait to find out."

Astraea

One Month Later

The new bedframe had proved a perfect first big project for Astraea, the size of it proving quite useful indeed.

The sun stretched over the villages and coasts of the realm. Its light didn't permeate the stone mountains, but its warmth reached, nonetheless.

"You weren't made to be a wielder," Saga said, "of weapons or anything else. You are poetry yourself. You are the art; you are the craft. You are more than what you do."

"So are you, Master Forger. In case it's been a while since anyone reminded you."

Saga grinned. "It had not. But thank you, Astraea."

Astraea shuddered in her arms. Her name, titleless. There on Saga's warm and clever tongue, it suited Astraea better than it ever had.

Saga's smile deepened. "I'll show you what I do, pretty thing. You just sit back."

Astraea felt made of honey. She wanted, suddenly and fiercely, to make Saga feel this way. She must have flinched—or else the smith could read her better than ever—for strong hands came to her thighs, holding her firm.

"Later. If you like. Let me take care of you."

"Fuck off," Astraea said, kicking her in the shoulder. "I want *this*."

Saga laughed, ears pink, and allowed Astraea to pin her to the bed. When Astraea climbed down her lover's sweet, sturdy body, she smiled to herself.

Not for the first time, a thought crossed her mind, a cheeky echo of a past life.

Eyes lowered, Stray.

There was absolutely nothing to prove. Nothing to do but what moved her, to better her day and the world. Her path, finally, was her own.

The one who harvests found something to sow. The bard in Astraea's heart brimmed with endless seeds for song.

And, at last, the Master Forger laid back against the pillows and let herself be the one remade.

"Aubade" is a standalone short by Maya Gittelman. A sapphic story of a prophesied Chosen One and the dwarven blacksmith destined to forge her world-ending weapon, it confronts the rhetoric of battles and glory in high fantasy: just because you were taught war is inevitable and necessary doesn't mean we can't pursue progress through nurture, not destruction. Something like a hobbit's take on human war, perhaps—"it is no bad thing to celebrate a simple life." Maya drew inspiration from a fascination with the mechanics of blacksmithing, and the song "Hammer and the Anvil" by The Longest Johns. Follow her at mayagittelman or bookshelfbymaya, wherever you follow writers. Hopefully by the time you're reading this, they'll have a website up.

Phoenix Tails Rescue, Inc.

Sara Codair

Sapphic Representation: Lesbian, Nonbinary

Heat Level: Low

Content Warnings: Danger to Cats, Dogs, and Birds, House fire, Arson

Serena might have been fireproof, but their clothes certainly weren't. By the time they found the stubborn cat hiding in this flaming deathtrap of a house and got out, it would be surrounded by firefighters, paramedics, police, and reporters.

Reporters with cameras.

The only way to not have their naked body being all over the news would be to shift to their gull form and fly away. But they hated being a gull. And gulls were not strong enough to carry cats. Too bad they weren't a full elemental who could actually control fire. Too bad they weren't a phoenix.

They hadn't been planning any heroics tonight. They'd been out running, their least favorite form of exercise but necessary for the triathlon they were doing to raise money for their animal shelter. They'd heard crying and found a kid hysterical about a cat, Teefs, and parents making very valid excuses about why they couldn't go back into a burning house for said cat. There were apparently some decent fireproof wards on the bedroom where the cat was probably hiding, but the wards had already failed on the ground floor of the house and it was far too hot to enter. Their only hope was that the fire crew got the blaze out before the bedroom's ward failed or some brave soul climbed a ladder and got the cat out through a window.

Since Serena was fireproof—rare even for magic folk—and the poor fool who would probably end up climbing through the window most likely would be at the mercy of cheap government fire-protection runes, they jogged around to the back door and walked through the flames, sacrificing their favorite joggers to save this cat. They were in the business of rescuing animals, but typically, that meant taking in strays or removing pets from hoarders, then rehoming them, not literally pulling people's cats out of burning buildings.

Choices had been made. They'd been the right choices, but now they were naked in some stranger's bedroom, hearing sirens, Serena admitted a bit more forethought would have come in handy. Serena lay belly down on the floor. Heat radiated from the tiles. They didn't have much time. The framed news articles on the wall depicting the kid winning national demon-summoning championships probably explained the super-hot fire, but also meant the news crews would be flocking to the scene along with the tardy fire department. The media—at least the non-magic variety—loved to trumpet how dangerous young sorcerers were.

"Teefs?" they shouted over the muffled roar of flames. They could see two yellow eyes glaring at them from under the bed. "Come on, Teefs. I'm going to get you out of here."

Teefs hissed.

Serena took a deep breath. Of course Teefs wasn't some friendly goofball who came to any stranger who called him. He'd probably sink his sharp little "teef" right into their hand if they reached under the bed to grab him, and they didn't have any treats or catnip with them.

Sirens wailed. Flames roared louder as the wards failed. Sirens ceased. Voices and radios crackled outside.

"Teefs, I know I'm a scary human, but you're going to die if I don't get you out of here." They always talked to cats like they could understand human.

Teefs replied with another hiss.

"You better be up to date on all your vaccines," they muttered and reached under the bed, grabbing Teefs by the scruff.

Teefs flailed, very sharp hind claws raking their arms. Of course their gut reaction to being clawed was to let go, but after years in animal rescue, Serena was very good at not letting go. Too bad they weren't as claw-proof as they were fireproof.

When they dragged him out from under the bed, his claws scrabbled at the tile. Serena wobbled to their feet, holding Teefs at arm's length as he tried to mangle their naked body. Smoke poured in around the edges of the door. Fire-resistant runes glowed and flickered, on the verge of failure. They had mere minutes to get this cat out of here.

Was that...someone behind the door? Surely no one else could survive this fire. Runes needed to withstand that heat would cost a fortune.

When Serena looked closer, the door was closed, with no hint of a figure. And Teefs was overheating. They couldn't take him out the way they'd come. The flames tearing through the rest of the house were way too hot for Teefs to survive. That left the second story window.

Serena had no problem going out the window thanks to a fluke of genetics that gave them some of their mom's fire elemental powers and their dad's were-seagull genes. They only needed to find a way to open the windo...

Crash!

Problem solved? Holding Teefs out, Serena ran to the window and found themself face to face with a woman in a firefighter's suit made for someone much bigger. Fireproof ward symbols glowed on the bulky red jacket. Constellations of freckles dusted what Serena could see of her face. Her blue eyes were oceans Serena could have stared into for hours.

"Are you okay, Ma'am?"

Serena blinked. Shit. They hadn't planned on human interaction.

Panic seized their brain, dousing logic quicker than water quenching fire.

"Here." They thrust the cat forward.

The door exploded behind them. Glancing over their shoulder, they swore there was a figure in the flames. Was that a sack in their hand? And a gas can?

"What about you?" asked the firefighter.

Serena panicked, shifted to their seagull form, and flew away.

* * *

Saturday came with a different kind of stress. Serena had been planning Barks and Brews with a local brewery for months. Adoptable dogs would be out in the beer garden, vendors would be selling dog-related products, and people would hopefully be adopting dogs and shopping. A share of the profits of beer and product sales would be going to their shelter, and they needed the cash. The shelter was getting low on food and the electric bill would climb as summer heated up.

Ten years ago, when Serena had inherited money from their aunt, they thought they were set for life. They'd invest the money wisely, live off the interest, and start an animal shelter. But interest rates were inconsistent and keeping two dozen small animals fed, sheltered, and in good health was more expensive than anticipated. The dogs, sometimes literally, ate through the money. Fundraisers—like Barks and Brews or Paddle for Paws— were what kept the shelter afloat. Barely.

But today, Serena felt like sinking.

"Is this one good with cats?" asked a person with gray hair and a cat button-up shirt.

"Which one?" Serena asked, cringing as Roko, a shepherd-mix, lifted his leg on a fake plant.

"That one." The woman pointed at Roko, who was now kicking his back legs. The plant tipped over. "But maybe I'll meet the smaller dogs first."

Serena darted off to grab the sanitizer and towels and almost made it to the pee when they saw a husky eat a sock that definitely hadn't been in his pen five minutes ago. That could be an expensive vet bill if the sock didn't come back out on its own.

Too late to stop the husky, they crouched down and sprayed deodorizing potion on the fake tree and was almost relieved to hear the husky puke the sock back up.

"Um, I think the husky just puked up a sock. He wouldn't be Cap, by any chance, would he?"

Serena looked up at the source of the voice. First, they saw well-muscled legs. Then black shorts with a rainbow stripe up the side. A cropped tank revealing defined abs but sadly no cleavage. Freckles. The frizzy red hair.

Serena paused at those mesmerizing summer sky eyes. This was the firefighter who had seen them naked. Their cheeks burned.

"Is the dog that just puked Cap?" asked the firefighter.

Serena nodded. "Um, yes. Were you interested in him?"

Maybe this person didn't recognize them from their brief encounter. That was probably for the best. It'd be a lot easier to ask her out if they didn't have awkward questions to deal with first.

"Yes. I'm Kat. I emailed Serena about him yesterday." Kat held out her hand.

"I'm Serena." They stood up and shook Kat's hand. Her grip was firm, and her fingers were rough and calloused. "Did you still want to meet him?"

"I'd love to!"

Serena glanced over at Cap. He was currently nosing a volunteer's treat pouch while they cleaned up his puke. "Max, can you please bring Cap over here after you clean up?"

The volunteer nodded.

"How is Cap with other dogs?" Kat said, trying and failing to get some red frizz away from her eyes.

"He loves them." Serena pictured how, before some serious training, he almost pulled them down trying to make friends with a big Bernese Mountain dog and another time with a little Yorkie mix. "But sometimes he comes on a bit too strong and gets himself in trouble. Do you have other dogs at home?"

"No, but a lot of people have off-leash dogs where I run. I'll work with him to not bug them, but I don't want to worry about my dog growling at everyone who tries to make friends with him, and..." Kat got a faraway look in her eyes.

"And what?" Red flags waved in Serena's mind.

Kat shook her head. "My brother lives in the apartment above me. His dog is missing."

"I'm sorry. Let me know if you need any resources." Serena kept a list of missing local pets on the corkboard in her office, just in case any arrived at the shelter by mistake. They wondered which one belonged to Kat's brother.

Kat's eyes brimmed with tears. "We tried everything and as far as we could tell, the dog was stolen while my brother was fighting a fire."

"Stolen?" Serena cringed. They'd heard of local dog-fighting gangs stealing dogs to train their fighters on. Those dogs were rarely recovered alive.

"Spot was a special dog." Tears and smiles mingled on Kat's face. "He was very smart, but some jerk started rumors that he was more than an ordinary dog. A few weeks later, he was gone."

Maybe it wasn't dog fighters, then. "Do the police have any idea who took him?"

"I have some ideas, but the police don't believe me."

"Like what?" Serena was getting drawn into this story. They should be paying more attention to what was going on around them. Was that barking excitement or stress? Did they smell poop? But that was all in the background, and their eyes were locked on Kat's blue ones wet with tears.

Kat broke eye contact and looked down. She picked at her cuticle. She opened her mouth to talk.

And 150 pounds of fluff and drool barreled into Serena at the exact moment Kat's phone beeped.

Kat shook her head like she was shaking off sleep as Serena struggled to grab the Bernese Mountain dog. Cap took that moment to prove he could, in fact, with minimal effort, leap out of his pen. He and the other dog took off running through the beer garden.

By the time Serena got the place back into something close to order, Kat was gone.

* * *

Later that day, when the dogs were either back with their fosters or in their kennels at the shelter, Serena sat in their office. The news was streaming on mute on one monitor, a list of pending adoption applications on another. But Serena wasn't paying much attention to either. There were looking at the wall of missing pets.

Serena had rearranged it so a group of particularly talented working dogs were in the center, one a Dalmatian with the very imaginative name of Spot, who belonged to Kat's brother.

Based on Kat's story, Serena had gone searching for more information. Half a dozen working dogs had gone missing in the weeks leading up to his disappearance. And Serena hadn't noticed it before because while they had looked for some of the dogs, they hadn't investigated the sources of their disappearance. That wasn't their job.

But now they had read the stories behind the working dogs' disappearances, maybe they *should* have been paying attention. It was clear these cases were related. Fire had been involved in almost every disappearance.

Then, a month later, there had been another string of what Serena was now convinced were acts of arson used to cover up the theft of animals, but this time, it was cats, not dogs.

Someone was setting things on fire and using it as a cover to steal dogs and cats.

Teefs.

Serena looked up every bit of news they could about the fire they'd pulled Teefs from. They had avoided the news about that for fear of seeing some reference to themself in it, but now, they devoured every article.

The media had blamed the kid for starting the fire, though both the kid and the family denied that was the case. The kid claimed they'd been sleeping when it started. The alarm hadn't gone off, but Teefs had woken everyone up then didn't make it out of the house himself.

There was mention of a brave firefighter who climbed in through a window and retrieved Teefs just before the wards failed, but thankfully no mention of a strange naked person's assistance.

The family said how lucky they were to have a beach house and were staying there while they rebuilt their main home.

Right before they shifted, Serena thought they had seen saw a figure in the flames behind the door. What if that was whoever stole Spot and the other animals?

They glanced at the news. The stream changed stories from a break-in at a local bank chain to a house fire allegedly caused by a stray firework at the beach. Panic shot through Serena's chest. What if it was the beach house Teefs' family was at? What if whoever set the first fire set a second and was trying to steal Teefs again? They knew what they were about to do was reckless. They knew if they stopped to think it through, they probably wouldn't do it.

Serena stripped out of their clothes, shifted into a gull, and flew out their office window.

* * *

Thankfully, a gull didn't look out of place on Seabrook Ave. The beach "cottages" lining the street were elegant and old and generally had the kind of charms modern mages had forgotten how to make.

But apparently, those old reliable wards had failed tonight. A stray firecracker landed on the roof, sending it up in flames. Even several houses away, Serena could feel the heat.

Serena circled high above looking for any sign of Kat or Teefs but the smoke made it hard to see, so they had to circle lower and lower. They gave up on trying to behave like an actual gull and perched on top of a fire truck, really hoping Kat wasn't already inside.

The family was outside talking to reporters. A girl was crying.

A man with red hair almost identical to Kat's was frantically clutching a radio.

"Kat, come on, it's not worth it. Get out of there!"

Static. Crackle.

"No! I'm so close."

Static. Crackle.

"It's just one cat."

Static. Crackle.

"It's not just about this cat. I need to know who's taking them. So I can find..."

Static...Static...

Serena launched themself off the firetruck at the house.

Fire exploded from the window just as they soared through it.

Heat raged in the air around their feathers, but it didn't touch them.

Inside, Kat was on the ground, not moving, surrounded by flaming boards. Ward marks flickered and glowed on her uniform. She had minutes left before they gave out. Teefs was nowhere to be seen.

A figure clad in a black suit lined with steadily glowing fireproof runes lunged toward Kat. The attacker's suit was less bulky than a firefighter uniform and apparently much more efficient at protecting its wearer, because this person leapt over flaming debris with no issue.

Serena opened her mouth to shout, but they were in bird form so all that came out was a squawk.

The mystery person didn't pause. They rolled Kat over and scooped Teefs out from under her, threw him in a sack marked with the same wards as their suit, and ran.

Kat's eyes flooded open, specks of cool blue in a sweltering sea of red.

Serena froze as they took in the inferno. They could chase the cat-stealer or save Kat.

Kat's eyes closed.

Teefs was alive for the moment and in a fireproof sack, but the wards on Kat's uniform were failing. Serena transformed back into a naked human and ran over to Kat, putting two fingers on her neck. She had a faint pulse but when Serena shook her and called her name, she didn't wake up. Kat's brother's voice crackled through the radio, but it was garbled. Serena picked up to call for help and the thing went silent.

"Shit." They tossed the radio into the flames. They crouched down, and lifting from their legs, slung Kat over their shoulder in a fireman's carry and prayed the wards on her uniform would last long enough to get her out of the house.

Thankfully, this house was one story and the wards just flickered for the last time as Serena tripped over the threshold and landed in a heap at the feet of a team just about to enter, armed with fresh wards and a firehose.

"She's alive. Get her help!" Serena said, before backing toward the flames. They were going to dramatically disappear into them, but they didn't want anyone else getting hurt or dying trying to find them in the burning house, so they transformed into a gull first and flew away. A tall shoot of flame reached up and engulfed their feathers, and for a moment, they pretended they were a mythical phoenix, an elegant firebird, not a clumsy fireproof seagull.

"Wait! Come back!" Shouts echoed beneath them, but they ignored them.

Serena soared above the house, still bathed in flame, circling just long enough to confirm Kat was alive and being treated, then went off in search of the cat thief. They didn't see anyone in an all-black bodysuit or carrying around a grumpy orange cat. They tried to peek in the windows of cars heading in a general direction away from the fire, but it was dark out and the streetlights glared on the windows. Eventually, their wings ached, and they returned home, defeated.

Before heading to bed, they looked at the list of missing pets and added Teefs to the board. The same number of cats and dogs had now been stolen. Did that mean the thief would stop? Or would they just switch to yet another type of animal? Or maybe there was no pattern. Maybe it was just random acts of arson and theft. Serena staggered to bed, hoping the animals were still alive, not being tortured, and that they'd find a way to reunite them with their humans.

* * *

A couple days later, Kat showed up at Phoenix Tails Rescue to pick up Cap. One arm was in a sling, a bruise surrounded her left eye, and her face had half a dozen scratches.

"How are you feeling?" Serena asked, trying not to stare at the bruises or sling.

"I've been worse." Kat sank into the chair on the other side of the desk. "But I have another appointment with the healers this afternoon."

"You sure you're ready to bring a dog home? I've been working with Cap on manners, but he still has a long way to go with impulse control."

"I'm on leave, so I'll get to be home while he settles in." Kat fidgeted with her curls, twirling red hair around her index finger. "I don't like having all that free time alone. I need someone to keep me busy. Keep me out of trouble."

"Well Cap will certainly keep you busy." Serena smiled, wondering if they, too, could help keep Kat busy. Their conversations had mostly been about dogs, but Serena found themself smitten with Kat's blue eyes and the idea that she risked her life to save a cat and catch the pet-stealing arsonist.

Kat glanced out the window. Her cheeks flushed red. "There is something I want to ask you, before I sign the paperwork. Something not about dogs."

Serena's hand froze over the print button. A jolt shot through them. "Oh? What?"

Kat bit her lip. "I'll take Cap no matter what you answer. But I just need to know."

Serena nodded, but nerves and excitement swallowed their words.

"Why did I see you naked in two different burning houses?"

"You recognized me?"

Kat nodded.

"You were unconscious in the second one."

"Mostly, but not the whole time." Kat narrowed her eyes and stared into Serena's eyes. "What were you doing there?"

"My job," said Serena even though it wasn't strictly true. "Rescuing an animal."

"But why naked?" Kat tilted her head. "You're wearing clothing now."

"Clothing isn't fireproof," said Serena, hesitantly.

"But you are?"

Serena nodded.

"Why not put fireproof wards on your clothing?"

"I can't afford them. I could feed ten dogs for a month with what it would cost to get one outfit warded long enough to last five minutes."

"But you're a fire witch, aren't you? Or some kind of phoenix?"

Serena couldn't stop the giggles that choked their way out of their throat. It wasn't the first time they'd been mistaken for a phoenix—a rare, shapeshifting fire witch who could be reborn from their ashes on the off-chance someone managed to kill them. Growing up, they'd had a cousin who insisted they were a phoenix, but Serena couldn't control fire, make runes, and certainly wouldn't be reborn from their ashes were they to die. But that cousin's half-serious insistence had led them to adopt the name for the animal shelter.

"Being a phoenix certainly would be more useful than being a fireproof were-seagull."

Now it was Kat's turn to laugh. "There is no such thing."

"There is no such thing as a phoenix either. Fire witches, sure, but the phoenix is just a legend." Serena fidgeted, hopes of scoring a date with Kat dashed.

Kat leaned forward, studying Serena's face. "Or maybe the tales of phoenixes aren't false, they're just not quite right. Stories change every time they're told."

Serena tilted her head. "What are you implying?"

Kat leaned even closer. "What if thousands of years ago, someone saw a fire witch turn into some kind of mundane bird, catch fire, and soar away, much like you did last week, and the legend of the phoenix was born? Maybe the phoenix was never a specific type of bird. It was just someone who got genes from a fire witch and a shifter."

Serena nodded, because they couldn't think properly with Kat's lips so close to theirs. Maybe their chances with Kat weren't ruined. Maybe Kat liked seeing them naked. Maybe Kat wanted to see them naked again and they could skip the date and get right to the naked part. They'd have to be careful of Kat's injuries, but Serena could be gentle.

"What do you know about the stolen pets?" Kat asked.

Serena had lots of ideas about what they could be doing with their mouth that didn't involve words, but they forced themself to speak anyway. "Not as much as I'd like."

Kat leaned back. Air escaped her lips. Her shoulders relaxed. She leaned back and smirked. "I think I believe you."

"Believe me?" Serena tried to straighten out her brain. She wanted Kat closer, not leaning back.

Kat nodded. "When I first saw you in Teefs' house, I thought you were the thief, but then you just handed him to me. So I did some research, and realized you ran the shelter I was already thinking of getting a dog from. I thought it couldn't be you, but I wasn't sure. I had to meet you. And then you saved my life. But if you're not the pet thief, you have to be working to stop them, right?"

"Not exactly. I do keep track of missing pets, but that's because sometimes people find animals outside and bring them to me. I need to make sure the pets that come through here don't belong to someone else before I put them up for adoption." Serena's knee bounced. "The first time I saved Teefs, I'd been out for a jog, saw the fire, and heard a kid crying about a cat trapped in a flaming house."

Kat leaned in close again. "And the second time?"

Serena flushed. "Well, after the meet and greet, I couldn't stop thinking about you and your brother's missing dog. Maybe I wanted an excuse to see you again. So, I started looking into it, and I saw a pattern. Then I turned on the news and saw Teefs' family's second house was on fire. I tried to find the thief after saving you, but I lost them, and all my research since has turned up dead ends."

Kat's face was temptingly close to Serena's again. "So, what are we going to do about this thief?"

"We?" Serena wanted to get up and pace, but Kat's lips were like a tractor beam, drawing Serena closer.

She shrugged. "Well, I can't take them on alone."

"I told you I hit a dead end. I don't know where to start."

"You hit a dead end. I didn't. I'm close to figuring something out." Kat winked. "Let's meet at Lakewoods on Saturday, take a stroll, then grab a coffee at Red's. Their patio is pet friendly. We'll talk strategy over coffee."

"Tell me a time, and I'll be there." Plotting a rescue wasn't exactly a date, but it was close enough for Serena, even if it did involve more clothing between them than they wanted...

* * *

Red's Coffee would have been the perfect place for a first date. But apparently, it was also the perfect place to plot a...was it a rescue or a heist? They were breaking into a highly secure something, but the pets they were removing had been stolen from their owners in the first place. And it wasn't entirely clear who they were stealing them back from. Kat had texted Serena a lot of theories, but there was no evidence that any of them were true.

For the first few moments of the conversation, Serena asked about how Cap was settling in and how Kat was recovering from her ordeal. Her arm was out of its cast thanks to a healer, and she looked almost back to herself.

Then Kat broke the illusion by pulling out a manilla envelope. "So, I can't really tell you how I got this without risking my source getting in trouble."

"Then I won't ask." Serena leaned back and took a sip of water.

Kat took out grainy pictures of an island and laid them in front of Serena. "This is where I think they took the cats and dogs."

"How far offshore is it?" A real gull could fly more than a hundred miles a day, but Serena had never pushed themself that far. Though they had noticed fitness in their human body translated to their gull form, and flying had gotten much easier since they started training for their triathlon.

"It's maybe twenty-five miles or so." Kat paused and looked down into her glass of water. "I got close on a boat once. The problem isn't the distance. It's the fire."

"Fire?" Serena was sure it would've made the news if there was a flaming island just twenty-five miles offshore, especially with all the pushes for renewable, non-magical energy and increasing divides between those with and without magic.

"The island just looks like a big, rocky island, almost porcupine-shaped, but there is a cave entrance and from what I could glimpse of the inside, it's blocked by a wall of fire." Kat picked at her lip.

Serena sat in silence for a moment. "So, what do you want me to do? Fly through the fire?"

"Yes." Kat peeked up and smiled. "You fly in, put out the flames, and I'll come in on the boat. We find the pets, load them up, and get out as quickly as possible."

"And what if I can't put out the flames? I didn't inherit any of my mother's ability to control fire."

"I don't think they're magic, at least not fully," said Kat. "When I got close, my instruments detected natural gas. I think you need to just get through and turn off a valve."

"Won't someone notice? Won't they have guards?"

"It's possible, but all my research leads me to believe this person is working alone and thinks the fire wall is enough to keep intruders out."

"But what if you're wrong?" Serena had dealt with some feisty animals in their life, but they didn't even know how to throw a proper punch.

"I can handle a few goons if necessary." Kat stirred her coffee, but she didn't take her eyes off of Serena. "You still with me?"

Serena nodded, deciding they weren't ready to know how Kat intended to handle the goons that may or may not be present. They weren't particularly fond of violence and people who used it, even with good intentions. It wasn't necessarily a deal breaker in the relationship if a person had a history of violence, say in the military or law enforcement, but Serena thought the relationship had a better chance of happening if they didn't ask for details too soon.

"Do you know why this person is stealing pets?" Serena thought this was a much safer question, and it was one they really wanted to know the answer to.

"There is a group of people online who think some animals used to be shifters, or their descendants were shifters, but they have since lost their ability to become human. It's not a theory accepted in the scientific community, but I think our thief believes it. I did talk to my cop friends about this, but they just don't have enough evidence to get a warrant or funding to search this island."

"If your evidence isn't enough for the police, are you sure you're right about this?"

Kat bit her lip. "My gut tells me I'm right."

Serena sighed. Their gut said to ask for more evidence, but Kat's smile, and her pretty eyes, overrode most of Serena's common sense. "All right. Let's do this."

* * *

Serena shivered on the edge of a rocky coastline on a foggy morning, waiting for a group of tourists with cameras to leave so they could shift.

If Kat was holding up her end of the plan, she was borrowing a lobster boat from a friend and swapping out the traps for dog crates. She'd get as close to the island as she could and wait for Serena to lower the flames.

Finally, the tourists left. Serena climbed down to a little cave they'd scouted out that didn't quite fill up at high tide and slipped out of their sundress. Then they shifted before anyone else came, and flew off.

Navigating to the island was easier than they expected. Sure, there were all kinds of distracting smells and winds and sensations, but they could feel the target destination, something magnetically off about it in a way they were more sensitive to in bird form. Something about the offness of the place called to them and they found when they arrived, there were dozens of other gulls circling around, all agitated.

Serena flew low, noting the wall of flames at the entrance to a rather large sea cave. Wanting to seem like a normal gull, they dove in a tidepool, snatched up a crab, smashed it on the rocks and ate its guts before flying back up. They flew back up, circling with the other gulls until they saw Kat drive the lobster boat in close and drop an anchor. Serena flew by the boat, squawking three times fast in front of Kat, then soared through the flames.

They were hot, but no hotter than any other fire. Then they were through.

No alarms went off. No lasers or wards attacked them.

They weren't sure what they were expecting, maybe cameras or spikes or lasers. But it wasn't an empty cavern.

Was this person so confident in their little fire wall that they didn't think they needed surveillance? Or did they have some other way of watching?

Granted, the empty cavern was creepy enough on its own. It was about two stories tall and the middle of it was filled with still, dark water. Even with the glow from the fire, there wasn't enough light for Serena to see how deep it was. Images from horror movies flitted through their mind. Anything could be lurking in those depths. Anything could have tentacles.

Perching on the highest outcropping they could find, Serena surveyed the area with keen bird eyes. The cavern wasn't entirely empty. There were spiders. Anemones. Crabs. Minnows. A whole slew of the kind of little sea creatures one would expect to see in a sea cave, and they made their seagull stomach growl even though they had eaten their fill of minnows on the way here.

There were no obvious guards unless they were lurking below the dark water.

What they couldn't see from the perch was a gas valve.

They flew lower, staying close to the edges where they had solid rock beneath them and were less likely to be grabbed by a tentacle. Granted, something with long enough tentacles could probably reach them.

There. They saw a pipe running along the wall, and a junction where there was a valve and another pipe. They flew lower, angling toward it.

Teeth and claws sank into their sensitive bird skin and tackled them out of the air. Serena shifted human and the teeth and claws seemed a lot smaller if still painful. They grabbed Teefs and held him out at arm's length even as the grumpy cat tried and failed to scratch their face. "You really should stop trying to murder your rescuers."

Teefs hissed.

Serena believed all animals were highly intelligent in their own way, but they didn't get how or why the pet-stealer could think this orange beast had descended from shifters. He clearly didn't have a large portion of the single brain cell internet memes claimed were shared by all orange cats.

Teefs stopped struggling and hung limp, glaring at them. "I'm going to put you down and turn off the gas, so we can get you and the other animals out of here. Stay close, but don't attack me."

Teefs narrowed his yellow eyes. Serena lowered him carefully and walked over to the gas valve, expecting at any moment that some monster straight out of a horror flick would come out of the water and drag them to their death.

But nothing happened as they inched closer, turned the knob, and watched the wall of flame disappear. Soon after, they heard the chugging engine of Kat's borrowed lobster boat.

This was too easy. Their stomach churned. Surely something was about to go horribly wrong.

Kat walked to the edge of the boat and handed Serena two packs. "As much as I like seeing you naked, you probably should put some clothes on."

Serena put them down as far from the water as they could. Teefs stalked over and sniffed them.

Kat leapt from the boat to the rock, landing with a wince. Serena grabbed and steadied her so she didn't fall in the water, their hand first brushing across one of two pistols holstered at Kat's hips.

They let go and backed away, then put their clothes on. Pistols never seemed very effective at fighting tentacle monsters in movies, but they sure did kill people.

"Any signs of trouble yet?" Kat asked.

Serena buttoned up the sturdy but flexible pants. "No, but that is unnerving to me. I am convinced something with tentacles is going to drag us into the water any minute."

"I don't think those kind of monsters exist outside of movies." Kat's voice was steady, but her hand twitched toward her pistols.

"But you believe in phoenixes." Serena tucked in their shirt. Once the shirt was tucked in, runes glowed to life. "If phoenixes are real, sea monsters might be too."

"I believe in you." Kat put a hand on Serena's shoulder. "But I also want to keep you safe. The runes make the shirt puncture proof against anything. So, if someone shoots at us or a dog bites you, then you'll be okay as long as the runes don't wear out."

"How did you afford this?" Serena thought of the runes that almost gave out on Serena's fire suit. If she could afford this, surely she could've had longer-lasting fire protection.

"I have a friend in SWAT who owed me a favor."

"We should get moving," Serena said before they asked more questions they weren't ready to hear the answer to. They weren't law enforcement's biggest fan, though they did maintain a cordial relationship with the local animal control officer.

Kat shone a flashlight around the cave. "It looks like there is an exit that way."

She and Serena walked along the narrow ledge. Serena supposed that by this point, if they hadn't been attacked by some tentacle monster, they probably weren't going to be, so they relaxed a little. And that was a mistake.

When they came to a door in the wall, they just opened it.

Serena barely managed to push Kat out of the way before a wall of flame roared at them. They held their arms out, trying to shield Kat from as much as they could of the fire. They felt the heat on their arms, but as usual, the flames felt like a warm bath.

"I thought you said you couldn't control fire." Kat's voice sounded far away over the rush of flames in their ear.

"I can't," Serena said, though their arms felt heavy, like they'd been at the gym lifting for an hour.

"Then what do you call that?"

Serena opened their eyes. The flames weren't touching them. Instead, they hovered a few inches away. Sweat dripped down their forehead from the strain of holding back flames being pushed toward them by a mechanism in the wall.

"Get clear," they said, panic cracking their voice. "I can't hold it much longer."

"Just hold on another minute." Kat was next to the door, too close to the flames, taking apart a switch on the wall. She fiddled with it for what felt like the longest thirty seconds of Serena's life and then it went out.

"What did you do?"

"There was a keypad on the door to enter a code. I didn't know the code, but I figured out how to disable it."

"How did you know how to do it?" Serena asked and their eyes wandered back to the two guns holstered at Kat's hip. "And how do you know how to use those?"

"Let's just say firefighting isn't my first career." Drawing a gun, Kat strode forward into a room with a lot of monitors showing a whole bunch of cowering animals. In front of them, sat a man in a swivel chair.

"Turn around with your hands raised," said Kat like she was a cop and not a firefighter.

The man got up slowly, lifting his hands as his body rose. Something about his look screamed politician. Maybe it was the slicked back brown hair or the cold blue eyes. Perhaps it was his angular face or arrogant jawline. Maybe it was the little flag pinned to his button-down shirt.

Serena glanced at the monitors, counting the animals they saw in cages, and noting the door on the other side of the room. Their heart raced. Could they make it to the door while the man was watching Kat? Or should they wait for Kat to do something like handcuff him or zip tie his hands or whatever people did to restrain each other?

"Turn around and stand still," Kat said as she moved toward him, taking one hand off her gun to get something from her pocket.

At that moment, the man turned and tackled her.

Serena thought for sure Kat would shoot him, but instead the gun went flying.

Serena froze as Kat and the man grappled on the floor. Their muscles tensed. Something soft brushed their legs. A pins and needles feeling shot up from their feet.

They had to do something, but they didn't know anything about fighting.

"Stop!" They screamed at the top of their lungs. Their face and the tips of their fingers felt hot.

They didn't stop. Frustration built within Serena. "STOP!"

Heat tingled on top of their head. Their hair burst into flames. Which was definitely a first.

Everyone stopped moving.

Kat was the first to recover. With a beaming smile she said, "I told you that you were a phoenix!"

Serena looked down at themself. They were alight with flame. A phoenix.

The man scrabbled to a file cabinet and stood, brushing dust and fur off his shirt. Kat was on her feet again with her other gun drawn, covering him. "What do you want? To steal my specimens?"

"These are people's pets. Their *family.* You stole them. We're bringing them home."

"Home to a life of enslavement," said the man. "All animals deserve to live up to their true potential. All animals could be weres. We don't know. You don't know! You make assumptions but *I* know what is best for these animals!"

Serena cringed. "I'm not the one keeping them in cages."

Kat stood, looking around the room. "These are *pets.* With my brother, Spot got two big meals a day, lots of treats, and he slept in bed with my brother. He worked with him. He helped him save people. Now you have him a cage, and he looks starved."

"They're shifters, not animals," the man said. "They're slaves to you people. I'm trying to teach them to think again."

"Spot had plenty of opportunity to think and problem solve with my brother, yet he never turned human," said Kat. "And he has been in many situations where having thumbs would've made his life easier."

"But out in the real world, he had a human to help. So he didn't need to shift. I can create situations where they are alone and desperate. Only I have the courage to truly push them. Only I can break them from their servitude on this island, then set them free."

Serena glared into the man's eyes. "Set them free where? They were raised as pets. They can't make it in the wild and they *aren't* weres. Trust me on this. If you care about these animals, you'll let us bring them home." Serena tried to think of what else they could say to persuade this man. They didn't have money to bribe him, and they weren't even sure if that would work. Kat could only threaten him with a gun for so long. At least Serena's hair had settled from "raging inferno" to "dying firecracker."

"Fine." The man sighed, deflating. "You win. Take these animals back. They're more work than they're worth anyway."

Serena was shocked for a moment, then skeptical. There was no way it was that easy. But Kat was putting away her gun, letting him go.

The man started walking toward the door, then dove for Kat's fallen gun. Kat fumbled for her weapon, but the man dove behind a cage with the gun.

Serena looked up at a scratching sound just in time to see Teefs knock a vase off the cabinet and right onto the man's head.

He collapsed, unconscious.

Teefs sat, purring with his chest puffed out.

"You brilliant, evil cat," said Serena while Kat zip tied the man's hands behind his back.

"I'll let you open the door, just in case," Kat said, dragging the pet thief clear of his own potential booby trap.

But when Serena opened this door, there were no flames. Just a cacophony of barks and meows of animals—regular animals—desperate to get out of their cages.

* * *

A week later, Kat and Serena sat at the local brewery, sipping fruity sours that didn't taste nearly as good as the can art looked. Serena licked froth off their lips in what they hoped was a suggestive manner. They'd always been hopeless at flirting.

"Spot and Cap are best friends," said Kat, eyes glued to Serena's lips.

"That's good!" Serena took a slow sip of their beer.

"Cap really helped Spot readjust. He was nervous when he first got home, but seemed to loosen up when he saw Cap being a goof. I'm letting Cap stay with Spot and my brother for a few days." Kat licked ketchup off her finger. "So, if we go back to my apartment later, we'll be all alone."

Serena smiled. "Then we should definitely go back to your place, because mine is overrun with cats and dogs who don't fit in the shelter."

"Have you practiced summoning or controlling fire anymore?" Kat asked as the server brought them the check.

Serena nodded. "I tried, but nothing happened. Maybe it was the strong emotion from when I thought you were going to die. I really like you."

Kat bit her lip. "Well, if heightened emotions are what it takes, I wonder if more positive emotions would work too." She reached out and put a hand on Serena's. "Fear sure did it, but what about...desire?"

"There's only one way to find out," Serena said, hoping their newfound ability didn't cause them to accidentally light, say, Kat's bedroom on fire if things got more enthusiastic.

"My place?" Kat winked.

"Please," Serena said, very much looking forward to the remainder of the afternoon.

Sara is the author of an odd assortment of novels and short stories. Learn more at **www.saracodair.com**. Follow Sara on Twitter and Instagram **@shatteredsmooth** for updates, cats, and dogs.

In the Mantle, An Inhale
N.L. Bates

Sapphic Representation: Lesbian, Ace
Heat Level: Low
Content Warnings: Coarse Language, Violence, Burning, Death

I.

Before time began

From within, a rumbling.

Stone rakes stone, edges grinding in the long, slow shift. Hot air puffs and stutters earthward, lifting itself from under the weight of the world.

II.

Now.

Raelynn arrived too late to stop the explosion.

Movement always felt slow here at the bottom of the Taaldin pit mine, like the sky had pooled into a current she had to swim against. Still, she broke into a run when the shouting started.

The source wasn't hard to find. There was only one large drill still active in Taaldin, and the three (*three*?) diamonds that powered it glowed star-bright, bathing the pit in something like daylight. Raelynn threw up a hand to shield her eyes. Around her, fellow miners grabbed buckets that crackled and sloshed.

Too late to stop the diamond pulse. The world rocked beneath her feet as the resonant power of the gemstones sent flames spitting from the drill. Then there was a great hissing as the water buckets were upended, and an erupting cloud of steam eclipsed the diamond sun.

Raelynn landed hard on one knee, coughing the damp and the heat out of her lungs. Steam blanketed her skin in a soggy embrace.

Blinking away the afterimage of the diamond pulse, Raelynn saw bodies on the floor of the mine. Living ones, she hoped, although some of those nearest the epicentre were lying awfully still. She saw someone wrest the cooling diamonds from the drill's housing. She saw people nursing blistered hands and sprained ankles. And, above the narrow access road that corkscrewed up and out of the mine, she saw movement, small against the distant sky. Their colleagues up at the surface, realizing something had happened. A plume of black smoke clawed its way heavenward.

She had time to wonder, briefly, if her wife was worried.

Voices poured into the silence left by the drill. The site medic, chivying the uninjured: Bring this over here, set up that cot over there.

Yes. That seemed important. Raelynn blinked water from her eyelashes and went to help.

She bandaged burns. She cleaned abrasions. She tried not to overhear the whispered conversations about the three unfortunates who'd been nearest the drill. They'd been trying to cool the diamonds with ice water and gotten lungfuls of hot steam for their troubles.

No one had died yet, but the tone of those whispers was not hopeful.

Eventually she ran out of minor injuries to tend and sat down on an unoccupied cot, meaning to rest only a moment. They would have to redo the dig schedule to compensate for this new delay. Get the injured to the surface. See if the diamonds could be salvaged, the drill repaired...

She must have dozed off, because an influx of voices brought her back to consciousness. It took her a moment to realize what the ruckus was about—the surface crew had sent help.

The mine was alight with chatter, a celebratory overtone masking the bright edges of anxiety and relief. Nearly the entire surface crew had come down, making the floor feel almost fully staffed again. But of the newcomers, Raelynn only had eyes for one. Because the last person to descend to the pit floor was Noelle.

Noelle Harrington: Miner, surveyor, and—though she hated when Raelynn said it—world's foremost expert on the phenomena of diamond resonance and diamond dimming. Raelynn's wife.

Noelle was petite, with wide-set brown eyes that held depths deeper than the Taaldin pit. Her umber skin, darker than Raelynn's sepia tone, was mottled with dirt. Her poker-straight hair had been swept into a sweat-slicked ponytail, and the too-big blouse Raelynn suspected she'd donned in a hurry all but hid the subtle lines of her hips. A black smear traced the worry lines along her forehead.

She was beautiful.

She was also not supposed to be here. The bosses always kept a surveyor with each crew, surface and floor, and there were exactly two surveyors still working the Taaldin mine: Noelle, and Raelynn herself. Raelynn saw her wife once every fortnight, when their entire skeleton crew received assignments for the next rotation. One day out of fourteen. Two, if they were lucky.

Noelle must have fought hard for permission to come down with the rest. The thought lit a pleasant spark in Raelynn's belly.

Noelle had spotted her too. The two of them met in the middle, Noelle wrapping her in a hug and going on tiptoe to brush her lips across Raelynn's cheek. "I'm glad you're alright."

Raelynn buried herself in the scent of Noelle's hair. "There was a pulse," she said unnecessarily.

"Not surprising." Noelle stepped out of the embrace, professional mask sliding into place, and that little spark sputtered a bit. Raelynn didn't want Noelle the professional; she just wanted her wife. "That drill was only rated for seven carats of resonance. The rocks loaded into that thing were closer to twelve."

"Twelve carats?" Raelynn breathed. That was way too much power for a drill that size.

"They were trying to compensate for the dimming, for one thing," Noelle said.

Her tone was so carefully neutral Raelynn almost didn't ask. "And for another thing?"

A pause. "The bosses told them to drill faster."

Dust stung Raelynn's lungs when she inhaled. "Of course they fucking did."

Noelle said nothing.

"We *told* them," Raelynn growled. Noelle had told them, really, passing out painstakingly carbon-copied charts to the small group of elites that represented the mine's owner. Charts that explained that yes, adding more diamonds could temporarily make resonant equipment work faster, but would likely destroy equipment and cause further delays. Because those were costs the Taaldin pit bosses understood.

Or not.

"We warned them. This exact thing."

"Rae." Noelle touched her arm. There were circles under her eyes, and her nails were dark with grime.

Raelynn felt a stab of annoyance on her wife's behalf. Noelle hated the feeling of dirt under her nails.

"This didn't have to happen." The ache in her jaw made her realize her teeth were grinding together. "And they don't care."

"I know," Noelle said, not quite gently.

"I'm sorry." Raelynn made herself take a breath. "It's just—people got hurt today."

Noelle's mask slipped, just for a moment. She looked away.

Raelynn should have said something, then. At least asked who didn't make it.

When she didn't, Noelle filled the silence. "You should get some rest. New assignment starts tomorrow."

Raelynn blinked. They were only nine days into the current rotation. Maybe ten? Too soon for a new assignment, anyway. Maybe the pit bosses had decided to switch things up, with half the surface crew already here. Maybe this was a contingency for the failed drill.

Maybe they'd finally arrived at the same conclusion Raelynn and Noelle had reached months ago: they'd drained Taaldin dry of diamonds. Maybe they were closing the mine, and she and Noelle were out of a job.

They'd be alright, eventually. Raelynn was sure they could find something before the money ran out. Maybe Noelle could finally apply for a job at the mineral museum. They could help the other miners get back on their feet somehow. Keep them out of the tenements. There were always the coal mines.

"...so who knows if they'll listen," Noelle was saying. "But it'll take time to access this new deposit."

"Deposit?" Raelynn echoed.

"The one we found after yesterday's explosion?" Raelynn was paying enough attention now to catch her wife's irritation before Noelle smoothed it from her face. Noelle had never liked repeating herself.

Raelynn felt her own professional mask snap into place. It was easier. "There's no more diamonds here," she reminded Noelle. Not once they were finally done with the current excavation, anyway. "We both signed off on that survey."

"Not in the pit. In the mountain." Noelle gestured to the wreckage of the drill. Behind it, the explosion had charred a recess into the north wall of the mine, where the Taaldin mountain lay.

It made sense. The Taaldin mine was literally a pit, a hole in the ground at the mountain's base, open to the sky. The mountain itself would hold the lion's share of the minerals—the trouble was knowing where to look. Finding a deposit suitable for excavation could take months of dedicated surveying, or else a chance discovery. Like an explosion in just the right place.

"We'll have to tunnel, of course," Noelle said.

Raelynn opened her mouth to say several things at once. What came out, eventually, was, "You think we can find a big enough deposit to make that sort of excavation worthwhile?"

Noelle rewarded her with a quick smile, teeth white against the dark of the pit walls. "I'm *sure* we can."

Realization dawned, and the pleasant little spark that had been flickering in Raelynn's middle threatened to gutter right out. "You're here on assignment. To map out the new diamond deposit."

Noelle nodded.

"I'll get ready to head up." At least a surface rotation would give her a break from the pit, her first in months. But she'd been so sure Noelle was here for her, not for the bosses. That they'd have a chance to be together, just for a little while.

Noelle shook her head. Did she hesitate for a moment? "We're on this one together."

"That's good," Raelynn said, because it was.

This time Noelle definitely hesitated. "I would have asked to come anyway, you know," she said quietly. "After the explosion. To make sure you were alright."

Raelynn swallowed words she didn't know how to shape. "I'm glad you're here," she said instead. It was true, after all. She wanted to be with Noelle, Noelle wanted to be with her, now they both had what they wanted, and nobody had even had to put up a fuss about it.

"You should get some rest," Noelle said again, and gave Raelynn another peck on the cheek. Then she was gone.

"I love you," Raelynn said to no one, and went in search of her cot.

III.

Earlier.

Diamond resonance is a form of influence. Yes, we've learned to use it, but we only know a bit about how it works.

The bosses are looking for an easy rule. They'll listen to me, so long as I can tell them how many diamonds it takes to make a drill that drills by itself.

But that's what I keep trying to explain: there isn't any such rule. Diamond resonance gives us patterns, but it does not give us rules.

This thing is so much bigger than us.

- From the observations of Noelle Harrington

IV.

Now.

Raelynn had done underground mining. So had Noelle, a little. Most of their crew had not. But at least they listened when Raelynn said things like, "No, the ventilation shaft is not optional."

From the swearing Noelle had been doing every time a telegram came in, the pit bosses not so much.

"If they think it can be done faster, they can come down here and show us how," Noelle panted, leaning against the pile of broken rock they'd been clearing from what would become their entrance into the Taaldin itself.

Raelynn grunted, wedging another chunk of rock out of the steadfast arms of the mountain with the end of her pickaxe. "I hope you didn't tell them that."

Improbably, Noelle grinned at her, lips chapped and black with dirt. "Don't worry. I signed my name to it."

Because they weren't going to fire one of their only surveyors, especially not Noelle with her resonance expertise. Raelynn found herself grinning back.

They were doing most of the excavating manually, with mundane pickaxes and a few resonance-powered hand drills not really suited to the task. The dimming had been bad lately, and Raelynn spent as much time fiddling with the drills as actually using them, adjusting the small diamonds that powered them in their casings in an attempt to get the drills to run anywhere near normal capacity.

Nobody suggested adding more diamonds. With two people dead and a third still fighting for survival in an infirmary at the mine's surface, the most recent explosion was fresh in everyone's minds.

They were shoring up the new entryway with a crossbeam they'd made from salvaged wood when a voice called out. "Noelle! New telegram for you!"

Noelle—stretched out on tiptoe to hold the crossbeam steady while Raelynn hammered it into place—growled deep in her throat.

"I got it," said one of the others, a straggly blond with the wispy beginnings of a beard, stepping in to take her place.

"Thanks," Noelle said, and disappeared.

She didn't join the crew again that day, or the day after that. She spent most of her time at the electrostat, muttering to herself and scribbling notes.

"How long does it take to answer a telegram, anyway?" someone grumbled. Raelynn didn't see who.

"Long enough for a nice little holiday," the barely bearded one grumbled back. Jonas, that was his name.

Raelynn made a point of clearing her throat. "I'm sure *my wife* is working just as hard as the rest of us." She hammered at the last dowel, hitting with more force than she'd meant.

Jonas' cheeks flushed. "Didn't mean to imply she weren't," he mumbled, looking away.

"Good." One more strike had the dowel firmly in place.

"It's just." He ducked his head. "I don't understand what she actually does, you know?"

"Resonance stuff," she hedged. In truth, Raelynn didn't fully understand what Noelle did either. Noelle kept trying to explain it to her, but there had always been one more drill that needed fixing, one more form that needed signing, before she was back to the pit floor for another two weeks. "It's important."

Jonas swiped at his eyes with a dirty hand. "Yeah? She going to fix the dimming for us?"

"We're looking into it," Noelle said from behind her, and Raelynn nearly jumped out of her skin. Damn her startle reflex. It was always worse when she was tired.

Jonas' expression turned sheepish; Noelle's was just grim. Raelynn couldn't tell how much she'd overheard. "Two things," Noelle said, and waited until she had everyone's attention.

"Lael didn't make it."

Some of the miners muttered a prayer to the dead. Raelynn allowed herself to join them, because there was nothing else she could do.

Then she took a slow, deliberate breath. "And the other thing?"

A muscle twitched in Noelle's forehead, like she was resisting the urge to frown. "We have to change the dig angle."

The mutters turned to full-throated groans.

"It's actually less digging." Noelle waved a piece of paper at them, creased and smeared with dirt. "We have to take a steeper decline, but this route will bring us right into an existing cave system, which is where we'll find our diamonds."

She sounded calm, assured. It was the tone of voice she used for relaying information that Noelle described in private as "fifty percent bullshit."

"What cave system?" Raelynn asked.

Noelle paused. "Kimberlite pipes."

Kimberlite, the rock that sometimes contained diamonds, came from deep underground, deeper than the floor of the Taaldin pit. It was ejected upwards by eruptions of magma—and the last eruption at Taaldin had been, in Raelynn's own best estimate, hundreds of thousands of years ago.

Which meant that, technically, they were mining an extinct volcano. But mining a volcano sounded dangerous, even a dead volcano, so the crew all just called it a mountain.

"How do we know where these kimberlite pipes actually are?" Kimberlite pipes were largely subterranean. It was part of what made them so hard to find.

Noelle's eyes flicked toward her, and Raelynn realized she'd blurted the question out loud. It was far from the first time Raelynn had questioned some message Noelle had delivered on behalf of the bosses. But never in front of the others, who were suddenly paying far too much attention.

"Resonance data," Noelle replied. Then, pointedly, "Plus, you signed off on the survey."

Which hadn't said a damn thing about any kimberlite pipes. But, it seemed to be good enough for the rest of the crew, who mostly turned back to their work. Noelle grabbed Raelynn's arm and steered her away from the group.

"Are you sure about this?" Raelynn asked as soon as they were out of earshot. "This is going to take weeks as it is. If we start guessing and we're wrong—"

"I know," Noelle snapped, and Raelynn clicked her jaw shut.

Noelle took a breath. "I'm sorry," she said, softer now. "I don't like it either. But the bosses aren't backing down on this one, Rae. They've got data from some fancy new machine they won't even let me touch, and they think there's a diamond jackpot just beneath our feet." She didn't sound convinced.

"Have you slept?" Raelynn asked, after the silence between them had gone on too long.

Noelle's head bobbed. "A little. You?"

"A little."

Noelle went back to the electrostat, and her telegrams. Raelynn re-joined the crew.

When it finally got too dark to keep working, Raelynn dragged herself to bed to find Noelle had pulled their empty cots together. A little ways away, she could hear the whir of the electrostat spitting out another telegram.

She found Noelle slouched over the device, hand hovering over the brass knob that sent a message back to the matching machine at the surface of the pit. Her stare was glassy, and she didn't react when Raelynn came up behind her.

"You should get some sleep," Raelynn said.

"In a minute," Noelle replied in a bleary tone that could have meant agreement, or dismissal.

"It's too late for them to change the dig again." Raelynn hoped. "It can wait."

"Last chance. We'll be down in the tunnels after this." Because the daily trek from the pit floor had stopped making sense. Tomorrow, when they went down to the tunnels it would be with all the equipment and supplies they thought they would need to last them to the end of the dig. But Noelle turned the knob to send the telegram anyway.

"Come to bed," Raelynn said again.

Noelle twitched away from the electrostat only briefly. "Shit, I forgot something. No, you go. I'll come soon."

Raelynn hovered for a little longer, but her vision had begun to swim in a way that suggested it was time to take her own advice. Noelle had still not budged from her position at the electrostat, so Raelynn went to bed alone.

V.

In the last few hundred years...

Lives, candle-brief, sift sediment for treasures, even while the world draws its power inward. Fire, smoke and drill pluck at diamonds spread like blood, pitting scars across earthen skin and bones.

The stones diminish. The world inhales, regardless.

VI.

Now.

Raelynn let the cool of the rock seep into her back, ignoring the uncomfortable something that jutted between her shoulder blades. Her back ached from a week of the nearly constant need to stoop. She squinted down at the headlamp she'd been working on and tried not to let her hands shake.

The dimming had actually started to improve as they went deeper into the mountain, but then came the first earthquake. And the second, and the third. The result of their mining activities, presumably.

It certainly wasn't the mountain. The Taaldin had been dead for a hundred thousand years or more.

After every earthquake, the resonance headlamps would start flickering pathetically, leaving the group bathed in darkness as often as not. The only steady source of light was the safety lamp Raelynn had insisted on bringing along in case of firedamp. So far, the colour of the flame had remained steady, so they were safe from dangerous gases, but it didn't provide much light.

Raelynn worked on the lamps, taking them apart to adjust the wiring. Sometimes, that was enough to get them working again. And it gave her an excuse to stop when Noelle stopped.

Her wife leaned against the wall across from her, swiping a hand across her brow. She made an irritated *moue* when the bangs that had escaped her ponytail stubbornly clung to her forehead. "This is what I get for seven rotations of surface duty in a row," she panted.

"To be fair," Raelynn offered, raising her voice to be heard over the constant percussion of metal against rock, "our last drill got pretty spectacularly busted." The insides of her eyelids felt heavy with grime. Balancing the safety lantern on her knee, she tried again to bend the headlamp's wiring back into place, but the fine metal just slipped through her fingers.

Noelle slanted a glance at her, and Raelynn realized what she'd said. They'd all avoided talking about the drill since Lael died.

But Noelle only said, lightly, "That drill wouldn't have fit down here anyway."

"And the drills we *do* have don't work half the time anyw—ow!" Her fingers twitched involuntarily, and the wire slipped from her grasp, biting into the soft skin under her thumbnail.

Noelle took the safety lantern and held it steady for her. "Now you're just trying to make me feel better."

"I am not!" But there was laughter in her wife's voice, so Raelynn laughed along with her. It felt good to laugh.

"Think I'm good now." Noelle picked up her scaling bar. But when she went to push the angled chisel at the tip between the rocks above her, the bar dropped back to the ground with a clatter. "Shit. I need another minute."

No joking around this time. Raelynn could hear the frustration in her voice. "We're all working too hard." She finally slid the wire into place, and the headlamp flared to life. Noelle was frowning at the fallen scaling bar like it had offended her.

"'Work as hard as a diamond.'" The sardonic quote came from Jonas, the barely bearded blond, inexpertly holding his own scaling bar a couple feet away. "Don't we just."

It was something the pit bosses sometimes spouted at them during shift rotations. The crew had mockingly adopted the slogan, sarcasm aimed firmly at the pit bosses. Usually. But something about the way he said it made her recall the way he'd talked about Noelle taking a "holiday" at the electrostat. From the way Noelle's expression had shifted, she remembered it, too.

Time to redirect the conversation. "You're holding it wrong. You'll have an easier time if you—" And she walked over to demonstrate.

"Why do we have to do all this scaling business, anyway?" he asked, though he allowed Raelynn to adjust his grip.

"To keep the mountain from falling on our heads," Raelynn replied. "You know what to listen for?"

"I got it." His scaling bar *ting*ed as he worked it. "Seems like one more thing slowing us down, is all."

"One *more* thing?" Noelle echoed.

Nearby, someone hit the rock face a little too hard and a particularly obnoxious cloud of dust erupted into the corridor, setting them all to coughing. Raelynn pulled a damp scarf over her face. It wouldn't protect her from stone lung—the best way to do that was to not work in a mine—but it was better than nothing. Noelle followed suit, then uncorked her water canteen and offered it to Jonas.

He took a swig, looking abashed. "Nothing in particular," he muttered. "Just seems like we're having trouble keeping up, is all." But he was looking at Noelle as he said it. Maybe only because he was handing her canteen back to her. Still, Noelle bristled.

"Keep it. I'm getting back to work." Noelle snatched up the scaling bar and marched down the tunnel.

"Noelle," Raelynn said, trailing in her wake. "Hon." Noelle ignored her, jamming the tip of the scaling bar into another crack in the rock face.

Ting. Ting.

Noelle didn't look at her. "Got your scaling bar?" she asked, wrenching the sounding bar out of the rock face and moving down the drift to another spot. "We wouldn't want to slow anyone down, after all."

"He was just venting," Raelynn said, less forcefully than she would have liked. It was hard to be forceful when she was trying to time her words around the angry *ting* of Noelle's scaling bar. "He wasn't complaining about you."

Ting. Ting, ting. "Wasn't he?"

"Noelle—"

"After all." *Ting,* went Noelle's scaling bar. "I'm the one having trouble keeping up."

Ting. Thunck.

The words dried in Raelynn's mouth.

"*Noelle!*"

The rumbling came from all around.

Raelynn lunged forward, almost tripping over the scaling bar she didn't remember dropping. She grabbed Noelle and hauled her backward up the tunnel, just as the ceiling started to crumble.

Someone was yelling. Maybe Noelle. Maybe her.

She yanked Noelle up the corridor, trying to get them both clear. This time, she did stumble, wrenching her knee with a nauseating jolt as her hands hit the ground. A spray of sediment showered down her back, hard enough she was sure she would bruise. She heard Noelle curse.

Another rock clattered to the ground behind her. Then there was nothing.

Raelynn forced herself to her feet anyway, grabbing Noelle's arm with a hand that she only now realized was bleeding. "Up the tunnel. In case there's aftershocks," she heard herself say.

"I *know*," Noelle spat. She was already moving, but when she saw Raelynn limping she threw an arm around Raelynn's waist and propelled them both forward.

The whole group retreated up the tunnel to their last rest spot. Raelynn had gotten the worst of the cave-in, her knee swollen and discoloured. She could put weight on it, but only just. And she'd taken several layers of skin off of the palms of both hands. Noelle had scrapes and bruises, and was seething quietly. At herself, Raelynn knew. Everyone else had cleared out in time.

After Noelle wrapped Raelynn's knee, she sat Raelynn down with a pair of long-handled tweezers and examined her hands with an intensity that felt hotter than the beam of her repaired headlamp. But her movements, as she fished tiny grains of rock out of Raelynn's bloody hands, were gentle.

"I made a mistake," Noelle said.

Mistakes happen. Especially when you've been pushing yourself as hard as we have. That's what Raelynn might have said, if she were thinking clearly. Instead, she mumbled dumbly, "It could have happened to anyone."

It was the kind of white lie she might have told to someone brand new to the pit floor. A comforting fib for someone who didn't know better, just before Raelynn arranged for them to be moved back up to surface duty for a few more rotations. And the set of Noelle's shoulders told Raelynn immediately that the words had been a mistake.

"You don't need to protect my feelings," Noelle said sharply. The tweezers made a tiny *snick* as she removed another grain of rock from Raelynn's left hand. "It was my mistake." And another.

"I can *handle* my own mistakes." Raelynn's participation in the conversation not required, apparently. "Hold still. This one's a bit stuck."

Raelynn tried not to grimace as Noelle carefully plucked the pebble out. "I'm sorry," she said, once the tweezers had *snick*ed again. "I shouldn't have—"

"I should have heard it." Noelle gestured so vehemently that Raelynn flinched. "Instead, I almost got you killed. And I slowed us down again."

"I'm sorry." Raelynn sifted her brain for the words that could fix this. She couldn't find any.

"I'm the one who fucked up. Left hand now." Raelynn held out her left hand, and Noelle drew in a breath and reached for the tweezers again.

VII.

Earlier.

Here's a fun pattern for you: diamond dimming.

All those sudden dips in diamond resonance—they're impacts. Our drills, our demolitions. Earthquakes and landslides too, though at least those are few and far between.

There's a larger pattern, too. The dimming isn't entirely linear, but it is increasing over time. One day—maybe not in our lifetimes, maybe not even in our children's lifetimes, but eventually—diamond resonance is going to fail us.

The bosses insist they've found a solution. Some sort of amazing data point that will fix all our diamond dimming problems. I could help them understand it, but they refuse to share it with the crew. They won't even share it with me.

But I doubt it will. Because that's the thing—you can't fix everything.

- From the observations of Noelle Harrington

VIII.

Now.

After the fifth shift—or maybe it was the sixth—where Noelle was the last one to put down her pickaxe, Raelynn took Noelle's kit from her and cleaned it along with her own.

After the seventh shift, Raelynn almost said something. Something like, *nobody thinks you're not a hard worker,* which was sort of true, now, or *you're pushing yourself too hard.* But then she caught Noelle's eye, and the words crumbled like mine dust on her tongue.

They were up to an earthquake a day, maybe more. It seemed like too many for a geologically dead area. She would have to ask Noelle. When Noelle wasn't so tired.

Near the end of the eighth shift, Noelle raised the pickaxe for another swing, and it bounced impotently off the rock face. Noelle cursed, adjusting her grip for another go.

"Noelle." The words tumbled out of her mouth unplanned. "Take it easy."

Noelle shook her head. "The data says we're almost there. The sooner we find diamonds, the sooner we can get out of these damn tunnels." She hefted the pickaxe again.

"We can't keep running ourselves like this." She hadn't meant to say that either. "It just leads to more mistakes." And mistakes got people killed.

She braced herself for Noelle to get defensive, but Noelle's shoulders sagged. Impulsively, Raelynn wrapped her in a hug.

"You're shivering," Noelle murmured into her shoulder.

However many shifts ago, they'd woken up to standing water in the tunnel. Either they'd drilled into a water table or there had been a really good rainstorm up top. Either way, the moisture came with a chill Raelynn had mostly stopped noticing. "I'm alright."

Noelle gave an exhale that might have been a laugh. "I don't think any of us are alright."

They widened the tunnel just enough to use as a rest spot. It took the last of their blast caps—not the only thing they were running out of. If they didn't find diamonds soon, they'd have to do another dig.

"Home sweet home," Noelle said wryly as they settled into their travel cots, set out in the dirt and the damp.

"At least you're here." Something else Raelynn hadn't meant to say.

Noelle's smile was half-hearted, but it was a smile. "Next time we're together up top, we'll have to take advantage."

"It's pretty dark in here. Who knows what we could get away with," Raelynn joked. But Noelle was already asleep.

The sound of her wife's breathing left her feeling surprisingly bereft. It had been so long since they'd been together. Maybe if she just...

Raelynn slid her hand into her pants.

She circled her clit with her fingers, probing for warmth, for pleasure, really for anything at all. When even that failed to penetrate the grey veil of exhaustion, she eventually followed Noelle into sleep.

The ninth shift started just like all the others, earthquake and all. Noelle was first to her feet after the bones of the earth had stopped rattling around them, and Raelynn knew she'd just keep pushing if Raelynn didn't intervene. She limped after her wife.

Before she could say anything, someone came sloshing up behind them. Jonas.

"Hey." He ducked his head. It was an almost comical gesture considering the near-permanent stoop most of them had acquired down here. "I just wanted to say I'm sorry. For poking fun at you before." He was looking at Noelle.

She considered him a moment. Her face was expressionless in the semi-dark. "I appreciate it."

But Jonas persisted. "I didn't mean anything by it. It's just—everyone's tired."

Raelynn saw the line of her wife's shoulders relax just a fraction. "Don't worry. I get it."

Jonas started to say something else, but then the world started to shudder.

Raelynn thought it was another aftershock, at first. The ground under her feet, or maybe the walls, started to rattle. But then the rattling intensified into something enormous. The tunnels around them were *palpitating,* or maybe that was just Raelynn's heart.

Then, in a ruin of flying rock, it was over.

Raelynn didn't realize she was on the ground at first. Her lip was split. Her knee was screaming. Her hands were covered in fine plaster dust, shards of olivine and mica and other minerals she couldn't identify. Her ears were ringing.

No, someone was crying.

"Raelynn. Raelynn, are you alright?"

Noelle. Noelle was in front of her, helping her up, hands steady but her face pale.

"I think so. You?"

Noelle nodded once, brusque and businesslike, in a way that suggested her composure was on the verge of cracking. "Yes. But." She gestured at the tunnel.

The tunnel was gone.

More accurately, the tunnel was buried. Piles of rock, from pebbles to boulders the size of Raelynn's whole self, had crashed down between them and the exit.

And the rest of the crew, apparently. The only other person still with them was Jonas. Noelle was kneeling beside him now. "It's not serious," she said, brusquely reassuring. "Press down as hard as you can. We'll wrap it after." Blood welled between his fingers. He was the one who'd been crying.

When Raelynn called out to the rest of the crew, no one answered.

"What *was* that?" Jonas stammered. "What do we do now?"

Noelle gestured to the pile of rubble in front of them, to the scar in the tunnel wall where it all must have come from. "We dig our way out." She looked at Raelynn, the question in her expression doing nothing to smooth away the worried lines around her eyes. "Rock burst?"

"Rock burst," Raelynn agreed. For Jonas, she added, "There's a lot of atmospheric pressure even on the pit floor, right? Well, we're even farther down than that. It makes the rock brittle, until sometimes it just...shatters."

Especially when some monkeys started drilling holes in the side of a mountain.

Jonas's eyes were wide. "That could've happened any time?"

"I should've realized it might," Raelynn admitted.

The kid's face went moon-pale. "We have to get out of here." He started to struggle to his feet.

"Not until you get that shoulder bandaged, for starters." He started to protest, but Noelle rolled right over him, in a tone that brooked no argument. "We might have to use your jacket."

Raelynn left them to it and went to investigate the rock fall.

Noelle was right: it looked like something they should be able to clear. Raelynn was spitting dust by the time she properly set to work, hoping she wasn't about to bring the whole mountain down on their heads. Eventually, Noelle and Jonas joined her. They worked the pile for...hours, Raelynn thought. She wasn't sure.

Nobody proposed stopping to rest. If they starved down here, it wouldn't matter if they starved tired. Raelynn's knee throbbed, but then so did the rest of her. Jonas had started making small keening noises under his breath, but he kept up.

"We could juice the drill a bit," he offered at one point, between gasps of pain he was trying to conceal. "I have some extra diamonds."

"Absolutely not," Noelle and Raelynn said together. The aftermath of the last diamond pulse burned bright in Raelynn's mind.

That was the last thing anyone said for a while.

It was Noelle who finally broke the silence, her voice holding more excitement than Raelynn had dared let herself feel. "I think," she said, her eyes fever-bright in the gloom, "we've almost got it."

The angle made obtaining any sort of leverage awkward, but they managed. Raelynn ended up wedged between the boulder and the tunnel wall, tiny pieces of rock crumbling onto her hair from overhead, grasping the handle of her pickaxe in both hands while Noelle counted down.

"On three...two..."

Raelynn planted her feet against the floor and heaved. She felt the strain in her arms and the sudden release of pressure, heard the strangled yell of triumph from Jonas as the boulder started to give way.

Then felt the sensation of air moving past her as the ground fell away beneath her feet.

IX.

Actually, Raelynn was grateful for the rocky shelf that slammed into her sternum. It probably saved her life.

She scrambled reflexively to the top of the ledge, lungs burning. The piece of rock that had just broken her fall was sizeable, a miscellaneous accretion of minerals built up over who knew how many centuries, looking out over a pipe-shaped opening. Peering down, Raelynn thought she could just make out the bottom.

It was hot in here, like standing at the edge of a hot spring, or—the memory came unbidden—like the pit floor, just after the drill overheated.

It might explain why the ground had given way. Heat stress would certainly contribute.

Overhead, she could hear voices arguing. "It's me," she called up to them. She had to try twice to force the air out of her lungs. "I'm alright."

The voices fell silent. Then:

"Rae? You're alright?" Noelle's voice was incredulous as much as relieved.

"I'm alright," she repeated, like a benediction.

"The way's clear," Jonas called. "Can you come up?"

Raelynn looked up, searching for the spot the voices were coming from. It took a minute to spot the telltale flicker of a diamond headlamp.

The rock face was uneven, with lots of little irregularities that someone might use as a handhold in a pinch. But it was also steep, and she'd fallen a good twelve feet or so. She could probably climb it, on a good day.

Today was not an especially good day.

"Do we have any rope?"

"We're looking." Noelle again. "Raelynn. Where *are* you?"

Raelynn took another look around the cylindrical cave. Much of the rock surrounding her had a pocked, coarse-grained surface and a bluish blush, though it was flecked with basalt, olivine, obsidian, other minerals. Even, here and there, the glimmer of raw diamonds.

"I think..." Raelynn swallowed. There was an odd heaviness to the air, making Raelynn wish she hadn't dropped her safety lantern. It would have been nice to know if she should be worried about gases. "I found a kimberlite pipe."

A pause. "I'm coming down."

There was a flurry of indistinct conversation that sounded like Jonas losing an argument, then Noelle came scrambling down the slope.

"You found a kimberlite pipe, alright." Her eyes were sharp with assessment. "You're okay?"

"Think so." Raelynn cleared her throat, which was starting to sting. "Still no massive deposit of diamonds, though."

Noelle flicked her gaze to the bottom of the pipe, just visible beneath them. "Maybe not here."

There were more indistinct noises from above, then Jonas appeared. He'd managed to unearth a coil of rope from somewhere after all. Still, the stubborn kid climbed down the rock face to join them.

"You could have just tossed it down," Noelle said, wiping a hand across her forehead. Her face was shiny with sweat.

"You said you found something," he replied. Sweat beaded across his upper lip. He coughed into his hand. "I deserve to see it too."

Raelynn and Noelle traded a glance.

"Suit yourself," Noelle said.

The rope got them close to the bottom. Once she blinked the sweat from her eyes, Raelynn could see the pipe round out beneath them, plunging down to a narrow opening like the stem of a champagne glass. It had an odd orange tinge that made it easy to see, even in the dim.

Jonas cleared his throat. "Should it be glowing?"

Raelynn heard Noelle suck in a breath.

Before Raelynn could object, Noelle let go of the rope and dropped to the bottom of the pipe. Then, she took the drill out of her pack, flicked it on, and jammed it into the rock near the champagne stem.

Raelynn dropped down as well as the rock started to fracture under Noelle's feet, followed by Jonas. The orange glow became more and more apparent as the three of them hammered away.

The stem of the pipe turned out to be relatively short, affording them an excellent view as the rock crumbled under their blows. Raelynn choked on a gasp as another chunk fell away, revealing the vast orange pool beneath them.

A magma chamber.

The surface of the magma itself was some distance beneath the pipe they were standing in. Raelynn could see the chamber walls, studded with cooling kimberlite, and yes, the gleam of raw gemstones. Mineral debris—some of which was still surprisingly solid—floated gently across a bright orange surface. Raelynn gaped down at the lake of magma, tucked away like a secret in the heart of this ancient, very obviously *active* volcano.

The sound of Noelle swearing finally snapped Raelynn out of her stupor. "*This* is the deposit we were sent here to find?"

"I think so," Noelle replied, her voice unusually small.

Raelynn cleared her throat. There was an astringent tang to the air, one that stung her eyes and the back of her throat. Jonas was coughing again. Raelynn pulled her neck scarf over her face and gestured for Jonas to do the same.

"They knew," Noelle said, her voice still soft. "Rae. The bosses *knew*."

Jonas coughed again. "We should get out of here."

As if to prove his point, the mountain—the *volcano*—started up a slow rumble. Somewhere, there was the rattling of rock. Another earthquake? Another rock burst?

Neither, Raelynn realized, as the magma below them began to bubble and sputter.

An eruption.

X.

One hundred thousand years from...

Stone roots quiver under the pressure of eons. Quiver, and then bow. Gemstones bubble in smoldering anguish, on the brink of becoming.

XI.

Now.

For a moment there was nothing she could do but stare. Then Noelle grabbed her arm, and they were moving.

She boosted Noelle up to the dangling rope. Noelle let go with one hand just long enough to help Raelynn up, and Raelynn offered a hand to Jonas in turn.

Then they climbed. Up, and up, while her muscles screamed in protest and her hands cramped around the rope. At least the pocked walls made it easy to find purchase, although at one point her foot slipped on a shard of obsidian embedded in the rock, and her knee wrenched in a painful reminder of the cave-in from a lifetime ago. Her ribs protested a much fresher injury.

Noelle was just ahead of her, Jonas falling behind. She couldn't stop to offer him a hand, not with the way her own arms were trembling. She heard him coughing somewhere below her. Her stomach roiled with the acrid tang of magma.

Somewhere partly up the interminable climb, the coughing stopped.

Above her, Noelle topped the ledge. She paused on the last slope, hands outstretched to help Raelynn up, face taking on a sallow glow in the brightening orange light. "Hurry!" she cried.

Raelynn crested the ledge and turned, hauling on the rope to bring Jonas up.

There was no resistance.

"Jonas!" she yelled.

Her words were swallowed by the magma, already filling the bottom of the kimberlite pipe.

Raelynn turned to Noelle and saw her stricken expression mirrored on her wife's face. But Noelle only shouted, "We have to go!" and tugged Raelynn's arm again.

Because magma would be coming this way.

They scrabbled and shouldered and squeezed their way up the last slope, through the opening they'd carved through the rock burst. Then they ran.

They ran for…Raelynn wasn't sure. Until they couldn't anymore. Far enough that the encroaching magma wouldn't fill the tunnel they were standing in and reward them both with a fiery, drowning death. Raelynn hoped.

She tried not to think about Jonas.

Noelle collapsed against the rock wall, gasping for breath. Raelynn joined her. It was hard to say which part of her body burned most.

"Raelynn," Noelle breathed after a few minutes. Or maybe a few seconds, Raelynn wasn't sure. "There's an entire damn magma chamber down there."

"Yeah."

"They had us dig a mine into an active fucking *volcano.*"

"Yeah."

Noelle took a shuddering breath. "This volcano is supposed to be extinct."

"Now that we know it isn't"—Raelynn took a shuddering breath of her own—"what are the chances they tell us we have to mine the thing anyway?"

Their eyes met across the tunnel. For the first time in—Raelynn wasn't sure how long—she knew exactly what her wife was thinking.

The drill overheating. The weeks in the tunnels, months on the pit floor. The rock burst. Lael and Jonas.

Raelynn said, "We can't let that happen."

Noelle said, "I have an idea."

Raelynn took a step toward her, then hesitated on the brink of an embrace. They should be running, or...whatever it was Noelle was planning. There would a better time. Like when the volcano they were standing in wasn't actively trying to kill them.

But that was the problem, wasn't it? There was always a better time.

Noelle closed the distance between them and threw her arms around Raelynn's neck.

Even the volcano that engulfed them stopped mattering when they finally came together.

Noelle's lips were hard and urgent against hers. Raelynn returned the urgency, the salt of Noelle's mouth on her lips, hand drifting down to Noelle's hip. Soaking in the smoldering heat of her.

Noelle broke away from the kiss and ran a hand down Raelynn's cheek. "I have an idea," she murmured again, lips brushing whisper-light against Raelynn's ear.

It almost didn't matter what her idea was. Just then, Raelynn would have walked right back into the magma chamber if Noelle had said it was a good idea. But the conspiratorial gleam was back in Noelle's eye, the one that was just for the two of them, and *that* mattered. It mattered so very much.

So Raelynn asked, "What's your idea?"

Noelle grinned. "We're going to have to break a few rules."

XII.

Earlier.

I can't convince them to call off this ridiculous dig.

They still won't share whatever magic data point that's convinced them there's a massive deposit just beneath us. I'd think they were having me on if this weren't such an expensive prank.

Keep your fucking secrets, then. I don't think the diamonds will care.

- from the observations of Noelle Harrington

XIII.

Now.

They didn't waste time hunting for exactly the right spot. There was still a volcano bubbling under their feet, after all, and they were geologists, not engineers. So, they defaulted to the universal standard of trades everywhere: a best guess.

The acrid tang of magma still hung heavy in the air, but nothing had trickled up after them. A slow eruption, then, not the kind that brought kimberlite deposits to the surface of the world. They'd have been crisped in less than seconds, otherwise.

This was an inhale, maybe. A warm-up act.

Noelle handed over the drill, and Raelynn stuffed the housing of its power supply with as many diamonds as she could physically pack in. Seventeen carats of resonance in a three-carat drill. "Last chance to change our minds."

The white of Noelle's teeth sparkled like diamonds when she grinned. "Let's do it."

The drill roared mightily when Raelynn powered it on. She shoved the bit into a fault in the rock face, where she and Noelle figured it would do a good bit of damage.

Then, they ran.

They ran as if they were facing down another river of magma. Putting as much distance as possible between themselves and the thing they'd just left behind.

Even with seventeen carats, it would take a bit for the drill to overheat. This time, though, there would be no one standing by with buckets of ice to cool it down. The result should be spectacular, collapsing the tunnel at the point of origin, closing off access to the magma chamber. Without collapsing the whole damn volcano and crushing Raelynn, Noelle, and everyone still up in the pit.

Hopefully.

Still, they ran.

There was no mistaking the explosion when it happened. The shaking started first, rattling Raelynn's ribs in her chest. Then the sound caught up, a peal of thunder that felt like it started *inside* her and clawed its way out.

Raelynn wasn't sure what was vertigo and what was real as the world shuddered around her. At some point Raelynn grabbed Noelle and hauled her to her feet, just before she did a faceplant on the stone floor. At some point Noelle pushed Raelynn out from under a piece of falling rock the size of Raelynn's head.

And then, at some point, it was over.

The ground settled into a series of gentle aftershocks. Raelynn looked at her wife. Noelle's face was a mirror: terrified exhilaration and just a little bit of awe.

"I think we did it," Raelynn said after a moment. Whispered it, really, as if their voices might somehow disturb the site around them more than what they'd just done.

"I think we did," Noelle spoke in the same hushed tones.

Raelynn cleared her throat. "Should we get out of here before this volcano decides to wake all the way up?"

Noelle looked around her as if noticing their surroundings for the first time. Then she offered Raelynn a hand. "Yes. Let's."

XIV.
One hundred thousand years from now

Built over millennia, appalling ordnance discharges in a blink. Magma rushes upward, bearing heat and stone, healing as it destroys. Old scars are remade, and diamonds, humming resonance, spread like autumn rain.

XV.
Now.

They found a few of the others higher up in the tunnels. Not everyone had died in the rock burst.

Together, they made their way to the surface. Raelynn had never been so glad to see the sky, even from the bottom of a pit mine.

She and Noelle set about evacuating the mine. Neither of them technically had the authority to do that, but the earthquake they had created had been felt even on the pit floor. It convinced the crew that packing up was a good idea, regardless of what the bosses thought. Judicious use of the words "active," "volcano," and "eruption" got them the rest of the way there. Noelle leaned a little hard on the phrase "could blow at any moment" for Raelynn's personal taste, but it certainly seemed to do the trick.

The fact so few of them had returned from their little journey into the mountain—into the *volcano*—probably also had something to do with it.

The bosses fumed impotently when they found out. By the time the order formally came to shutter the mine, most of the workers had already left.

Raelynn walked through the quarters she and Noelle had shared, and found she wouldn't miss them.

She did find Noelle, packing away a few final things. "All ready to go," she remarked when Raelynn walked up.

"Do we know where we're going?" Raelynn asked.

Noelle hesitated. "I was thinking I could apply at the museum."

"Makes sense," Raelynn agreed. "I'll find...something. Somewhere other than a mine."

Noelle huffed a laugh. "Oh, god, anywhere but."

"We'll figure something out," Raelynn said.

"We will," Noelle agreed. Another hesitation, then, very unlike her. "But maybe...some time off first?" And then, before Raelynn could reply, "Together?"

Raelynn thought she might laugh, until she realized she was blinking away tears. "That sounds amazing," she said, and meant it.

Noelle looked up at her with those enormous brown eyes. Then, she nodded.

Raelynn reached for her.

This kiss wasn't like the one they'd shared in the volcano, hot and hard and urgent. This one was slow, and careful, and sent long tendrils of warmth humming into parts of herself Raelynn had barely realized were dormant.

"I love you," Noelle murmured into her shoulder when they finally broke apart.

"I love you too," Raelynn murmured back. She folded herself into Noelle's embrace and let her wife's heat draw her in.

XVI. / I.
One hundred thousand years from now / before time began

From within, there is a rumbling. Hot air puffs and stutters earthward, lifting itself from under the weight of the world...

"In the Mantle, An Inhale" is a story by Canadian author N. L. Bates. When she's not dreaming of diamonds, she writes and performs music as her alter ego Natalie Lynn. To keep up with her work, visit her at www.nlbates.com or www.natalielynnmusic.com

Flame Retardant

Heather Tracy

Sapphic Representation: Lesbian
Heat Level: Low
Content Warnings: Burning building, Extreme cold

A descendant of Hestia shouldn't have this much trouble keeping her clothes on. It's bad enough that I keep inadvertently setting fire to the furniture in my apartment without wanting to, but to keep burning my clothes clean off is really starting to get on my nerves.

When my dads told me I was likely to get some kind of superpowers when I turned thirty—being a descendant of Hestia, Greek goddess of the Hearth—I'd have liked something like invisibility or flight. Nope. All the women in our line get some kind of fire power. Not that every Greek god or goddess's powers are only passed down to certain genders, but as Hestia never married, her powers are only passed down to the females in her line. My great-grandmother could start fires by snapping her fingers—something that probably came in handy during WWII. My grandmother's body would vibrate such that she was able to heat an entire building. My aunt can shoot lasers from her eyes like Superman, and she has to wear special glasses so she doesn't burn the world down.

So, what fire power did I get? Gods, all of them. The whole kit and kaboodle. My whole body bursts into flames at a moment's notice and I can shoot fire from my hands. I also run hot all the time, so I live in tank tops and shorts, even in the winter. From what I can tell, I feel like I'm having a constant hot flash, and my skin stays hot enough to burn, but I don't perspire unless I'm in full flame-mode. I do have to drink about a gallon of water per day, though, to keep myself hydrated. I've had the powers for six months now and have gotten more control over them, but I just can't figure out how to keep my clothes on when I go full Firegirl...Flame Woman...ugh. I haven't come up with a good superhero name yet.

I could let the media come up with my name. Some superheroes do. The boring, uncreative ones. The rest of us prefer to come up with our own names. Ever since my aunt, Mimi, was christened as "Hot Pants"—mostly because of her suit—the women in my family have always chosen our own names and given them to reporters.

That's why I'm heading to Judy's Fabrics today; to see if I can find some kind of fabric that will stand up to the flames. Without a flame-retardant suit, I'll be left standing stark naked in the streets when I use my powers. I'm a pretty decent seamstress and I know I can make myself a nice suit to wear under regular clothes. I only need to know what fabric to use.

When I get in the store, I go straight to the cutting counter. I can sew, but I don't know fabric well. I take a number—thankfully the line is short today—and wait behind a woman with at least ten bolts of quilt fabric to be cut. After a seemingly interminable amount of time, during which I survey the wide variety of scissors and cutting boards, my number is called. I approach the counter and see the employee is putting the last of the quilt fabrics on the returns cart. Her short teal hair is styled in an asymmetric bob, and I'm sure her baggy hoodie is covering up a lusciously curvy figure considering the way her leggings are hugging her muscled thighs and backside. *No, Tana. You're here to pick up fabric, not girls.*

"What can I help you with today?" the employee, whose nametag reads "Carrie," asks when she turns around. She smiles pleasantly and has her scissors at the ready.

I shake my head slightly because she's even more lovely than I'd thought seeing her from behind. She's got these large, blue eyes—akin to a Disney princess—and her bow shaped lips look supremely kissable. I really don't need this distraction. I'm here on a very important mission.

"Hi. I...um...would like some assistance picking out some fabric," I manage.

"Sure, I would be happy to help. What project are you working on?" she asks, setting down her scissors and walking around the counter.

I knew I was going to have to answer this question, and I'd rehearsed how I was going to answer it, but now that

I'm standing here catching the faint scent of vanilla from her perfume or shampoo, all those words fly right out of my brain. "I'm...uh...like this superhero." That's a *great* start. Her eyes widen, but she doesn't interrupt. "Yeah, and my power is fire, so I'm having a terrible time with keeping clothes on when I...you know..."

I don't know what I was expecting her response to be, but I swear she's blushing and her eyes get even wider. I'd expect no less. I mean, superheroes aren't completely unheard of, but it's not like we're everywhere either. Really, Judy's should be cashing in on us superheroes. I can see the tagline in their email ad now: "Find the fabric for *your* powers here. All superhero fabric 20% off! Some exclusions apply."

Carrie clears her throat and says, "You're probably looking for something flame retardant then. What kind of fabrics have you tried?"

I start ticking them off on my fingers. "Cotton, which just went up like tissue paper. Wool took a little longer to burn, but was still gone by the time I cooled off. Spandex melted, thankfully it didn't adhere to my skin. I looked at a couple that are treated, but I haven't tried them yet. I've basically been wearing my regular clothes and just sacrificing them to the cause."

"I see." She looks up to the ceiling for a moment then back at me before she speaks again. "I think we should look at some of the flame-retardant utility fabrics, and work from there. Come with me."

She leads me to the back of the store where they have all the home décor and outdoor fabrics, which is a section that I very rarely think about when I'm in here because I don't do any home decorating and I don't have any outdoor space at my apartment. It's hard to have lots of pillows and curtains around when you're a walking lighter. My furniture is either metal or coated very heavily in fireproofing paint. We turn toward the clearance section when I see the utility fabrics she mentioned. There's a little tag that mentions "flame retardant."

"Let's see what we have here," Carrie says as she starts pulling down the enormous rolls of fabric down with ease. *I bet she's got some amazing arm muscles going on under that hoodie.* I could feel heat start to rise up from my belly. *Knock it off, Tana!*

"This one might work for boots or a belt or something." She holds out a roll of heavy-duty chocolate brown fabric. I reach out to touch it, and it feels like stiff leather or vinyl. Stiff and not going to work at all for a suit. But, she's right, it might work for some nice boots.

"Boots would be cool," I reply.

She nods and sets that roll to the side. She pulls another roll forward, this one an orange woven fabric that looks like it's a little less rigid than the last one. "This is a new flame-retardant duck cloth. It still might be a little heavy for what you're looking for, but see what you think." She unrolls it a little and holds it out to me.

I rub the fabric between my fingers and she's right, it's still too inflexible and thick for a whole suit. "Not quite right, but we're getting closer."

Carrie shows me a few more fabrics in this section, but they're all more suited to making tents or cushions for outdoor furniture, not something to wear. I'm about to lose all hope and go home in defeat to start scouring the internet again, when she holds one finger triumphantly up in the air.

"Wait a minute!" A huge grin breaks out on her face. "I completely forgot we just got in this totally new fabric that would be perfect for your suit. We haven't even put it on the shelves yet. If you promise not to touch anything else, I'll take you to the storeroom to show it to you."

"I promise," I say, meaning it. I try very hard not to touch things as a general rule these days.

Carrie grabs my hand to lead me back to the storeroom. "Ow!" she exclaims, dropping it like a hot potato—which, it kind of is.

"Oh my gods! I'm so sorry. Are you okay?"

She shakes her hand a bit, then looks at it and even I can see it's red, but she doesn't have any actual burns. "It's fine. I just wasn't expecting that is all."

"I feel terrible. I'm usually able to warn people before they touch me. Really, I should just wear gloves all the time. I'm so sorry." I didn't want to scare her off with my powers. Especially because holding her hand for even those couple seconds set off fireworks in my core.

"It's okay, really. It feels better now." We look back at her hand and the color is already returning to normal, which is a little unusual because most of the time people will at least get small blisters from my touch. But, maybe we didn't touch for as long. "That must be hard for you, not being able to have human contact."

I see such genuine sympathy in her eyes that I almost start to cry. That has been one of the hardest things about this whole superhero thing. People think it's so amazing to have powers, but they don't think about how isolating it is—literally. Forget having a relationship. "It has been hard. I have to put on long sleeves and gloves to hug my dads."

"That's awful. I can't even imagine what that's like, um...sorry, I didn't catch your name."

"Tana. Tana Loukas."

"Tana Loukas, I'm Carrie Pendleton. It's nice to meet you." She starts to put her hand out to shake, but I put mine out for a fist bump, as I've found those are more easily tolerated. She bumps my fist with hers and gestures for me to follow her. "C'mon. Let's go to the back."

I don't know what I was expecting from the back room at Judy's Fabrics, but probably something akin to a fabric and craft wonderland—neatly stacked shelves of well-organized fabrics in rainbow color order, elegant cubbies with skeins and skeins of yarn, etc. That is absolutely not what I find.

It is, in a word, chaos. Disheveled boxes of every shape and size stacked haphazardly on the floor. There is fabric stacked on shelves, along with other craft items, but it is by no means organized. There's basically a small trail to walk through—probably for OSHA standards—an employee break room in the corner, an office and that's about it. It's a flame-ridden superhero's worst nightmare!

I must have been standing there dumbfounded, because Carrie walks back to get me. "That fabric is over here."

I follow her carefully through the maze of boxes and shelving—careful not to touch anything—until she turns to a particular stack of boxes, spreads her arms wide and says, "Ta-da! These boxes are full of the new Provelon fabric. It's supposed to be fireproof, waterproof, rip proof...basically everything proof. I haven't tried it myself, but you're welcome to look at the brochure."

She hands me a brochure from the manufacturer—A Kut Above Fabrics LLC—where they tout that it's the "*Perfect fabric for all your superhero needs.*" Apparently, they've decided to cash in on the superheroes of the world, and I'm sure they'll make a bundle. They show photos of it being lit on fire, submerged in water and stabbed with a knife, but it resists all types of damage. Of course, those photos could be fabricated, but it's definitely worth a shot. I'm surprised I haven't heard of it before now, but Carrie did say it was brand new.

"Can I see it?" I ask.

She nods and pulls a box cutter out from her forest green apron to slice open the box nearest us, labeled: Dragon's Breath (orange). "I have been dying to get into one of these boxes to see what this stuff feels like, so I'm really glad you came in. Plus, the color names are fantastic!"

I look at the other color names on the back of the brochure, and she's right, they do have some fun names.

Aside from Dragon's Breath, they have Pomegranate Seed (red), Solar Flare (yellow), Squid Ink (black), and Peacock Kiss (blue).

When she opens the box, there's plastic covering the fabric, but she tears this away easily and pulls out one of the bolts. It's shimmery red-orange fabric that has what looks like raised dots all over it. Carrie holds the bolt out for me, and I take a deep breath to make sure I'm feeling cool and calm before I take it. When I do, I feel the silkiness and that those bumps are just an illusion on the fabric—it's as smooth as satin. I can tell that it's sturdy, but it is not as stiff as the other fabrics we looked at, so I could definitely make a suit out of this. Whether it will stand up to my rigorous demands remains to be seen.

"How much would you like and in what colors?" Carrie asks, obviously sensing I'm in love with this fabric.

"I'll take everything you have in Dragon's Breath, Pomegranate Seed and Solar Flare," I reply.

* * *

After several days of sewing, I have what looks like an actual superhero suit. Since my body stays hot all the time, I steered clear of tights or leggings and went with mid-length biker shorts instead—because I'm not about to wear what amounts to panties or a leotard out in public either. For the top, I made a wide strap, fitted tank top that is plenty long enough to tuck into the shorts without gapping. I went with Dragon's Breath for the base color, with a couple Pomegranate Seed stripes on the sides of the shorts, and more stripes up the sides of the tank top that merge up into the straps. I plan to use the Solar Flare fabric for my emblem, if I can ever come up with a name. Firestorm, no...that's taken. Ugh.

Before I go out to test the new suit, I need to pick up one thing I forgot at Judy's. In my haste to purchase all the Provelon, I completely forgot to get any of that heavy-duty fabric for making myself some fabulous boots. So, I throw on another tank top and shorts over the suit and head for the store, secretly hoping Carrie is working today so I can show it off.

However, on the way, I'm stopped at a traffic light when I see people start streaming out of a vaguely familiar-looking office building. Some of them are frantically getting into their cars and trying to drive away—creating a bottleneck in the process—others are just running like mad down the sidewalk. I look at the building, and nothing immediately jumps out at me as being amiss, but then I feel it. A vibration rumbles beneath my car right before I hear it.

BOOM!

Just what I need. *Awww, c'mon. I haven't even made my boots yet!*

I pull my car up onto the sidewalk and leap out. I pull off my outer layer of clothing since I have my new suit on underneath. I scrape my long, dark hair into a quick ponytail to get it out of my face. As I approach the building, I see what looks like glass shards shooting up out of the roof. Definitely not something you see every day, and people are alternately screaming and pointing at the glass shards.

That's not glass, that's ice!

I know exactly who's behind this: Blaine Van Houten aka Winter Storm.

Every superhero has to have an archnemesis, and Blaine is mine. He's also a descendant of a Greek god—Boreas, god of the cold North Wind and the Bringer of Winter—but, mostly, he's just a douchey guy who won't take no for an answer. I mean, if our college had had a lacrosse team, he'd have been on it.

We met in history class my senior year, and Blaine sat next to me the entire semester. He was nice enough at first, but when we were working on a group project, he decided to mansplain the entire thing to me like I was a five-year-old. Then, he kept pestering me to go out on a date with him even after I told him I was a lesbian. I kindly explained that I wasn't interested, but he would not let it go. I've run into him a lot over the years, and every time I see him, he does everything he can to get me to go on a date with him. The word "no" is not in his vocabulary.

I take a deep breath as I enter the building, steeling myself for the fight to come. *At least I get to test out the new suit.* I feel my body temperature rise as I walk toward the ice shards. I hope against hope that the Provelon works.

Blaine stands across the two-story lobby with his arms up in a fighting stance, right behind one of his frozen creations. His black and blue pinstripe suit is sleek and tailored to perfection. He's lucky his powers allow him to wear whatever he wants.

I see him pouring his focus into creating another giant shard, so he doesn't notice me coming up beside him. Sirens wail in the distance.

"Blaine, this is getting a little old, don't ya think?" I ask, barely containing my molten energy.

He turns to face me, defiance in his eyes. "Tana. New suit? Hope this one doesn't burn off like the others," he chuckles. "Or, maybe I do." He lifts his eyebrows suggestively.

I roll my eyes. "Give it a rest."

"Blah, blah, blah." He mimes talking with his hand. Tiny ice crystals fall from his fingers. "You keep saying you're a lesbian, but I've never seen you with a woman, a man, or anyone for that matter. You're just playing games with me because you know I love the chase. I mean, how could anyone not want to be with me?"

I know there's no way to reason with him; he's the very definition of toxic masculinity. So, I set about trying to diffuse the icy situation at hand. I remove my gloves and attempt to direct a little bit of fire from my right hand at the nearest ice shard. I'm starting to get a handle on my powers to where I can control them sometimes, but Blaine standing there all cocky has me flustered, and the heat rises through my entire body. When it reaches my hand, flames gush out in a stream that send me reeling backward as if I've fired a rifle. Not that I've ever fired a gun, but I can imagine the kickback.

The blaze melts the shard I was aiming for, but it also catches the nearest wall on fire. Thankfully, the sprinklers come on and put it out quickly. Blaine laughs behind me, but I press on, moving closer to the ice so I can place my hands directly on it instead. This works much better, if more slowly.

"You do know they'll melt on their own, right?" Blaine asks, leaning against a nearby column, inspecting his frost-tipped fingers. "I don't know why you bother."

"Because if this much ice melts on its own, the building will flood. If I heat it up, the water will evaporate faster. I'm trying to minimize the damage. You took science in elementary school, didn't you?" As I'm melting the next pillar of ice, I notice a sign by the elevator that mentions Data Structures Inc. Then I realize why he chose this particular office building to destroy: we worked here together briefly five years ago. "Did you hate working here that much that you had to destroy the building?"

"Took you long enough," he says, smirking. "I didn't mind the work too much, but it was the place where you told me you would never date me if we were the last two people on earth, so I don't really have fond memories. Plus, I thought it would get your attention."

I shake my head. "Well, I think you've officially run out of places to ruin in which we have a history." He'd already hit the café where we ran into each other once, the gym we both belonged to—he joined after me and I quit shortly thereafter—and the history building at our college, where we first met.

"You could just go out with me and save all this fuss."

"Leave me alone."

Just then, we hear the police pull up outside. Blaine hunts nervously for the best exit. The police love working with superheroes like me who are trying to do good with their powers, but they are constantly trying to catch the villains like Blaine who are only out for destruction. They keep beefing up their armor and tech so they can catch villains and bring them to justice. And none of the superheroes or villains are invulnerable, that we know of.

"I'm going to leave the police for you to deal with. But you'll see me again. You can count on that, Tana." He creates an ice slide out the back of the building and disappears from view.

With Blaine finally gone, I finish melting all the ice shards and the building returns to normal, albeit with new skylights in the roof. I go outside and speak to the authorities to explain what's happened.

When I get back to my car, I look down and see that my new suit has remained mostly intact, save for a few spots where the seams have opened up. It's probably due to the thread not being as durable as the Provelon. At least I didn't leave the scene naked again! Although I hate seeing—and battling—Blaine, I am glad I got to do a trial run with the prototype suit. I now know that I need to put some reinforcing fabric over, and maybe under, the seams, with heavier-duty thread. *I could add more stripes and make the reinforcement decorative!* I think. I head back home to start sewing, but I definitely want to go tell Carrie the good news about the suit.

* * *

"You're back," Carrie says, smiling, when I show up at Judy's the next day. I find her crouched on the floor restocking yarn. "How did the Provelon work for you?"

"It worked like a charm," I reply. Then I explain about the seams opening up and the reinforcing I did.

"That's great," she says, pushing the hair back from her face. From my vantage point above her, I see a couple strands of silver glinting in the fluorescent light. Must just be my imagination. "I'm glad you thought to reinforce the seams with the heavier thread. Hopefully that will work much better for you. But, I'm really glad the Provelon held up."

"Would you like to see what I made?" I ask.

Her eyes light up. "Yes, absolutely!" She checks her watch, which is this really intricate steampunk fob pinned to her apron. "I have my lunch break in fifteen minutes. Can you stick around?"

For that beautiful face, of course. "Sure," I manage. "I was going to pick up a couple things I forgot the other day anyway."

"Great. Meet me by the stockroom door in fifteen and you can show me the suit." She shoots me another 1,000-watt smile and my face heats up, but it's not Hestia's powers this time. If I didn't know better, I'd swear I'm falling for her.

While I'm waiting, I grab that heavy-duty fabric for my boots, some stainless-steel buttons, and some more heavy-duty thread, and head to the cutting counter. Several of the old ladies give me sidelong glances—probably because I'm wearing a tank top, biker shorts and elbow-length gloves on the coolest day of autumn so far—but I do my best to ignore them. I check my phone and see lots of news articles about the incident with Blaine yesterday. The media are very clear on who Winter Storm is, but they have no idea what to call me. Some refer to me as Hestia's descendant, some say Fire-Girl, and others just call me Flame, for lack of anything better. *I have got to come up with a superhero name, and soon!*

I get my fabric cut, then stand in the never-ending line at the checkout. But, by some miracle, I'm done with everything in fifteen minutes. When I head back to the stockroom door, I see Carrie already waiting.

"C'mon," she says, grabbing my gloved hand and pulling me through the door. "I'm dying to see your Provelon suit!"

She leads me toward the breakroom but makes a sharp turn away from it. "I thought we were going to the breakroom," I say, not really caring that much as long as she keeps holding my hand.

"I have a better spot back here that's a little more private." She winks, and my cheeks flush more than normal. *Does she feel this too?* I take a deep breath to calm myself down because I definitely don't want to lose my cool around all these boxes, fabrics, and materials.

We finally get to the Provelon spot. The boxes are just how we left them, and I think vaguely about buying even more now that I know it works well. Carrie flops down on top of one of the boxes, her green apron spread across her lap. She rests back on her elbows and looks at me expectantly. "Alright, let me see this suit."

I stand in front of her and get suddenly nervous with the fact that I'm basically going to be stripping my clothes off in front of her—even though I have another complete outfit on underneath. Up until a few days ago, I was appearing naked in front of strangers—albeit by accident— on a semi-regular basis. This time feels different, though, because this time I want to.

Sexy striptease music starts running through my mind, and I shake my head to jettison that. To not make this any more awkward, I decide to turn around and remove my top layer of clothing as quickly as possible. I continue taking deep breaths while doing so, really glad it's cold in the building so I'm at less risk of overheating.

When I'm finished, I turn back to Carrie and strike what I hope is a commanding, superhero-esque pose—hands on hips, chest out, legs apart. "Voilà!" I say, almost as nervous as if I was standing there naked in front of her.

She looks me up and down for a moment, pondering. "I absolutely love it." She gets up from her seat and walks around me to get a better look. "I mean, top marks for craftsmanship. This stitching is excellent. And, I love the way you have the stripes going up the sides. Really shows off your figure."

Her gaze traces my entire body. I take another deep breath as she comes to stand right in front of me. There are mere inches between us, and I'm torn between wanting desperately to crush her body to mine and not wanting to burn her.

"Hi," I whisper.

"Hi," she whispers in kind. "You're so warm."

"Heh. Yeah. Comes with the territory." I shrug.

"Well, I feel like I'm always cold, especially lately." She gestures at her hoodie. "Maybe I need someone warm in my life. Someone who knows her way around a sewing machine and has a keen fashion sense for superhero suits. Know anyone like that?"

I haven't felt this kind of attraction for someone in a really long time. I feel like we're magnets being drawn together, fabric dealer and seamstress, superhero and Critical Love Interest. "I know someone who might fit that description. But I don't want to burn you."

"I'll take my chances," she says as she steps closer and gently presses her lips to mine.

It's my lips that burn when we meet, an eclectic mix of desire and need and confusion. How are her lips not being scalded? How hot can I be before I combust? Instead of pulling away, she deepens the kiss, and I will explode if we continue. No amount of deep breathing is going to keep the flames inside this time. I step back from her and pull my arms close into my chest. Closing my eyes, I will myself to control it for once. *C'mon, please, just this one time!*

"Tana, are you okay?" Carrie asks, concerned.

"I'm...just...trying to keep from...burning up...the stockroom," I reply through gritted teeth.

"Anything I can do?"

I sigh heavily. "Stand back, just...in case."

She moves back behind the boxes near the wall. Meanwhile, I'm doing everything in my power not to combust in this extremely combustible area. My heart is pounding, and I think I can almost hear it in my ears.

"Um, Tana..." Carrie says, trailing off. She's staring at a point behind me, and her eyes are wide.

As I turn, I hear a commotion like screams and the sound of metal crunching. That wasn't my heart I heard pounding in my ears, it was the crackling of ice shards penetrating the roof.

Winter Storm is here.

* * *

I can feel the chill in the air even though I was just about to catch fire, and I see Blaine on the other side of the stockroom throwing ice every which way. *How did I not think that he would follow me? He is always following me!* His suit jacket is on the floor next to him—I've never seen him not be in a full suit, since he got his powers, that is. But this suit looks new. *He probably bought a new suit because he saw mine.* His movements are precise and sure, and I can see his muscles ripple through his crisp, white shirt. He shoots me a look that says, "I'm not playing around this time," and a shiver runs down my spine. *He saw us kissing.*

"Get out of here! Run!" I turn and yell at Carrie. She stares at the scene behind me, eyes wide, and hesitates. I reach out my gloved hand and cup her cheek. "Carrie, please, just go. I'll take care of him."

She leans forward and presses a kiss into my palm. "Be safe. I'm not done kissing you."

It's a miracle any of my clothes still exist. "I'll do my best," I reply, winking. I wait for her to start running for the exit before I turn back to Blaine. I don't have much time to think about the fact that Carrie just touched me again without burning.

"Alright, Blaine, let's finish this," I shout over the sound of crackling ice. The ice must have tripped a breaker or cut a wire, because the lights go out and the emergency lighting comes on. I stride toward him in the dim light, discarding my gloves to one side, and I stop trying to hold the flames back. The heat starts at my toes and moves quickly up to the crown of my head. A glow surrounds me. I have my own fire and the fire of arousal—I am *unstoppable.*

His arms still for a moment and he rounds on me. Fury is etched on every feature of his face, amplified by the light of my flames. "I can't believe you'd want to be with *her*"—he spits out the word with disdain—"instead of me."

"Oh my gods! You seriously need to get over it. It's been *years,*" I reply, still not believing I'm having to go through this with him yet again. "Putting aside the lesbian part, you and I are—quite literally—fire and ice. Even if I was into men, we could never work!"

True to form, he either doesn't listen or still doesn't comprehend my words. "Just go on one date with me and you'll see that we were meant to be!"

I heave an exasperated sigh and start throwing fireballs at the smaller ice shards closest to us. They melt instantly, and all that's left is a large puddle. That's the thing about men and villains like him—they're more consistently irritating than earth-shatteringly dangerous. I turn to start working on the larger ones which will take a lot more time and effort to melt.

Blaine moves to stand right in front of me. He holds his hands up, threatening to impale me with ice.

Scratch that previous thought. Apparently, me kissing another woman turned this from petty annoyance to an actual battle.

I take one large step back and to the side and put my arms up. My dads had me take a self-defense class a while back, but I think this is going to be a little different. Blaine strikes me as the kind of guy who does taekwondo or Muay

Thai or something. I'm also keenly aware of the incendiary nature of the entire area around us. One false move and this whole store will go up in flames.

As I suspected, Blaine fires a dagger of ice from his right hand. I manage to lean to the left just in time for it to fly past me. I don't take time to gloat over this small victory because I see he's already gearing up for another shot. I dodge this one as well. Then he starts throwing them faster and faster, from both hands, and I know I can't move quickly enough to dodge them. As much as I didn't want to, I'm going to have to use my powers to combat his. Hopefully Carrie will forgive me for destroying her store.

I toss small fireballs at his ice daggers, trying to time my movements precisely with his. Things are going really well until I see something shiny move just beyond the closest shelves. It's enough to throw my rhythm off just slightly, and one of the daggers slides across my left shoulder. I gasp in pain as the searing cold melts away the fire on my skin. It almost feels like I've been...*burned in reverse*. And that patch of skin isn't glowing like the rest of my body. There's no visible wound, but I can't feel the heat in that area anymore.

I don't have long to investigate what's happened to my shoulder, or what the shiny thing was, because Blaine is still throwing ice at me—possibly even more earnestly now that he sees he can hurt me. I duck behind the nearest bank of shelving and continue to combat his frozen blades with fireballs, but my right hand has to do most of the work. I can only make very small flames with my left side. There's a disconnect between my body and the lower part of that arm that had better be temporary.

Blaine looks over his shoulder at something I can't see. *Maybe he's seen that shiny thing too*, I think. He moves closer to the shelf nearest him—which is full of cake decorating supplies—all the while still firing ice in my direction. I stalk closer to him trying not to draw too much attention to myself while he's distracted. My right arm is getting very tired from picking up the slack from my weakened left arm, and it's all I can do to aim properly to avoid hitting the shelves full of flammable materials with fire.

"What're you doing?" Blaine says to no one that I can see. He has turned himself around to face the shelf behind him now and his hands are still for the first time since we started fighting. While he's distracted, I take the opportunity to quietly move closer to him.

There's no vocal response to his query, but all of a sudden, I see that shiny movement again. Leaning over and peering past Blaine through the shelves, I can tell it's actually a person—a woman, if the generous mounds of flesh...no...metal on the chest are any indication. Generous enough that it really does look like... *Wait, is that...could it be, Carrie?* Her whole body is shining like polished metal, and even her hair shines silver in the light from my firelight.

"Carrie?" I call, completely stunned.

"Yep, it's me!" she replies, sounding anxious. "Apparently, I have powers too. Not sure how or why now—maybe the stress?"

"I...I...that's great!" I say, meaning it.

She steps closer to me, and her skin, her clothes, everything gleams like stainless steel. It's almost like she's got armor. "Gotta admit, I'm a little freaked out, but I'm sure you'll help—"

"Hate to break up this little love session, but we were in the middle of something," Blaine interjects. He throws an enormous ice shard right through the shelf between Carrie and I. Shelving and cake decorating materials fly out to the sides, and I am hit in the chest by a large tub of fondant. I'm knocked down onto my backside by the impact as the undamaged container rolls off to the side. I rub my chest briefly before pushing back up to my feet.

"Tana! Are you okay?" Carrie calls.

"All good. You?"

"I'm good." She steps out from behind the ice and gives me a thumbs up.

I turn toward Blaine and see him gearing up to throw another large piece of ice. I let the rage from "Let me take that, a man is much better equipped to change the toner in the copier" combine with the memory of Carrie's lips, and send as much heat as I can out to my right hand, aim directly at his hands so I can stop the ice shard as it starts, and fire. Red-orange flames hit Blaine's just as the ice is forming. It melts immediately and my fire is doused at the same time. But, it worked!

Blaine fumes and his hands summon more ice. I continue to melt his ice the moment it forms. Bingo! It takes a larger concentration of flame, but less effort overall because I'm not constantly shooting fireballs from both hands—especially since the left one is still feeling the effects of the ice burn.

Not liking this turn of events, Blaine rounds on Carrie—his back to me now—and rapidly fires ice shards at her. I can feel a chill, even through my flaming skin, which means his ice has only gotten colder. Carrie blocks them with her metal skin/armor at first, but soon I start to see cracks appear on her "skin." She's grimacing in pain as they strike her, and I know I have to do something to either help her or stop Blaine.

Does her skin act just like metal? If so, I might be able to make her stronger, like a blacksmith quenching a hot sword. I gather all my energy and send it out to my right arm. Using my left hand to steady the wrist and help direct the flames exactly where I want them to go, I send a large burst of fire out through my hand. It hits Carrie squarely in the chest and I see her head snap back with the impact. I'm scared I've done too much, but then I see the cracks in her armor soften and meld back together, and her whole body glows orange with my flame. The look on her face shifts from shock to pure bliss.

Then, Carrie stops absorbing the flames and directs them out from her chest toward Blaine. He doesn't see this coming because he's turned back to fire at me. The fire hits his hands and he's sent reeling onto the floor. I stop the spray of fire from my hand, but not before the back wall is hit with a sizable burst of flame. Unfortunately, that wall is covered in linen and cotton fabric and ignites instantly.

"Oh my gods! Blaine, can you put out the fire?" I yell.

"Why should I help you save your lover's shop? Without her, you'll have to choose me!"

"I can't choose anyone if we all die in a fabric fire, you idiot!"

He sits up—suit a little singed, but otherwise looking okay—and tries shooting ice at the burning wall. Nothing happens. His normally frosty hands are a typical skin color, and there's no ice anywhere. "I...I can't. I...don't have my powers," he whimpers. "She did something! What did your harlot do!?"

"Defended herself." Seeing the flames only getting larger and spreading as we stand there, I take deep breaths to put out the fire on my body. "Carrie, Blaine, let's go!" I call as I start moving for the exit.

"Right behind you," Carrie replies.

Turning back, I see Blaine limping after her just as the next wall of fabric catches fire. Sensing his distress, Carrie runs back to him and hauls him into a fireman's carry. I reach the back exit and fling the door open, heedless of the "Emergency Exit Only: Alarm Will Sound" warning. The security alarm blares intermingling with the sirens of the emergency service vehicles arriving on the scene.

I hold the door open and wait for Carrie to bring Blaine through before closing it again. Then I put my hands on my knees, bending over in exhaustion. Carrie gently sets Blaine on the ground where he clutches at his ankle—and looks ashamed that a girl had to save him. We all take in big gulps of fresh air as smoke pours from the openings in the roof made by Blaine's earlier ice shards. Carrie, meanwhile, has started to look like her usual self, as the metal "skin" has disappeared, and her hair is back to its teal hue. But, she now has a lovely streak of silver running through her hair. Perhaps another indication of her new-found powers. I guess I wasn't imagining those silver strands earlier after all.

Within a few moments, the authorities come and haul Blaine away in handcuffs. He spews some choice phrases at the arresting officers, and whines about how we "stole" his powers. They take statements from Carrie and me, then say they'll call us if they need anything else. I can see Blaine still shouting in the back of the police vehicle as they drive away.

Tired and in desperate need of showers, Carrie and I are left standing behind the store while the firefighters work to put out the blaze. She reaches over and puts a hand on my left shoulder.

"You okay?" she asks.

"Yeah, I just wish none of this had happened."

"None of it?"

I shake my head. "Okay, not none of it. I'm definitely glad I met you, but the whole thing with Blaine was a lot."

"But, at least that's over now." Brightening, she says, "Plus, I really enjoyed seeing your new suit in full firelight."

"Heh. Thanks." *Hey, wait a minute. What did she say? Firelight. Firelight.* "Hey, what do you think about Firelight for my superhero name?"

"Oooo, I like it. 'Winter Storm taken down by Firelight,'" she says in full newscaster voice. "It has a nice ring to it."

"That's it then! That's the name I'm going to give the reporters before they leave," I say, so thrilled to finally have a superhero name.

"After that, wanna go back to my place so we can finish our earlier conversation?" Carrie asks.

I look into her sparkling eyes. "More than anything."

* * *

Even though we're both desperate to pick up where we left off, we decide to take things slow and take separate showers...this time. Also, I have no idea how to control my powers during another emotional surge like the one I had with her before—we'll have to figure that out as we go. But, as the battle knocked out the power to the area, I did get to act as the "Firelight" for Carrie's water heater. Five minutes of full-flame was enough to heat up plenty of water for both of us.

"So, I guess I must be related to Hephaestus somehow," Carrie explains as we sip tea—heated up by yours truly—in her living room. She's back to "normal" now and I'm going to help her explore her new powers later on. "I'm adopted, and I don't know anything about my birth parents or my lineage."

"Wow. It must have been hard to get powers you weren't expecting and not even know it was going to happen in the first place," I reply. "It was hard enough for me, and I knew I was at least going to get something."

"At any rate, mine are a little less destructive than some other people's I know," she says, nudging me in the left shoulder.

My shoulder still isn't quite right, but it's starting to feel warmer. I've never gotten blasted like that by Blaine, so I'm not sure how this works. My guess is, the full force of his ice power was enough to cool off that section of my body, at least temporarily. Time will tell whether I regain my full powers on that side. Blaine, on the other hand, got a full blast of fire redirected by Carrie, so who knows if that melted his powers for good or not. He's at least behind bars and awaiting justice for his crimes. Carrie suffered no ill effects and I'm wondering if she'll actually be stronger now that I blasted her with flames.

I laugh. "Ha, ha, ha. I'm sure you haven't realized the full extent of what you can do yet."

"Well, I'm glad of one thing," she says, a gleam in her eye.

"Yeah? What's that?"

She reaches a hand up to brush the hair back from my face. "I'm glad I can take all the heat you can dish out."

Fire floods my body, and there's nothing I can do but kiss her and hope she has fire insurance.

Heather got the idea for this story from a Twitter thread by @katiehahnbooks that's been circulating around the interwebs since May 2020. It suggested a story about a lesbian seamstress and the fabric store employee who falls in love with her every time she has to ask, "so what are you making with this?" Her title was "Girlfriend Material," but changes were made to make the story fit the themes of fire and female power. The idea for Blaine came about from another thread that posited what if all female superheroes' villains were just douchey guys who wouldn't take no for an answer. Unfortunately, she couldn't find that one again to give credit, but if you know who wrote it, feel free to send it to Space Wizard Science Fantasy.

This story is also dedicated to all my friends who have ever worked at a certain fabric store. Hope the ending makes you smile.

Fallout

J.S. Fields

Sapphic Representation: Lesbian
Heat Level: Hot!
Content Warnings: Claustrophobia, Childhood trauma

On the second highest volcano in the Cose Mountain Range, baking in the midday sun, Auna Firestill finally triumphed. "I did ittttaugh!" she managed before a meter-long slab of obsidian pushed up from the viscous lava bed to her left. Auna teetered, desperate to regain her footing, when a gust of wind pinned her to the stone slab, the orb she'd been hunting dropping just out of reach.

She was so close, damn it. Another centimeter and she'd have the orb. Then it would just be a matter of freeing herself, hitching a ride back to her volcano, and spending the next month gloating that she, Auna Firestill of the Margrud Fire Witches, Vice President of the Cose Volcano Safety Committee, had found the Elemental Orb. She'd found it safely, relatively quickly, and had disturbed no protected ecosystems to dig it up. No small feat, especially for a fire witch who had never left her mountain village before.

Then the Cose Volcano Safety Committee would release the elemental magic trapped within and end the Margrud Curse that kept the fire witches trapped on the active volcano range.

The Cose Volcano Safety Committee had spent the past six months triangulating magic pulses across their ancestral mountain range. They had pinpointed the orb's most likely location. By popular vote and because Auna was the most risk-averse and safety-conscious among them, she had spent the last week first with a detection spell, then with a shovel and pickaxe, meticulously digging down into a two-meter squared section of pumice only a handful of meters from active lava flow. Two meters down her shovel *clinked*. She'd tossed it aside, slid her arm down into the narrow hole, and pulled the magical nuisance into the light. Fresh lava had bubbled up—she'd likely hit an active tube, but it didn't matter because *she had the Elemental Orb!*

But now, thanks to a slab of obsidian and a rogue wind, she was orbless *and* trapped. It was a very undignified way for a vice president to meet her end.

"Let go!" Auna screamed as she stretched her foot forward. The wind eased just enough that Auna could wiggle her bare toes against the shiny silver and white metal of the orb, but failed to bring it any closer. Sweat beaded where skin had touched metal, and two droplets of saltwater *pit patted* to the ground.

Sweat. Liquid sweat. From a fire witch. Blended elemental magic was ridiculous.

"The orb is dangerous. My family has been trapped, *trapped,* on this mountain for six generations. If I want to dig up the Elemental Orb and end the curse, damn it, I will! I don't need complications. A tiny excursion I can handle. A complicated adventure is entirely off the table." Auna screamed at the universe, at the Margrud Curse, and at the wind that stole her words the moment she uttered them.

Pebbles jittered across the uneven pumice, blown by a now hot, volcanic wind. One of the pebbles struck the edge of the orb, knocking it closer to the hole from which Auna had fished it.

More curse? Or just a really troublesome wind? "No!" Auna yelled at the orb. "I'm taking you to Cose's safety committee where we will shatter you under a durable fume hood. Then every single one of the Margrud Fire Witches is going to walk down off the mountain range and never look back." Well, *most* would. Auna had a perfectly fine house on the mountainside. And if she left, who would run the Safety Committee?

A tinny, angry voice said, "Go home, fire witch." The unrelenting wind forced the orb to the edge of the hole, teetering so precariously that Auna's breath could knock it over.

Curses didn't talk.

Wind didn't talk.

Orbs *certainly* didn't talk.

Damn it.

Auna had been certain she was on the mountain alone. Yet another miscalculation. One more hit of wind and the orb would be lost for another century.

Auna screamed. "Whoever you are, wherever you are, call off the wind! You push it down that lava tube and my people will never get off this mountain range." Beads of liquid fire dripped off her eyebrows and down her neck. The wind carried the distinct smell of singed hair. "You think we enjoy spending our days absorbing heat so it doesn't erupt and wash away the foothill villages? Maybe if we had a choice, sure. But someone thought it necessary to force us to do it and that is unconscionable!" Then she screamed, a little unhinged, "Justice for the Margrud Fire Witches!"

"A curse doesn't mean you break other people's things." A tendril of wind so fine it could have been a sigh curled through Auna's fringe, across her lips, then down her legs, tickled the ground, and then tipped the Elemental Orb back down into the now very active lava tube.

In a blink, the orb was gone.

Forever.

Auna had failed. She'd left her village, traveled up a volcano, and gotten absolutely filthy, for *nothing*.

"Please," Auna whispered, her tears burning the fine hairs on her cheeks. "Retrieving the orb is my job. We have to destroy it. It's the only way out."

Warm wind twirled across Auna's cheeks. "Have you tried walking down the mountain?" the voice asked. The warmth dropped away, but the breeze remained—strong enough to keep Auna against the obsidian, but gentle enough that molten tears could still slide down her face.

Auna herself had never gone more than a handful of meters past her village's (decorative) border wall. Until this week. But other fire witches had. "What do you think?" she said. "Would I be digging up old magic on a mountain if walking were an option? My cousin toddled across as a baby and all we have to remember her by is a handful of soot. My friend Ioke's mother tried to cross to get village medicine and now she sits on Ioke's mantle in a glass jar. We deserve the right to come and go as we choose."

The wind stilled in contemplation. Auna could have run, but why? What purpose did it serve, to return to Cose empty handed? Instead, she wiped liquid fire from her face and decided that her only remaining option was diplomacy.

Finally, the wind said, "That isn't fair, what happened. It isn't fair to be cut away from your family and friends."

Auna brightened. "Can you bring the orb back?"

"Don't be silly," said the wind, in an exasperated sigh. "That lava tube only leads to death. You'll be lucky if the orb shows itself again this century, and it wasn't yours to take, nor yours to break. But I...I do feel for you, even though you have legs and arms and a head and I'm...this. No one deserves to be trapped."

Auna squinted up at the bright blue sky, half expecting to see a face peering down from the clouds. "Honestly, we had no idea something...some*one* lived up here with us." She shivered. "We've been trapped here for a century. Are you...a witch? Another elemental witch?" Another elemental witch would be a lot less weird than sentient wind. Auna had been voluntold for a treasure hunt, not...whatever this was turning into.

"I'm not magic," huffed the wind.

"Uh, oh," Auna said. There was a reason she was never elected to collect offerings from the villagers at the Margrud Mountain foothills. Auna could run a meeting with calm aplomb. Small talk just hurt. "Um, well, regardless. There's no excuse for theft. I'm very sorry. Could we perhaps discuss a barter for the orb? Could you find it again? Could you direct me to it? I don't mind a hike, so long as we keep the surprises to a minimum. I am *not,*" Auna said through clenched teeth, "looking for a quest. Or an adventure. So how can I help you, so that you can help me? Help me *safely*."

Auna was once again driven back against the obsidian. The wind turned cloying, braiding through Auna's golden curls and feeding the tiny flames that bloomed across her skin. "Yes, little witch. I'll help you."

"With...the orb?" Auna asked as a flush smoked from her cheeks. "Could you back down the wind a bit? If you keep with the close contact, I could set the little vegetation here ablaze. This is a protected ecosystem."

"My apologies." The air around Auna stilled again and she sloughed from the obsidian, onto her knees. "Fire doesn't blend with a lot of ecosystems, does it? We'd need a place where your temper wouldn't cause too much damage. Tell me, do you like trees?"

"I'm a fire witch. Trees don't like *me*." Auna stood and backed well away from the obsidian. There was nothing else for the wind to pin her to. There was nothing but barren pumice, a handful of ground shrubs, and burning lava for kilometers in every direction. "Where are you? *What* are you? Another curse? Are you bound to the orb?" Auna asked. "Are you tasked with guarding it? Is that why you won't get it back for me? Oh! Would destroying it destroy you?" That made a lot more sense. "The Cose Volcano Safety Committee takes its charter very seriously. Breaking the orb was the easiest option but we can look into simply draining the magic, or even altering the spell. I'm sure with your help we could—"

A sharp breeze kicked up, pushing Auna's head west. "Stay down and close your eyes. Don't want those ducts to dry out. You're going on a trip across an ocean. A very small ocean, but an ocean nonetheless."

Ocean? Fire witches did not cross water. Fire witches didn't go swimming, or take baths, or shower. Dead skin and smelly bacteria burned away as easily as they washed away. Aside from all that, crossing an ocean definitely violated Auna's "no adventure" rule. "How are you going to get me over the border without me combusting? And I don't want to leave the range, I just think we should have the option to do so," Auna protested, but the words desiccated in her mouth. Wind swirled and whipped until Auna had to squeeze her eyes shut or risk losing her eyeballs. "I can't leave!" she shouted, but her words disappeared as quickly as she formed them. "I'm Vice President of the Cose Volcano Safety Committee and belong to the Margrud Mountain Range!"

"Calm down, pretty little meddling fire witch. I heard your wish. Wind can go where fire can't and at least one of us deserves to be free."

* * *

Rainforests, Auna concluded, were just as wet as the ocean itself.

Today's rain beaded and hissed when it landed on Auna's long-sleeved, long-hemmed, balloon of a wool dress. That really fine, vapor-like rain was her least favorite as it tended to roll from the fabric instead of being absorbed. What good was a heavy wool abomination of a dress if it was saturated with water? Dry wool itself could handle a little fire, sure. But if Auna got stung out in the forest by a hem-haw ant or forgot her lunch *again* and had to spend the day with a gurgling stomach, she'd stress-light the entire dress to charcoal in under ten seconds. While Auna had made the trek to town naked before, it was not an experience she wanted to repeat.

She'd been living in a lean-to in a tropical rainforest for the past week. There'd been a lot of indignities, especially at first, but none as horrific as trying to negotiate the price of a fabric bolt while all the hair on your naked body smoldered...including the hair between your legs. Was it better than living in a barren, mountainous prison? No. Walls aside, Auna genuinely liked the Margrud Mountains. Or rather, she liked the familiarity of the mountains. It was definitely better than being pinned to a rock while the wind alternately teased you, then tried to give you frost bite. It did *not* help her solve the problem of her people's imprisonment and that there was clearly a loophole in the boundary.

Auna had absolutely no idea where the wind had dropped her. Several Margrud mountains crested about the clouds, and on a clear day she could see the curve of the planet. In all that span Auna had never seen more than tiny patches of the forest and she could not comprehend that any forest this wet would be anywhere near her dry mountain range. If she was going to set out on a trek home she needed reliable clothes, and shoes, travel-stable food and, most importantly, a map. Her foraging basket now had enough mushrooms to trade for one. In theory.

"Another day in paradise?" the wind asked without a drop of sarcasm as Auna placed another handful of oyster mushrooms in her basket. "Or did you want somewhere with more topography, for hiking? You weren't specific."

"This isn't what I asked for, and it isn't helping me find the orb," Auna said sourly. "I want to go home."

The arrow-shaped leaves just above Auna's head rustled. "What do you mean? I thought you wanted to escape. This is a pretty place, isn't it? Do you like the village? Have you tried the hot springs?"

Auna pointed south, then west. "I don't have a lot of time for hot springs. My people, wherever they are, are trapped, my parents probably think I'm dead, and I've spent a week foraging mushrooms under a leaky sky. How did you even get me here?"

"I told you," the wind said. "You flew with me. Wind can go where fire can't."

"Two elementals together? Is that what you're saying? Or did the orb wash so deep into the mountain that whatever hold it had over the fire witches broke?"

The misty rain sizzled as it fell into Auna's eyes. Somewhere, a water witch was laughing at how sodden and sorry Auna knew she looked. "I went up that mountain to break a curse, not to run away." Auna stomped her bare foot, withering the leaves of some no-name understory plant with heat of her heel. "This isn't what I wanted. You have to take me home!"

The leaves in the collective overstory shook, just once, in tandem. A seed pod swirled lazily from a branch above Auna's head, telling her that her wind spirit / disembodied witch / tormentor had moved on. Looking up, the sun was already at its apex. Days were short, wherever Auna was, and it wasn't safe to be outside her lean-to once the sun dipped below the tree line. If she was to make any trades today, she had to get moving. And Auna was done arguing with the wind, done foraging, done with being soaked to the bone day in and day out. She'd spent the last five years with the Cose Volcano Safety Committee. She'd memorized every rule book and operating procedure. This wasn't an adventure, rather a more of a mishap, and Auna knew how to clean up messes. She'd prepared enough. She'd saved enough. She was going to the market tonight to get her map, then she was going home. With or without the wind's help.

* * *

The closest village to Auna's forest shanty consisted of seven family huts and three longhouses. The northernmost one held a small market, and it was here that she headed. No one spoke the regional Margrud language, nor her Cose dialect, nor did Auna recognize any of the words she heard as the languages spoken by the free people at the base of her mountain range. Hence Auna relied on a mixture of grunts and shoulder shrugs to get her point across. That her sweat smoked from her skin in the humid air had not endeared her to the local population.

"Map?" Auna asked the fabric dealer she most often dealt with. She scooped a handful of round, white mushrooms from her basket and held them out. "Picked today. All yours, for a map of the region."

Wind—regular wind—whistled through the longhouse roof thatching. With it came the smell of salt—a sure sign that a storm was blowing in. Auna's mountain range ran alongside an ocean. In theory, if she could find the body of water she could walk along its shore and maybe, eventually, see some familiar scenery. The wind had said it was a small ocean, right? How long could the trip take?

The fabric vendor's mild smile melted to genuine delight. He moved two thick bolts of cotton from his booth, then opened a wooden case—the inside filled with silver and gold jewelry.

"No, not jewelry," Auna said, and tried to mime opening her hands like a book. "Whooosh. Wind. Ocean. Mountains." She pointed to different places on her palm. "Something that shows me where they are."

A furrow came to the man's forehead. He bent under the table to rummage then emerged triumphant, another wood case in his palm.

"Not jewelry!" Auna insisted. "Look, would you just—"

The vendor flipped the latch and lid open in the same motion.

Inside, resting on a bed of flower petals, was the Elemental Orb.

"*Oh.*" Auna picked the orb from the box and ran her fingers across it. The weight and shape were identical to the one she'd found on the mountain. Auna's fingers stuck to it with the same draw of magic, and it hummed with the same promise of power. But it couldn't be the Margrud Elemental Orb just...sitting here in a moldering forest waiting for a basket of mushrooms in trade?

"Map," the vendor said, putting emphasis on "M." Auna had clearly stumbled on a parallel word between the two languages. Parallel sound, with very different meanings.

No matter. Auna held the orb, clutched and nearly crushed it as she waited for the wind to take it from her, to tease her, to once again snatch the victory from her hands. But the air remained still, the vendor expectant. And the fire that perpetually sparked across Auna's eyelashes and the wisps of her curls extinguished. The sodden ground firmed under her feet.

"How much?" Auna asked, offering him the entirety of her mushroom basket.

The man cheered. Ignoring the basket, he took the orb from Auna's hands and, with an awl and mallet, promptly punched a hole dead center, and clear through.

"Don't do that without any safety protection!" Auna screamed. Heat seared under her wool dress. The damp moss and dirt under her feet smoked and tiny flames leapt from fingertip to fingertip. From outside Auna could hear waves crashing against a breakwall as the wind whistled violently through the rafters of the longhouse. Outside the longhouse Auna heard a *thunk* and a woman's confused scream. Dropped tree branch, likely. That was the danger of living around so many damn trees.

The vendor threaded a cheap chain through the hole. He then placed the necklace over her head. The metal of the orb, when it touched Auna's skin, was dead and lifeless. "Map."

The ocean quieted. The wind stilled.

The tips of Auna's hair smoldered. Heat blazed through her curls.

Broken orb. *Broken.*

What did that mean for the curse?

What did that mean for getting home?

Auna's internal fire turned her fingernails a cracked, charcoal black. A whole orb she might have been able to use to bribe the wind to take her back home. But that was fine. She could still find a map. She could still do this alone. There was less pressure now, right? Now that the curse had maybe been broken? Or was that silly, wishful thinking?

The fabric vendor poured a bucket of water over her head.

Auna's flame, and her temper, promptly went out.

"I didn't know fire witches were big on fashion. Or rainforests. Do you live nearby?"

Had she just heard the Margrud language, in Cose dialect?! Auna spun around to find a tall, willowy woman with charcoal hair. A pretty woman, with a petal pink flush to her cheeks from the evening air, sensible-if-outdated leathers that hugged her form, and a welcoming smile the like of which Auna hadn't seen since arriving in the rainforest. The left side of her body was caked in fresh dirt, as was the right side of her cheek.

"I didn't mean to startle you."

"You didn't," Auna stuttered. "But I don't see many wearing leather in this climate. Where are you from? Did you"—she pointed to the woman's cheek—"get knocked to the ground just now?" The set of the stranger's eyes and the sharp bridge of her nose suggested a shared lineage with the locals, and her two long braids were in the same style as everyone Auna had met in the rainforest thus far. But this woman was a good head taller than the tallest man and her clothing was downright impractical.

"I'm Eir."

Unhelpful. "Your question dodging is as smooth as your Margrud."

Eir snorted. "You're rude and you don't belong here."

She deserved that. Auna touched the orb resting against her throat. "I'm...sorry about the tone. You're right, I don't belong here. I'm trying to get home to the Margrud Mountains. Can you help me find it? Are you, are you from one of the foothill villages?" That would explain the leathers. With fire witches absorbing volcanic heat, the weather in the foothills could be downright chilly. Excitement spiked within Auna, sending licks of fire onto the remains of her wool dress. "Is that how you know my language? Or..." She leaned toward Eir and whispered, "Are you a fire witch? Did…" She lowered her voice, "Did a sexy wind bring you here, too?"

"I'm sorry?"

Auna shook her head. "I'm reaching, and you're far too pale to have come from an active volcanic site. I need a map, or a guide. I want to go home. Can you help me? Translate maybe?"

"Do you have any money left?"

"I think this guy just claimed all my mushrooms."

"How much for that?" Eir pointed at Auna's neck. "I like it." Long fingers reached out, the tip of one just gliding over the orb's surface. "I like it a lot."

"The priceless magical artifact is not for sale," Auna said automatically.

"Oh. I see." Eir's fingers fell from the orb to brush Auna's collarbone. Tiny licks of flame rose on Auna's skin, chasing the unexpected coolness of Eir's touch.

"You feel like…" Auna trailed off before finishing her thought. Margrud language. Cose dialect. Delicate, cold touches. The Elemental Orb. Auna swallowed her very wild theory. She had other issues at hand. If the orb was broken and the magic gone, then Auna didn't need it, did she? Her people were already free.

Did she need to go home?

Did she *want* to go home? What even was home, if the rules around her entire world had been punched through with a single stroke of an awl?

The entire market had gone quiet. This made sense as the remains of Auna's wool dress were smoldering, and the tips of her hair burned a bright blue-orange.

"We don't want any trouble, fire witch," Eir said, her hands raised. The villagers in the longhouse had moved to the periphery and were slowly edging their way to the door. "Maybe you could calm down?"

"I'm not agitated, but yes, I see your point." A normal reaction to a pretty woman touching you was hardly cause for concern, especially in a rainforest. Nevertheless, Auna sucked in a long breath and drew the fire, the heat, back into herself. Eir's tone was entirely unfair, noting Auna hadn't destroyed a single plant or building since arriving. To hold an officer position in the Cose Volcano Safety Committee you had to show a fire-free record for at least five years. Auna hadn't accidentally immolated anything since she was seven and opened her heel against a particularly jagged piece of pumice.

When the wool once again hung dead against her body and her hair lay limp and flame-free, Auna said, as seriously as she could manage, "I'm in need of a map." To where, she was now uncertain. She ought to at least *check* on the Margrud Mountains though. She owed her family, and the Safety Committee, knowledge that she wasn't a pile of ash somewhere before they scattered off the mountain.

Eir contemplated for a long moment, eyes jumping between Auna's now much-higher hemline, and the charred ring of dirt around her feet. "You're currently in the southern continent. There's an ocean between you and your home, and no land bridge for you to walk."

"I'm sure I can trade for boat passage. How many mushrooms do you think it would be?"

"It would take weeks to cross the Chichuck Sea. The wind itself needs four and a half hours."

Surprisingly specific. "Well then what do you suggest?!" Auna slapped an indignant hand on the nearest booth. Her fingertips left charcoal outlines in their wake. "If I can't go over the water, can I go under it? Do you have any channels or tunnels? How did you learn my language if not from being raised in the foothills? How did *you* get *here?* If you're not a Margrud villager, then you either got hit with released magic when the vendor punctured the Elemental Orb or..." Auna decided not to add "...or my tormenting wind spirit got a body." That sounded ridiculous.

Eir straightened and said, brightly, while entirely avoiding the questions, "I have an idea! Lava flows underground and heats the hot springs just south of the village. They run under the ocean and to the northern hemisphere, where your mountains are. But"—whatever light had briefly kindled in Eir, extinguished—"that's still a very long walk, even if you won't get burned by the magma. It's shorter, underground. But it isn't safe. There's air enough, but food is scarce."

Home sounded more and more alluring the more Auna thought about her bed, and her father's firebread muffins, and how it was her turn to deliver the status update presentation for the Cose Volcano Safety Committee. Besides, she was a fire witch. What did she have to fear from magma? "I'll leave tonight if you can show me the entrance?"

Eir stared at her. "Help you find a hole at the bottom of a hot spring? Help lead you to your death? My father's house was there. There was...another village there." Eir's lips pursed. "Items float up into the pools from time to time. Shoes. Hair bands. A concerning number of bones."

"Orbs?" Auna asked, grabbing the one at her neck.

"Maybe," Eir whispered. She stroked her clavicle, in the same place where Auna's orb rested.

"I need you to lead me there."

"The sun has set," said Eir. "It would be safer in the morning. It's not wise to walk at night in a forest."

"Even with a fire witch to protect you?" Auna lit her entire head aflame. Potentially overkill, but time was wasting.

A smile cracked around the corners of Eir's mouth. Auna supposed a head full of flame did make one look scarier than whatever lurked in the rainforest. Auna had certainly never had any trouble during her last week of habitation.

"I...suppose that does help. Follow me," Eir said, in a whisper that felt like it carried through the entire longhouse.

Auna extinguished her hair and followed.

* * *

The wind remained still and the air humid as Auna and Eir picked their way across the village and along a well-worn path. The springs were no more than ten minutes away—a series of circular pits steaming the night air and no village in sight.

"This one is the shallowest," said Eir, leading them to the second pit. "It's the one I spent the most time in as a child."

"You're a southern hemisphere native then?" Auna asked as she set down her pack and sat at the pit's edge. "I don't see any houses out here, not even foundations. Was there a fire? Flood?"

"Do fire witches swim?" Eir asked.

"No. Never. I won't be the one to start, either. Is there a reason you won't answer my questions?" She put her palm flat on the water's surface and sent heat—a lifetime of absorbed heat—into the pit. Steam rose, hot and thick, and Auna gagged on the night air.

"You can't evaporate a whole pool!" Eir cried as she choked on the humidity. "Can you?"

"They're seasonal, from what I can tell of the evaporation lines. They'll come back next year. How else will we get access to the tunnels?" Auna used the sleeve of her dress to clear the condensation from her forehead. "Ironically, a little wind would be great about now. Your humidity is stale."

"The wind used to blow through here," Eir said, her voice as eerily still as the air.

Auna coughed into the endless steam. Evaporating out an entire hot spring was hard work. Not as hard as keeping a volcano from erupting, but close. "A few more minutes of this. Could you find a frond to fan, maybe? I'm hoping the water gives out before I do."

A cool, long-fingered hand wrapped around Auna's upper arm.

"Helpful," Auna barked through the steam. "But not as helpful as a fan."

Wind came then, a cool, salty ocean gust that fed the fire on Auna's skin as it pushed the steam away, back into the forest, as quickly as Auna could generate it.

Auna didn't have the ability to look at her helper, not while she focused on the heat. Breath after breath she bled fire into water until the fire chapped her suddenly overly dry skin, until her lungs cleared, and she could see the substantial drop before her.

"The bottom!" Eir said, her voice so close that Auna flinched. There, approximately six meters down the muddy bank, was a basalt-encrusted hole wide enough for a pony to fit through. As long as it didn't rain and they didn't break through whatever thin barrier existed between the lava tube and the groundwater, they'd be fine.

"Perfect." Auna rubbed her eyes, failing to clear the fatigue, and said to Eir, "Take the rope from my satchel and tie it to a tree and I'll use the other end to scale down."

Eir did not move, her hand still gripping Auna's arm. "How much magic did you just spend? You need time." Her fingers were as cool as the wind that had traced Auna's ear, that had pinned her to a slab of obsidian. "Moving that much water takes a lot of magic."

"Do you know much about magic?" Auna asked her, the words coming out more exhausted than she'd meant.

"I...no. I don't think so?"

"You sure?" Auna took a step forward and stumbled, her legs wobbly. "No chance you're a wind witch?"

Eir caught her and for a moment Auna's cheek pressed against cool, dry leather—an impossibility in a rainforest. "What kind of riddle is that?" she asked in a voice of absolute confusion. "Will you let me take you back to the village?"

"I...no." Were Auna's data showing correlation instead of causation? Gods help her, this woman *was* her wind witch, wasn't she? "I think we should," Auna stumbled as she backed away. She'd wanted to say, "I think we should sit and talk," but her body shivers had turned to shakes. "I need to recover, but I won't get that at the village. I need to get to the magma." There was warmth to the air, yes, that she could absorb, but nothing short of active fire or boiling magma would let her truly recover. "Help me?"

"You'll die down there, in the lava tubes."

Eir's emotions were as shaky as Auna's legs. Auna smiled, as reassuringly as she could. "You can't kill a fire witch with fire."

"Magic can do a lot of unexpected things." But Eir took the rope from Auna's bag, tied it to a tree and to Auna's waist, and helped her down into the hole. The heat curling from the magma helped soothe Auna's limbs and raised her body temperature. She was still exhausted, but not so much that she couldn't poke her mystery helper. "Help me out with something? That wind that came. It helped move the sublimed water vapor. You don't think a wind witch called it?"

"What wind?" Eir double checked the knot at Auna's right hip. "The air has been dead still all night."

It was always nice to meet someone with bigger problems than yours. "Has it?" Auna put a hand over the orb that rested under her wool dress. "Tell me, how did you get to the market?"

"I walked," Eir responded.

"From where?"

"A...my house?" Eir's mouth remained agape. "I needed to buy...no. I was swimming. I was swimming and Katerina dared me to touch the bottom of the pit. The...wind had moved the water? No, I *told* the wind to move the water, so I could do the dare. I..." She blinked at Auna. "I don't know. I don't *know*."

Auna didn't know either, but she could make an educated guess. "It sounds like you and the wind were on good terms. Like you knew how to command it, the same as I do fire. How old were you when you went swimming?" Auna asked, as gently as she could. "How old was Katerina?"

"We were girls."

"Could Katerina command the wind, too?"

"Of course. Everyone in the village could," Eir said with a dismissive wave of her hand.

"Of course," Auna murmured. Louder she said, "And what happened then? After the wind moved the water and you touched the bottom?"

Eir met Auna's eyes—wide and confused. "And then I walked up to you in the market. But I can't control the wind, Auna. I'm not a wind witch."

"What are you then?" Auna asked. "What have you been doing since that night with Katerina?"

"I..." Eir's eyes grew wide as she stared, blankly, at the star-filled sky. "I don't know."

Auna let out a long, exasperated sigh. "This means I'm not allowed to be angry with you, doesn't it, for keeping me from the orb?" She gave the rope one more check, then offered Eir a hand. "I think you should come with me. Maybe you'll leak a few more memories as we walk."

"I don't want to go down there," Eir whispered with a shake of her head.

"Why?" Auna asked. "Is there someone here waiting for you? Your village? All I see are trees. That lava tube doesn't have trees, but it might have your memories. And it's my way home. We both win."

Eir turned in a slow circle, scanning the canopy, the dangling liana, the foxfire-dotted ground.

"What do you have to lose?" Auna prodded.

"My life."

Auna did not care for the flatness of those words. "I thought we agreed, you don't have to be afraid when you've got a fire witch." The Margrud villagers had been afraid *because* of the fire witches, but they didn't need to get into Auna's sob stories. Being trapped without a body, without family, without friends, was far worse than several hundred fire witches imprisoned on a volcano. Together, maybe, they could solve both their problems. Auna didn't quite know *how* yet, but she wasn't going to abandon a cursed wind witch, either. Besides, if Auna had to go on a downright dangerous adventure, she needed a safety buddy. That Eir was a particularly pretty and endearing safety buddy, well. Maybe there were solid reasons to miss a Cose Volcano Safety Committee Meeting after all.

"It's not the fire I'm afraid of," Eir said, but she let Auna tie her into the rope and clung to her as tightly as a terrified child, as they descended.

The magma popped and boiled only two meters from the opening, making the descent mercifully short. Auna made sure to hit the ground first, absorbing the heat, cooling the magma and hardening it. The relief was instant, sending shocks of warmth into her bloodstream, flushing her cheeks, her sweat again dripping in delicate licks of fire. Steam swirled in the air around the two women and up into the greater forest.

"Ready for you," Auna said, tapping the dark, firm ground with her bare heel. She helped Eir ease down off the side of the pit and, when her feet were back under her, unfastened the knots that held them together. "You did great. It's just walking now. The magma will cool ahead of us. Fire witches don't have a lot of tricks, but this one we do really well. Well, that, and this." Auna held out her palm and a tiny flame ignited, poorly illuminating the tunnel beyond.

Eir stared blankly ahead. In the distance, Auna heard the skittering of rocks pushed by thermal vents. The *skritch skritch srittle* sent Eir to shivers. "This is a bad place," Eir whispered.

"Not with me," Auna said. She knew nothing of the internal mechanics of volcanos and had never dreamed that she'd have to physically impregnate one for her freedom. But Eir didn't need Auna's fears on top of her own. "Magma and steam and magic make for strange bedfellows. That's rocks you hear, not insects or animals. Take my hand."

Eir's fingers intwined with hers. "There won't be enough to eat. It's too far to your volcano. More than days."

Without bothering to consider, Auna kissed the top of Eir's hand. They might starve. They might be crushed. But Auna had stagnated on the Margrud Mountain Range her entire life. She'd taken a chance to find the orb, and this was where her path had led. Turning back now would be asinine. Fire couldn't go back. Fire could only move forward.

"What was that for?"

"I just wanted you to know I understand."

Eir looked quizzical.

"I still have my satchel of mushrooms. I forgot to give it to the fabric vendor. I can..." Auna briefly considered the intersection of physics and fire magic. "Water I can make from the steam of cooling magma. Poison gasses from the volcano...those probably won't hurt elemental witches."

"How does that help me?"

Right. None of those facts would help a broken wind witch with lost memory.

"You have me. I'll protect you. I promise. Fire magic is versatile."

"Not as versatile as the wind." But Eir wiped her eyes with the back of her hand and pulled Auna forward, down the tunnel.

"Magic is such a mess," Auna muttered to herself. The only way out was through. If there was dangerous magic ahead, well, they'd solidify that magma when they came to it.

* * *

Eir reached around Auna's neck, unclasped the necklace, slid the orb off, and held it up to her nose. Her touch still held the pleasant shiver of the wind, but the tease had bled away, replaced by a repressed melancholy.

"What do you know about it?" Auna asked.

Eir's head turned right, then left, then right again as she examined the orb. "It's soft, like aluminum. Lighter even." She handed it back to Auna. "It's shaped like a squashed potato." She frowned, creating an adorable "V" between her eyebrows. "What is it supposed to do?"

How long they'd walked before needing a break, Auna could not tell. She'd kept the frayed ends of her curls lit, which now gave off the only light in the lava tube. They were far enough down now—the first several hours had been a down grade—that Auna couldn't hear the ocean anymore. That they were underneath it she had no doubt, if only from the crushing atmospheric pressure. Eir led with a confidence of stride that sat in complete opposition to the worry on her face and had only stopped when Auna voiced concern over their ability to keep the pace on empty bellies and no sleep. Thus, they'd snacked on button mushrooms from Auna's satchel and now sat on the recently cooled magma.

Auna smiled at Eir and Eir smiled back—the movement more mechanical than sincere. Auna said, "The myth says it balances elemental power. It can grow trees on hot lava, find a spring in a desert, still the wind on a mountain top, that sort of thing."

"If it is capable of all that, why are you still sweating fire?"

Auna wiped her brow with her sleeve, singeing the wool. She flipped her hands over to find tiny flicks of fire across her palms. "There's a lot of heat down here, as you can imagine. It has to go somewhere, and most is going into me. And this orb has a hole in it." She pointed to where the chain pierced the metal. "It's broken. Which is great, because after spending three years studying those old myths, the Cose Volcano Safety Committee determined there was a greater than fifty percent chance that the orb keeps the Margrud fire witch population chained to our mountain system."

"Are they free now?" Eir flipped the orb over and ran a finger along the edge.

"I won't know until I get back. But I think this orb also belongs to a friend of mine, a wind witch." Rest time could also be memory prodding time. "Do you know anything about wind witches?"

Eir ignored the question. "We have only one way to go until the tunnel branches. The air will only get hotter. No one will come if we scream." As she pulled away her fingers slid across the necklace chain, just grazing Auna's skin. The coolness came again, leaving a short halo of steam in their wake.

"S...scream?" Auna's breath caught. It was the same touch as the volcanic wind, the same from the market, yet Auna's reaction compounded exponentially.

"Did I hurt you?" Eir asked.

"No. No it's very hard to hurt a fire witch. You can drown us. That's about it. If anything, the wind, you know, and fire. They uh. They get along." Those had been completely unnecessary sentences to say out loud. Gods it was murderously hot in the lava tube, even for a fire witch. Vibrations from the planet's core kept the small bits of rock jittering against the ground, the scraping of unforgiving stone echoed in the long tunnels. Auna ached for a breeze, for that cooling touch down her arms, across her neck, down her thighs. "Do you remember how it felt when you touched me on the mountain?"

"No. Yes? I feel like I've been cold my whole life. Your skin it...I shiver from the heat. It's so cold on the mountains. It's so quiet. Then you were there, softening the magma, lighting the ferns to ashy soil. Your shovel scraped the ground, and your hands beat the stone and when I pressed you to the obsidian, I felt *alive*. I..." Eir pulled her hand back as if stung. "I am being wildly inappropriate. My apologies. I don't know where that...memories are starting to untangle but they're still so out of order."

Auna had absorbed a great deal of heat since their descent and did not need to be making more of her own. Cool touches and sweet / awkward words could wait until they were topside. Auna tapped the orb at her neck. "What about memories of your last time down in this tube? Can you tell me what is waiting for us down here?"

Eir's hands dropped away. "The more I push, the more the memories scatter. It's like the whole lot are trying to come through at the same time, through a hole the size of your pendant loop. I see you on the mountain, then I see my mother staring down the lava tube, then comes a memory of playing with my sister in the forest. Each one whips up my insides." Eir blinked, cocked her head, and said to Auna, "I was rude to you, wasn't I? On the mountain? I..." She studied Auna then, like she'd only just realized Auna was a real breathing person. "You're very pretty."

What in the Margrud Mountains was Auna going to do with that? Especially right now? "Thank you," Auna said, hoping she sounded sincere. "Let's try to sleep, even just a few hours. Who knows what will come in your dreams?"

Auna stretched out on the magma, well used to the hardened surface. Eir spent a moment assessing her options before curling up next to Auna and resting her head on Auna's chest. Eir's breathing evened almost instantly.

"May sleep bring you answers. And I'm sorry I didn't bring a pillow," Auna whispered.

Eir replied as she drifted off to sleep, in the cool voice of the wind, "I'm not. See you in the morning, fire witch."

* * *

The memories that did come in the next several days were, unfortunately, more about Eir's childhood, and less about being an asshole that liked to pin fire witches to mountainsides. The more Auna prodded in that direction, the faster Eir shut down, or changed the subject or, on one occasion, broke into a run until she collapsed into a heaving pile of magic-touched villager.

There'd been some movement however, even if only subconscious. Elementals were incapable of hiding their power, almost as if they'd been designed that way. Eir's elemental power stayed buried in her lost memories until stress triggered—like Auna needing help moving steam from a hot spring. It snuck during periods of deep relaxation too, like last night, when Auna absorbed too much heat and hadn't been able to sleep. A wandering chill had blown across her forehead, around her neck, along her arms and fingers and, just once, across her stomach, until she'd finally fallen asleep.

"You've been quiet," Eir said, looking back over her shoulder. "Do we need to stop for a rest? How did you sleep last night?"

"I slept well, thanks to you." That she'd hoped Eir's wind would have found its way farther under her tattered dress did not need to be voiced. "How far do you think we've come?"

"Too far," Eir replied. "Not far enough. Does it matter? We have a half day of food left. We either reach the destination in the next few days, or we die. Maybe we die sooner."

"Stop." Auna grabbed Eir's shoulder. The heat from Auna's fingers went right through Eir's thin cotton. Steam hissed at their connection. "You're safe here. With me. Remember?"

"We need to walk faster."

"Why? What is ahead?"

Wind came, smelling of sulfur and bad eggs. It picked up the tiny bits of shale as it blew, and Auna had to shield her eyes. She pulled Eir in, pushing Eir's head against her shoulder. "See?" she said over the whistle of the wind through the tight passages. "It's easier to protect you if I know what is coming."

"Our *death* is coming!"

"But from what? Magic? Another elemental? Starvation? Insanity? What happened to you down here, Eir? I need you to remember!"

A rock at least the size of Auna's fist hit her in the calf. She buckled, bringing Eir down with her to the ground. Their knees hit the cooled magma in tandem, the wind dying as suddenly as it'd begun.

"That's going to slow us down." Auna rubbed the forming bruise. "Are you alright?"

Eir swiped at the moisture collecting at the corners of her eyes and refused to look at Auna.

"Eir." Auna traced a fallen tear down Eir's cheek, evaporating the water trail.

"We don't have time to talk." Eir stood and offered Auna her hand. "We're almost to your mountain range. The outcome could be different, this time. I suppose. With you here."

Auna started to speak, then thought better of it. She took Eir's hand, and they continued on, albeit at a slower pace due to Auna's newfound limp.

They didn't speak for the next two hours and stopped only long enough to eat a few handfuls of berries. An hour later, just as Auna was about to request a longer break to cool off and check her calf, they came upon a fork in the tube. One tube curved right, the other carried on, ahead. Auna chilled the magma in both directions just to be thorough. To the left was more of the same darkness. To the right, the tunnel glowed a faint, eerie green.

"I went right, last time," Eir said with certainty. "We should go left. Right is...the incorrect choice."

Auna was perfectly willing to avoid potentially magically glowing tunnels, but if she had been a child, well. Glowing green would have been her first choice. "But you got out. Wouldn't that mean right is the correct choice?"

"No."

Auna headed right, intent upon at least tossing a fireball down the floor to see as far along as she could. She made it four steps before Eir pulled her back by her shoulders. "Don't go down there!"

"A look won't hurt, will it?"

Eir's fingers ripped apart the wool like ice. The chill spread down across her chest, down her legs, setting her skin to gooseflesh. "There's magic down there."

"I'd say that's apparent." Auna took another step in. "Can the magic get us home more quickly?"

"It's the *wrong way*."

Auna unwrapped Eir's fingers, but the chill remained on her skin, radiating down to her bones. "What kind of magic?"

"The kind that can't protect us from starvation. We are wasting time!"

"Except something down that forbidden tunnel helped you once before."

"Listen to me!" Eir grabbed the orb from Auna's chest, pulling on Auna like a leash. The leather cord snapped, and Eir's hand opened, allowing the orb to fall down the front of Auna's dress, into the loose corset around her chest. The metal crackled against her skin, like ice in liquid magma. The sound of icicles falling from tiled roofs, of steam escaping a kettle, ricocheted from the orb, through the cavern and down into the right-side tunnel.

Auna had never shivered. Not once in her life had she ever felt cold. Now she could not control her shaking, the fire inside her dying to cool embers. She drew out the orb and held it out, first to the left, toward the tunnel Eir wanted them to take. The metal warmed, mildly, in her hand. Auna then spun back around and took two more steps toward the forbidden. The orb split in half, icicles flowering on its cracked surface.

The Elemental Orb had come from this tunnel.

A very large, very concerning part of the Margrud Curse fell into place.

"The orb," Auna said. "Where exactly did you find it?"

Eir bit her lip. "It was the wrong way to go."

"Are there more? If I can find the source, I can make sure the Margrud fire witches are never cursed again."

"Go that way and die." The impossible breeze—Eir's wind—lapped at Auna's ankles.

"You didn't die," Auna said, her voice as light and gentle as she could make it. "Did you?"

"I wanted to."

Auna pulled her companion close, until their noses touched. Had Eir cursed the Margrud Fire Witches to a century of imprisonment? Yes. Had she paid a price? Yes, many times over. "Wind Witch, what happened?"

Auna's words broke through some unspoken, invisible barrier between Eir and her memories. The gaze that suddenly met Auna's blazed with the heat of a forest fire. Eir's fingers, those impossibly long, surprisingly dexterous fingers wove into Auna's hair and pulled her to Eir. Eir found her lips and kissed her, sending an entirely different kind of heat through Auna's core. A fierce wind dove through the cavern, all but lifting Auna's feet up, pressing both of them against the warm cavern walls.

"The wind," Eir breathed against Auna's lips. "I'd forgotten. How could I forget?"

"You just needed a friendly reminder," Auna said. She pressed back into Eir, determined to enjoy the small victory, when Eir stepped back.

"Did I do it wrong?" Auna brushed her lips with her fingers. "Did I hurt you? I've never kissed a non-fire witch before."

Auna had, in her twenty-seven years as a fire witch, kissed a grand total of two people. The first had been a boy of eleven on a dare during one long, particularly dry summer of Auna's tenth year. He hadn't been expecting the kiss and his cheeks had flamed so hot rock under his feet had liquified, nearly sucking him down into an underground lava tube. Which was fine. His lips had tasted like stale sulfur anyway.

The second attempt had been last year on the spring solstice. A fire witch from the next mountain village over had come to visit extended family and run into Auna during an early morning walk. They'd picked red lehua blossoms which Auna had, brazenly, braided into the woman—Ioke's—hair. Ioke had leaned back, just enough that her head hit Auna's shoulder, and kissed her. This kiss had tasted like a fruit Auna could not name—something bright and tart that would have come from a village, not the mountains. They would have stayed there under the lehua tree all day except a bitter breeze had blown in, chilling them and driving them back to the village. Ioke had left the next day, as scheduled, and Auna had not had the courage to visit her.

"Eir?" Auna prodded.

"I'm really glad," Eir said, "to be off the mountain. Thank you for finding the orb. But I can't go back. Wind witches and fire witches," she said, clearly deflecting. "Can you imagine the destruction?"

"No one is asking you to go anywhere." Auna used the tip of one finger to turn Eir's head and kissed first the tip of her nose, then her chin then, finally, her lips.

Eir yielded this time and Auna melted their bodies together. Auna broke that first kiss only to reposition, to take nips across Eir's jawline and down her throat. Wind rushed across her backside, up under her dress, across her breasts as Auna spread a soft heat across Eir's hips as she pulled her closer.

The air felt electric. It smelled of volcanic minerals and salty bodies and Auna would not let go. Not ever. Forget her mountain, forget the curse, because Eir's wind had turned her nipples to frozen peaks. It had slid between her legs, replacing the native fire with a nip of ice in critical locations.

"You're cheating," Auna growled. She searched for tie that belted Eir's tunic. "The only way I can get under your clothes is to burn them off."

"There's enough smoke in here already," Eir said with a grin. She stayed focused on Auna's face but that damn tendril of wind slid back and forth between Auna's legs, alternating heat and cool. It thrust up, finding the place where Auna could not help but yield, her knees buckling.

"Still unfair," Auna gasped. Eir gripped her elbows, holding her up, but Auna did not want to be standing. Every part of her screamed to pull Eir down to the floor, burn off all their clothes, and see if her fire was as versatile as the wind.

She started to suggest just that, but her words came out in a cough instead. It was smokey in the cavern, although Auna was certain nothing was actually on fire.

"We have to go," Eir said, pulling the collar of her tunic over her nose. "I can't breathe." A black smoke clogged the air, cutting out her burning hair and the useable oxygen. Auna would have lost Eir completely if not for the hand she suddenly found slipping into hers.

"Agreed. This way. To the right." Auna coughed the words as she gagged on the smoke.

"Auna!"

"Eir, just run! Argue when you can breathe."

They did run then, down the righthand corridor, both gasping and coughing, molten tears staining Auna's cheeks. They ran until Auna's foot caught on a raised piece of basalt and she fell, face first, onto the cooling magma floor. Her satchel flew to one side, her hair extinguished. Eir, too close behind, tripped on Auna's heels and landed on top of her, further scratching Auna's face on the basalt.

"Sorry," Auna scrabbled to her feet. "Are you alright? Can you breathe better? The air is clearer here, but I still can't see you. Hold on. I need to catch my breath before I can relight."

Except, as Auna's eyes adjusted, she saw the tunnel was dimly lit by little crystals—green dots scattered over the ground glowing from no discernable source.

"I'm back," Eir said. "Back here again."

"Where?" Auna asked as she picked herself up and probed for scratches. Nothing major. Wounds cauterized fast on a fire witch.

"*Here.*" Eir kicked one of the crystals, dislodging a ball of green light to tumble across a silvery-white floor—the same color as the orb. The crystal stopped when it hit Auna's satchel, which had itself landed on what appeared to be a small pile of decaying clothes.

With a sinking weight in her stomach, Auna restrung her satchel and pulled apart the cloth pile. Side by side she laid out a stained pinafore, a tattered black dress, and the torn remains of a lace shift. None were longer than her arm.

Creating a bright flame took sustained effort—not something she could employ for hours without a lot of food and rest, but Auna lit a small loop of light across her palm anyway. She raised her hand up, then slowly brought it down, letting light and shadow chase their way across the tunnel walls. There was Eir, back against the wall, eyes lost in memory. There were the clothes of a six-year-old child, Eir's clothes no doubt, moldering at Auna's feet. And all around her the walls and floor of the cavern shone orb-silver. The color—the mineral? Metal?—outcropped unevenly from the basalt, sticking out like blunt daggers.

Auna sliced off a chunk of the metal with her foraging knife in a shower of bright green lights. Her fingers wrapped around the oblong shape in her hands, like she might wring the past from it. Instead, the congealing spray of sparks knitting her skin back together faded away. Her sweat turned to saltwater.

"Lithium comes from the earth," Eir said, her voice as small as a child's. "It reacts with water. It reacts with air. It combusts as readily as a fire witch."

Auna took the orb from her pocket and held it next to the wall. The materials were identical. She understood the science. She understood the magic. Still. *Six generations* the Margrud Witches had been cursed, bound to the mountain range.

Eir knelt by the clothes, folding each piece into a delicate triangle and stacking them like they were about to be put back into a dresser. She closed her eyes, and with a clenching of her hands, sent the clothes flying about the cave. Not with her hand, but with a gale of wind that ripped down the tube and whirled around the cavern like a cyclone.

"Wind witch," Auna said as she fought to keep blond curls from her face. "Explain."

"I was little, and the volcano wasn't as active. The magma wasn't flowing, the springs weren't as warm. I wanted to touch the bottom of the tube, and we'd spent all day practicing, using our wind to move the water from one hot spring to another. We emptied one, this one, and I made it all the way down but when I pulled the rope for my friend to bring me back, she didn't respond. The rope end fell on top of me. I waited all night, and the next day, and when no one came I started walking. I thought I could find an exit. But the farther I walked, the hotter the ground became. The wind cooled the floor but not nearly enough. My shoes melted. My feet blistered. I made it this far and took the right corridor but by the time I came here the soles of my feet were burned off. But it was cooler, in this cave, leaning against the lithium. I had no food. I had no water. I had a foraging knife, so I carved for hours until I was too tired even for that. When I laid down that final time, I wished. Maybe I prayed. I should have taken the left side. I just wanted to go back. To escape. To see my family the fastest way I could. And then I'd make sure everyone in the village stayed safe. Stayed cool. Away from fire, and lava, and the danger of the volcano."

This close to the wellspring of elements, buried under a metal that could borrow and regulate, and *reshape* elemental magic...Eir was lucky the result hadn't been worse. Well, worse for her. They'd definitely been worse for the Margrud Fire Witches. At least magic had seen fit to let Eir emerge as the adult she'd become, instead of the child she'd been. "Magic can be so specific and yet so simplistic," Auna sighed. "Six generations of bondage because a child had an unfortunate adventure."

Sharp eyes met hers—clear and angry, with all the energy of the disembodied wind that had teased Auna on the mountain. The side of Eir's personality untampered by memories of friends or family. "I didn't, I mean, I should have died. I lost my body to this thing"—she slapped the orb remains from Auna's hands—"and became tethered to your mountain range. We're right below it, so you know. Directly above, that's where this orb surfaced, and me with it. I've been a bodyless wind witch for almost three hundred years. Do you know what that does to a woman?"

Now was not the time for pithy retorts. Rhetorical questions were best left alone.

"I was feral after that long. The orb is a part of me, and you wanted to destroy it. I thought that would destroy me! After three hundred years I want to live, just not as fucking wind! But knowing now that I..." The steel in Eir's voice melted. "I had no way to break the orb. It never occurred to me to...to ask one of you for help. I could have freed all of us. But I didn't. I was a self-absorbed coward."

"You were a child," Auna said. "A child all alone under a mountain. And now you have a body, although how I'm not clear on, but you have a body, and a friend, *and* I think I know a way to make sure no other little elemental witches end up on the wrong side of this magic." Auna looked up at the silver and white speckled ceiling. She reached up to one of the low points and brushed some of the white powder away. "We're right under the Margrud Mountain system?" she asked.

"Right where you found the Elemental Orb."

"Perfection. We have fire, me, and the magma. We have air, you. We have earth, or mineral lithium, in this case. Lithium being a highly reactive alkali metal. Highly *flammable* metal. That's what happened back at the junction. Little heat, little wind, condensation from magmatic water and...we make our own magic."

Eir squinted at the same spot on the ceiling. "I don't understand. I'd advise against making a wish, too, unless you want to become a non-corporeal lava ball."

"Not a wish, and an action highly inadvisable without at least some face protection. I think...I think I'm talking about making out."

That got all of Eir's attention. "I...now?"

"Yeah, yeah I think so. You'll need to stay really close, and I don't know if I can absorb all the heat from the reaction. Probably I can, but there are risks."

"Risks to what?"

Auna grinned, slow and wide, bringing her palm to her face so Eir could see it. What she was proposing was wild. It broke every tenet of the Cose Volcano Safety Committee. There was no way to contain the results, no way to quantify their impact, no way to mitigate disaster. Yet it was—noting Eir's past and trauma—perhaps the most healing means of escape.

"Auna, *what?*"

Auna took Eir by the shoulders and pressed their bodies together. She kissed her lips, hard and demanding, then said, with all the bluster of a fire witch, "Want to blow the top off this mountain?"

* * *

The first thing Auna saw upon opening her eyes was the severed tops of the Margrud Mountain range. Eir stirred next to her, the wind witch's head pillowed on a mound of burnt lithium so fluffy and white it looked like a ball of cotton. The burnt lithium capped around them, broken only by a soft grey ring of cooled lava.

"Uggggh," Auna said as dizziness forced her back down, landing on the crook of Eir's shoulder. "That was a really bad idea. Useful, but still bad."

"We're out?" Eir carefully moved Auna's head as she shifted out from under her. "We're *out!* And we're...traveling very lightly."

Auna forced her eyes back open and confirmed that both she and Eir were naked. A secondary consequence of the explosion. Wool could only withstand so much heat, and Eir's leathers had crisped and shredded to bacon somewhere in the explosive process. "See?" Auna said when the dizziness receded enough that she could sit up. Before Eir could respond Auna added, "You're free, Eir. You're *free.* Now we can go—"

"Auna, your mountain!" Eir pulled on a mango sapling to stand up. "You fingered a wind witch in a lithium mine. Half the mountain range is gone. I don't think the explosion went entirely up."

One look at the carnage of her mountain stilled every thought but one. "The fire witches! We have to go. We have to get to Cose. We have to see—"

"Gods have mercy! Auna is that you? Is that why the air reeks of absolute chaos?" Ioke appeared from behind a small grove of trees, waving wildly. "Who is that with you? Are you alright?"

"We already know we're naked," Eir said.

"She's not talking about that," Auna said as realization dawned. It was where they were, so low on the mountain they were technically in the village foothills. Auna tapped the ground, then punched it. Her knuckles came back covered in dirt. *Dirt.* Where her shoulders had been was the semi-soft lava from the Margrud volcano system. Her feet were pillowed in a soft red clover. Her naked bum sat in a ring of bare dirt—the uncrossable boundary between the fire witches and the foothill villages. "I'm not ash," Auna said, grabbing the dirt and letting it run through her fingers. "I'm not ash! Ioke, come down here! Bring the village!"

But Ioke was already at her side, helping Auna to stand. Completely unconcerned about the formerly cursed soil on which they now both stood. "Old news. The magic fell days ago. There isn't a single witch left on the mountain. Good thing too, since you just blew it apart. Wind blew the detritus to the other side of the mountains, too. Convenient. Good job on retrieving the orb. Did you break it underground?" She grinned, wide and mischievous. "As the president of the Elruin Volcano Safety Committee, your sister safety committee, I may need to revoke your membership. But I'm pretty certain the former city of Cose will want to give you a reward, so that should help."

"I...we did it. Eir, we did it!" The fire witches were free. Auna's home was gone in the process but...oddly that didn't matter as much anymore. Her family was safe. The curse was broken. Home was where she made it. And Eir...

Eir still clung to the mango tree, her face squinting at the perfectly blue sky.

"How's your memory?" Auna asked her. "How are you? The explosion. The escape. Did it help? How do you feel?"

"Warm," Eir said. She turned back to Auna, but where Auna had expected sadness, she saw only relief. "Auna I'm...I'm sorry. For the mountain. The orb. I'm sorry for making the Margrud Curse. I'm not sorry I kept the orb from you though." She put her cheek against Auna's and whispered, "Thank you, fire witch, for saving me."

Magma pooled between Auna's legs.

"What now?" Ioke leaned in like they were spilling national secrets. "Your new friend cursed the Margrud Mountains? Were you going to tell me?"

Auna pushed Ioke back and kissed Eir, sending tiny sparks of fire across the other woman's tongue. Eir squeaked but sent swift retaliation across Auna's backside.

"Auna, what is going on?" Ioke demanded.

Auna pulled back from Eir just enough to say, "The witch who cursed the mountains died centuries ago. This is Eir. She's recently broken out of a curse herself. I think...I think she and I might travel together for a while. There's a lot of world neither of us have seen."

Eir bit her lower lip. "Thank you," she mouthed.

Ioke bristled. "I think you owe a report first to both Volcano Safety Councils—"

"Another time, Ioke. Eir, you pick first. Where do you want to go?"

"You're sure about us? Together?"

Auna nodded.

Eir's grin was so contagious that Auna giggled. "Maybe a quick trip to the village where your people went? For clothes?" Eir asked.

Auna held up a hand before Ioke could respond. "Why? We're probably just going to burn them again. Think bigger. We just dissolved a curse. We harnessed magic. With those credentials we could go anywhere."

Eir snickered and lifted Auna into her arms. "Anywhere?"

Auna nodded. "Your choice. Just maybe we could avoid overly damp forests this time?"

"Auna you absolutely can*not*—" Whatever Ioke said next was lost a rush of wind as Eir left the ground, speeding them away from the mountains, away from the forests, into the unknown. As long as her people were safe, Auna did not care about the Cose Volcano Safety Committee. She had spent her whole life tied to a mountain, Eir had spent several decades tied to a combustible metal, and both of them deserved a chance to see the world. Together.

Together, they were dynamite.

"Fallout" is a stand-alone short by J.S. Fields. You can read more of their science fiction and fantasy work at **www.patreon.com/jsfields** or check out their website: **www.jsfieldsbooks.com**

The Ferry Maiden

Dee Lyle

Sapphic Representation: Lesbian, Bi
Heat Level: Hot!
Content Warnings: Coarse Language, Violence, Dead People

With only a short time left before the signal bell tolled, the Gondolier felt the needles of impatience tighten her shoulder blades. Though truth be told, none of the gondola's occupants were getting any older. The majority had lived full lives—faces creased with a lifetime of laughter or scowls, skin paper-thin and spines crumpled from the weight of decades. A few showed the hollow-eyed signs of illness, youth snatched away before ever leaving bloom. Lastly, six soldiers sulked at the stern of the boat, the last to arrive. One had a split skull, another his detached left arm in his right hand, two carried multiple gaping punctures in their torsos, and the last shuffled in awkwardly, holding his head still so as not to jostle his broken neck.

"Ey, gondola Maiden!" an old, jowly farmer barked, rapping his cane against the side of the boat. "Can we get this carnival moving? I want to see my focking wife. I got to tell her that I finally bagged her sour-faced gourd of a sister and brag that I outlived her by nearly six years."

The Gondolier turned her head slowly toward the knobby-kneed old codger, well aware that her deep hood hid her features from the souls on the boat. She didn't say anything, spearing an unflinching gaze at him. The living could be tedious, and although she devoted her existence to ensuring their safe passage to their final afterlife, they would not make demands of her.

One of the others in the boat nudged him. "Don't antagonize her. What if she never takes us across?"

"Pah! We'd walk the long way."

Eons ago, that was the way of it. Souls of the dead would land on the shores of the fiery lake and have no choice but to walk the long way around within the heavy, dark shadows. None of the light generated by the waves of fire could penetrate the velvety black mist, where unnamed things shifted. Not even The Gondolier understood what lived out there or why so few souls completed the trek, but if one stared directly into the dark, sometimes they could catch a glimpse of something staring back.

A wave of fire slapped against the wooden hull of the gondola, rocking it and the people who had already gathered there. The lake itself was an unforgiving mistress. If the souls weren't already dead, the heat would have scorched their mortal bodies, making charcoal from their frail skin.

More of the gondola's occupants turned on the old man, hissing for him to shut up. For the first time, a look of worry passed over his jaundiced eyes. He glanced toward the edge of the boat where wood met flame, then to the Gondolier and her boat waiting to collect the dead. He broke his gaze away from her darkened features, gnashing his worn teeth and grumbling under his breath.

A white light bloomed upon the beach. All of the fallen warriors perked.

A figure in battered, blood-spattered armor jerked upright with a sharp gasp. A singed plume on her helmet quivered and bobbed until she doubled over and let gravity pull the helmet into her cracked gauntlets. Upon straightening, she flicked a sweaty mass of wheat colored hair over her shoulder. Strands clung to her neck and cheeks, smearing beads of sweat. Three pikes jutted from her blood-and-filth spattered chest plate.

Slamming the helmet into the ashy ground next to her, she grabbed hold of one of the pikes and gave it an experimental wiggle.

"Well fuck me, that's in there good."

The Gondolier stared. People of all types dropped onto the lakeshore to be taken to their afterlife. Sooner or later, death came for everyone. Faces blended together after millennia, but on occasion, one stood out.

The warrior had a fine squared jaw and a hooked nose that most would consider too large, but instead gave her face a sense of regalness, aside from the crook across its bridge. Her eyes were emerald, framed with pale lashes; her cheeks freckled from a life spent under the sun. For all of her strong features, her lips stood out as oddly plump and delicate. At least, until they broadened into a luminous smile.

The warriors all stood up in the back of the boat, erupting with hollers and cheers. One slapped his buddy's back with his own detached arm and another's head flopped back and forth as he gripped the edge of the gondola.

Unfazed, the warrior on the beach hopped nimbly to her feet, moving with the grace of a lion in spite of her heavy, clinking armor and the pike jutting out from it. "So, this is it. Lake of fire and everything! Look at that boat, just like my nan said there'd be! And a creepy, black-cloaked Gondolier and all!" She turned in circles, glancing around at the smothering shadows on either side of the beach, then at the boat and its occupants. "Oh, hey, there *are* six of you. I knew you were dead! Your body is up top twitching, just about faked me out," she told one of the other soldiers, jerking her thumb over her shoulder.

He made a rude gesture in return.

Ignoring him, she said, "Let's look at this boat! Beautiful craftsmanship. Did you really build this yourself?" she asked, directing the question toward the Gondolier, but not waiting for an answer.

The warrior took strides forward on long legs, reaching out to touch the gondola, but the Gondolier stepped into her path. She jarred to a halt, looming over the Gondolier by a whole handspan.

"You must pay for passage. You may not board the gondola without paying the toll." The Gondolier held up a pale hand expectantly, the only skin peeking out of her enveloping robes. She had to angle her body carefully so as not to get jabbed with the end of one of the pikes.

Blinking those large, emerald eyes, the warrior took a measured step back. "Right. Yes." She patted her pockets. "I'm a bit shallow in the pockets right now, but that's all right. I won't be staying for long. And don't you worry one bit, love, this job is going to earn stacks as fat as a prized sow. I'll be loaded up by the end of the week."

"How are you going to get your money if you're dead as the rest of us?" one of the soldiers in the boat crowed.

Scraping her golden hair off her square jaw, the warrior just grinned. "Don't you worry about me, lads." She suddenly fixed her attention back on the Gondolier. "Can I ask you something? What's under the hood?"

The Gondolier's slender, pale hand remained raised between them, palm up. "The boat is almost full. If you cannot pay, you will have to walk the long way."

Turning, she looked into the darkness that swallowed the path leading around the lake, her eyes brightening. "Don't tempt me with a good time, love."

Nobody ever seemed *thrilled* at the prospect of walking. The occasional fool, perhaps. The Gondolier tried to convey her disapproval through the darkness of her hood, but the attempt broke over the warrior with no visible effect.

"You know, in all the stories my Nan ever told me about Death's Ferry Maiden, she never gave you a name. Do you have one?"

The Gondolier stared impassively, not interested in formal introduction.

"Pity. My parents called me Layla. Seemed a bit prissy growing up, but I've grown into it, don't you think?"

"You must make a decision, Layla." The name tasted like honey mead on her lips. The Gondolier clamped her teeth together at the absurdity of the thought. Shaking it off, she plowed forward. "You must make a decision. You either pay the toll or you walk. You may not linger. When the bell chimes, the boat leaves this shore, and then the shadows will close around you."

Layla continued grinning, nodding up with her chin. "Give it a few minutes, love."

One of the stooped old women already seated in the boat raised a frail finger. "I have an extra farthing in here I can pay your passage with, dearie. My sons loaded my pockets to make sure I had enough to make the crossing."

"That's mighty kind of you, and speaks well of your sons, but I'll be just fine. My Nan would whack me with her rolling pin if she knew I'd taken an old woman's final wealth."

"The bell will chime soon. If you are not on the boat, you will be left to the shadows," the Gondolier warned, a sick feeling creeping into her stomach. To leave Layla on the ashy beach as she took the gondola across the fire... Like so many others, she would be gone by the time the boat returned.

The warning bell would chime any minute.

"Another may pay your crossing. The deal she offers is acceptable."

Layla cocked her head, resting a hand casually on one of the pikes. "What do you do with the money."

The Gondolier blinked. "Excuse me?"

"Do you buy an endless supply of billowy black robes? Do you have to purchase supplies? Do you eat?"

"That's none of your concern."

"When am I ever going to have another opportunity to learn the answer to these things? Do you have a pub over there on the other side and drinking buddies?"

Once again, the Gondolier tried and failed to radiate disapproval through the darkness of her hood.

"You're no fun," Layla huffed.

And she still had not paid the toll for safe passage. The Gondolier could not force anyone to board her boat, although she never had actually wanted to before.

On the beach, near where the metal helmet remained, white light bloomed. A new figure formed within it and a man appeared, laying facedown on the ground with a battle ax sticking out of his back.

"Hey, that's mine!" Layle cried indignantly, whirling away from the Gondolier and stomping over.

The man had on the same red and gold livery as the other soldiers in the boat, all who groaned and hissed their displeasure at seeing another comrade appear.

Before the Gondolier could think to warn her, Layla slammed a heavy boot into the back of the soldier's neck, grabbed the haft of the ax with both hands, and yanked. The ax, of course, was not the actual ax that had killed the man, but a shade of it. It was now a part of him, as much as it was a part of his story. The two could not be unbound quite so easily.

Layla bellowed in rage, adjusting her grip, her foot grinding into the poor man's neck as she heaved, a vein on her sweaty forehead popping out.

"Give me my ax, blackguard!"

The soldiers in the boat all rose again, but the Gondolier whipped toward them and hissed, "Leave the boat and you won't step foot back onto it," which succeeded in stalling them from jumping out.

Robes billowing out around her, she stalked over to where Layla continued attempting to pry the ax out of the soldier's back. He caterwauled and thrashed his limbs around but did not succeed in throwing her off.

The Gondolier laid a hand on the exposed skin of Layla's arm between the end of her pauldron and beginning of her bracers. Even in death, she scorched like the flames of the lake.

"Enough. Leave him."

Layla exhaled noisily through her nose and stepped off the soldier, who finally managed to push up to his hands and knees, spitting ash. He tipped his head back and his throat gaped open. Layla's ax might have sent him to the ground, but a knife across his throat had finished him off.

"Keep it. I'll have enough money soon to buy a better one," Layla growled.

Removing her hand from the scorching skin of her arm, the Gondolier swallowed thickly and addressed the soldier, raising her hand. "If you wish to cross the lake, you must pay the toll."

Eyeing Layla suspiciously, he began patting his pockets and reaching for his belt. "I...uh...I'm a little light." Looking to the boat, he spotted his friends, one of which waved his detached arm. "Can one of you spot me?"

"Again, Dag? I've got it, but this is the last fucking time, I swear!"

Before escorting him to the boat and accepting the toll to allow his passage, the Gondolier turned one last time to Layla, who was trying to tame her wild, sweaty tresses in irritation.

"Please," the Gondolier murmured, too low for the others to hear. "The bell will chime any minute and the boat will leave. You must be on it."

That wild grin stretched her lush lips. "Sweet of you to fret, Ferry Maiden, but I won't need your boat quite yet. Maybe next time."

As if summoned by the insane confidence of the warrior, a white light blossomed at Layla's back.

"About time! You keep a spot on that boat warm for me, though. I'm sure I'll be back before long."

Fixing the Gondolier with those brilliant green eyes, Layla winked, and then vanished from the beach. The only evidence she had ever been there were boot prints in the ash and a dented helmet with a crooked plume sticking out of it.

The boat erupted in roars as the soldiers expressed their shock and rage, demanding to know where she had gone. To the Gondolier, it was clear. Somehow, she had crossed the barrier from death going the opposite direction.

From far across the lake, the warning bell began to chime. The shadows already felt thicker, deeper, creeping slowly to swallow the beach an inch at a time. They were out of time.

Normally, such an event would have annoyed the Gondolier, as humans were not strictly supposed to be able to cheat the one thing that equalized them all. But the beautiful warrior would be back, allowing the Gondolier to gaze upon her face again. Perhaps more than once, as long as she remained friends with a necromancer.

* * *

"...and that's how I killed my fourth husband," the old woman chortled, running her bejeweled fingers down the snow-white mink coat she wore.

The pox-ridden young man next to her nodded, eyes wide, mouth slightly agape.

"Have you ever been married?"

He shook his head.

"Would you like to be?"

He shook his head again more vigorously, one of his pustules bursting open on his neck and oozing into the threadbare collar of his shirt.

The Gondolier hid a smile within the darkness of her hood as the elegant old woman launched into a soliloquy about her fifth husband's life and untimely demise. The woman had an admirable penchant for orchestrating accidents that never led back to her.

Over on the beach, the bright light erupted to signal a new arrival. Most of the occupants of the boat didn't even seem to notice, enraptured as they were by the tale of a piano being hoisted aloft, a bumbling husband following a trail of rare gold coins scattered on the ground, and a rope that hadn't been well secured.

A splash of water followed the materialization of a figure in plate armor, sprawled out on her back with arms and legs akimbo. A sopping golden head raised briefly, then fell back onto the sand.

"Damn it. I should have known she'd pull me in and drown me."

The Gondolier's heart scuttled around in her chest for a moment before she managed to lock it down again. Time didn't mean much in the land of the dead, but endless boat passages had come and gone since the warrior's first visit to her beach. She had been patient, knowing that sooner or later they would meet again.

Rolling onto her side, Layla spat a mouthful of water and dragged a tangle of sopping blond hair back on her head. She looked, impossibly, a bit less round in the face, not that she had much softness there to begin with, her jawline and cheekbones both sharper, a few new nicks and scars on her face, and the beginning creases of laugh lines that disappeared and reappeared around her emerald eyes with the changing expressions on her face. They bloomed again quickly when she once again broke into a smile.

"I suppose all my mates were right—no matter how pretty the fish-girl is, they will definitely drown you if you try and kiss one. Let that be a lesson to all of you, not that any of you actually need the wisdom now. Whatever. It was worth it. I'd do it again." Her gaze traveled over the occupants of the boat and onto the Gondolier, those eyes softening. "We meet again, my shrouded friend!" She scrambled awkwardly to her feet, waterlogged in her armor as she was. It poured out of all of the joints as she made it to her feet.

"Do you have a coin this time, or would you prefer to wait?"

"Yes, and yes. They'll fish me out of the bottom of the bog sooner or later. But here. I know sometimes folks come through with empty pockets. Why don't I pay a few in advance?" She began patting her armor as if it contained pockets until she found a little pouch tucked away and extracted it with a jingle.

The Gondolier frowned. "It doesn't work that way."

"Why not? You let people pay for each other all the time. It's in half the stories. My Nan says that's why she always makes sure her friends have two coins on them after they...you know..." She mimed choking, getting one's throat cut, and what appeared to be an ax murder. "Just in case."

"I know, but they're not here yet. It isn't done like that."

"That's a stupid rule."

The Gondolier opened her mouth to argue, but Layla had already uncinched the pouch and flung the coins across the sand.

"Oops. It appears that I've dropped *all* of my coins. It sure would be a shame if someone who might have died without any money stumbled across one."

Crossing her arms, she tried to glaring at the warrior through the darkness of her hood, but it bounced right off of Layla as it had the previous time they met, who lit up like a ray of sunshine. A soggy ray of sunshine, but luminescent, nonetheless.

"Oh! Oh, fuck me, I almost forgot!" Again, she began patting down her armor and yanking at her chest plate to try and wedge an arm underneath it, her bracer getting in the way. "I've been carrying it on my person for two years now. Didn't want to not have it on me if I died next in a place where my friends can't get it in my hands before I get whisked off to the underworld, like at the bottom of a bog. It did get cracked once, but the glass is quite hardy and has survived more battles than it really ought to have."

She continued wrestling around, tugging at fasteners until she finally extracted a glass bottle from the small of her back. She presented it proudly to the Gondolier. As mentioned, a crack marred its otherwise smooth surface, and within the bottle, was a little boat identical to the one bobbing next to the beach.

"I had it made based off of memory, but I think I got it. The little wave carvings on the prow and the rows of seating and the stick thing you use to propel it."

"It's just called an oar," she murmured, stunned by the accuracy of the tiny gondola in its glass container.

"Do you like it?"

The Gondolier bent closer, inspecting the details, which weren't perfect, but charming, nonetheless. She had crafted the boat herself, eons ago when she first decided to begin offering safe passage to souls across the lake of fire. She'd made a pact with an ancient incense cedar for its wood and traded favors with her cousin for his craftsmanship to temper it against the lake's flames, but personally carved each feature herself, hoping to make the gondola inviting for the souls for their final passage.

"It's wonderful," she breathed.

"Take it!"

"What?"

"I had it made for you!" Layla eagerly thrust the bottle closer to her.

"What for?"

"Because I thought you'd like it."

The Gondolier reached out a slender, pale hand from within her robe, then pulled it back. "What do you want in exchange for it?"

"Nothing. It's a gift."

She shook her head, her fingers curling inward. "I'm not...I can't...it doesn't work like that."

"Work like what?"

"A being such as me cannot owe a debt. You must ask for something in return."

"Huh." Layla cocked her head, mouth twisting those full lips to the side. "I suppose my Nan always did say that the gods love a trade. And never to expect anything for free. She should have warned me about kissing pretty fish, but that's neither here nor there." Straightening her head, the creases around her eyes deepening, she said, "All right, then in exchange for the boat, will you show me your face?"

The Gondolier was knocked a full step back, retreating deeper into her hood. "My face?"

"They say no mortal has ever seen the face of the Ferry Maiden. Can I? Can I be the first?"

Her impulse was to refuse the warrior's demand, but the longer she looked between the little boat encased in glass and the woman's wide, green eyes, her defenses crumbled and the word "no" seemed to flee from her vocabulary.

"I...yes. I'll show you."

Layla perked like a flower greeting the sun. "Really?"

Glancing over her shoulder at the boat full of waiting souls, she reached out her hand and touched Layla's arm below the pauldron, drawing her further away so they might have a sliver of privacy. They strolled down the beach, as close to the swirling, swallowing shadows as she dared, and turned her back on the gondola so no one else would see.

In the beginning, her intention had been to be an equalizer, as death leveled the playing field for all mortals. She did not want her appearance to influence anyone from fearing or embracing death, so she had selected her shroud. Now, after ages upon ages of ferrying souls, it seemed rather arbitrary, but was not a habit she could convince herself to change.

For a moment, all she could manage was to twist her fingers together while her heart thudded noisily against her breast. She should not be so nervous for someone to see her face, but logic had long since exited the conversation. Raising her hands to the edges of her deep hood, she hovered there without moving, gathering what courage she could find.

"May I?" Layla asked, but without waiting for an answer, also raised her hands up to the opening of her hood, the thin fabric pinched between her strong, callused fingers. "You nod when you're ready."

The Gondolier exhaled. Then nodded.

Before she could regret her choice, Layla flipped the hood back. Then gasped. For a horrible moment, she thought the gasp was one of horror or shock or repulsion, but the laugh lines quickly reappeared as her grin spread and those green eyes drank her in.

"You're beautiful!" she cried, her voice tinging toward outrage. "All that secrecy over *this*? You're just a normal, pretty—albeit very pale—woman. I thought you probably had a bare skull with spiders living in your eye sockets, given how secretive you are. Now I know the historians and clerics have been misspeaking this whole time! You're not a Ferry Maiden, you're just a *fair maiden*."

Her rough fingertips traced the Gondolier's cheeks and brow with unearned familiarity, but she couldn't bring herself to push Layla away, the touch sparking an odd, squirming heat that started in the pit of her stomach and flared out from there. Her thumb grazed just beneath her lower lip, and she lost the reason she thought the touch might be too familiar. Layla just continued grinning at her, more and more smug by the second.

"You're so beautiful," she repeated. "If you were part fish, I'd kiss you in a moment!"

Before the Gondolier could scramble any words together to reply, Layla held out the boat in the bottle like a prize. The Gondolier grasped it, pulling it to her chest where her heartbeat surely should have been heard clanging against the glass. She was infected by the other woman's smile, her lips lifting into the barest arc of a smile.

"The trade is fair," she uttered at last, her voice oddly reedy.

They just continued to stare at each other's faces and smile like fools.

"Can I brag about this?"

"About seeing my face?"

"Yes! I want to tell everyone, especially that weasel of a ranger, Perry, who doesn't even believe that we met the last time I died. He keeps making fun of me for trying to protect the boat in the bottle every time we get into fights. Just wait until he dies and gets a mouthful of sand when he lands here and realizes it's all true. I want him to eat his words. And the sand. And hopefully he dies somewhat embarrassingly."

Words abandoned her, so the Gondolier simply nodded.

"I think this makes us proper friends now, don't you think? And if we're going to be proper friends, I have one more question. You must have a name. Can I know it? I can't just go on calling you the Ferry Maiden, can I?"

"I...I have many."

"Any you particularly like?"

"No." If only because her mind had abandoned her, and she suddenly couldn't remember any of them.

"Huh." Layla opened her mouth for whatever bold statement she would next exclaim, but a flare of light cut her off, encasing her fully. "Ah, looks like my friends scared the pretty fish away and got my corpse back to shore. Until next time, love?"

Still clutching the glass bottle to her chest, the Gondolier watched as the light pulled Layla back to her friends in the realm of the living until she was fully gone, leaving nothing but boot prints on the sand of the beach. Once the light had fully dissolved away, she pulled her hood back over her glossy, black hair and pale face, composing herself as best she could. She could hardly hear over the ringing in her ears, more eager than she ever thought she could be for a mortal to die and visit again.

* * *

Mortals died at an inconsistent rate. Sometimes, the Gondolier could bring her boat to the beach where she collected them and have hundreds already waiting for her, and more landing in the sand each second. Other times, hours might pass between single deaths.

The day started without a single soul needing passage, which was unusual within itself, but time lingered on quietly, the only movement coming from the shadows cast from the lake's surface and the roiling darkness on either side of the shore. The Gondolier perched on the edge of a newly constructed bench—made by her and installed next to the dock. The bench was made out of the same, pleasant smelling incense cedar as the boat. It came from the same ancient tree, in fact, and had been a nice diversion for the Gondolier to visit her old friend again. The tree had delighted in catching up and listening to the service the Gondolier had provided mortal souls with its wood.

More people used the bench than she ever thought would want to. Many of them had coins in hand, ready to pay the toll to cross, but wanted one last moment to linger and reflect on the lives they left behind. Others simply wanted a quiet place to wait to see if a loved one would join them before the bell rang out across the flames and they needed to be off.

Sitting on the bench for the first time since its installation, pale hands folded neatly atop her lap, the Gondolier simply surveyed the shoreline and empty gondola and relished the quiet while it lasted.

Before long, a bright light on the beach bloomed, heralding the first soul of the day.

She knew who it was before the light fully faded, just from the posture of her armor-clad figure, although this set seemed slightly better quality, fitting against her strong form as if it had been customized to her measurements. It didn't carry any visible cracks or dents on its polished surface. She wore no helmet, much like last time, but instead her golden hair was draped with a chain of little white daisies.

"Oh, you have got to be *shitting* me!" she cried when she took in the beach. She slapped a hand over her shoulder, spinning in a circle and giving the Gondolier a glimpse at what had delivered Layla this time.

A knife stuck out from her back, punching straight through her armor, her scapula, and into her heart.

"Isn't the purpose of the armor so that type of thing doesn't happen?" the Gondolier asked, swallowing against the knot in her throat and trying not to appear *too* pleased to see the warrior, given the circumstances.

Layla whipped her gaze toward her. Her freckles had multiplied, as well as the lines around her mouth and eyes, which were now visible even between smiles. Even though a thunderous rage built behind those deep green eyes, a silent promise lived on her face that laughter was never far off.

"That little shit stabbed me in the back! At a solstice festival! A *festival*! I'm supposed to be eating little pastries off of the full bosoms of bar wenches, not...not..." She finally got her arm around far enough to grab the pommel of the dagger and begin yanking at it fruitlessly. Her bicep bulged where it was briefly visible between pauldron and bracer. She gave up after a few hearty attempts. "Right. These don't come out, do they?" Huffing indignantly, she turned finally to the Gondolier, whose steps had drawn her forward without either of them realizing, erasing much of the distance until they were an arm's length apart. "Greg will get me back up once he finds my body, and then I will go smash Rupert into pulp. At least, I think it's Rupert behind this. Is there a way to know who killed you if you didn't see it happen?"

The Gondolier shook her head.

"Typical." Layla exhaled in one last huff. "I'm certain it was him anyway. Enchanted dagger is exactly his style. But enough about that, are you well?"

The Gondolier blinked. "Am I well?"

Nobody had ever asked her that, much less a mortal.

"Yes. It's been, what, seven years since we last spoke? A lot can happen in seven years. I slew a drunken dragon, defenestrated a great mage, planted a lovely garden outside my home in Feldruin that won the Annual Feldruin Outstanding Horticulture Award, and then burned that house to the ground for reasons that shall not be named—but Finch Whistlebottom knows what he did and why it had to happen. I'm sure I'm missing something, but those are the interesting bits. Oh, and I got stabbed in the back by a world-renowned flutist, obviously." She gestured vaguely to the knife sticking out of her back. "So? How do you fare?"

The Gondolier couldn't make her mouth cooperate. She meant to say something along the lines of being an eternal being with a consistent structure to her existence who had not deviated a single moment from her duty in thousands of years. Instead, what came out was, "I want to hear everything you've ever done."

Layla's scowl softened. "That, my friend, is going to be a very long conversation. And we probably don't have much time, depending on how long it takes for my body to be discovered and resurrected."

Blinking and shaking off her nerves, the Gondolier slowly and delicately reached up to lower her hood, a quick glance around confirming that they were, indeed, alone on the beach, aside from what unknowable creatures lurked in the shadows away from the lake's firelight.

The gesture pulled another quick smile from Layla. "It's good to see you again."

"Does anyone believe you've seen my face?"

"Most people have a hard time believing all of my stories. That's just what I get for living a life so abundant."

Pushing aside a swell of shyness, the Gondolier gestured for her to follow. "I want to show you something."

It didn't take Layla long to spot the bench next to the gondola. "Well that's new!"

She walked her over to it, explaining, "It occurred to me that if someone wanted to wait instead of boarding my gondola immediately, that they didn't have anywhere comfortable to do so. People have been using it as a spot to reflect, so it's gotten quite a bit of use. Do you like it?"

"I love it! It's got the same little wave patterns as the boat." Spinning, her armor clanking slightly, she plopped down onto the left side of the bench, tossing an arm over the back and sighing, angling her body so that the knife hilt didn't hit it, long legs sprawled out in front of her.

The Gondolier lowered down onto the other side, her fingers twisting in her lap.

After a moment, Layla's expression sobered, although the laugh lines remained. She sat up, leaning forward to brace her forearms over her metal-clad thighs. Her flower crown sat lopsided on her golden head of hair, strands falling to frame her square face. She looked, for the first time, melancholy. "Can I ask you something?"

She knew that this question would come. "Yes, Layla. She was here."

Though her eyes were turned away, she could see her pale lashes flicker up and down as she blinked rapidly.

"I thought so. Was she okay? Did she make it on board the boat?"

The Gondolier nodded. "Of course she did. It was wonderful to meet her. I knew instantly who she was. She had your eyes, and your smile." Reaching across the divide between them, she laid a hand over Layla's sun-kissed fingers. "We talked a lot about you."

"And she wasn't hurt or anything? She wasn't in any pain?"

"Are you in pain? You have a knife in your back," she pointed out gently.

"I guess not." Layla sighed, swallowing heavily, turning her hand so their fingers could wrap each other more easily. "I miss her. I always miss her when I'm out adventuring, but this is different. It's not the same coming home and Nan isn't there. She raised me more than my parents did, you know. They were always busy working, so I was always at Nan's."

"I know. She told me." She squeezed Layla's hand. "She also told me how proud she was of you, for going out and finding a life beyond where you began. She even told me about your award-winning garden, and the dragon that got into the mead hall, and the mage defenestration, and so many other things."

Layla gave a little, indignant gasp. "So, you've heard all of my stories already!"

"Some of them," she corrected. "But I'd still like to hear them all from you. Besides, you still have more things to do once you go back. You'll be packed with even more stories before we see each other again."

"Unless Rupert assassinates all of my friends first," she snorted. "Then I'll be in trouble. I forgot my coin purse at the jousting tourney."

"Layla," the Gondolier scoffed, "your Nan made it to these shores with coins in all of her pockets and sewn into the linings of all of her garments. I'm not even sure how she got around, it was so heavy, and totaled in almost three hundred gold pieces. Even with giving them away freely since I ferried her across, there's still well over two hundred left."

The warrior choked on a laugh and swiped her free hand under her eyes. "I worried she'd get here and not have anything."

"She used one coin to cross and insisted on leaving the rest."

"I thought that wasn't how it worked."

"I made an exception for such a remarkable woman."

Layla squeezed her hand, glancing up at her through damp eyelashes. "Thank you, fair maiden." She brought the Gondolier's hand to her full lips, pressing the barest hint of a kiss to her knuckles that nevertheless sent a full shiver down her spine. "Speaking of," she whispered against her fingers, "you never did tell me what name you like best."

Unsticking her tongue from the roof of her mouth, she could only string enough words together to say, "I suddenly can't remember any of them again."

Layla's smile flashed into something wicked. "Is that so?"

She nodded, her hand tingling where the other woman's breath whispered against it. "Whatever you call me, I would answer."

Using the grasp she had on her hand, the warrior pulled her in to close what little distance remained between them. Their heads inclined together, so close that the Gondolier could only smell honeysuckle and sunshine, and she was utterly trapped in Layla's emerald eyes.

"What if I called you *'mine'*?"

She found herself nodding. "Yes, I think that would work for me."

It came as no shock that Layla was almost grinning too broadly to even kiss her, their lips pressing in fits and pauses as she laughed into the Gondolier, which made her let out a broken series of giggles in return. She couldn't even say why they were laughing, other than Layla completely entranced her with how brightly she shone in the shadow of the underworld. She craved the sunny warmth of her lips and the scorching calluses that wrapped the back of her neck under her sleek, black hair. She snaked her arms around her broad shoulders, made broader by her armor, trying to cling to the vibrant life her soul still carried into death. Strong arms encircled her waist and hauled her up and into Layla's lap. The Gondolier's robes were a tangled obstacle that made them both laugh harder as she wrestled them in order to get straddled across Layla's thighs.

Framing the woman's face in her slim hands, she dared look into those emerald eyes again. The Gondolier let herself be hypnotized by them as their kisses turned urgent, swallowing any lingering laughter, shallow gasps and delighted hums replacing it. No ambrosia had ever tasted as sweet as the warrior's lips against the Gondolier's, no chiseled god had ever been as tempting. She sank willingly into the mortal's chaotic charm, imaging much more than the bench she would someday craft in her honor.

As if conjured by the thought, Layla pulled back briefly, the grin and subsequent laugh lines returning to her face. "You said you built this bench for me?"

The Gondolier hummed noncommittally, once again bereft of words, pressing kisses down her sharp jaw and to the beating pulse just beneath.

"I ought to trade something in return for it, yes?"

The Gondalier paused, the taste of sunshine lingering on her lips as she also pulled back. "I...no. It's for you, but not *for* you."

"Clear as a wooden post, love." Before she could find the right words to articulate the sentiment, Layla pressed on. "I'm trying to come up with a reason I can perform a favor for you. Let me have this."

If she had been mortal, she would have died from the spasming in her chest. "I need no favors from you. You are more than enough as you are."

She stroked a strand of hair away from her eyes. "You're a darling, my unnamed goddess of death, but I really would like to offer you a sampling of my talents, if you are so inclined."

"I'm not actually a goddess of death, I'm more of a courier than anything..."

Layla exhaled noisily and interrupted her. "We may not have time to argue the semantics, depending on where anyone's at with finding my body and tracking down my necromancer. Do you want to continue kissing for that length of time or may I taste you more thoroughly?"

Her mouth snapped shut. "Oh. I see." It was a small miracle she managed human speech at all in that moment. "You may."

Before she could wrap her brain around any of the logistics, Layla had picked her up, spun her around, and plopped her onto the bench. Layla lowered down to her knees in the sand between the Gondolier's parted legs. Layla's callused fingers skimmed up the Gondolier's ankles and calves as she pushed her black robes up above her knees.

"But this isn't an...an exchange," she stuttered out, determined to make that clear. "I put the bench in for anyone like you, who wishes to rest instead of board the gondola im...immediately...*oh. Oh fuck.*"

Layla wasted no time, yanking the Gondolier's hips to the edge of the bench, pushing her thighs apart and pressing a wet kiss to her center before parting her lips with a hot and efficient lick. The Gondolier's pale fingers snapped to Layla's golden crown of hair between her legs, accidentally crushing the wreath of daisies there. Half the little white and yellow flowers fell to the metallic pauldrons and slid off into the sand, the rest caught between the Gondolier's fingers and the soft strands of hair wound around them.

The heat coming off the lake had nothing compared to Layla's mouth. The Gondolier had no concept of the last time she'd blushed so furiously. The blush would not recede, not with Layla crouched before her, letting out an appreciative groan. The Gondolier pressed a fist to her teeth to smother a choking noise, her hips bucking unceremoniously in response to the first clever little licks as Layla explored.

Green eyes that reflected the fire of the lake peeked up at her, a quick check-in before returning to task when the Gondolier breathlessly nodded. Pale lashes fluttered close against freckled cheeks. She tried to burn the image into her memory, stroking Layla's gilded hair back from her forehead.

The next noise the Gondolier gasped out, she didn't attempt to smother. Layla worked her from entrance to clit with practiced, diligent strokes, alternating pressure and suction in dizzying patterns, perfectly timed to the way the Gondolier tightened and relaxed the grip in her hair. What was left of the poor daisy crown shredded between the tangled strands of hair fisted in her hands, the rest lost to the sand.

Wrapping her strong arms under the Gondolier's thighs, the warrior yanked her even closer, nearly pulling her off the bench. Her mouth yet remained soft and warm, her tongue extracting exquisite pleasures that stole the breath from the Gondolier's lungs. She tried to speak, to praise her or beg her for more, but the words tripped over each other into an incoherent pile. The string of syllables that tumbled from her parted lips may have created words, but thankfully only the roiling shadows were there to witness the attempt. By the time Layla pressed two fingers into her slick core, the Gondolier had given up entirely on coherency. Whatever noise she uttered, Layla only laughed into her, pulling back to nuzzle the tender skin of her inner thigh.

"Perfect, you're just perfect, love," she crooned, grinning up at her. The Gondolier matched the grin, unable to string a coherent sentence together if she wanted. "Fucking adorable."

She smugly returned to her task.

The Gondolier lost herself to the rise and fall of the rhythm Layla built for her. Kisses, licks, bites, touches—all of it became an endless tide of sensation. For eons, she had asked for nothing more than her purpose of ferrying souls, had never thought to reach beyond the task she had assigned herself for anything. Or anyone.

She didn't fight the building pressure or overwhelming affection that choked her. Her thighs trembled. She could barely keep her hold on the snarls of hair that were the only thing keeping her anchored. She needed to hold onto her mortal, her Layla, even as the rapture within her swelled. Jagged cries burst from her throat, and she flung her head back so hard she cracked it on the back of the bench.

Layla's laughs reverberated through her, following the aftershocks that rocked her body. Pressing kisses to the crease of the Gondolier's thigh, Layla playfully tickled the backs of the Gondolier's calves and knees while she caught her breath.

"Plenty more where that came from," the warrior began with a little eyebrow waggle. Then, more sober, she asked, "Wait. Just to be sure…I'm not going to get pregnant, am I?"

She blinked, taking a beat before replying, "It doesn't work like that."

"I don't know if you've noticed, but I never have any idea how it works in this place."

Leaning forward, the Gondolier claimed her mouth in a scorching kiss, only pulling back when an eruption of white light pulled her attention, signaling an end to their privacy. She snapped to her feet, shifting her robes back into place and yanking her hood forward.

Grinning so broadly her cheeks looked about to crack, Layla quickly wiped her mouth and checked her own armor's placement.

"Another time, then, love."

Beyond them, a little old woman stooped over a cane appeared from within the flare of light, her white puff of hair floating around her head like a nimbus.

The Gondolier needed to collect her toll and get the woman onto the gondola. Her legs didn't quite crumple as she finished composing herself and strode forward to greet the soul.

"Oh!" Layla gasped before she could make it more than a step. Light also bloomed around her. "Think they found my body!" Before the necromancer could fully snatch her back to the land of the living, Layla raced forward and ducked into the Gondalier's deep hood with her, snatching a quick kiss. "Be seeing you again soon."

Before she could formulate a reply, the warrior was gone, leaving behind footprints in the sand and a scattering of crumpled white petals and stems around the bench.

"See you," she sighed, already missing her.

But Layla would be back, one way or another. Necromancer or no, one could only run from death for so long.

* * *

Daisies bloomed out of the black sand of the beach.

The Gondolier had never seen anything grow in this part of the underworld, especially nothing that came from the mortal realm. Little yellow and white flowers poked out and unfurled in clusters, persisting in the hostility of the realm without any explanation. Over time they spread, creating their own soft, little oasis.

The Gondolier sat with a small child and showed him how to string them together in a crown, much like how they had arrived on her shore. The child wore his crown proudly as she held his hand and helped him board her gondola once he was ready.

He had barely boarded for the journey when the entire beach lit up in a way that the Gondolier had rarely ever seen it. Light after light after light after light. Souls pushed the boundaries of the beach to the shadows, clogging every inch of sand between the fiery shoreline to the black, roiling walls of darkness.

Then a familiar voice rose above them all.

"Ha! Get *fucked*! You're dead! You're also dead! That's right, you're dead, too. Thought you could outmatch Layla the *fucking* Knight of the Lilies, Champion High Queen Tatiana of the Summer Court, Slayer of the Midnight Moore Shadow Beast, Flamebringer, Mimic Tamer, Friend to Dragons, and Slayer of Dragons. Welcome to the afterlife, blackguards. Hope you remembered to bring your coin purses. Now where's my girlfriend?"

The Gondolier lowered her hood, having grown accustomed to showing her face a little more often to the mortals who entered the afterlife.

Layla shoved her way through the crowd of her enemies, chortling and cackling the whole way, taunting them on some failed plan.

"Did you single-handedly take out an entire army?" the Gondolier called when she finally spotted a golden head bobbing amongst the rest.

"Bah, barely half, but it's enough. My friends will clean up the rest. Better get these assholes on board or walking, because I guarantee more are coming."

The warrior shoved the last few bodies separating them aside. She wasn't dressed in her usual armor, but a simple linen tunic and breeches, her hair a wild mane of gold and silver that cascaded around her shoulders. Her face held more creases denoting a life of mirth. Instead of her ax, she carried bags. Many bags. Several packs, pouches tied to belts crossing her body and around her waist, pockets bulging, several extra satchels thrown over her broad shoulders. She was radiant.

Flying forward, she threw her arms around the Gondolier, bags clinking and jangling awkwardly.

"You would not believe how easily these cowards fell into the trap I set for them."

"If they fell for it, why are you here?"

"Someone had to stay behind to spring it."

"And how long until your friends retrieve your body?"

Pulling back, Layla studied her face, beaming. "Afraid my body's going to be a bit difficult to retrieve this time."

Freezing, she eyed her skeptically. "You're not going back?"

"Not this time. You got room on that boat for me, right?"

"As long as you can pay the toll."

Her grin broadened, the creases around her eyes deepening. "Don't you worry, love. I knew I wasn't going home after this one, so I came prepared." Swinging one of the pouches forward, uncinching the top and revealing the coins practically bursting out of it. "Figured if this was going to be my final adventure, I better plan ahead.

Brought my fortune, or as much of it I could carry, at least. Adventuring truly has been good to me over the years. How many boat rides do you think this'll buy me?"

Scanning over the amount and size of the bags Layla had on her. "I...it...it doesn't..."

"Work like that?"

"I actually don't know. Nobody has ever tried it before."

"Want to see how it goes?"

"Absolutely."

Layla reached forward, grabbing her hand and bringing it to her lips. "Perfect. And when I run out, I'll take my chances walking the long way. I've always been curious about what's out there and how hard they are to kill."

"You don't have your ax."

She shrugged. "Eh. I'm resourceful."

Leaning down, the warrior pressed a sweet, gentle kiss to the Gondolier's lips, full of all of the warmth and life she had brought with her from the other side. She grasped her hand, scarred and callused and inexplicably now missing half her pinky on the right side, and escorted her to the gondola, almost giddy she finally got to seat her love into it. She had so many things she wanted to show Layla about her world in the afterlife, things they had never had time for with the woman being plucked out of death so quickly each time.

Layla tossed her a coin and climbed aboard. "Fantastic. Can I row the stick thing?"

"It's an oar. And you know, no one has ever rowed *me* across the lake."

"Do I have to pay extra for the privilege?"

"Of course not. Maybe you could finally tell me about all of your adventures instead."

"Good thing I brought all this gold, because we're definitely going to need to a few trips to get through all of them."

"The Ferry Maiden" is a stand-alone short story by Dee Lyle and is her first publication. You can find Dee on social media @deelylewrites.

Please take a moment to review this book at your favorite retailer's website, Goodreads, or simply tell your friends!

ABOUT THE AUTHORS

Rosiee Thor began their career as a storyteller by demanding to tell their mother bedtime stories instead of the other way around. They spent their childhood reading by flashlight in the closet until they came out as queer. Now, they write stories for all ages, including young adult novels *Tarnished Are the Stars* and *Fire Becomes Her*, the picture book *The Meaning of Pride*, and tie-in novels for franchises like *Life is Strange* and *Firefly*. Their short fiction appears in many anthologies, including the Lambda award nominated *Being Ace*, and Junior Library Guild gold standard selection *The House Where Death Lives*. Rosiee lives in Oregon with a dog, two cats, and an abundance of plants. You can find them online at www.rosieethor.com or on social media @rosieethor.

William C. Tracy (he/him) writes tales of the Dissolutionverse: a science fantasy series about planets connected by music-based magic instead of spaceflight. He also has a standalone epic fantasy with seasonal fruit-based magic, a nonfiction book about body mechanics and correct posture, and a hard sci-fi trilogy with generational colony ships and a planet covered by a sentient fungal entity.

William is a North Carolina native with a master's in mechanical engineering, and has both designed and operated heavy construction machinery. He has also trained in Wado-Ryu karate since 2003, and runs his own dojo in Raleigh, NC. In his spare time, he cosplays with his wife, and they enjoy putting their pets in cute little costumes and making them pose for the annual Christmas card. Follow him on Bluesky (@tracywc) for writing updates, cat pictures, and thoughts on martial arts. Find him online at spacewizardsciencefantasy.com or www.patreon.com/wctracy.

N. Romaine White (she/her) is a writer living in the wilds of central Maryland. A Hood College alum, she got her professional start as a local arts and entertainment journalist. Romaine experiments with incorporating Mid-Atlantic history and experiences into her fiction writing. By day she masquerades as children's book author and illustrator Nilah Magruder. Nilah's work has appeared in Uncanny Magazine, Fireside Magazine, books published by Harlequin Teen, Scholastic, and Macmillan, and in television and film. She won the Dwayne McDuffie Award for Diversity and was nominated for a Hugo Award. When not working, Romaine is baking, gardening, and hanging with her dogs, cats, and chickens.

Robin C.M. Duncan (he/him) is a Scot from Glasgow, a Civil Engineer by profession. He began writing in 1980, but only pursued publication from 2013. Robin's debut novel *The Mandroid Murders* appeared in 2022, its sequel *The Carborundum Conundrum* in 2023, his latest *The Rigel Redemption* in 2024. Robin's stories feature in Space Wizard's *Distant Gardens, Farther Reefs, Lofty Mountains*, and *The World of Juno* anthologies, and in GSFWC's Gallus anthology. His short story "The NEU Oblivion" was long-listed for the 2019 James White Award. Robin belongs to the Glasgow SF Writers' Circle, Edinburgh SFF, Reading Excuses, the British Fantasy Society, and the British Science Fiction Association.
Visit robincmduncan.com, and message at @robinski.bsky.social.

Maya Gittelman (they/she) is an Ignyte nominated queer nonbinary Fil–Am and Jew-ish writer and critic. She writes on queer trans diaspora belonging, anti–imperialist liberation, joy, ache, and love. They review genre media for Tordotcom, and their cultural criticism has been published in *The Body is Not an Apology* among other publications. Find their fiction in *Lofty Mountains, Night of the Living Queers*, and the forthcoming sci-fi YA anthology *Why on Earth*. Formerly the events and special projects manager at a Manhattan branch of Barnes & Noble, she is currently at work on a novel.

Sara Codair (they/them) is a community college Academic Coach and author of speculative short stories and novels, including *The Evanstar Chronicles* and *Earth Reclaimed*. They partially owe their success to their faithful feline writing partner, Goose the Meowditor-In-Chief, who likes to "edit" their work by deleting entire pages. You can follow Sara and Goose's writing journey on Twitter and Instagram (@shatteredsmooth). You can also learn more about Sara on their website, www.saracodair.com.

N.L. Bates (she/her) is a Canadian author of science fiction, fantasy, and slipstream stories, and is the moderator of the long-running critique group Reading Excuses. When not writing stories, she enjoys biking, dancing, and tabletop RPGs. She also writes and performs music as her alter ego, Natalie Lynn and filks occasionally, usually by accident. Connect with her on Twitter (@nlbateswrites) or Bluesky (nlbateswrites.bsky.social).

Heather Tracy (she/her) is a travel agent by day, and a masked copy editor and writer by night. As a travel agent, she plans Nerdventures—travel for the nerd in all of us. These can be anything from visiting New Zealand to see as many *Lord of the Rings* filming locations as you can to visiting castles in Europe to following in the footsteps of your favorite author.

As a copy editor, she's found hundreds of typos, comma splices, and other grammatical nitpicks for Space Wizard Science Fantasy since before 2016. With over 30 titles copyedited, this year she turns her hand to her first published short story in *Fiery Deeps*, and her first novel, *Only a Chapter*, which features some of her personal journey surviving breast cancer.

Heather lives in Raleigh with her husband of over twenty years, William C. Tracy, where they have two rambunctious cats and several beehives. They enjoy taking their own Nerdventures—as much as they can be away from their small businesses—and cosplaying at various markets and cons throughout the year.

You can find her on Instagram as @melvinstraveladventures for her travel agency or as @hunnyjar319 for her author page.

J.S. Fields (@Galactoglucoman) is a scientist who has spent too much time around organic solvents. They enjoy roller derby, woodturning, making chainmail by hand, and cultivating fungi in the backs of minivans. J.S. lives with their wife and kid in the Pacific Northwest, along with a Flemish giant rabbit named Sir Chip Edmonton III.

Fields' writing spans across science and science fiction / fantasy. Their *Ardulum* series was a Forewords INDIES finalist in science fiction, and a Gold Crown Literary Society finalist in science fiction. Their YA fantasy *Foxfire in the Snow* was also a Foreword INDIES finalist in YA, and their adult fantasy *The Rosewood Penny* was a Queer Indie Award nominee. All of their writing, from published to drafting, is available on their Patreon: http://www.patreon.com/jsfields. You can keep up to date on their work at http://www.jsfieldsbooks.com/

Dee Lyle's love of telling stories began before she could read when she found her mom's copy of *Jurassic Park* and began carrying it around, making up her own story about what it was about. She only began writing those stories down when, as a pre-teen, she read a book with an ending she disliked and decided that she could probably do better. She couldn't but it began a journey of learning how to tell a good story, and she has been honing her craft ever since. She spends her days doting on her dog, two cats, and jungle of house plants. She has since read the actual *Jurassic Park* novel, and agrees that it was probably better than what she, as a toddler, was telling people. This is her first publication. You can follow her on social media @deelylewrites.